HYBRID LORE
ORIGINS

J.D. PARKER

ISBN: Paperback 979-8-9899980-0-5
ISBN: Ebook 979-8-9899980-1-2

Design and publishing assistance by The Happy Self-Publisher.

Parkers Publishing

Contents

Prologue

As Captain Cooper approached security checkpoint three in the USSF secret underground facility outside Philadelphia, he pulled his clearance ID. The master sergeant by the metal detector didn't even look at it. He waved Cooper through, saying, "He's been waiting for you."

At the end of the hall, Cooper rapped twice on the door designated *Director* and entered.

"Captain Cooper," said the man behind the oversized mahogany desk. "Come in."

The captain noticed right away that the rumors were true. The director strongly resembled George Clooney. But he knew better than to say it. This was a powerful man who could make or break your career with a word. Cooper had been counseled by three different officers in the chain of command with the same advice. Get in, get out, don't ask any questions. Still, Cooper had to stifle a smile.

"Director Lange," acknowledged Cooper, "I finally found the terrorist known as Jubal by backtracking through his bogus IP addresses until we hit the real one." He paused for an *atta boy*. After all, Cooper had done in a week what others had spent two years working on. Lange was waiting, impassive. Cooper felt slighted but continued. "Turns out he was Robert Hazer's son. They're working together."

"I thought we put Robert Hazer away?"

"We did, sir, but he was released on parole recently."

"Well, that's a fuckup I'll have to pursue. You would think after all we put him through, he'd know better than to go back to that life. You caught them?"

"We got Robert, sir, but Jubal escaped."

"Unfortunate," said Lange, a look of irritation on his face.

Cooper tried to stay upbeat. "We found a ton of their research, though, and we have his computer. But this parchment was in his safe and I was told to bring it straight to you."

Cooper offered a twenty-four-inch round cardboard tube across the desk. Even with the cap on, Lange could smell the age and decay wafting from inside of what he speculated would be sheepskin.

When Lange ignored the tube, Cooper took it back and offered him a file with his other hand. "Well, here's what we translated from it, sir."

Lange took it and said, "Run the scroll by Portis at NASA II for authentication. He probably wrote the damn thing anyway."

Not understanding the reference, Cooper said, "Did you say he wrote it, sir?"

Lange responded with a stare and Cooper avoided his eyes. They had warned him—no matter how innocent or relevant—Lucy Lange did not tolerate questions.

"Jeez, what an asshole," Cooper thought.

Lange snapped, "What did you say to me, Captain?"

"N…N…Nothing, sir," Cooper stammered.

"Get the fuck out of here," Lange said.

Confused and flustered, Cooper slunk out of the room. Lucy opened the file and began to read.

Translated ancient Greek from the Rosahi Famo Manifesto, circa 312 B.C. Discovered in an archaeological dig outside of Athens Greece in 1984:

Aliens exist. Countless different civilizations with advanced technologies have traveled the universe for millions of years. What we know for sure about all of them is they need endless volumes of natural resources to function. Tens, maybe hundreds of thousands of years ago, our solar system was discovered by a race of aliens the ancient Sumerians called the Anunnaki. These beings began to immediately harvest the find of a millennium. The third, fourth, and fifth planets from the sun teamed with gold, silver, mercury, quartz crystals, and many other elements and minerals that were coveted by technologies of the future. Soon, other alien races arrived, demanding that such a bounty be shared. A bitter war ensued between many of the alien factions. The fifth planet from the sun between Mars and Jupiter, then called Ceres, was completely destroyed. Nothing remains now but an orbiting mass of rubble called the main belt. The fourth planet, Mars, was left a barren rock. Earth, the richest of the planets, was all that remained. War continued to rage until the aliens realized Earth also faced annihilation. Led by a gleaming race known as Errans, everyone came together to negotiate a treaty. Legend says that the aliens divided the earth among themselves using the world's natural magnetic ley lines as boundaries. Anunnaki, Reptilians, Errans, Greys, and Mantis were some of the names of aliens that were preserved from antiquity in religious texts and historical documents as Gods. Gods who shaped the history of the Earth. Gods who bred monsters, demons, and freaks. Gods who created man in their image.

The director mumbled, "Gleaming race my ass." He let the paper slip from his fingers and waft into the trash can.

CHAPTER 1

MR. JOHNSON

The humidity was a heavy blanket pressing down. Mr. Tilman Johnson took a left onto 22nd Street. He trudged along with his small bag of groceries, hoping the rain would hold off until he made it home. Only a short jaunt to the Quick Shop, but it seemed so much farther now that he was in his eighties. He didn't know exactly how old he was, just what his father always told him. "Till, my boy, your mother died right after the Great Depression was gearing up and you were a baby then. That's the closest I can get to an actual birthdate."

Mr. Redden waved and hollered a greeting from across the street. Everyone knew Mr. Johnson, as they had his father and grandfather. Tillman had lived here in the East End of Newport News, Virginia, his entire life. In fact, Tillman still lived in the same house that Mulberry Johnson, his grandfather, had built sometime in the late 1800s. He crossed Crow Avenue—almost home. A shrill greeting rang out from behind him. Sounded like Lemisha Brown. He waved back but kept moving. At a stooped six foot six and always wearing his tan fedora, he was easy to spot.

Mr. Johnson squinted a half a block down at a group of teens standing around the fence gate that opened onto his sidewalk. Everyone called them Knuckleheads, but he called them punks. They called themselves gangstas. Punks couldn't even spell.

The East End had hit bottom. The crime rate, the drugs, the violence—all out of control. He had heard a rapper on TV talk about downtown Newport News, except he called it Bad Newz. Police avoided the area and most of the people that had grown up there now lived their lives in intimidation and fear. All because of the Knuckleheads.

Mr. Johnson thought back on his life here in the East End. When he grew up, the area was mixed: White, Black, even a section that was mostly Korean. It was clean and everybody got along fine. That all changed after the civil rights riots in the sixties. The Whites and most of the Blacks left. The houses decayed and crime rates went up. In the seventies, it became a sanctuary for the blossoming drug trade. By the eighties, it was a dirty, dangerous ghetto. But it was in the nineties that the gangs of Knuckleheads appeared and never left. Except for Mr. Enoch across the street, Mr. Johnson couldn't remember the last time he had seen a white person living downtown. He wasn't even sure if Mr. Enoch still lived there since he hadn't seen him for at least a year. Still, that dark-skinned girl who lived with him showed up now and then. What was she anyway? Indian maybe? Funny how those two never seemed to look any older.

LaToya, who lived next door, had told him once, "Tillman, that girl runs around the backyard buck naked like she's crazy."

"Wouldn't mind seeing that show," Mr. Johnson said to himself.

As he walked up to his gate, five Knuckleheads pulled in together blocking it. "Ya'll git from here," he barked at them. "And you, get off my fence."

They all wore the same uniform. Hoodies hiding their faces and baggy shorts showing their underwear and hanging below the knee. Mr. Johnson pushed his way through the laughs and taunts and opened his gate. He looked back when the gate wouldn't close and saw the tallest one holding it.

"Show respect, old man," said the thug. He pulled back the corner of his coat, revealing a 9mm pistol stuffed inside his waistband.

Mr. Johnson snatched the gate free and leaned in, nose to nose. "You punks don't scare me," he said.

And then he saw it. The eyes. The punk's eyes became yellow with black slits like a cat or a snake. Then they were round again. It shook him to his soul. Mr. Johnson was a believing man and he believed he had just seen the devil.

Turning and stumbling, he hurried into the house. Unnerved, he dropped the groceries to the floor and went straight for the hall closet. After a few seconds rummaging the top shelf, he felt it. His 1911 .45 caliber pistol. It was the first time he had picked it up since returning from the Korean War. It felt good and strong in his hand and the fear left.

He turned, feeling a bit foolish. There, eye to eye—inches away—the demon eyes were back, staring right through him. He tried to shoot the .45 but nothing happened. Mr. Johnson looked down. The gun was still in his hand, but his hand lay on the floor, separated from his arm. Blood spurted out from his empty coat sleeve, forcefully matching his heartbeat. His legs weakened and he knew he was going into shock. A scaly red hand grabbed his throat. Chameleon-like, it became the same color as Mr. Johnson's own skin. There was a sharp pain under his left rib and Tillman Johnson knew he was about to die. The last thing he heard as his life escaped him was a loud hissing sound.

The hand that held Mr. Johnson's throat released and he crumpled to the floor. The killer's appearance went back to a normal teenager and the slits became round pupils. A deep grating voice said to the other punks in the room, "I'll dust him and get rid of any traces. Go start tearing out the floor in the garage. Quietly."

CHAPTER 2

MEET THE ARCHERS

Jimmy Archer was a light sleeper. On the floor next to his king-sized bed lay two sixteen-pound cairn terriers, Connor and his brother, Petey McPhee. Serious hunters, a proud and stubborn breed that loved their momma. Both were rescues and near impossible to tell apart when they were puppies. Their soft whining to go outside woke Jim. He opened his eyes and was face to face with their cat Tippy. It was a bit annoying, but that's how he was awakened every day. Tippy hopped down and Jim leaned up to survey the room. It was still dark out, but he could make out Nick and Molly asleep in their beds. Nicky looked like a beagle and even had pedigree papers. But he was probably twice the size of a normal one. An old breeder once pointed out to Jimmy some blue speckles on his coat and speculated that there was a blue tick hound in the woodpile somewhere. Still, as was typical of his breed, he was affectionate, fast, loud, and always sniffing around. Molly was a mix. Basically, she looked like a big doberman with long hound dog ears. Protective and loyal to her inner circle and no one else.

All the "kids" were canines except Tippy the cat. He was a Maine Coon, the largest domestic cat breed in the world. With a shimmering solid gray coat except for some black stripes on his face and one black spot on the tip of his tail, the name Tippy suited him. He wasn't named that by Jim. He and his wife Debbie always used people names for their children. Jim's sister Shirley had named him Tippy. Like most people, she liked descriptive pet names. When she was little, her stuffed animals were named Skunky, Teddy, Cowie, and such. Years earlier, Jim and Debbie were just supposed to keep baby kitty Tippy while Shirley moved into her new house. Now, all thirty pounds of Tippy was turning twelve.

"Let's go," Jim whispered.

Tippy, Connor, and Petey ran to the bedroom door. Being careful not to wake her, Jimmy gently untangled himself from Debbie's arms and legs. He put on some sweatpants, slippers, and a Captain America hoodie. Even though it was summer and hot out, mosquitoes were a factor. If they wanted him, they would have to work for it. Molly had moseyed to the door as well, but Nicky the beagle was still sound asleep under his blankey.

"Nicky," Jim called softly. He said it louder and stressed the A at the end, as in "Nick A." The other kids were getting antsy. Jim made a sheep noise, "Baaaaah." Nick was up and over. He was a sucker for animal sounds.

Jimmy eased open the door and they all went down the long hall, across the den, and out to the screened back porch. As the kids filed through the doggy door and onto the back deck, Jimmy went back inside to check the time. He flipped on the overhead fan light and the Bugs Bunny wall clock read 4:30 am. Then he saw Bocephus asleep on the recliner/couch combo and quickly turned it back off.

He had forgotten. They bailed Bo out of jail yesterday and he'd spent the night. The house was four thousand square feet with five bedrooms—technically, six—a mother-in-law suite on the far end next to the double garage, and another two-story detached garage in back they called the shop. Even with that much space, Bo always slept on the couch in the den when he stayed over.

Jim could see through the glass that it was beginning to get light outside when he heard the beagle howl once. Then all the dogs started barking. It had to be a critter. Living this far back in the woods, it was common for an opossum or racoon to show up. Even deer and coyotes could get over the side fence section, which was only forty inches high.

Jim ran across the back porch and through the screen door, grabbing a machete he kept hanging there for emergencies as he went by. From the top deck, he could see the dogs across the yard. Nick was stationary, locked in place and howling. Molly saw Jim on the deck and ran toward him. That's when Jim spotted the commotion in the tall monkey grass around the pear tree. It looked like a fight scene from a cartoon episode with a blur of fur, paws, leaves, and grass flying up in the air. Jim broke into a sprint, the dew on the grass soaking his slippers. About twenty feet from the ruckus, a snake flew out of the fray and landed at Jimmy's feet. Nicky kept his post, howling, while the terriers charged after it. "No! Stay!" Jim called with his hand up. Connor and Petey jumped, barked, and spun in circles but stayed back. Molly the Doberman watched from behind him, with no intention of getting involved with a snake.

The snake headed toward the fence, moving awkwardly. Jim caught up and held it down behind the head with the flat of the machete. He looked at the arrow-shaped head and vents under the nose. Definitely a copperhead, venomous, and he was badly hurt. Two serious wounds on his upper body oozed blood and innards. The terriers had been busy. Without hesitating, Jim raised the machete and mercifully separated the head. Being careful to avoid the dead bite, he slid the head onto his blade, then picked up the rest of the body. Nicky and the terriers were going crazy. After putting the snake parts on top of the fence, Jim convinced the dogs to follow him onto the back porch. On the way in, he saw Tippy sitting on the upper deck railing, eyeing the snake parts. Tippy seemed calm except for the twitching tail. Jimmy smiled. "You too. Come inside," he said to Tippy. "It's dead, but it can still bite you for a couple more hours."

Jim closed off the doggie door and filled the food bowls. Dogs on the floor. Tippy's meal went on the glass table. He needed to wake Debbie. Not just to tell her what had happened but also to check the kids for snakebite. He stopped cold by the couch and tried hard not to laugh out loud. Morning light was creeping through the French doors and Bo had kicked off his blanket. Bocephus' boxers had ridden up his crotch, exposing his balls. Jim ran to the bedroom and woke up Debbie. Then he went rummaging excitedly through the dresser drawers, looking for his camera.

Debbie got up slowly, a little groggy. She liked to sleep until 7:00 am. "What are you doing?" she asked in a pissy tone.

"I need the camera. There's a lot going on."

"Use your phone. What's so important?" she inquired, still grumpy.

"I need to take a picture of Bo sleeping on the couch. His balls are showing." He cackled out loud.

"You're crazy, Jim."

Jim grabbed his phone from the night table. "And the dogs got into it with a copperhead."

Wide awake now, she said, "I'll get dressed. We need to check them for snakebite right away. Have you checked them yet?"

"No."

"I'll meet you down there."

"Okay, as soon as I get some pictures of Bo."

"Bo's gonna kill you." Her voice trailed off behind him.

They checked the dogs for snakebite and found one. Connor yelped and pulled back when Debbie felt under his throat. They held him up to look closer and there it was. The two fang holes had become widely separated because of the swelling. Debbie shaved the area with an electric razor while Jim called the emergency vet. The vet confirmed what they already knew. The copperhead venom only killed the cells it touched. Their venom didn't attack the system. Connor would have a painful sore for a while, but there was no threat to his life. Not like little Percy that they'd lost ten years earlier to a water moccasin.

Connor was so brave while they cleaned and put antibiotic cream on the wound. Jimmy told Debbie in detail the whole story of what had happened while he held Petey.

She looked at Connor standing on the kitchen counter wagging his tail and said, "You're my little man. You're my little badass." She began to riffle his head, repeating, "Who's my little badass?"

Connor barked back at her as if to say, "I am, Mom." He was always a talker.

Awakened by the commotion, Bocephus walked into the kitchen in a sleepy stupor. "What's going on?" he asked after a big yawn.

"Well," said Debbie, "I'm going to see Shirley and Jean Anne. You two are going to the lawyer's office to address your current predicament. Then you guys are going to collect our very last rent from 22nd Street. Misters Connor and Petey McPhee took on a copperhead snake this morning. Oh, yeah," pretending it was an afterthought, "and Jim took pictures of you asleep on the sofa with your balls hanging out."

"What the..." Bo began. But Debbie interrupted him.

"Bo, go get some clothes on so we can eat breakfast."

Bo realized he was just wearing his boxers and quickly left the room, grumbling.

"We're going to seriously talk later," he called out to Jimmy.

Knowing Bo's phobic fear of snakes, Jimmy called back, "After you get dressed, I'll show you the copperhead."

"No you won't," Bo shot back.

"You guys are taking your Lexus," Deb hollered to Bo.

"Okay," came the response from the den.

"Then Jim can ride back with me, and you'll have your car."

"Okay."

"So whether you come back here or go home, it won't matter."

Bo stuck his head around the kitchen door. "I get it already. Take my car."

"You're gonna get it," Debbie said and threw a rubber spatula at his head.

Bo caught it and tossed it aside in time to parry Debbie's follow-up left jab. His palms went up and they started the routine. Left, right, duck, left right, duck. With Bo's encouragement, Deb punched harder and picked up the pace. Then, without warning, Debbie let go with a side kick to Bo's solar plexus. She held back, but it still dropped Bo to one knee.

"That was sneaky," Jim said, laughing.

Bo stood up, smiling and wagging the naughty finger at her. "Thas Deb," was all he said as he left the room.

"I think he was embarrassed that you saw him in his underwear," Jim said.

Debbie shook her head and laughed. "Sometimes he's like a child."

Jim watched Debbie go back to loving up Connor and felt happy for the first time in quite a while. They had been through a rough patch, but things would work out. They always did.

CHAPTER 3

WHITE BIRD

Shewuma of the Hopi Indian Nation walked out into the backyard of her house at 2424 22nd Street in the East End of Newport News, Virginia. Shewuma meant White Bird in English. Her mother gave her that name because a dove flew into their pueblo while she was being born. It was considered an important sign, since there are no doves in the Arizona desert.

The morning was misty, and everything was still wet from last night's rain. Shewuma loved the morning air, her favorite time to work out. After windmilling her arms around to her chest, she made the symbol of her people with both hands. She preferred training naked, but despite the six-foot privacy fence, the prying eyes of neighbors had become an issue for Enoch. He recently began insisting that she always wear clothes outside. An odd stance for him to take considering he rarely wore a stitch himself.

What was Enoch? Calling him mate, lover, or companion were all accurate but also incomplete and misleading. He was an Erran from the Pleiades constellation. In the Erran language, they were Crevetch. His tongue was complex and confusing. Even after so many years of teaching her, she still found translating Crevetch—or most of their words for that matter—frustrating at best. She let it go. He had become obsessed about not attracting attention, so she would humor him.

For working out, Shewuma had her long, jet-black hair in a single braid. She wore what her people called a manta, a traditional dress of the Hopi women that Shewuma had made herself, with a few adjustments. As was customary, it was green and strapped only over the left shoulder. But it was also very short, with a small slit up the right side partly for mobility and partly because she liked showing off her legs.

Like all the old downtown houses, a three-inch sewer pipe was attached to the rear outside wall. The pipe came out of the ground and traveled up the two-story house, stopping a few feet above the roof line. Using her hands, fingers, toes, and balls of her feet, Shewuma latched onto the pipe and scrambled up like a squirrel climbing a tree. Standing on the steep pitched roof, Shewuma looked down at the small tattoo of the winged Sun God on her left forearm. A Hopi medicine man had given it to her when she turned sixteen. Tracing around it with her fingers, she said a Hopi prayer to greet Mother Earth. Gazing out across the seemingly endless splay of rooftops, she breathed in deeply. Her incredible sense of smell told her that something was off. The usual scents were there: neighbors, fireplaces, car exhaust, sex, food cooking, and pollution, of course. No Mr. Johnson across the street. He must be off visiting his niece. But something else. Faint. A Drachonian smell, she realized. The Lizard People. It happened occasionally. She might pick up their scent in any number of places since they walked freely among humans in disguise. Still, she would mention it to Enoch. He had the sight, as did most of his kind. If something were up, he would know.

Out loud, Shewuma said, "I am Kachina. Time to go to work." She adjusted the tomahawk and the array of fighting and throwing knives on her battle belt and dove off the roof.

About fifteen feet out, she caught a relatively thick branch of the oak tree in the corner of the small yard. The branch bowed and let her down until she gently dropped the remaining two feet to the ground. Then she threw herself backward into one-handed cartwheels. One, two, three, then four, ending with a midair somersault into a defensive crouch. She continued around the yard, spinning, somersaulting, flipping, and rolling with incredible speed. Back into the tree she went, then down onto the privacy fence running across the top of the thin boards. Diving up and onto her hands, she vaulted off the fence into a twisting layout and landed lightly on the grass, never breaking a sweat.

Enoch would have enjoyed that landing. She wished he would join her. They had spent the last hundred years working out and sparring together. But for the past few months, he had kept mostly to himself, avoiding any physicality. And now he had begun the Transcending, his culture's time of veneration for their religion. That meant no exercise, no food, no sex, just meditating for about the next month. Something was on his mind. But as was his way, he never spoke of it. He was the keeper of the Sanctum and she was his Crevetch. That's just how it was.

Shewuma tried to remember what year she had left the tribe to join him, but it was so long ago. She aged slower than most, but Enoch seemed never to age at all. Oh well. Could've been worse. He could've been ugly. Maybe she was just horny.

Hanging in the tree with one hand about eight feet up, Enoch called to her telepathically. "Come in now," he said to her mind. "Hurry!"

Shewuma swung forward through a backflip and hit the ground running. Mentally, he pulled her upstairs to the bathroom that hid the entrance to their underground sanctuary. Coming down the hall, she saw him: tall, lean, platinum blonde, and incredibly handsome. And those emerald green eyes. God, he was sexy.

Then she caught a scent that filled her with dread. The familiar, sickly-sweet smell of a Drachonian soldier.

Enoch's face was grim. "We are under attack," he said into her mind.

"How is that possible?"

He gave her a plasma rifle and his Cric, a thin, two-inch piece of quartz crystal that his race used as computers. Touching her cheek, he told her without speaking, "Hide it and be ready. We are one."

Shewuma held the Cric next to the yellow wings of the Sun God tattoo. Just as she had practiced, she said "Hide," in the Hopi language. The Cric disappeared under her skin behind the tattoo.

The plasma rifle was fully charged, and she clicked off the safety. Shewuma preferred her traditional weapons—bow, knife, and tomahawk—but deferred to his judgment.

Enoch stepped into the bathroom and vanished. What looked and even felt like a vanity was actually a secret door to their hidden underground chambers. Enoch called it a physical hologram. As with all his people's technology, she didn't understand it.

The Drach stench became strong. They would be here to steal the Sanctum and must be stopped at any cost. "I am Shewuma, Kachina of the Hopi," she said under her breath. She had spent her life training for just this moment. Waiting patiently, she kept her breathing calm while energizing her body's adrenaline. They had to come up the stairs. Enoch would be securing the Sanctum down below and then they could make a break for it. Minutes went by and nothing happened.

"Enoch," she called over her shoulder. "Enoch!" again, louder this time.

From behind, a low grating voice said, "Enoch's busy."

In a blur, she spun into a crouch and fired. The plasma stream went through one Drach's chest and exploded another scaly head behind him before burning through the plaster wall and continuing into space. Then Shewuma saw a bright blue light, and everything went dark.

CHAPTER 4

LEGALITIES

Jimmy and Bocephus waited patiently at the receptionist desk of Alicia Jones, the lawyer. There sat a very young, very white female. With painfully slow movements, she shuffled some papers and scanned a notebook.

Finally, she looked up and said his name. "James Archer?"

"Yes, same as it was five minutes ago when I told you." The regular receptionist was his fifth cousin Susan. "Where's Susan?" he asked, reaching his limit.

"Susan?" she asked, looking at him. She seemed frozen in time.

He was becoming more annoyed by the second. "Susan, the regular girl. Where is she?"

"Oh, I'm a temp," was all she said.

The receptionist was maybe twenty. Her looks were nondescript, her face blank. And was that even a hair color? Jimmy felt people under thirty should be banned from the business world.

She turned her attention to Bo. "Bocephus Dean?" For the first time, her blank expression changed to genuine surprise. "You're African American?"

"So?" said Jimmy.

"Well, it says you are both here on a family issue."

Jim shook his head. "Are you an idiot?"

Bo put his hand on Jim's arm and winked at him. Figuring what was coming, Jimmy looked aside to hide a smile.

Bo said, "I got this, Jimbo." Then, in his best offended tone, "Are you saying we can't be related because he's White and I'm Black?"

He was pretending to play the race card for fun. He often did that with young people. Say the words race or Black to a Gen Z and they tended to fall apart. He leaned in with his mean face. "Are you saying Blacks and Whites should be separated?"

"No, no…I…I'm sorry. I didn't." She trailed off, visibly shaken. Hanging her head and watching her hands, she seemed to be trying to compose herself. Without looking up, she finally said, "Please wait in the conference room. I'll inform Miss Jones that you're here."

Jimmy motioned for Bo to follow him as he headed down the hall toward the back offices.

"Sir! I need you to wait in the room," she called after them, not sure what to do.

"Read my T-shirt," he replied. It read, "Rules are for fools, wise men use judgment." "We're going to Alicia's office. She'll need her computer," he said to Bo.

Bo couldn't resist and yelled, "Dr. King," back at the girl.

"Dr. King?" she repeated quietly and wondered what he meant.

"She has no idea what you're talking about, Bo."

With resignation, Bo admitted, "It's sad but I think you're right."

Jim and Bo entered the last room of the long building, the office of Alicia Jones, P.C. Stacks of files sat on the coffee table, the loveseat, and different areas of the floor. Several files were fanned out across her huge mahogany desk.

Alicia glanced up from her screen and saw Jimmy. Her freckled face lit up and she squealed, "Jimbo!" and came around the desk with the speed and dexterity that thirty years of softball had given her. Jimmy had to lean over to allow her 5'1" frame to hug his neck. She promptly turned and introduced herself to Bo. "Hi, I'm Alicia Jones. Call me Alicia. You must be Bocephus Dean. I've heard so much about you, but nobody told me about these." She squeezed his biceps as if testing them, obviously flirting.

Bo seemed a little embarrassed, even tongue-tied. But that was Bo. Put him up against a businessman or a gang boy and he was wide open. But against a cute woman flirting with him, he was defenseless. Debbie always said he had no game, none whatsoever. Jimmy had never known Bo to date any White women, though many approached him for obvious reasons. But once, in a rare moment of candor, he told Debbie he was fascinated by redheads.

As if he knew what Bo was thinking, Jim said, "Here's your big chance, buddy." Alicia looked at Jim quizzically and he explained. "Bo has always had a penchant for the red carpet."

Bo looked at Jim horrified. "Jim, what the…Wait, did Deb tell you that?"

Bo expected Alicia to be offended. Instead, she seemed intrigued. "Look at a big handsome guy like you acting all shy."

Flustered, all Bo could offer was, "I can't believe he said that."

With a light punch to the arm, Alicia said, "Don't worry, Bo. I don't pay any mind to what Jim says. Everybody knows. How does Debbie put it? Not rude, not crude, just nasty? Come on, guys." She gestured for them to sit. "We'll play later. We have a lot of work to do."

The guys moved piles of files from the chairs in front of Alicia's desk and sat. Alicia also sat, purposely crossing her legs to show plenty of thigh. Bo's eyes lingered long enough for Jimmy to clear his throat, hoping to move things along.

Alicia had always been playful and flirty. Debbie swore that once she had even hit on her. But that didn't affect her skills as a great lawyer for them and their property management company, Archer's Acquisitions.

Years back, when Jim and Debbie took a risk and bought their first fixer upper, random chance selected Alicia to be the closing lawyer. Alicia was a new junior associate in a big law firm at the time. Then Archer's Acquisitions grew, along with Alicia's client list.

Now, Alicia had her own practice and two junior associates of her own. Unfortunately, Jimmy was there to discuss Archer's Acquisitions impending bankruptcy.

From the beginning, Jimmy and Debbie were real estate naturals. They fixed up the first house in three months. A good appraisal came in and they refinanced, retrieving the renovation expenses plus a few thousand extra. That tax-free profit was used for the next and then the next. The rent from the houses paid the mortgages and left a modest profit each month. The targets were homes in low-income, rundown, predominately Black section of Newport News known as East End.

Everyone advised against buying downtown, but they were wrong. The houses were cheap, the appraisals came back high, and the rental market was strong. The only downside was the occasional brush with local gangs.

The first five houses were renovated by Jimmy and Debbie themselves. After that, Jimmy began subbing out the remodels and just supervising, while Debbie handled the management side. They spent most of their day searching for bargains, tracking down owners, and inspecting properties. It was the most fun they ever had and if possible, brought them even closer together. Soon, investors and speculators were coming to them for help investing in downtown using the Archer's model. Jim and Debbie would find a good rental prospect, fix it up, and manage it. Within eight years, the Archers owned more than fifty rentals and managed another two hundred.

It was during this time that Jimmy originally hired Bocephus Dean to do landscaping. Bo Dean was the hardest working man Jim ever met. Bo kept taking on more responsibility until he became foreman and then limited partner. Over time, all three became very close and a strong friendship developed. When Jimmy and Debbie renewed their vows in a big ceremony, Jimmy asked Bo to be his best man. From then on, they were family.

Bocephus Dean had grown up in East End and his past was dark. Many was the time that Jimmy was approached by a businessman or tenant from downtown, asking if he really knew who Bo was. Jim knew, but Bo's past life and time in prison were inconsequential. Family.

In early 2008, a series of events took place that would change their lives. Years before, Old Bill was one of the first to invest in East End through Archer's Acquisitions. In addition to being the largest private real estate holder in Southeast Virginia, Old Bill owned more than two hundred rentals. His real reputation, though, was as master of the flip. He bought high-end houses for cash that needed updating, fixed them up, sold them quickly, and boom, $30,000 to $50,000 profit. After selling about twenty a year for a long time, Old Bill was very rich.

Old Bill came to Archer's Acquisitions with the offer of a lifetime. Nineteen houses, ready to be remodeled and flipped. He would personally hold the mortgages. Jimmy and Debbie discussed it at length. One million in profit in less than two years, then sell their rentals and the management company, probably to Bo. They could retire young and live the good life.

Some said Old Bill was tired of real estate; others said he wanted to retire. But many figured he just knew what was coming.

Old Bill and Archer's Acquisitions made the deal. Eight months later, the real estate market crashed. Overnight, Jimmy and Debbie's sixty-two rentals were worth less than what was owed on them. Worse, the drop in value of the high-end fixer uppers, many almost ready to sell, could lose them $30,000 to $40,000 each. It was a nightmare. They worked harder and longer, borrowed money, and took on as many new rentals as possible. But it was no use. It was like trying to climb out of a flushing toilet. Spread too thin and bleeding money, the first foreclosure happened. It was a crushing blow to their spirits, their legacy, and their credit. The second foreclosure wasn't as hard to take. Then the rentals fell, one after another. Rents had dropped and no longer covered the mortgage payments. But they couldn't be sold because they were worth less than what was owed to the bank. Of the nineteen potential flips, two were sold at a substantial loss, and $400,000 of fix up money was gone forever on the others. Old Bill eventually took back the houses that were left and wrote off the debt. It was a magnanimous move but no real help. The Archer's credit was destroyed, and they were deeply in debt. A fortune was lost, the damage done. In 2007, Debbie and Jimmy were looking at early retirement. Now, in 2019, they had come to Chapter 7. The business was over.

The only remaining managed rental was 2424 22nd Street. It was a rental they had acquired four years earlier when Herbert retired. It was a gem. The tenant was named Enoch Erran and they'd never even met him. The lease required the tenant to pay city taxes, handle all maintenance and repairs, and pay the rent in cash each month. Until this month, it was always in the drop box on time. This month it would be over. One last rent payment and the property went to Berkley Management.

Jim and Bo sat and talked with the lawyer about the end of life as they knew it. Alicia explained the normal bankruptcy routine and its potential consequences over the next few years. She had all the paperwork ready—just a few asset questions to clear up. Jimmy answered them all. Okay then. The last rental was officially gone when they received that month's rent…*check*. Jim and Debbie's house had been in a trust for eight years and was safe…*check*. Do not declare Jimmy's weapon collection or Debbie's jewelry…*check*. How easily twenty years was just gone.

Alicia turned her attention to Bo. "Okay, let's talk about your issues, Bo. I don't normally do traffic violations. But the Archers consider you family, so I'm all yours. Double entendre intended. So what's the deal?"

Edging out Bo, Jimmy jumped right in. "Bo was pulled over for no brake light but ended up getting a ticket for driving without a license."

"So pay it and we're done," Alicia said and clapped her hands with finality.

"Okay, wait," Jimmy said. "That ticket was his third and that apparently makes three strikes."

"Fine," said Alicia. "What were the other two?"

"Same thing. No license," said Bo.

"So Bo, I'm guessing you have no license."

"No ma'am," he answered.

"We can still work this out. You may have some serious community service. And we'll get you a license so they can suspend it for a while. It's very doable."

"So you'll represent him?" asked Jimmy.

"Sure," she said, turning to her computer. "Just let me check… something…" Alicia went at the keyboard, humming almost whimsically. Then her hands dropped into her lap and her brow wrinkled in concern. Or was it confusion? Alicia read the screen for several minutes with no change in her expression. Jimmy began to fidget. Having been in this situation many times, Bo remained calm. Alicia looked at Jimmy and then back at Bo as her face morphed into a look of helpless realization. She had just learned what most downtowners already knew. Bocephus Dean used to be a very dangerous man.

"Well, where do we start?" said Jimmy, pulling her out of her fog.

She looked at Bo as her eyes welled with tears. "Honey, you're going to jail." She was so caught off guard that she seemed close to sobbing.

"No, come on," said Jimmy. "I know he did some serious time, but that's all over now. And they're just tickets for Christ's sake!"

"You don't get it, Jim." She wiped her eyes and became all business. "He was in for attempted murder, kidnaping, robbery, and torture. And those were just the convictions. When a judge sees this, it'll snap his head back." She took a sip of water to compose herself.

"It sounds worse than it was," said Bo, causing her to involuntarily spit the water across the desk.

Jimmy wanted to speak, but she cut him off and said to Bo, "You got out in ten years because of a special state program combined with parole for good behavior. The three strikes have violated both. You could go back for twenty more years, Sweetie. You need a criminal lawyer, a badass one. I need to make some calls right away."

"Alicia," Jim began. But she cut him off and came around the desk.

"I'm sorry, Jim. I'll get Bo the best lawyer I can, but this is way out of my league. There's nothing else I can do. I'm surprised you even made bail," she said to Bo. "It must have cost a fortune."

Jimmy was upset and had more questions as Bo calmly but firmly steered him out of the office. Bo looked back at Alicia's distressed face. To her surprise, he said, "Thanks, Alicia. Don't worry. It'll be okay."

Jimmy stopped Bo once they were in the parking lot. It was all so unexpected, and he was still trying to process. "You're too calm. I don't think you understand what Alicia was saying, buddy."

"We'll figure it out," Bo reassured him. "But right now we need to get that rent from 22nd Street and then meet Debbie at John and Anna's for lunch. If we're late, Deb will be pissed. We can talk about it more at lunch." Jimmy caught Bo by surprise and gave him a hug before they walked to the car.

CHAPTER 5

LAST RENT

As Jimmy had pointed out to him many times, if Bocephus had to drive like an old woman, why do it in the left lane?

"You're just upset," said Bo while moving over into the right lane at just under the 55 MPH speed limit.

"Damn right I'm upset. You going to jail for a ticket? It's bullshit."

"Look, Jimmy, whatever happens, it'll be okay."

"But you could go to prison. I don't think Debbie would accept that. How can you be so calm?"

"If I must go, I'll go. I can do the time. I just need somebody outside to take care of my stuff and watch my house."

"Well, you know we've got that, Bo. But I'm not giving up on this yet. I'm going to get everyone I can think of—that councilman downtown we helped, renters, clients—whoever. I'll have them write recommendations for you and be character witnesses in court. We'll make you look like Mighty Mouse. The judge will be giving you a hand job before it's over."

Bo laughed and said, "You're crazy."

"I'll start making calls today. By the way, how could I have worked with you all these years and not know you didn't have a license?" Jim asked. Bo looked like he'd caught him stealing a cookie.

"Nobody in East End has a license," he said matter-of-factly.

Jim laughed and then continued thinking about his strategy for keeping him out of jail.

Bo took the Chestnut Avenue exit off I-64, considered the main entrance into East End. Bocephus Dean was well known downtown. On every block, someone waved, shook a fist, or flipped the bird at his Lexus.

Bo turned onto 22nd Street and had to stop. Four Knuckleheads were slowly—painfully slowly—crossing the intersection against the light. They had an air that dared anyone to challenge them. Bo blew the horn several times. The punks began to circle the car but stopped when they realized who it was. It was Bocephus Dean and the White guy he worked with. There was a rumor downtown that the White couple working with Bo Dean were in the mafia. Debbie and Jimmy had always figured Bo started the rumor. There was also a story that the White woman, called Miss Debbie, had once taken out Anthony Washington at the Quik Store on 36th Street by herself when he talked trash to her. That one was true.

The Knuckleheads were uneasy about confronting Bo Dean, but reputations had to be considered. Bo hit the horn again and one of the Knuckleheads put his hands on the hood of the Lexus. Bo threw it into park and jumped out of the car. Jimmy pulled a .380 Ruger out of his pocket and put one in the chamber. The punk backed up two steps and put his hand under his coat, implying he had a gun.

Bo pointed at him and then each of the others in turn as he spoke. His face was stone as he said, "You know me. Get away from here now or you're all dead. Now!"

Amid a variety of comments and gestures, they walked away. Bo got back in the car quite pleased with himself.

"What if he had pulled that gun?" Jim asked.

Bo laughed. "That guy can't shoot. I saw him and another guy empty their clips at each other in a crowded hotel room once and nobody even got hit. Besides, I knew you'd be ready."

Putting the compact pistol back in his pocket, Jim said curiously, "What made you so sure?"

"Because," Bo began as he drove on, "I remember the first sub job you gave me at the Hampton Avenue house. I was just about to fire the sheetrock guy for being high when you and Debbie walked in. I grabbed his stilts and told him to git. He put his hand on his hammer. You two stepped up behind him on either side. Even though I didn't know y'all that well yet, I could tell if he tried something, y'all were going to take him out."

Jim remembered it and joked, "Yeah, Debbie probably. Not me so much."

Bo chuckled. "Thas Deb."

Jim harkened back to the other story, surprised how much he was learning about his best friend. "Should I even ask why you were in the hotel room?"

"Nope." And that was all he said.

The Lexus pulled up in front of 2424 22nd Street. Bo and Jim went up to the front door and rang the bell. There was no answer, so they knocked and rang again…and again…and again.

"What you think?" Bo asked.

"Let's go meet Debbie. We'll come back Sunday morning. If no one answers then, we'll go in." And they left.

CHAPTER 6

Help Me

About thirty feet below Jim and Bo's assault on the front door of the rental in an underground chamber—a buzzing sound brought Shewuma to consciousness. She could only raise her head a little, just enough to see the red light blinking over an archway each time the buzzer next to it went off. Someone was ringing the doorbell upstairs. No matter now. She realized she was tied to the old kitchen table they kept down there for reading and such. All four limbs were tightly secured, one to each table leg. Two more ropes, one just under her breasts and another above her pelvis, held her in place. Her mind was fuzzy, but she knew she was naked. The stench of dead Drachs filled the room.

The Drachonians had a gland under the right armpit that created a poison deadly to most life. Its acidic nature also caused non-metals, a human body for example, to quickly disintegrate into dust once in the system, and it smelled hideous. That same poison would also eliminate a Drach's body once it was dead, though it took longer. Despite their tremendous power and influence in government and finance all over the world, Drachonians strived to stay concealed as a race, so they never left evidence or witnesses.

Shewuma knew she was hurt. How badly was impossible to ascertain. She couldn't focus and most of her body was numb from the restraints. Her incredible sense of smell told her that one Drach and her Crevetch,

Enoch, were at the other end of the room. She could smell that he was alive, but she could also smell his blood and his misery. The sounds of bludgeoning and hacking meat were occasionally interrupted by the Drachonian asking the same question.

She strained against the bindings to raise her head a little higher. The horror she witnessed burned into her soul. The Drach had initially started on her in the hope that Enoch would quickly give in to protect her. When that strategy failed, he went to work on Enoch. How long had this been going on? Enoch was Erran and they were extremely hard to kill. He could have been suffering for hours, even days.

Consumed with despair, she thought, "Oh God, my poor Enoch."

It was all in vain of course. Enoch would never break, and she didn't have the knowledge sought by the torturer. All seemed lost. Her mind drifted back to her early training so long ago. The Medicine Men of the Tribe always told her, "When you have nothing left, keep your faith." Shewuma hung her head back over the edge of the table and spoke the words. "Masauwu Keeper of Fire and Spirit of Death. I am Shewuma, I am Kachina of the Hopi Nation, I am a Starchild of the Realm of Man. Please Help Me!"

A voice from Hell said, "There's no help for you, little girl."

CHAPTER 7

THE GIRLS

Three women stood on the front porch laden with both plastic and paper bags. Jimmy's sister Shirley fumbled in her purse for keys to unlock the front door of her rancher in the upper middle-class neighborhood of Newport News. She was getting irritated as one of the grocery bags in her other arm began falling. Debbie Archer was standing next to her and shifted her own bags. She snatched a falling cabbage from free fall and righted Shirley's slipping bag all at once.

Jean Anne, Shirley's twenty-five-year-old daughter, squealed with delight. "How did you do that, Aunt Debbie? You're so fast."

"Oh, she's so quick you wouldn't believe it," Shirley mumbled, still searching for her keys. Finally, she gave up and confessed, "I think I locked them in the car."

Debbie put her bags down and asked, "Where do you keep the spare key?"

"In the house," Shirley replied, apparently not understanding the question.

"Do you have a spare key under the bumper or hidden outside or something?"

"No."

Debbie laughed. "I'm surprised. Jimmy keeps a house key in a fake rock and a spare key on every vehicle. Also blankets, a change of clothes, and weapons and tools too, for that matter.

Shirley sighed. "No spare key."

Jean Anne chided, "Uncle Jimmy and Mom have absolutely nothing in common. So, what do we do now?"

Debbie laughed to herself. Jean Anne was one of those people who inserted herself into everything. You either loved her or hated her. It ran about 60/40.

Debbie and Jimmy were on the love side. Debbie moved Jean Anne from in front of the living room window. She flicked open a purple lock blade that seemed to just appear in her hand and popped the screen out of the window frame.

"I'm not really dressed for this. Pardon my lack of modesty," said Debbie as she pulled up her short, tight black skirt.

"Mom, I think she's breaking in," said Jean Anne excitedly.

Shirley nodded and watched with interest. Debbie slid the blade up where the windows met in the middle. With a twist, she pushed the latch back. Then she threw up the sash and climbed through the open window effortlessly.

"Damn," said Jean Anne. "Look at that."

Debbie opened the front door and gestured to them.

"Wow!" exclaimed Jean Anne.

"If you think that's something, you should see her fight," said Shirley as they brought in the bags.

Jean Anne asked her mom, "So you've seen her fight?"

"Just recordings. Still, it's crazy to watch. It's been a long time since you fought, Debs."

"Not in the ring anyway," Debbie said with a grin.

"Why did you quit, Aunt Debbie? Get tired of it?"

"Not tired of the fighting. Tired of the healing afterward."

"You have a black belt or something, right?" asked Jean Anne.

Shirley interjected, "You have two black belts, don't you?"

"Three," Debbie muttered humbly.

"Three black belts, Aunt Debbie! How about teaching me to fight before I go back to the Congo?"

"That place is dangerous. Especially for someone like you, Honey. You shouldn't even go back there," said Debbie.

"I have to," said Jean Anne. "I'm a missionary. I have to go where I'm sent, where I'm needed."

"You carry a weapon though, right?" Debbie asked her.

"No. I'd be arrested for having a gun."

"How about a knife? I can pick you out something good from Jimmy's collection to take with you."

"No way," said Jean Anne. "They search everything at the airport. They would take it. I can't even sneak a candy bar into that country."

"What about mailing it?" Debbie suggested.

"They check the mail too," she said glumly.

"Okay, I give up," said Debbie. "I'll get Jimmy to show you some self-defense in case you get in trouble."

Jean Anne was surprised. "Why not you, Aunt Debbie?"

Debbie had to search for the explanation. "Look, Jean Anne, if I had six months, I could teach you to kick some serious ass. But in an hour or two, I would just set you up to get hurt. Tomorrow at the picnic, Jimmy can show you some tricks to defend yourself or get away from someone trying to hurt you that don't need training and practice. Different logistics."

"How does Uncle Jimmy know so much about it?"

Debbie looked at Shirley and said, "He's Deep Creek trained."

"Deep Creek?" Jean Anne looked at her mother. "Where you guys grew up?"

Shirley waved her off. "I didn't run with those crazy Deep Creekers he ran with."

Debbie smiled at Jean Anne. "She was adopted from the Indians. You know the story." They both laughed.

Debbie hugged them both and started for the door. "Gotta go, guys. Meeting the boys at John and Anna's for lunch."

"Aunt Debbie, wait." said Jean Anne. "How did you learn the window thing?"

"Hey, Babe, twenty years as a property manager. You learn about getting into houses."

"Oh," said Jean Anne, nodding.

"But," Debbie continued, "Jim showed me that particular move."

"More Deep Creek stuff?" asked Jean Anne.

"You bet," said Debbie.

"Damn, Mom, shame you were adopted. You missed all the good stuff."

"You know I wasn't really adopted, right?"

"I'm starting to wonder," Jean Anne shot back.

Shirley and Jean Anne waved goodbye to Debbie as she drove off in her white SUV that she called Miss Interceptor, because it came stock with a police interceptor engine. Debbie waved back and squealed the tires a little to show off.

"Boy," said Shirley, "I wish I was built like her."

"She really has it all, doesn't she?" mused Jean Anne.

"Oh, you haven't heard?"

"What?"

"They're losing the business, all the rentals. Supposed to be filing for bankruptcy. I think they're in real trouble."

"That's weird. Everyone in the family thinks they're rich."

"Yeah well, we'll see what happens," said Shirley.

"I'll ask them about it tomorrow at the picnic," said Jean Anne.

Debbie drove out of sight and Shirley sighed. "Let's get to work. There's still a lot to do for the party."

CHAPTER 8

LAST LUNCH

Debbie waited alone in the back booth at John and Anna's restaurant because Jimmy and Bo were late. She impatiently watched a clock hanging next to a huge picture of the Piazza Navona in Rome. The three meet there for lunch every Friday at 1:00 pm. It pissed her off a little. She preferred being the person who was late.

A tall, handsome, middle-aged man in a double-breasted suit near her booth cleared his throat. "Are you free for lunch, Miss?" he asked with a charming smile.

Until then, Debbie had been completely unaware of how she was sitting. She looked down and saw her feet jutting out past the end of the booth. The black skirt was riding dangerously high up her muscular legs and the buttons on her blouse were opened at least one too low. "No wonder he's hitting on me," she thought, and snapped at him, "Fuck off!"

Without a word, he quickly turned and left.

She swung her legs under the table. "Enough," she thought, and went for the cell phone in her purse. Just then she spotted Bo's Lexus pulling into the parking lot.

Jimmy and Bo saw Debbie's ominous visage while approaching the booth. Realizing how late they were, a *yikes* look passed between them. They knew only Debbie was allowed to be late.

Jimmy sat by Deb, and Bo sat across from them.

Debbie unloaded on them right off. "Where in the hell have ya'll been? It's 1:30 and I've been here since 12:45." Neither of them believed that. "I've got guys hitting on me left and right and Lisa is gone."

Bo stood up. "Which guys?" he demanded, scanning the dining room.

"Well, just one guy actually," Debbie admitted.

"It's okay, Bo. Sit back down. What do you mean Lisa is gone?" Jim asked.

"She's gone, out, vamoose."

"Was it that white guy in the suit?" asked Bo, still on his mission.

"Let it go, Bo. Sit down and look at the menu. Gone on vacation?" Jimmy tried.

"No. They said fired."

Jim said too loudly on purpose, "Oh come on. Lisa's been here since John opened the place thirty-four years ago, I think."

"It's that daughter," Bo said, finally sliding back into the booth. "Ever since John retired and gave it to his daughter, this place has been going to Hades."

A laugh escaped from Debbie. "Did you just say Hades? Say Hell, Bo. Come on, just say it. Hell. You can be so odd."

"I can't believe they would fire my girl," he murmured.

Debbie was struck by one of her famous insights. "Wait a minute. Bocephus Dean, did you sleep with Lisa?"

Bo avoided her eyes and tried to change the subject.

"Answer my question, Bo Dean. You told me you'd never slept with a White woman."

Bo answered sheepishly, "She's Asian. I don't think that counts as White."

"Oh my God, he did," said a stunned Jim. "You fucked Lisa, our waitress? She's been working here since we were kids. She's old enough to be your mother. It's like before today I never knew you."

Debbie elbowed Jim on the shoulder. "I could see it. She was awfully attractive for her age. How could we not have known there was something going on between them?"

"We didn't know he doesn't have a license either," Jim pointed out. "Booocephus, after all this time, you still surprise me. Hey, I'm thirsty."

"I ordered drinks before you guys got here. I don't have high hopes, though. She didn't write anything down."

The waitress arrived a few minutes later. "This is Lynn, our alleged waitress." Lynn shot her a dirty look. Debbie had ordered a Mr. Pibb and black coffee for Jimmy and unsweetened iced tea for Bo. He never, ever ate sugar. For herself, water, no lemon. It annoyed her that in the last few years, it had become necessary to specify no lemon. Why would they presume? She had fallen into a seriously crappy mood and needed to let it go. Leaning back, she watched Lynn place the drinks. Jimmy got Pepsi. No coffee in sight. Bo sipped his tea and spit it back in the glass. It was sweetened. Debbie's water had a big old lemon wedge in it.

All three let her have it, piling it on. Stifling tears, she went for new drinks.

"You didn't write it down again," Debbie called after her.

"Maybe we were a little hard on her," Bo said.

"Why? You gonna sleep with her too?" Debbie said sarcastically.

"Boy, you're in a mood," said Bo flatly.

"Yeah, right," Debbie snorted. She looked at Jimmy and he nodded in agreement. "Sorry. So, what did Alicia say today?"

Jimmy and Bo hesitated.

Not understanding the pause, Debbie said, "Come on, guys. Talk to me."

Jimmy blurted it out. "Alicia said that Bo broke his deal from prison and broke his parole. He has three strikes from the tickets and a hideous criminal record. She says he's going back to jail and is currently trying to find us the best criminal lawyer to be had around here. It'll cost us a lot of money we don't have for a lawyer who can't really help us anyway."

Jimmy got a little excited before going on. "Now all that being said, I've formed a plan to keep him free."

Debbie was reeling from the news. "You are not going back to prison." Debbie stated as if it were her decision. "How much will the lawyer cost?"

"Don't know yet but listen to my plan. We get everyone we know to give written recommendations and then come and be character witnesses at the trial. We show how he's a good father and always pays his child support. We show all the work he's done in the community."

"Okay," agreed Debbie, "I see where you're going. Then we throw in a really good lawyer."

"Stop it, guys," Bo interjected with more force than intended. "You two need a reality check. I've been in this situation a few times. I will almost certainly go back in."

"No. No. Not gonna happen," Debbie insisted.

"Look, I'll do the time and it'll be okay. It's really gonna happen, Debs."

Debbie slumped her shoulders and hung her head. "How long would it be?"

"Could be up to twenty years. The state program and the parole took off ten apiece. There's always the chance of a lighter sentence but the odds are way against it. So we need to be prepared. One day we'll be sitting in court and they'll just come and take me away. I want you two to be ready for that. The same situation nearly killed my mom."

"So what is this almighty state program?"

"It was classes, therapy, and job training. That's where I learned to lay brick and got my barber's license."

"Oh shit. The barber shop. You've only been open for two weeks. What about that?"

"Jerome, the tenant from 27th Street, already rents a chair and opens for me. I just need to find somebody to close. Maybe Nini. She runs the salon next door. I was thinking you two could watch the finances and make sure my mortgage gets paid."

"We'll do whatever you need, Buddy," said Jim.

"Of course we will," added Debbie. "Looks like you're all over this thing. And you're so calm about it."

"Well, as you White people say, it's not my first rodeo."

They sat in contemplative silence until the drinks came, then ordered lunch.

The waitress left and Bo said, almost to himself, "I love you guys."

"We're family. You know that," said Debbie. After a pause, she continued. "I hate to even bring this up now, but what about the bankruptcy?"

"Well," said Jimmy, "Alicia is emailing you a couple more things, but we're good. The house is safe and solid in trust. She was very specific that we need to be discreet about our guns, knives, and jewelry to be sure and keep them. Which we should never mention again. She could get in big trouble for saying that. Also, we can only keep two of the five vehicles."

Jimmy went on for several minutes with more of the minutiae.

Debbie nodded through the flow of information without comment. She was having trouble keeping her mind off Bo going to prison.

The food finally arrived. Chef's salad with house dressing and extra olives for Bo. Pepperoni pizza with extra cheese for Jimmy. Lunch portion lasagna for Debbie, with extra sauce on the side. Thank God the daughter had kept the old cooks.

They ate quietly until Debbie took over.

"Boss mode, Boss mode," Jimmy and Bo joked back and forth.

Debbie ignored them. "Okay, here is how I see it. We have to stop eating out, of course." Jimmy and Bo laughed hard enough to draw Debbie in also. The laughter faded. "But really, we have expenses and no income, so generating some cash is a priority. Bo Dean, anything you make from the barber shop will go directly toward your child support and legal fees. I've been stashing cash for years, so we can last for a while. But no more expenses unless absolutely necessary. I'm so glad we paid the house off when we sold that two-story in Suffolk."

"You've been stashing cash for years?" asked Jim, a bit astonished. "You're amazing."

He looked at Bo, who agreed. "She is definitely amazing."

"Yes, I am, Baby. Did you get that rent today?"

"No. Nobody home," answered Bo. "We're going back Sunday morning."

"Jim, when we get back home, pull the file on them. See if there's a phone number, references, employment info, you know the drill." Jimmy nodded. "Bo, why don't you follow us back to York County and spend the next few nights? You can go with us to the family picnic tomorrow, and Sunday morning we can all go for the rent together. Maybe after, we can work out or run or something. Then we're having dinner with your mom."

"That sounds good," said Jimmy. "I haven't worked out for three days."

"Me either," said Bo.

"Unlike you lazy bums," said Debbie, "I ran two miles this morning and worked the heavy bag for forty minutes before I went over to Shirley's."

Bocephus pointed at her and said, "Thas Deb."

Debbie was fishing a hundred out of her purse when John's now infamous daughter, known only as Miss Russo, was suddenly standing at the booth with a very serious expression on her face. "Excuse me," she stiffly directed to Debbie. "The gentleman sitting by the bar said you were very insulting to him. And my waitress said you were mean and made her cry." She crossed her arms, waiting.

"What...? Let me up, Jim," Debbie demanded, pushing him.

"Oh man," Bo murmured.

Debbie scooted out and got right up in Miss Russo's face. "That asshole was hitting on me, and your waitress screwed up our order. And you fired Lisa, you little shit." The daughter appeared frightened as Debbie's finger pushed against her forehead. "I've been coming here to eat since this restaurant opened. You weren't even born yet. I've known your father well for at least twenty of those years." Everything that had been happening to her, Jimmy, Bo, and the business seemed to be exploding out of her at the poor woman. "I watched your bratty ass grow up running around this place, and you don't even pretend to know who I am or look me in the eye."

Miss Russo turned to escape, but Debbie grabbed her hair and bent her roughly over the table. Shoving the hundred-dollar bill down the back of her yoga pants, Debbie leaned in close and whispered in her ear, "Keep the change, bitch."

Debbie stood up and composed herself. Everyone in the place was watching with either shock or amusement. Several phones were in the air filming the outburst.

"You guys ready?" Debbie asked them calmly. Miss Russo seemed unwilling to stand up just yet.

They walked out to the parking lot in single file.

"Wow!" said Jimmy. "That was awesome, Debs."

"You truly are Wonder Woman," added Bo.

"Just, uh, too much at once," said Debbie, feeling a bit self-conscious about the outburst. She shook it off. "Okay, Bo Dean. Follow us."

Debbie backed Miss Interceptor out of the parking space with Jimmy in the passenger seat, basking in the afterglow of her performance. As she drove past Bo standing by the Lexus, she saw him pointing both fingers at her and mouthing the words, "Thas Deb."

CHAPTER 9

FAMILY PICNIC

It was crazy hot, even for July. The noon sun reflected piercingly off the immaculate 1975 mandarin orange Trans Am with the black and gold bird on the hood. It made a hard right turn off the highway onto a residential road. Bo gripped the passenger door arm as Jimmy accelerated up a steep hill and onto a street right out of *Leave It to Beaver*. Jimmy squealed the tires and shot forward past an old man yelling at him to slow down. Bo knew he should have left earlier and ridden with Debbie. Jimmy was his best friend. Bo had been the best man at Jimmy's vow renewals. Bo was a Black ex-con and Jimmy couldn't care less. Bo loved Jimmy like a brother, but he dearly hated riding in this car with him.

Jimmy called his Trans Am the Muscle. It was forty-four years old, and except for a small cigarette burn on the passenger seat from 1994, it was perfect inside and out. Bo often wondered what terrible fate befell the person who lit that cigarette. He commented apprehensively on Jimmy's speed. After all, they were in a residential neighborhood.

Jimmy laughed. "You don't understand." He explained to Bo for the thousandth time, "This car has a 455 cubic inch engine, two to one steering, five-speed manual transmission, four-barrel carburetor, quad tip exhaust, and a high output cam. It's meant to be driven, not coddled."

"Don't forget about the full documentation," Bo added, still nervously wedged into his seat.

"Yes, that's important," Jimmy replied, ignoring the sarcasm.

Bo finally relaxed as they pulled up in front of a brick rancher in suburban Newport News. Jimmy's sister Shirley loved this house. When she married her second husband Brian four years earlier, he wanted her to move into his six thousand square foot stone estate on the James River. She absolutely refused. This three bedroom, two bath with a large, fenced backyard and a garage full of accumulated *stuff* was her baby. She would never move again.

It was the Archer annual family picnic and cars lined the street. Jimmy found a spot to park three houses down. The picnic had taken place without fail every year of his life. As a child, family members would rotate hosting the gala at their homes. Then there was a ten-year spell when it was held at the park. But Shirley had been hosting it for the last five years and she made it special.

Jimmy and Bo crossed several yards to reach Shirley's front driveway. Jimmy dangled the keys in Bo's face. "You wanna drive back?" he teased. Bo reached for them, and Jimmy snatched them back at the last second. "No way. You drive like an old woman."

Bo gasped and looked to the left. Jimmy turned in reaction, realizing too late that it was a ploy. Bo grabbed the keys, and it was on. Jimmy hooked Bo's arm and lateral dropped him to the grass. He loved wrestling with Bo. So few people in his life had ever been a challenge. High school wrestling champion and a wrestling scholarship to college. If not for that damn torn ligament, Jimmy was sure he would've been in the Olympics. So wrestling most anyone was over very quickly. But Bo had also wrestled in school. He was experienced and savvy on the mat. But the difference was his strength. Mutant strength, Debbie called it. Debbie had a black belt in ju jitsu, and she would not go to the ground with him. They had grappled on the lawn for a few minutes in the hot sun when Debbie's voice stopped them cold.

"You two stop wrestling right now!" she shouted. "Jesus Christ, you're like children. Get in here. Oh Lord, look at your clothes." Both Jimmy and Bo's jeans and dress shirts were wet with sweat and spotted with dirt and grass stains.

"*My* clothes! Look at you," Jimmy spat back. He thought she dressed too revealingly as a rule. But a family picnic? Debbie was so hot with her large breasts on that fit, muscular body. Add her braided blond hair reaching the small of her back and those big blue eyes. Jimmy just didn't understand. She was wearing a denim mini skirt, three-inch heels, and a tight, V-neck T-shirt that read across the front, "I kiss my dog on the lips." "You can't wear this to the family picnic. I'm gonna get my spare coat out of the trunk for you to wear."

He turned but she held him in place, trying to dust the grass and dirt off his clothes. "I'm not wearing your stupid coat. I think I look good."

"Right. You look too good. Help me out, Bo. Tell her."

She was brushing Bo off now and he said, "Yeah, Deb, you look really good."

Exasperated, Jimmy said, "That's not what I meant, Bo. Thanks a lot." Then to Debbie, "All those damn Creekers will be staring at you."

"And don't you forget it," she said, smiling.

"Then they'll start hitting on you."

"No they won't. They're too scared of you."

"They're probably scared of you too," Bo said.

They followed her inside and watched her walk through the living room and the dining room, then out of the French doors to the back deck.

"Damn! You're a lucky man, Jim," said Bo.

Jimmy elbowed him playfully. "You were no help. You encouraged her."

"Thas Deb," he said.

The hosts, Shirley Peck and her husband Brian Donnely, appeared from the hallway and greeted Jimmy and Bo. No one knew exactly why Shirley kept her old name when she and Brian were married, but Brian didn't seem to care. The older women in the family on both sides did seem to have issues with it, though. Not their business was Jimmy's opinion.

The four crisscrossed hugs and handshakes, but Bo received an especially big hug from Shirley. They always spent Christmas together, but this was Bo's first family picnic.

Most of Deep Creek was somehow related to Jimmy's family. After years of hearing about Creekers, Bo had avoided these affairs whenever possible. So, Jimmy had to explain to him that Creekers didn't dislike Blacks. They disliked everybody. There was also the fact that Shirley, Jimmy's other sister Darlene, Debbie of course, and even Shirley's daughter Jean Anne had all called him separately and pleaded with him to attend. Bo relented and here he was.

Shirley tried to whisk Bo off to meet the relatives, but Jimmy insisted on introducing him to his Grandfather first.

"Where did Granddaddy set up shop?" Jimmy asked his sister.

"Oh man, he's in the kitchen," Shirley replied. "He and Nanny got here two hours ago. He went straight to the kitchen, turned a chair around, sat down and started drinking vodka. He's been there ever since."

"Where's Mom?' Jimmy asked.

"She's in the back bedroom. We set it up for the babies and tots. You know her and kids. Okay, listen Jim, everyone is out in the backyard. Brian is about to put the burgers and dogs on the grill. There's tons of food on the table already. There's soda, beer, wine, and liquor."

"Any tea or juice?' asked Bo.

"Sure," said Shirley. "I almost forgot. No booze, no sugar. Good thing you like women or you'd have nothing to do." She laughed. "How do you keep those muscles without eating any real food? I'll get you a glass of tea." She headed out to the backyard.

"Unsweet," Bo called after her.

Jimmy took Bo's arm to get his full attention. "Okay, call Granddaddy Cap'n Dick. That's what everybody calls him. Even Papa."

"Who's Papa?"

"His father," was the answer.

"Captain Dick," Bo said.

"No. Cap'n Dick." He enunciated it slowly. "And don't take it wrong when he calls you Boy. He calls everybody that. Except me. He calls me John Henry."

"Why?"

"Cuz he likes me. I'm his favorite."

"No. I meant why doesn't he call people by their names?"

Jim thought for a second. "I guess he doesn't remember names. Or maybe he doesn't care. I don't know. He calls the girls Lucy. Except his favorites. He calls them Becky."

Bo smiled. "That's odd. Does he call Debbie Becky or Lucy?"

"Oh, she is definitely a Becky."

"Thas Deb," he replied.

They entered the kitchen and Bo realized his preconceptions of Cap'n Dick were way off. Cap'n Dick was sitting in the corner facing the door. His dining room chair was turned around backward, and he straddled it, forearms resting on the back and holding an empty tea glass. Though not exceptionally tall, he was massive across the chest and shoulders, with a huge belly. At least three generations of kids had slid down that belly. He was also wearing a tan, worn out fedora. "Old school," thought Bo.

Jimmy yelled, "Granddaddy!" and gave him a loud kiss on the cheek.

Cap'n Dick didn't move. "Granddaddy, this is Bocephus Dean."

Cap'n Dick looked Bo up and down before saying, "Hey, Boy." He said it fast like it was one word.

"Nice to meet you, Captain Dick."

"I ain't in the Army, Boy," he countered, impassive.

Bo remembered Jim's words: Cap'n, not Captain. "Right. Jimmy talks about you a lot."

But Cap'n Dick wasn't listening. He looked at Jimmy and waved his empty glass while pointing at an empty pint of cheap vodka on the counter. Jimmy knew his Granddaddy. He would have brought that pint with him. Granddaddy wouldn't be caught dead without his liquor. Looked like he had finished it off quick. Maybe Jim could slow him down some.

"How about some wine, Granddaddy?"

Shaking his head, Granddaddy said, "Tastes like water."

"A beer?"

"I don't drink that horse piss."

Okay. He tried. Jimmy pulled a 1.75-liter bottle of Kettle One vodka out of the cabinet where Brian kept his booze. He held it up and offered it. "Good?"

Cap'n Dick nodded and held out the tea glass. Jimmy began to pour slowly. When the level reached halfway, he started to pull back. But Cap'n Dick's scowl prompted him to keep pouring. About a half inch from the top Granddaddy grunted, and Jimmy put the bottle down. Bo watched in amazement as this man—in his eighties at least—pursed his lips and delicately but steadily drank more than half the glass at once. His only visible reaction was a sniff and some slight reddening of his cheeks. This man was absolutely not one to overreact, thought Bo.

"So, Boy," addressing Bo, "you that Black boy that stood up at John Henry and Becky's wedding?"

Bo wasn't sure if it was a statement or a question. But at least he could talk to him now. "Yes, sir. But it was a renewal of their vows, technically not a wedding."

Cap'n Dick squinted at Bo and seemed uninterested. He shifted to Jim. "John Henry."

"Yes, sir."

"Have you heard from J. R.?"

J.R., or Jay to many, was Jimmy's father. It had been years since the incident caused him to disappear. Only Jimmy, Debbie, Jimmy's other sister Darlene, and Cap'n Dick knew that J.R. moved to Oregon and changed his name. Jimmy's mother didn't even want to know where he was.

"No, Granddaddy. I haven't heard from him in quite a while."

"I'd go and visit him again if I knew where he stayed." Granddaddy sighed.

Apparently, Cap'n Dick had gone to visit J.R. a year after he left, with the express purpose of delivering him a gun. J.R. couldn't get one in Oregon, so Cap'n bought a .32 caliber Colt and took it to him. At the time, Jimmy tried to impress on Granddaddy how dangerous and illegal it was to take him a pistol under the circumstances. His daddy was a wanted fugitive. Cap'n Dick explained to Jimmy, "All those Mexicans are packing, and my boy needs a piece. Besides, in Deep Creek, illegal is a sick bird."

Jimmy's dad later told him how Granddaddy stayed for four days and refused to set his watch back the three-hour time difference. Every day, Cap'n Dick would go to bed at 6:00 pm and get up at 3:00 am.

Jimmy grabbed Shirley's little square kitchen table and dragged it over by Granddaddy. He put his elbow on the corner and said, "Let's pull arms, Granddaddy. I've been working out and I'm ready for you now."

Bo was curious. By Jimmy's reckoning, arm wrestling was the Deep Creek national pastime. Jimmy was sure that pulling arms and making dares were the only reasons that Creekers didn't kill each other off. Bo had pulled arms with Jimmy many times. Bo usually won, but it was always a long and painful battle. Jimmy had told Bo many stories about his Grandfather's legendary strength in Deep Creek. Cracking pliers with one hand, lifting a beam that two normal men couldn't budge. Bo could see power in the old man's build. Cap'n Dick's forearms were as big as Jimmy's biceps. Still, the man was ancient. Bo's interest was piqued.

Granddaddy put his elbow on the table and sniffed twice. He and Jimmy interlocked thumbs and spent a good minute adjusting, situating, trying to improve their grip. Jim looked Granddaddy in the eyes and said, "Let's go on three."

Cap'n Dick nodded almost imperceptibly.

Jimmy began counting, "One…two…" All at once on two, Jimmy grabbed Cap'n Dick's arm with both hands, pulled them to his chest, raised up off the chair and threw himself backward with everything he had. Cap'n Dick's arm moved about an inch and stopped cold. Then Cap'n Dick easily pulled his grandson's whole body up onto Shirley's kitchen table.

He let go of Jimmy and laughed. It was the first real change of expression Bo had seen in the old man.

Cap'n Dick's eyes twinkled as he said, "That was sneaky, Boy. You almost got me. Keep practicing. I got high hopes for you."

"Try him, Bo," Jim offered.

Bo realized his mouth was still open. "No thanks."

Jimmy put the table back, saying, "Okay, Granddaddy, we have to go see Mom. Love you." He kissed his Granddaddy on the stubbly cheek, cocked his head at Bo, and they headed out.

"Nice to meet you, sir," Bo called back.

Cap'n Dick yelled at them, "Hey, leave that bottle on the counter." But they were already gone.

As they passed through the French doors to the back deck, Bo said, "That man is a piece-o-work."

"Right?" Jim agreed.

Jimmy looked around the yard, squinting while his eyes adjusted to the harsh summer sun. Between the potential for sunburn and the sheer number of inappropriate body types, it was crazy how some people dressed for these shindigs. Tank tops, halter tops, skintight clothes, short shorts. And where else could you see so many men in shorts, black socks, and sandals? Jimmy glanced down at his shirt, jeans, and hiking boots and laughed to himself. There was a line of sheet-covered tables borrowed from the church and packed full of southern fare: macaroni and cheese, corn pudding, ribs, hot dogs and hamburgers from the grill, barbecue—not pulled pork. Yankees said pulled pork. In the South it was just barbecue—corn on the cob, okra, collards, fried green tomatoes, soft crabs, and many different cheeses. Mmm, Jim was hungry. There were also condiments: mayonnaise, hot sauce, mustard, ketchup, pickle relish, old bay, and ranch, among others. Desserts were also plentiful: peach and blueberry cobbler, pound cake, banana pudding, pecan pie, and all manner of cookies. There at the end of the table was a lone bucket of KFC chicken. Jim hoped it was the original recipe. On the ground sat a galvanized tub of beer and wine packed in ice.

Bo leaned over and asked low, "Anybody here packing?"

Jimmy answered, "A lot of the men and at least one woman."

Bo laughed. "Thas Deb."

"Thas Deb," Jim echoed.

Shirley's backyard was like the fairgrounds packed full on Independence Day. Easily, over a hundred people were spread all over, mostly in small gatherings at randomly placed tables or clusters of yard furniture. A special table specifically for pulling arms was set up next to a firepit. A few men waited in line for their turn at the next winner. A mix of kids and adults were playing volleyball, while croquet was set up in another area. It was Shirley's usual. Brian was cooking on his big grill next to the house, meats sizzling and smoke billowing. Lawn chairs crowded the deck, and down the steps on the attached patio was a round picnic table covered by a large umbrella.

In the shade of the umbrella sat Debbie with three of her favorite girls: niece Jean Anne and two of Jimmy's cousins. Similia, or Simmy as Deb called her, sported a sizeable gauze on her bicep. No doubt from her latest tattoo. Next to Simmy sat Corrine, Jimmy's best friend in the world. Only two years difference in age, they grew up together, learned guitar together, and ran together, as Creekers called it. To Debbie's knowledge, Corrine was the only girl of their generation beside herself to be considered a Creeker. Corrine saw Jimmy and unleashed her electric smile, made even brighter by her dark complexion. She hadn't seen him in almost two years. At 5'8" and one hundred forty pounds, she looked fit. Her long dark hair had grown past her shoulders. She ran to Jimmy and jumped into a hug. He spun her once and kissed her on the cheek. They caught up—how good each looked, how long had it been. And the cancer? So far so good. Four years ago, radiation, chemo, surgery, and then remission. It seemed to Bo that they hugged a long time for cousins. And her husband Daniel? He was well and off drinking somewhere with Mr. Bulles and Papa. They were so happy to see each other that it made Bo smile.

"You remember Bo?" Jimmy gestured and Corrine shook his hand.

Pulling Jimmy's hand, Corrine insisted, "Come sit with us, Jimsy."

"I'll be there in a few," Jim said. "I have to go see Papa."

Corrine went back to her seat next to Debbie, which was now occupied by a blonde woman unknown to her. Corrine dropped her smile and barked, "Get the fuck out of my chair, woman."

Shocked, the blonde left indignantly. She walked away saying, "I'm telling Jeff."

Shirley appeared on Bo's arm. "Come on, Bo. I'll introduce you around."

Bo had spied Jimmy's Uncle Willy and told her, "In a minute. I want to say hi to Willy first."

Jimmy scanned the yard looking for familiar faces. Family on his dad's side was huge and most of his mother's people were there also. With so many, it was common to not recognize some of the attendees. All the family characters were there in all their glory. A lot of the old timers were called Uncle, Aunt, or Aunty no matter what the actual kinship was. There was Uncle Eddie, seventy-four years old and still doing backflips. Aunt Minnie with stage three lung cancer and emphysema, alternating between the portable oxygen and a camel cigarette with no filter. Her morbidly obese daughter Joan scolded Aunt Minnie while she hacked and coughed. Uncle Dan walked toward the girls at the umbrella table. Everybody knew Uncle Dan hugged too long, patted and touched too much, and rubbed shoulders too deep. When he realized Debbie, Corrine, and Simmy were sitting there together, he just waved at them and veered off toward Aunt Syani. Those three could be dangerous. Over by the food, Jimmy spotted Uncle Willy and Bocephus prodding each other playfully and talking. Bo and Uncle Willy hit it off from their first meeting. Willy had spent his life as a cop. Street officer, detective, and then retired after a term as sheriff. He was one of the few in the family that knew Bo's loaded past. It was as if their different paths with the law somehow bonded them.

In the shady back corner of the yard, Jimmy's great Granddaddy was drinking with Bishop, Mr. Bulles, and Corrine's husband Daniel. His Great Grandfather's name was Beauregard Reginold Archer. Most, even his own son Cap'n Dick, called him Borey. But to Jimmy and all the grandkids, he was Papa. Jimmy headed that way. He loved him some Papa and hadn't seen the man for months. Mental note: Go see Papa more often. Papa was well over one hundred now but still looked good. Like his son Cap'n Dick, Papa was broad shouldered and never went out without a hat. He wore a brown top hat with little holes on the side. But that's where their appearances ended. Papa was tall and thin, almost gangly, with large hands and a long face. He had taught Jimmy many things that most people never considered while growing up: driving a tractor, knocking down a hornet's nest, moving the donkey without being kicked, and growing and picking tomatoes. But the best thing he ever learned from Papa was shooting matchbooks. Jimmy remembered that first lesson.

"Snap your fingers, Jimbo. Snap em," coached Papa. Jimmy did several snaps. "Now hold the tip of the matchbook and keep your middle finger behind the flat part. Raise your elbow till the matchbook is level. Now snap!" Papa could send a matchbook across the room and knock over a glass of water. It was an amazing feat to a young boy. Jimmy promised to practice until he had it down. For a time, the matchbook would sputter and fall on every try. It was becoming disheartening. Then one day the matches took off, zinged across the room, and hit their beagle, causing a yelp. He upped his practice and learned to control it. It was a skill he cherished. To this day, Jimmy could put a welt on someone's face from fifteen feet away. Later, he learned in college that beer bottle caps flew even harder.

Jimmy wasn't halfway to Papa when he heard Jean Anne calling him. Damn. He'd forgotten that Debbie had promised her he would show her some moves.

Papa saw him and waved. Jimmy waved back. Shaking his finger, he yelled, "I'll be back, Papa."

Jimmy grabbed Jean Anne's hand and pulled her around to the side of the garage, hopefully for a little more privacy. It would also be cooler out of the sun and the grass was thicker and softer. The shade was not helping the humidity and Jimmy noticed that Jean Anne was wearing a skirt, neither of which were conducive to physical exertion.

"Are you sure you want to do this?"

"Oh yes, Uncle Jimmy. Definitely."

By the side garage door, men stood talking, smoking, and drinking beer.

"Ronnie!" Jimmy yelled.

"Reg!" the big man called back.

Ronnie had started calling Jimmy Original Reginold when they were six years old. It had been Reg ever since. He and his brother were named Ronnie and Donnie, a set of twins as different as night and day. He and Jimmy had grown up and run together for many years. Both had serious reps of their own; as a pair, they were legend.

Ronnie was always bigger than everyone else. All city tackle in high school, he was so feared on the football field that his right arm was called Flippa by his opponents. He lettered in wrestling too and never backed down from a fight. He and Jimmy had many tall tales together, as Debbie would say. Ronnie moved away at twenty-five and this was the first time Jimmy had seen him in many years. So here he stood fat, bald, and married with three kids. Jimmy gave him a huge bear hug. Ronnie said he was only in town for a few days. He set Jimmy down and motioned to his left. There was Charley Mooncliff, also a cousin and a Creeker, kind of slow but always reliable. Jimmy shook his hand and they greeted each other. The third man to Ronnie's right was Jeff, supposedly some distant relation. He didn't step forward and there was no cheer in their acknowledgement of each other.

Jeff was also raised in Deep Creek, but he'd never been considered a Creeker. For some reason, he'd always blamed Jimmy. Jimmy didn't understand why and didn't care either. He considered Jeff an asshole and never had any use for him anyway.

"So, ya'll know Jean Anne, Shirley's daughter?"

They did and all exchanged greetings. Charley looked her up and down and asked her how long she'd be in town. Ronnie flicked his ear sharply to remind him they were related. She explained to them that she was going to live in the Congo soon and Jimmy was going to show her some self-defense moves.

Ronnie cocked his head at Jimmy. "Self-defense moves, Reg?"

"Dirty Deep Creek tricks," Jimmy clarified.

"Gotcha," Ronnie said.

Jeff spoke up for the first time. "Perhaps, Miss, you'd rather have my help. Jimmy is just an old wrestler, whereas I have a brown belt in karate."

Charley interrupted him, saying, "Funny you say that after what happened here at this very picnic for the last two years, Jeffy."

Jimmy laughed and Ronnie insisted on hearing all of it.

To Jeff's chagrin, Charley explained that two picnics ago, Jeff and Jimmy had some words. As usual in Deep Creek, it would be settled with a dare. A crowd gathered as Jeff bragged about his newly acquired yellow belt in karate. And not only could Jimmy the wrestler not hold him in a head lock, but Jeff said he could escape the hold with one finger. Jimmy accepted the dare. Jeff began leaning forward in anticipation of a classic WWE style headlock. With his own left hand, Jimmy grabbed Jeff's right wrist and extended the arm. With his own right arm, Jimmy reached around Jeff's neck and grabbed the upper bicep. Jimmy did all this in one smooth, quick motion and hip checked Jeff to the ground. Jimmy then cranked everything up. It was nothing like the headlocks you saw on TV. Through his grunts, Jeff tapped out on Jimmy's shoulder with his free hand saying, "That's not what I meant. That was two years ago."

Ronnie was laughing and jokingly pushing Jeff, who was visibly pissed off and a little red-faced.

Charley continued. "Then last year, Jeff comes to Jimmy saying he has a green belt in karate now and there is no hold Jimmy can put him into that he can't get out of."

Nodding and pointing at Jimmy, Ronnie told Jean Anne, "I've won so much money on this guy putting people in wrestling holds. You wouldn't believe it."

Charley went on with the story. "Well, Jeff gets on all fours and Jimmy does this thing where he slides his leg in and reaches over or something."

Ronnie knew Charley was describing what some called a stretch or a back lock, but they called it a guillotine. That annoyed Debbie, because in her ju jitsu, a guillotine was something entirely different. It was one of the few wrestling moves that has no counter.

Charley got tickled as he went on. "So, Jeff not only couldn't get loose, but it must have hurt bad cuz Jeff starts pleading for Jimmy to let him up."

Jeff broke in. "Okay, okay. We get it."

"No." Charley was talking directly to Ronnie now. "Jeff was getting up off the ground and saying Jimmy could never have done that if he hadn't let him. Well, Jimmy jumps back on him and whoosh, bang, they went right back into it."

Jeff stepped up to Jimmy, his lips set, and said, "Well, I have one for you that you're going to eat this year, tough guy."

Jimmy looked at Jeff, slightly amused. Without warning, he kicked him hard in the shin. Jeff hopped back, cried out in pain, and then quickly took a fighting stance. Ronnie grabbed Jeff by the collar and tossed him to the ground like a bag of groceries.

"Go on, Jeff, before you get hurt." Ronnie's tone was menacing.

Jeff got up and left—humiliated but not willing to incur the wrath of Flippa. "Wait until next year," he thought. He'd have a black belt. Then he'd show them.

They all agreed to get together before Ronnie left town. Charley wanted to stay and watch Jean Anne practice her moves, but a kick by Ronnie to Charley's behind persuaded him to head back to the picnic.

Jimmy spent the next hour giving Jean Anne a crash course in defending herself. He went over the most vulnerable attack points: eyes, nose, throat, solar plexus, knees, and of course, the balls. But only for grabbing, not kicking. Punching and kicking took practice and experience, he explained, so attempted shots at the groin or the midsection of a seasoned fighter could easily just piss them off. He showed her how to disarm a knife attack, though he figured she could never pull it off. But the other lessons were productive. Biting, eye gouging, fingernails, bending fingers, popping the ears, and his own technique that he called the windmill, a way to diffuse an attacker and take someone down. He explained how people look and act if they're going to attack and to always strike first if you see it coming.

"You mean like when you kicked Jeff?" she asked.

"Exactly like that."

When they were sufficiently soaked in sweat, they returned to the party. Jean Anne assured him she would practice what he'd shown her and continue learning self-defense when she was settled in the Congo. He hated that she was going someplace so dangerous, but it wasn't his call.

Back at the party, not knowing when he might see them again, Jimmy went and planted himself between Papa and Cap'n Dick. Apparently, there was only one fight at the party, a new record. To Jim's delight, and not surprisingly, he heard Bo had knocked someone out with one punch. Debbie, Corrine, and Simmy got pretty schnockered and all went for Simmy to get a new tattoo. They were gone for a couple of hours. Cap'n Dick's wife was named Eva, but most called her Nanny. It was an odd thing, since Jimmy's maternal grandmother was also called Nanny because that was her actual name. So the distinction of Nanny Archer or Nanny Gaston had to be made. Nanny Archer, like any good Southern Baptist, never drank alcohol. But that day she was unknowingly eating the fruit that had been soaking in the rum punch all morning and getting tipsy for the first time in her life. A wasted Nanny Archer got into it with Gladys over Elton's supposed indiscretion with Mabel. Gladys threw a glass of tea at Nanny Archer before Shirley broke it up. There was a reason that Gladys' husband called her the Battleaxe. And Cap'n Dick would be sure to remind Nanny she'd gotten drunk for the rest of her life. Unlike many previous family picnics, the day went relatively smoothly. Dunner showed off his tree climbing skills by shimmying up the tall pine tree twice. On a dare, Cap'n Dick broke a pair of pliers just by squeezing them with one hand. Joe Fretus did the slow walk, one of Debbie's favorites. Bernard White told stories of riding out storms on the James River. Red Horton showed the little kids how to open a bicycle lock with a paperclip. It was a good time all around.

As the sun went down and night crept in, people began leaving. Except for Mom, who had fallen asleep in the back bedroom an hour earlier, only a small group of Jimmy's core family remained by 10:30. There was Jimmy, Debbie, Corrine, Daniel, and Corrine's dad, Uncle Ricky. There were also the sisters, Shirley and Darlene. Then Brian, Jean Anne, and Bocephus. They sat on lawn chairs in a circle around the roaring, crackling fire pit. The booze buzz was all but gone by then. Some were relaxed. Others—like Shirley—were exhausted. There was a ton of cleanup still to be done. But it was late and nice, and no one wanted to break it up just yet. Once a year, right? Separate little conversations developed here and there, then faded out. Uncle Ricky became interested in an exchange between Jimmy and Brian.

"No, Brian. Not contrails. Chemtrails."

Brian was unwavering. "There's no such thing."

"Yes, there are." Jimmy wouldn't concede, but neither would Brian.

"I flew in the Air Force for thirty years. I know what contrails are. They go away in a couple minutes."

"Right," Jimmy said. "That's why these are called chemtrails. They don't go away. They get bigger and spread out."

Brian leaned forward. "That sounds like bull hockey. You're saying the Air Force is making clouds using chemicals from fighters?"

"Yes, sir. That's what I'm saying."

"Why? Where? Come on."

"Here," Jimmy insisted. "Debbie and I delivered newspapers for six years. We would see them early at first light all the time. One or two planes would travel back and forth crisscrossing the sky. The contrails would swell and get thick, then spread out. In no time, a clear sky was overcast and covered with clouds. Sometimes our windshield had a soapy film afterwards."

Brian snorted a laugh and sat back, shaking his head.

Uncle Ricky jumped in. "It's true, Brian. Chemtrails are real. Some speculate it's camouflage to hide bases from satellites."

"That makes sense." Debbie was in now. "Look at all the military around here. Norfolk Naval Base, the Farm, Eustis, Langley and NASA, Naval Weapons, Dam Neck, Coast Guard Base."

"The Shipyard and Jefferson Labs," Jimmy threw in.

Uncle Ricky said, "Or maybe they're drugs to affect the population."

"Na, no way." Brian wouldn't budge.

"Brian," Bo joined in, "Jimmy and Debbie told me this stuff and I thought it was silly. They called and woke me up one morning at 5:00 am and said to go outside. So I did. And I watched these planes go back and forth for a half hour and bam! A clear sky was cloudy. It's true."

"Jimmy was up at 4:30 am checking the sky every morning for a week just to prove it to Bo Dean," Debbie was saying to Darlene.

Everyone was in the conversation now, exchanging opinions and making comments.

"I'd have to see it," Brian decided.

Uncle Ricky said, "The government does lots of things we don't know about and wouldn't like."

Shirley commented, "You sound like Jean Anne's old conspiracy boyfriend."

"Who?" Corrine asked.

Debbie explained. "John was Jean Anne's boyfriend. Some kind of sniper in the Army until he went nuts. He would go on and on about how the government was behind every bad thing that happened. You know, conspiracy theory stuff. Where is he now, Jean Anne?"

"In an institution," she said while twirling her finger around her temple.

The *Ohs* from the group showed that everyone understood. He was crazy.

Daniel said quietly, "They probably put him away because he knew too much."

There was a spooky moment of silence until Brian said, "Next you'll be saying that aliens run the government."

In all seriousness, Ricky said, "Not running it, just in cahoots."

"Oh Jesus Christ," Shirley blurted.

"Maybe Jesus was an alien," Uncle Ricky said jokingly.

Shirley took offense. "That's not funny, Uncle Ricky. Don't mock our Lord and Savior."

"Easy, Shirl. It was just a joke," Jimmy told her.

"Maybe, maybe not," said Uncle Ricky.

Bo saw trouble brewing and figured it was time to change the subject. "Let's talk about something else. This is as bad as talking about politics. How about Santa Claus or Bigfoot?"

Corrine stood up, her hands out. "You guys won't believe this. Me and Daniel, we saw a Sasquatch one morning. (She pronounced it Sassquatch.) It was early, and we heard this long kinda howl. Buck was growling. We looked out back and saw one by the edge of the trees. Then whoosh! It was gone."

"How big was it?" Jimmy asked.

"Oh, come on. You don't believe in Bigfoot, do you?" Darlene asked him.

"I believe Corrine," he said firmly.

Darlene turned to Corrine. "You really saw this thing?"

"Yes," she insisted. "It was what?" she said as she looked at Daniel and held her hand up high.

"About eight or nine feet tall easy," said Daniel. "I checked later and found a track." He took his cell out and passed around a picture of a massive footprint.

"Maybe someone was playing a joke on you," said Brian.

Corinne and Daniel looked at him amused as she asked, "Our ranch is backed up to an Indian reservation on three sides. You think the Choctaw were playing a joke on us?"

"Okay." Shirley stood up and clapped her hands together. "I've enjoyed all this I can stand. Who's going to help me clean up?"

That killed the conversation, but the mood hung in the air. The picnic was over, and they all pitched in to put away some of the food and halfheartedly clean up the trash. It was late and Shirley insisted they'd finish the rest in the morning so everyone could leave without feeling guilty.

The last of the party headed to their vehicles. Jim and Bo stood on the front porch saying their goodbyes to Shirley and Brian when Jimmy saw Corrine and Daniel getting in their four-wheel drive Jeep. He quickly kissed his sisters and ran out to catch them before they left.

Daniel put down his window as Jim trotted up. "Nice Jeep, guys."

Corrine leaned over and said, "Come on out and visit us in Oklahoma. We'll go booney stomping and I'll show you what it can do in the mud."

"With the business gone, why not?" Jim replied. "We might just move out there."

Corrine knew he was joking but said anyway, "You know ya'll are welcome anytime for as long as you want. We got plenty of room."

Daniel was nodding in agreement.

"Come over to the house and hang out," Jimmy offered. "You can spend the night."

"I wish we could, Bubba," Corrine said. "But we got a gig Tuesday night."

"Damn. Going back so soon?"

"Yeah," said Daniel. "Next time, though." They shook hands through the window.

As they drove off, Jimmy yelled, "Take care of her."

"Always," Daniel yelled back, waving out of the window.

Jimmy met Debbie and Bo at her SUV. "Bo Dean wants to ride with me," Deb informed Jimmy.

"Chicken," Jimmy teased.

"No. Wise," said Bo.

"Well, turn on the CB and we can play 'Who Is It' on the way home. I already have one."

"It's Vanessa Williams," Debbie hollered to Jimmy as he headed for the Muscle.

He stopped and looked back. "How did you know that?"

Debbie pulled up beside him in Miss Interceptor and rolled down Bo's passenger window. "Because, dear husband, you're obsessed with her. Race you home," she challenged and hit the gas.

"I'm not obsessed with her," he mumbled to himself. He jumped in the Muscle and took off after her, tires squealing and smoking.

Shirley shook her head at Jimmy's departing spectacle. "He's so immature," she said to Brian.

Later, as Shirley and Brian were finishing up the last of the dishes, Shirley said, "Brian, what do you think about all that weird stuff they were talking about?"

"Chemtrails, Bigfoot, and aliens? I think they watch too much TV."

"Yeah, you're probably right."

CHAPTER 10

BREAKING IN

It was Sunday morning and Debbie awoke to an empty bedroom. It always seemed so big when she was in there alone. At twenty by thirty-six feet with two walk-in closets, a sitting room, and two large full baths, that was no surprise. As always, Jimmy and the kids were long gone without disturbing her. She knew the bedroom door was shut and the deadbolt locked. It was one of her safety quirks. She liked deadbolts on the interior doors as well as the exterior doors. Jimmy didn't mind. It actually jived with his obsession of overly securing windows and placing weapons strategically around the house *just in case*. Some might consider them paranoid. But in Deep Creek, they would be called prepared. He was such a Boy Scout. She loved that guy.

Well, 7:00 am. Better get up. Finishing up what they called a whore's bath, she repeated the Deep Creek definition. "Wash up as far as possible. Wash down as far as possible. Then wash possible." Saying it always made her laugh.

She left her bathroom and went to the next door down on the left. It was her walk-in closet. It was so perfect she'd named it Versailles. Two walls were for hanging clothes, with different height rods critically placed for maximum efficiency. On the next wall were row after row of shelves for shoes, purses, and whatever she wanted folded. Sweaters, pajamas, coats, active wear, jeans, and denim skirts. Despite Jimmy's objections, she liked her skirts short. Around the next wall, there was a full-length mirror, lingerie bureau, chest of drawers, a catchall chair, and two standing jewelry boxes. Debbie loved her some jewelry. On the side of a jewelry box and next to the entrance door, two weapons were attached for quick access—courtesy of Jimmy. A Walther .22 magnum pistol and a ninjato, a ninja short sword. Debbie could live the rest of her life happily in her walk-in.

Picking through her lingerie, she decided on a pink, lacy, bikini panty/bra set. It always made her feel sexy to wear slinky underwear, even if no one else was going to see it. Although Jimmy would see it. She'd make sure of that. Next, a pair of argyle ankle socks, tight blue jeans, and her bebops. That was her name for the high-top Sheins she wore most of the time. Now came her favorite part. Opening the top dresser drawer, she picked through an array of specialty made T-shirts. And there it was, a picture of Daryl from *The Walking Dead* on the front. On the back was a big X. Underneath were the words, "If you can read this, you are in range."

Smelling something yummy, she sniffed the air and realized it was fried potatoes with onions. But back to the task at hand. The topper as always was jewelry. She felt that no self-respecting woman should ever leave the house without jewelry. First and foremost came her wedding band and customized engagement ring containing a two-carat diamond, flanked by two half-carat diamonds. Though it was a thing to have an accessory theme, Debbie decided today she would mix metals. A silver and gold chain necklace. Next to the wedding rings on the middle finger was a gold Capricorn ring. On the right hand were three silver rings. A coiled, two-headed snake with a blue topaz on each head. A spoon ring of a flower. And a stainless steel knuckle buster. Never know when a person might need a lesson in manners. The final touch was a black-faced Movado watch on the left. And on the right, a collection of thin silver bangles. She checked herself in the mirror. Perfect.

Jim was in the kitchen cooking breakfast at his dream stove in his pizza face apron. Debbie still couldn't believe he paid $3000 for it.

It was really nice—six gas burners, a middle grill, and double ovens. This from a man who wouldn't buy Heinz ketchup over generic just to save a few cents? She didn't begrudge him his toy, though. It was the only thing he'd ever spent serious money on besides her, and he truly did love to cook. In fact, Debbie couldn't remember the last time she made a meal. He cooked; she drove. That was their way.

Jimmy took four sausage patties out of the pan and paused before cooking more. "Bocephus," he yelled into the den. Bo didn't hear him. Playing with four dogs and a cat with two balls and a thick piece of knotted rope all at the same time took real concentration. "Bo," he yelled again. Bo heard the second one and responded while trying to calm the frenzied kids.

"You don't eat pork, do you?"

"Right."

"Do you want some beef or fish or something with your eggs and potatoes?"

"No, just the eggs are good," he replied, finally getting the kids settled.

"Shit," Jimmy said. "I forgot. No potatoes. How about some sliced tomatoes? I bought some monster homegrowns from the old lady on Centerville Road the other day."

"Perfect," said Bo.

Then Jimmy yelled "Get em, kids. Get Bo."

The animals knew exactly what *get em* meant and it was on again. Debbie came down the hall to great smells from the kitchen and sounds of chaos from the den. She was glad Bo was staying over. No one said it out loud, but they all wanted to stay together as much as possible for now. Could he really go back to prison? She put it out of her mind and joined the fray in the den.

They had a wonderful Sunday breakfast while discussing the family party. Bo said he hadn't seen that kind of crazy combination of people since Mecklenburg Prison. In great detail, he told Debbie about Cap'n Dick, Borey, and Aunt Minnie as if she had no idea who they were. Debbie asked him if he had really knocked out Jeff.

He said, "Well yeah. There was really no choice under the circumstances."

"What circumstances?" asked Jimmy.

"He was talking trash about you," Bo replied.

Jimmy smiled, leaned over the table, and they bumped fists. But Bo seemed especially interested in Cousin Simmy with the tattoos.

Debbie caught the hint. "I never figured you for a tattoo guy. Particularly on a pale white girl like Simmy."

"Why is that?" asked Bo while pouring everyone more coffee.

Jimmy drank his coffee black. And he winced as Debbie put four spoonfuls of sugar and flavored creamer in hers before she went on.

"I thought Black guys liked pristine skin, no scars or tattoos or anything."

"Where did you come up with that?" asked Bo.

She replied playfully, "I don't know. Maybe Eddie Murphy or Chris Rock."

"Black men can like tattoos just like you White men," Bo said to Jimmy.

"Oh no," insisted Jimmy. "I'm not a tattoo guy."

"Well, that's bullshit," said Debbie. "What about Angelina Jolie and that Princess woman you watch in the John Carter movie over and over?"

Jimmy felt like he needed a snappy comeback, but all he could think of was, "They're good actresses."

Debbie and Bo both dismissed his answer and laughed.

"Is Lady Gaga a good actress too?"

"Yes, as a matter of fact she is," Jimmy shot back.

"Bad example." Deb couldn't let it go and threw out, "I meant Miranda Lambert."

"Okay, we get it." Jim seemed annoyed.

"Thas Deb," Bo said, smiling.

The dogs all sat around the table hoping for scraps of people food, while a most unusual family enjoyed each other's company.

They all helped with the dishes while discussing plans for the day. First up was the rent from 22nd Street. If the tenant didn't answer today, they would go in. Debbie and Bo wanted to run the trail around Mariners Museum in Newport News. Jimmy didn't like running, mainly because of his left knee issues and especially a five-mile trail. But Debbie and Bo loved to run, so he would tough it out this one time. Then to Miss Dora's for fried chicken. Bo's mom made some serious fried chicken. It would be a full day. It was time to leave, and Bo offered to drive them in his Lexus. Jimmy was only partly joking as he pointed out that Bo shouldn't drive since they needed to get to Newport News before dark. So, Jimmy offered to drive the Muscle.

Bo only said, "Come on, man."

Debbie took over and informed them she would drive Miss Interceptor. She always named things that were important to her. The Beretta was Calamity Jane, her compound bow was Lightning, her walk-in closet was Versailles, and her big stuffed panda bear was Hank. Another one of those things about her that Jimmy adored.

"Well, let's take the dogs out and go," said Debbie.

"I got it," said Bo. He went to the back door and hollered, "Outside!"

Stampeding sounds came from every direction of the house. Jimmy and Debbie watched from the French doors as Bo ran back and forth across the yard with the kids. It brought a smile to Jimmy's face. He looked over at Debbie and she seemed sad. Her whole demeanor appeared melancholy. Tippycat sensed her mood and jumped into her arms, meowing for attention. She petted him absentmindedly, deep in thought. Jimmy ran his hand down her long blonde hair until it rested on the small of her back.

She looked at Jimmy and said, "I called Alicia at home last night. They're going to take him away, aren't they?"

He took her hand and said, "We'll come up with something." But he didn't really believe it.

Finally on the road, they weren't five minutes from the house when Miss Interceptor merged on to eastbound I-64 traffic. Even on Sunday, the construction caused the cars on the two lanes—squeezed by Jersey walls—to travel well below the temporary, fifty-five mile per hour speed limit. The highway expansion had been going on forever. But soon, very soon, thank God, it would be finished.

"So, what did you find out about this guy, Enoch Erran, at 22nd Street?" Debbie asked Jimmy.

"I found the lease on him out in the shop, but there wasn't much there. What is there, though, is very interesting. We got him from Herbert Newton when he retired. The lease was written in perpetuity in 1911 and the tenants handle all the maintenance and taxes."

"You don't see that very often," said Bo.

"Was East End even around in 1911?" asked Debbie.

"Oh yeah," said Bo. "Mr. Johnson's house across the street has been there for a hundred and fifty years."

"Jesus, how old is this Enoch guy?" Debbie asked.

"I don't know," said Jimmy. "Anyway, the rent automatically increases by three percent every four years. We missed that, by the way. Probably because he always paid in cash in the drop box. The owners, where we send the money, was just a PO box in New York City. That's the important stuff."

"Have either of you met him?" asked Debbie.

"Not me," said Jimmy and looked back at Bo. "You?"

"I only went there once," said Bo. "I had to meet the city guy about a sewer backup on the street. We went under the house, which looked really good. I could tell they had a deep basement. But I never saw anyone there."

"Don't see many deep basements around here with this water table," said Debbie. "Well, we'll see when we get there."

"Jimmy, put on some tunes," said Bo from the back seat.

"How about Joni Mitchell?" suggested Jimmy.

"Who?" asked Bo.

"No, I got it," said Debbie. She opened a CD and inserted it, with Jimmy bitching about her paying attention to her driving the whole time. "Let's Stay Together" exploded from the speakers and Jimmy turned the volume down a little. Then held his fist for a bump from Bo in the back. Al Green, Bo's favorite singer.

Bo leaned up between the seats and asked Debbie mischievously, "Does Black peoples always has to sit in the back, Miss Daisy?"

Debbie laughed. "You know I love driving you around East End in the back seat like a carpetbagger. Do you want to go to the Piggly Wiggly, Bocephus?"

He looked over at Jimmy and said, "Thas Deb."

Everyone was rocked forward as Debbie braked hard for one of their usual traffic backups. "Shit," said Debbie, craning her neck to see down the road. "This might take a while."

"Let's play movie quotes," proposed Jim.

"Okay," said Debbie. "Bo Dean, you go first."

Jimmy and Debbie loved playing these games, but Bo wasn't that fond of it. Going over movies in his mind, he took so long that Jimmy and Debbie began prodding him.

"All right," said Bo. "Give me a minute." Seeming pleased, he finally said, "Say hello to my little friend."

Jimmy and Debbie said *Scarface* simultaneously. "You can do better, Bo," Deb scoffed. "Jimmy, go."

Bo made a face at her from the back.

In a bad English accent, Jimmy said, "Do you want me to wash your dick, you little shit?"

Debbie said, "*Arthur.*"

"I don't know that one," said Bo.

"Really," said Jim. "It's a Dudley Moore comedy. Probably the funniest movie ever made."

Bo shook his head. "I got nothing."

"Okay," said Debbie. "How about this? Are you crazy? The fall will probably kill you."

"I know that," said Jimmy. "Butch Cassidy and Sundance."

"*Butch Cassidy and the Sundance Kid*," Bo said quickly. He saw Debbie looking at him in the mirror and added, "I knew you'd correct him, and I wanted to beat you to it."

Deb stuck her tongue out at him and said, "You're up, Bo Dean."

"I'm gonna make him an offer he can't refuse," said Bo.

"*Godfather*," Jimmy and Debbie said together.

"Jim, you're up," said Debbie.

"We're gonna need a bigger boat," was Jimmy's quote.

Bo shook his head. "I can't place it."

"*Jaws*," said Debbie. "Except technically, it's *you're* going to need a bigger boat."

"Really?" asked Jim. "Okay, Deb. Go."

"What the fuck, Cooper. I almost put it on YouTube."

Jim and Bo thought hard and Debbie smiled. She was sure she had them.

"I know this," said Jimmy.

"I don't," said Bo.

"You give up, guys?"

Jimmy blurted out, "*Spy*."

"Good, Baby," said Deb. "Bo, you're up."

"You know this isn't fair, right?" said Bo.

"What isn't fair?" asked Debbie

"We're doing White movies. If I started quoting Black movies, you two wouldn't have a chance."

"Give me your best shot," Debbie said smugly.

Jimmy smiled. He knew something that Bo did not. Debbie had always been fascinated by Black movies and watched them quite often.

"Are you sure?" asked Bo.

Debbie just said, "Go."

"Did you see his hair? MF looks like a predator," Bo said and sat back confidently.

"Lean up here, Bo Dean," said Debbie. He leaned up and she answered it. "That's from *Booty Call*, except he said motherfucker, Bo, not MF. Mother…fucker."

Bo was surprised and more than a little impressed. "You know *Booty Call*?"

"Of course, Bo. It's a classic."

"She loves Black movies, Bo," said Jimmy. "She makes me watch that one with Vivica Fox and Anthony Anderson with her a couple times a year."

"Thas Deb," said Bo, still smarting. "Okay, you're up, Jimbo."

Jimmy held up one finger and said, "I can only vouch for the bird."

Bo shook his head, but Debbie immediately said, "*A Touch of Class*."

"Damn," said Jimmy. "You're too good."

"Now, this one is for Bo. You won't know it, Jimmy."

"I might."

"No, Honey, you won't. But you should, Bo. The funny thing is, on the outside I was an honest man."

As Debbie predicted, Jimmy came up blank.

"I know this," said Bo proudly. "*Shawshank Redemption*."

"Excellent," said Debbie. "Okay boys, we're changing the game. Think of the best-looking actress or famous person ever. Best-looking woman, as long as she's famous."

When the guys were ready, Debbie said, "Me first. Michelle Pfeiffer." The guys nodded their heads in agreement.

"Good pick," said Jimmy.

Bo added, "White gold."

"Damn right," said Deb, enjoying the Bruno reference. "Jimmy, I already know your pick, but go ahead."

"Vanessa Williams."

"And I was right, of course. Bo, your turn."

To Jimmy's enjoyment and Debbie's apparent annoyance, Bo said, "Rita Hayworth."

"Bocephus," Debbie said in her bossy voice, "Rita Hayworth is an inappropriate answer, both age wise and race wise."

"What have you got against Rita Hayworth?" Jimmy asked.

"Wait a minute." Bo cut in and leaned up between the seats. "Jimmy picked Vanessa Williams. Isn't she age and race inappropriate for him?"

"No. He's been obsessed with her since she won Miss America, so it doesn't count.

"I'm not obsessed," Jimmy said defensively.

"You're definitely obsessed," Debbie insisted.

"That makes no sense," said Bo. "But I'll change my girl to Zoe Saldana."

"Oh, hubba-hubba," said Jimmy. "I love the Green Whore."

"But Bo, she has small breasts," said Debbie.

"Since when do they have to have big breastises?"

"Tell me you didn't just say breastises, Bocephus Dean." Debbie jeered.

"She's pissed because nobody picked her," Jimmy told Bo.

"No, I'm not."

"But she said famous," Bo said to Jim.

"She thinks she's famous," Jimmy answered, only about half joking.

"You two stop talking about me like I'm not here."

And so it went for another fifteen minutes while Al Green sang in the background.

Miss Interceptor took the Chestnut Avenue exit from I-64 and turned left into East End.

"Black folks love them some Jesus," said Bo and it was evident that Sunday morning. Chestnut Avenue had a church every couple of blocks and the main thoroughfare was teeming with well-dressed people heading to worship. After Miss Interceptor turned onto 22nd Street, the only people they saw were two Black guys sitting on a knee wall in front of an old, dilapidated house. As they drove by, one waved while the other looked away.

"You know them, Bo?" asked Jimmy.

"Yeah. The ox is called Big Mo. He's okay. I spent a year with him in lockup. The other one is named Gransy or Granby or something. Anyway, they call him G. He's a fool and a Knucklehead. And that's a crack house, by the way." They arrived and Debbie backed into the driveway of 2424 22nd Street.

Debbie, Jimmy, and Bo called it confirming a rental. They had done it too many times in the past to count. Enter the property by any means necessary, confirm if the tenants still lived there and acquire any helpful information in the process. Everyone went into their set routines. Bo headed off to check the garage doors, the windows, and the back door. Debbie went straight for the front doorbell and began alternating between ringing it and knocking loudly. Jimmy pulled out his ring of master keys and started trying them in the deadbolt one at a time. Unknown to most laymen, standard rental locks had a finite number of keys. If you had a large collection of master keys—Jimmy had eighteen years' worth—odds were good that one of them would fit any given rental. These actions were their step one. Step two, if necessary, would be to break in. Bo came around the house shaking his head at Debbie.

Still ringing and knocking, she asked, "No luck?"

"We'd have to break some glass," he answered.

Jimmy was trying the second to last key on his ring. Bingo. The deadbolt turned. He made quick work of the doorknob lock with his driver's license and the front door swung open. They went in cautiously and the first impression was that the tenant had moved. The living room, dining room, and hallway were bare. Bo went straight upstairs.

Debbie called out, "Be careful, Bo-Bo," while she and Jimmy went to the kitchen in the back of the house.

There were signs of life in the kitchen. Two wooden high back chairs sat in the center of the room facing an old-style JVC television. Hooked up next to it on the kitchen counter was a combination DVD/video tape player. Debbie went to check the garage while Jimmy went to the refrigerator. The freezer was packed full. Half was TV dinners and half was frozen steaks, mostly ribeyes. There must have been fifty or sixty steaks. The fridge had two gallons of whole milk, a half empty case of grape soda in cans, a deli size roll of bologna, two loaves of bread, three dozen stacked cartons of eggs, several jars of peanut butter and different jellies, a squeeze bottle of yellow mustard, and two bananas, the skins almost black. Very unusual. Also unexpectedly, the kitchen was exceptionally clean. Even the oven and drip pans under the stove burners were shiny and spotless. Jimmy began to rummage through all the cabinets and drawers, mainly looking for mail. He found some silverware and dishes and a variety of sundries. But one thing he found in abundance were stacks of illegally burned black market DVDs and CDs. Another drawer was full of only Cameron Diaz movies. Obviously, a big fan lived there.

Debbie came back wide-eyed and said, "Jimmy, you have to see this garage. It has a lot of regular junk. But there are weapons hanging all over the walls. Bows, arrows, knives, tomahawks, whips, even a flail. And there's a box of what looks like folding machetes."

Jimmy's eyes lit up. "I've never heard of a folding machete." Wouldn't be the first time he acquired some nice weapons for his collection from an abandoned rental.

Alarm in his voice, Bo yelled from the second floor, "Jimmy, Debbie, you gotta see this." They hurried upstairs and joined him at the door to the upstairs bathroom. There was a puzzled look on his face. "This is weird, guys," he said and motioned them to look in.

There was a good-sized square hole in the wall between the toilet and the bathtub where the sink should have been.

"Where's the vanity?" asked Jimmy.

"In the bedroom down the hall," said Bo.

Light was glowing from the hole and they could see stairs going down.

"I say we check it out," suggested Debbie.

"I don't know," said Jimmy.

Without comment, Bo started down the stairs.

"Okay, we're going in," said Jimmy and followed him.

Debbie closed and locked the bathroom door before joining the quest. They went down three flights of a stairwell that was dimly lit from no readily apparent light source. They ended up in a fifteen-foot square room that was hewn out of solid rock. A tunnel exited the room and then split into two directions. They stood at the Y, trying to look down each hallway.

"This is creepy," said Jimmy. "There could be anything down here. Haven't you two ever seen a horror movie?"

"Terrorists maybe?" said Bo.

That comment prompted all three to produce a pistol. Debbie's .40 caliber Beretta Calamity Jane came from her holster, Jimmy's .380 Ruger from his pocket, and Bo pulled a 9mm Colt from the back of his waistband. The click of bullets entering all three chambers was almost simultaneous.

"How is this possible?" whispered Bo. "This should be flooded. We're right by the bay."

"We should go back and call the police and the city," Jimmy suggested.

With a finger to her lips, Debbie whispered, "I hear something," and headed off to the left.

"Or not," Jimmy said as he followed her.

"Thas Deb," said Bo, right behind him.

As they moved along, the noise defined itself as a rhythmic thumping with intermittent grunting sounds. The tunnel opened into a long room and all three were shocked by the bizarre scene. A large, scaly, yellowish Lizard man was on top of a woman bound to a table and humping her. Reacting before thinking, Bo yelled, "Hey! Get off her!"

The creature leapt lightly from the table and landed facing them, sporting a huge, crooked erection. All three tried to shoot but their guns wouldn't fire. The vertical slits in the creature's snake eyes pulsated as he studied them. The beast uttered a low hiss and black curved claws sprang from his fingertips. Acting on instinct, Jimmy pocketed his .380

and pulled an Old Timer lock blade from the leather case on his belt. He opened it Deep Creek style with one hand and took two steps toward the thing, garnering its attention.

He yelled, "Bo, flank him!"

But Bo was already attacking. The Lizard man slashed out toward Bo's face. Bo ducked under it and delivered a crushing uppercut to the scaly chin. Jimmy once saw Bocephus knock a two hundred fifty-pound bartender out cold with that same punch. But it seemed to have no effect on the monster, who then grabbed Bo by the throat with both hands and lifted him off his feet. Bo was frantically punching, kicking, and gouging, but he couldn't free himself from the monster's grip. Jimmy's peripheral vision picked up Debbie coming in from the left. A vicious kick to the scaly knee—followed by a flurry of blows to the face and throat—got the brute's attention. He dropped Bo's now limp body and forced Debbie back with flailing claws. Debbie was too fast for him to hit and quickly deciphered his rhythm. She dodged his attacks with counterstrikes that had no discernable effects. Jimmy didn't have her reflexes or boxing skills, but he had to do something—now. Watching the beast's pattern of moving his left leg, Jimmy saw his opening. He had done it a thousand times wrestling. When the left foot came down again, Jim leapt on the reptilian mutant. It was all there, almost too easy. He slid in his left leg, reached around the back, grabbed the right arm, and came up and over the head. By the time the freak knew Jimmy was on him, they were going to the floor. He locked in the guillotine. And for the first time in his life, he wasn't going to be able to hold it. The creature had strength like he couldn't imagine.

"Debbie! I can't hold it. Kill it. Kill it now!" he yelled to her.

Debbie came in with her Gerber lock blade and stabbed it repeatedly in the chest while Jimmy barely held on. The knife strikes had no apparent effect and seemed to just be making it angrier.

"I'm losing him," said Jimmy desperately.

Debbie heard a weak voice coming from the woman the Lizard had been raping. "The throat. Not the chest. The throat," was barely audible.

Jimmy felt a gush of green blood on his face and thought he could see Debbie sawing at the creature's throat. He felt it begin to go limp and he released his hold to help her. It took only seconds to all but sever the head from the body with both of them slicing together.

Jimmy heard Debbie say, "I think it's dead."

Soaked with the green blood and consumed by the dead weight and stinging stench, he almost freaked out in his frantic efforts to get it off him.

"You're okay, Babe," said Debbie, helping him up. "It's dead and you're okay."

"Are you all right?" he asked her.

She came in for a messy hug. In her ear, Jimmy said, "Bo's right. You are Wonder Woman."

She pulled back. "Bo," she said. "I'll check him. You check her on the table."

"Keen eye, sharp tooth," he said, quoting Rikki-Tikki-Tavi, and kissed a clean spot on her cheek. Jimmy hurried to the table and winced. The woman was lashed to the table with nylon rope. Her dark complexion and jet-black hair suggested American Indian. Her body and face were so covered with bruises, cuts, and red blood as to make her otherwise unrecognizable. She looked as bad as he'd ever seen. The knots holding her were unfamiliar and complicated. When trying to untie them became frustrating, he pulled his Old Timer and just cut them.

Debbie screamed, "Jimmy, come here quick! I think Bo's dead!"

Jimmy ran to Debbie's side and dropped to his knees. Bo had no pulse. But that didn't make sense. The creature had him for only a few seconds, not nearly enough time to strangle him. Debbie cleared Bo's throat and began CPR. She pushed his chest fifteen times. Jimmy pinched his nose and gave him two breaths, just like they'd learned in CERT class. Under the next round of compressions, his chest just collapsed. They pulled back in horror as his shoes fell off as if his feet were gone. His pant legs went flat, and they watched his hands turn to dust.

"What the fuck!" Debbie cried out.

Bo was disappearing. First his body, then his clothes. Only metal remained in the pile of dust. Eyelets from his shoes, a belt buckle, a zipper, the 9mm, and where his face was, a gold tooth lay in the sooty remains.

"It's poison," said the woman on the table.

Debbie's eyes were blank. Jimmy thought she was going into shock. He took her by the shoulders and shook her. "Debbie, we have to go. There could be more of those things."

Looking stunned, she said unemotionally, "Bo's dead. He's gone."

"I know, Baby, and we need to go too, okay?"

"They'll be coming," he heard the woman say. He looked over and saw her sitting unsteadily on the edge of the table. "They're coming," she said again and fell back on the table, out cold.

"Debbie!" He shouted and slapped her across the face. Recognition crept back into her eyes. "We have to go now, Baby."

"Okay." She nodded. Confused and bewildered, Debbie rose to her feet and headed back in the direction they'd come. Jimmy took ahold of the woman's right arm and pulled her up into a Fireman's Carry. Catching up with Debbie at the base of the stairs, he mumbled, "I must be getting old. This woman feels like she weighs a ton."

Debbie seemed clearheaded again as she climbed the stairs two at a time. Carrying the woman across his shoulders, Jimmy fell behind, laboring with each step. Before entering the bathroom, Debbie called back, "You okay, Babe?"

"Yeah, keep going. I'm coming."

Outside, as she descended the front stoop, Debbie saw the two Black men from earlier standing beside Miss Interceptor. She pushed the button on the key fob to open the side door and back hatch, startling both of them. The one Bo called G came toward her as he reached under his oversized T-shirt. Debbie pulled Calamity Jane and stepped into a vicious front kick to his chest. After what happened in that basement, she wasn't sure if the gun would fire, but he didn't know that. Lying on his back and trying to regain his breath, he felt her knee come down on his throat and looked down the barrel of her Beretta. She pulled a 9mm from his waistband and tossed it in the truck. Big Mo looked from Debbie to Jimmy carrying the woman from the house and took off.

Debbie pushed the barrel against G's forehead. "Are you ready to die?" she spat at him, eyes blazing. He shook his head frantically. She stood up. "Then run. Run!"

He crabbed across the yard until he made it to his feet and then disappeared behind the house across the street.

Completely exhausted, Jimmy rolled the woman off his shoulders and into the back of the SUV. He headed for the driver's seat, but Debbie stopped him. "No, Babe, catch your breath. I'll drive." He hesitated. "No, I got it," she insisted. "Sentara Hospital is only about twelve minutes from here."

Too tired to comment, Jimmy simply nodded and went around. As they drove away, Jimmy and Debbie didn't see the viper eyes watching them from Mr. Johnson's front window.

CHAPTER 11

THE HOSPITAL

Blowing the horn, Debbie pulled up to the emergency room entrance. A security guard stuck his head out of the double glass doors as Jimmy yelled, "We need help!"

Carrying the dark-haired woman, he was met by two nurses pushing a stretcher. Covered in both green and red blood must have been a sight. Lying her mangled, naked body down, he pulled the sheet up as the nurses backed up. They were eyeing him warily and didn't move closer until he stepped away. Then one pushed the gurney into the building. While still leaving ample space between them, the other nurse began asking him questions.

"Does she have allergies?"

"I don't know."

"Does she...."

Jimmy cut her off. "I don't know anything about her." He turned and searched for Debbie in the parking lot. She was parking Miss Interceptor in the back.

The security guard had been watching closely the whole time. When they entered, he ushered them to the front desk, keeping a respectable distance. The only thing he said was, "Miss, you can't bring that firearm in the hospital."

Jimmy prepared for the worst, but when Debbie saw only a radio and nightstick on his belt, she turned and ignored him. He stayed a few feet behind them as they spoke to the receptionist. Whether it was their current physical state or the gun and bad attitudes, Jimmy couldn't say, but the receptionist had trouble looking them in the eye as she began asking questions of Debbie.

"Are you two okay?"

"Yes, we're fine."

"What happened to her?"

"We only know she was being raped."

"Does she have allergies?"

"I don't know."

"Contact number or next of kin?"

"I don't know."

"What are you two covered with?"

Debbie hesitated and Jimmy said, "Mud."

"I'll need you to sign here," she said, spinning a form around in front of Debbie and laying a pen next to it.

"Whoa!" Debbie put on the brakes. "Does signing this in any way make me responsible for her bill?"

"Well, technically, I guess so."

Annoyed, Debbie said, "Technically as opposed to emotionally or spiritually? Hell no, we are not signing anything. I told you. We don't know her."

Debbie was getting louder, and Jimmy saw the guard shifting uncomfortably behind them. "Easy, Babe," he said to her. Then to the nurse, "We accept no responsibility for this woman," and spun the form back around.

A tall imposing woman in her fifties with a tight bun of gray hair on her head and a clipboard appeared confidently behind the counter. Veins stood out on her forehead as she spoke to them through bright red lipstick. She looked like a demented Cloris Leachman from the film *High Anxiety*. The receptionist shrank away from her. "I'm Mrs. Stormworthy, administrative assistant manager." She poked the back of her ink pen at the name on her flat chest. "You two brought in a patient," she stated, then paused.

"Yes," said Debbie, sighing impatiently.

"I want her name." It was more a demand than a request.

"And people in hell want ice water," Debbie snapped back.

Jimmy deflected Mrs. Stromworthy's reaction of indignance by saying, "We don't know."

"What happened to her?" she commanded.

"We still don't know," said Jimmy, looking down and shaking his head.

"Hey, Nurse Ratchet," Debbie's voice was rising as she leaned over the counter a bit. "Talk to the girl over there that's scared to death of you. She already asked all these questions."

Stormworthy addressed Debbie in a scornful tone. "Look, lady, that patient has serious injuries. We have reason to believe she's been tortured and raped, and you two come in here looking like this. You better show some cooperation."

Stormworthy stepped back as Jimmy's finger came across the counter and invaded her space. "I've had about enough of you," he snarled.

The security guard put his hand on Jimmy's shoulder. "Sir, you need to step back and calm down."

Before Jimmy could react, Debbie had snatched the guard's hand. With the pain from a wristlock, she moved him several steps back, then blocked one foot so he plopped into a waiting room chair. Her face was stern as she told him, "Now you stay here and don't touch my husband anymore. Understand?"

"Yes, ma'am," accepted the frightened guard.

Just then a pale, slight man in a charcoal gray, off-the-rack-suit—followed by two uniformed police officers—came through the oversized glass entrance doors.

"She attacked the security guard," yelled Mrs. Stormworthy, holding up her clipboard like a shield and pointing at Debbie.

Debbie looked at the cops defiantly as Jimmy moved up beside her. The officers put their hands on their sidearms. Debbie did the same. The man in the gray suit stepped up with his hands out. "Easy everybody. Just take a breath… guys," he said over his shoulder. The policemen took their hand from their pistols but remained alert. Debbie relaxed a little. He walked deliberately toward Deb and Jim. "I'm Deputy Sergeant Reubens. I can see that you two have had a rough morning."

"You have no idea," said Jimmy.

"Come on," he said calmly. "Let's go to the cafeteria. We'll get some coffee, and you can tell me what's going on. You want to wash up first?"

"Yes, thanks," said Debbie, considering for the first time how they must look. She saw the cops still eyeballing the Beretta on her hip. "I have a concealed weapons permit," she said to the sergeant.

"Understood," he said. "But how about I hold onto it for now?" Debbie drew it quickly, startling the policemen, and handed it to the sergeant. Jimmy held back a smile. Debbie was fucking with them. She was a nut. He kept the unseen Ruger in his pocket. After the morning they had, he felt better keeping it handy. "Let's get cleaned up." Reubens gestured them down the hall towards the men's room.

While the two policemen waited outside the door, Jimmy and Debbie went into the men's room together. They washed up as best they could. Just inside the cafeteria entrance, Sergeant Reubens told them, "You guys get a table and I'll get us some drinks. Coffee?"

"Yes, black," said Jimmy.

"Hot chocolate," decided Debbie.

"Hungry?"

They both said no. "I'll be right back," said Reubens.

Debbie and Jimmy picked a table by the wall and sat with their backs to it. It seemed safer. The officers sat at another table nearby. Sergeant Reubens returned with a tray of coffee, hot chocolate, two bottled waters, and a bag of potato chips. Jim and Debbie both took long drinks on the water. They were tired. For the first time since the incident, as it came to be called, they felt at ease. The sergeant was patient and thorough in his interview. After a time, Jimmy and Debbie sipped their now warm drinks while the sergeant went over and talked to the officers at the other table.

"Sampson," The sergeant said to the bigger man, "here are their concealed weapons permits and driver's licenses. Run them both for driving, criminal, and anything else you can think of. And check on that woman they brought in. Jordy," he said to the other one, "you might want to get you fellas something to eat. We're going to be here for a while."

Back with the Archers, Sergeant Reubens restarted the questioning from the beginning. Debbie told the sergeant what had happened pretty much verbatim, with two exceptions. She changed Bo's role. It seemed like a bad idea to tell a cop that Bo had melted into the floor. She also held back that the villain was a Lizard man. When he asked for a description, she said he was big with funny eyes. Jimmy backed her up completely and told the same story. The interrogation seemed over, and Jimmy asked if they were done. Reubens was amused. "No, we have to go through it again." Over an hour later, Sampson the cop came back and signaled the sergeant across the cafeteria. "I'll be right back," he told the Archers and motioned Officer Sampson to another table.

They sat down and Sampson pulled out a small notebook. "Here's what I found out. They had a property management company for quite a while. It went out of business this year and they recently filed for bankruptcy. The driving records are pristine. Their credit is shit. And I think they may be a handful."

"Why do you say that?"

"He was born and raised in Deep Creek." Cops knew the reputation of Creekers. They had been a problem for generations. "He's had two arrests for assault but no charges filed. She did a short stint as an MMA fighter, and you saw her with the gun foolishness. He may be trouble, but boss, I think she's dangerous."

"Was she any good?"

"She won three times and then quit. And your gonna love this."

Sergeant Reubens came back to the table. It had been well over two hours, and he could see that Jimmy and Debbie were getting very restless. "Any word on the woman we brought in?" asked Jimmy.

"She'll live and we're doing forensic testing for rape," was all he would offer.

"Can we go now?" asked Debbie. "We've been gone a long time, and we have a lot of animals at home.

"Not yet," he said. "We need to go over it again." Exasperated, the Archers shifted uncomfortably in their seats.

"What did you do when you got up this morning?"

After another round of the same questions, he left the cafeteria for about twenty minutes. When he came back and sat down, he asked again for the description of the alleged perp. Jimmy was exhausted and Debbie was looking rough. He'd had enough. "Look Sergeant, we don't need to do this anymore. Debbie needs some rest and I desperately need a shower. Why don't you just go to the house and check it out yourself?"

Jimmy stood up, prompting Officer Jordy to do the same. The sergeant signaled him that all was well and stood up also. "Mr. Archer, the police have already spent half the day at the house and the fire department has been there since right after you left. The house burned to the ground shortly after you two arrived here at the hospital. We also found the basement. It contained a table, ropes, blood, and a 9mm pistol but no dead body of a big man with funny eyes."

There was an awkward silence until Debbie said, "So what now?"

"I guess we're good for now. But I know you're holding back. And I intend to find out what really happened in that basement." He paused and when they didn't respond he went on. "I'll call you in a couple of days after I have the Beretta tested. Don't leave town."

Jimmy took Debbie's hand and pulled her with him as they left the cafeteria. Walking through the hospital, Debbie said, "He doesn't believe us."

"Fuck em," said Jimmy. "They got nothing."

With a harsh expression and arms crossed, Mrs. Stormworthy watched Debbie and Jimmy plod across the emergency waiting area. Debbie could see her reflection in the glass doors. Without looking back, Debbie flipped her off as they exited the building. Jimmy offered to drive and walked Debbie to the passenger side with no resistance. He put Miles Davis in the CD player and turned it on low. Holding hands all the way, they drove home in silence.

Back at the house, the kids sensed their mood and their excitement waned quickly. Debbie showered first while Jimmy robotically fed the kids, took them out, and made a ham and cheese sandwich for them to split. During his shower, Jimmy began rinsing out the clothes, but the lingering smell was rank. As he watched green blood swirling down the drain, he said under his breath, "What the fuck, Bocephus?" He decided to throw it all out in the morning. Afterward, in the bedroom, Debbie was in bed and the sandwich remained untouched. He wasn't hungry either and ended up feeding it to the kids. While putting on some boxers, he could tell Debbie was crying softly. Sliding up behind her in the bed, he put his arm across her belly. That seemed to comfort her and she fell into a troubled sleep.

Monday morning at 4:30 am, Jimmy woke and was startled to see two floating yellow eyes with black slits looking back. Whew! It was just Tippycat like any other day. But it wasn't any other day. From habit Jimmy went through his morning routine. Take the kids out, feed them, wash any dishes in the kitchen sink, make coffee in the electric percolator, check his phone for messages, and check the weather forecast. Finally, with a bit of nervous anticipation, he pulled up the local news highlights. There it was. A house in the East End of Newport News had burned down. Bocephus being gone had felt like a dream, but not now. He read the article while he used the bathroom. Then checked all the other headlines and the police log. Nothing about the woman they took to the hospital. He thought that was odd. While showering, shaving, and brushing his teeth, he relived the day before over and over in his mind. Petey was whining at the door as he put on his workout clothes. Damn, he forgot the tub water. Petey loved to lick the tub water off his calves and ankles after he showered. He opened the bathroom door and Petey—along with all the kids—was sitting there patiently. Animals always knew when something was up. "Sorry, Pete," he said. They followed him back to the kitchen. After an eternity, it was finally 7:00 am and Jimmy went to the bedroom to wake Debbie. The kids jumped on the bed to wake her with their morning ritual, but it wasn't the usual celebration. Debbie got up, barely paying the animals any mind. She went straight to Jimmy and hugged him until Jimmy gently pulled her back and asked if she was okay.

"Yes," was all she answered as she kissed his cheek.

He left and came back with a cup of coffee just the way she liked it. Four spoons of sugar, three heaping spoons of French vanilla creamer, and a shot of cinnamon. Already dressed in sweatpants and a loose T-shirt, she sipped the steaming cup of extra sweet coffee eagerly. "I checked the news," said Jimmy. "The house burning was there but nothing about the girl."

Debbie wrinkled her forehead and said, "I don't want to talk about that yet."

"Okay," he agreed, and they headed for the kitchen.

Debbie sat down, distant while nursing her coffee. Jimmy didn't feel like cooking, so he pulled out a box of Frosted Flakes and a box of Rice Krispies. Jimmy always mixed his cereals. Add a half gallon of milk and that was breakfast. Instead of their usual dishes, he went to the China cabinet and took out her favorite bowls. Blue stoneware from Japan with Shinto gods painted on them.

"Oh, I love these," she said, and he felt a little better.

Over cereal, Jimmy started talking. "What do we tell Bo's mother?" he asked, not looking up from his bowl.

"What?" said Debbie, deep in her own thoughts.

"Miss Dora." Jimmy looked at her. "What do we tell her?"

"I don't know." The question surprised her. It came back to her *hard* that Bocephus was dead. She hadn't even considered the fact that nobody else knew. They were supposed to have gone to Miss Dora's for dinner yesterday. Checking her phone, she saw three messages from Miss Dora and one message from Bo's sister. "Jesus, Jim, Dora doesn't even know. Nobody knows." Jimmy nodded and put down the spoonful of cereal he was about to take. Debbie pushed her bowl away.

"You haven't eaten anything since yesterday, Babe. You should eat something. Want me to cook you some eggs?"

"You're not eating either," was her answer.

Jimmy stood up and the kids reacted. "I'm going to work out and hit the heavy bag for a while."

"Really?" Deb asked. "Right now?"

"Yes, I need to hit something. You want to join me?"

"No, not now. Maybe later."

"Okay, I'll see you in a little while. Outside!" he called as he went through the French doors. All the children scrambled to the back door except Tippycat. He jumped into Debbie's lap and began to purr rhythmically. "Love you," he called out as he shut the door.

"Love you back, Jimsy."

As Jimmy approached the detached garage, Connor, Petey, and Nick took off to explore and play in the yard. Only Molly stayed with him. Downstairs was what they called the shop. It was a two-car garage with pegboard walls covered with hanging tools of all types. Debbie had sectioned them off into hand tools, mechanic's tools, building tools, small power tools, and antique tools. There was also a section of old license plates and a small part of Jim's astonishing weapons collection. There was a three by ten-foot workbench along the back wall and it was a do-it-yourselfer's dream. Jimmy used to keep his Trans Am, the Muscle, in the garage as well. Since closing Archer's Acquisition's, the shop was packed full of appliances, office furniture, filing cabinets, and lots of what Jimmy considered junk. Jimmy and Molly weaved through the clutter and ascended the stairs to the second floor. Jimmy turned on the light to their homemade gym over the shop. There was a heavy bag hanging from an open joist in the center of the room. On one wall was a wide array of exercise paraphernalia. Pairs of single weights from one up to seventy-five pounds. Stretch bands of multiple colors indicating tension strength and different sized medicine balls. On a makeshift shelf, an old TV and a DVD player with stacks of exercise videos they'd accumulated over the years. Over by the window, an older but still effective weight machine. It had every function an individual would want. Any press or curl possible up to six hundred pounds. Also, bars for pull-ups and dips and even a slant board for inverse sit-ups.

"Boy, Bo Dean dearly loved this machine," Jimmy said to Molly. He needed to get to work and clear his mind. "Go lay down," he said to her. Molly wasn't much for romping in the yard like the terriers and the beagle. She claimed her favorite spot on the old wrestling mat that had come from Jimmy's high school. That acquisition was quite a coup. Jimmy had taken the one section when they threw out the existing mat for a new one. Jimmy loved the fact that it was the same one they'd used when he wrestled there. Unlike grass, carpet, or even yoga mats, it was perfect for wrestling, drills, calisthenics, or yoga. He put on his practice mitts and began hitting the bag.

Inside, Debbie sipped her coffee and stroked Tippy while she listened to Diana Krall sing about the girl in the other room. Suddenly she felt lightheaded and there was a pain behind her left ear. By the time she rubbed her eyes it was gone and she disregarded it. Then a thought occurred to her. Tippy jumped to the floor as she stood up quickly. "Come on, Tips. Let's get busy."

Jimmy hit the heavy bag for about a half an hour. Then he ran Molly off the mat, growling with irritation, and went into his own pattern of wrestling drills. It was going well until he tweaked his left knee. "Shit," he said out loud. It was really sore from holding the Lizard guy and carrying that woman up the stairs. He said, "Fuck it," and skipped to the end of his routine. Ten dips, Ten reverse dips, and then pull-ups until he was toast. That was it. He turned off the light, dripping sweat. It was going to be another hot one. "Come on, Molls," he called, and she followed him down the stairs. In the backyard, Petey and Connor grappled in the grass while Nicky rested comfortably under the shade of the mimosa tree. "Let's go in," Jimmy called out and they raced for the deck. After a quick shower, he put on his uniform. Black khakis, white sox, and steel-toed hiking boots. He tucked in a tan T-shirt that read "Work twice as fast and finish in half the time." A Swat four-inch lock blade went in his left pocket, and the Ruger .380 went in his right. He found Debbie in the front corner bedroom that was also their home office. "What are you doing, Babe?"

"I was doing some research while I waited for you. Did you know that there is a whole mythology about Lizard Men? They're called Drachonians or Reptilians and a lot of people think they've been trying to take over the world for centuries."

"Yeah, I knew that. You know I've been watching those *Ancient Alien* shows for years. That's just the kind of stuff they have on there."

"You've never mentioned it before."

"I never believed it until yesterday."

She turned off the computer and stood up. "Let me put on my boppers and we're gone," she said urgently.

"Gone where?" he asked, looking her up and down. She was wearing a pair of cut-off jeans with an inch of lace trim around the bottom. The lace was the only thing keeping her butt cheeks from peeking out. She was also wearing a favorite T-shirt of his. On the front, a picture of Xena, Warrior Princess. On the back, it read, "I Have Many Skills."

"We're going to the hospital to find out from that woman what the hell is going on."

"Dressed like that? I don't think so," said Jimmy.

She ignored his remark and said, "I called Sentara. They said she was moved to Riverside hospital this morning. They have her in room 341. Under the name Jane Doe."

"Surely you're not serious," said Jimmy.

"I am," said Debbie. Then in unison they both said, "And don't call me Shirley."

They both started laughing. It was the first time they'd even smiled since the incident.

"Do we have to go right now?" asked Jimmy.

"Why not?"

"Because you look amazingly sexy."

"Really? Because you just implied that I looked kind of slutty."

"And?"

"Read the back of my T-shirt."

"I can't take my eyes off the front," he said, and came in low. Picking her up and throwing her over his shoulder, she squealed with delight. He ran to the bedroom and kicked the door shut behind him.

An hour later, Debbie exited her walk-in closet wearing white, low-waisted sheer lace panties while putting on the matching underwire bra. On the king-sized bed watching her lay Jimmy, the beagle, both terriers, and Molly. Tippy watched from his precarious perch on top of the brass headboard.

"Do you think it's wise to wear one of those bras?" Jim asked.

"You don't like it?"

"Hell yes. It's spectacular. But it kinda makes you stand out, you know?'

"It'll be fine. You need to get dressed so we can go," she said, enjoying all the attention.

"As long as you look like that, I'm not moving a muscle," he said, and raised his phone.

"Don't you be filming me like this," she shrieked and ran back into the closet, slamming the door behind her. When she came back out, she was fully dressed in the same outfit as before.

Jimmy looked at her shoes. "I thought you were wearing the boppers."

"I am."

"Then what are the bebops?"

"The bebops are the high tops. These are the boppers," she said, pointing at the New Balance sneakers.

Jimmy jumped out of bed naked and wrapped his arms around her. "My mistake," he said, and kissed her deeply. He put his uniform back on while Debbie went back for jewelry. She came out wearing only silver.

"Let's go, Baby," she said.

"I'm ready when you're ready and ready when you ain't ready," was his Deep Creek reply.

"All you guys be good. We love you, and we'll be back soon," she said to the kids.

Debbie decided to drive Miss Interceptor so there would be plenty of room to bring the woman back.

"You're kidding, right?" said Jimmy. Debbie's answer was to hold up and shake a paper bag she brought with her.

"What's in there?"

"A dress, flip flops, water, and a granola bar."

"You're really serious about bringing her back home?"

"As long as she's alive, I'm as serious as a heart attack. And don't ask me again," Debbie said as she pulled out of the driveway.

When they merged onto I-64, Jimmy asked, "What about Dora? Bo can't just disappear."

"I called Dora and texted Bo's sister. I told them both what I told the cops. Bo went to check on Mr. Johnson when we went in the rental, and we haven't seen him since. I don't see any other option right now. I couldn't bring myself to tell her he had died and disintegrated. She wouldn't believe it anyway. Besides, that's what we told the sergeant, and we have to keep our story consistent."

"You're right," said Jim and looked at his phone. "Waze says we are clear to Riverside Hospital, about twenty-five minutes. So, here's my question to you. Prompted by your T-shirt, who wins the fight? Xena or Buffy?"

"Ah," said Debbie. "The game is afoot, and the door is ajar. This is a tough one." She paused.

"Talk it out," prompted Jimmy.

"Well okay. Buffy is the slayer after all." Jimmy nodded. "But Xena is so badass." She thought about it more while Jimmy started grinning at her commitment. "Xena is bigger than Buffy. But that doesn't mean she's necessarily stronger. Of course, Xena has the sword and that chakram. But Buffy kills armed demons and monsters bigger than her all the time. And she has her stake, of course."

"That's all true. What do you think?"

Debbie finally decided. "It's a gut call, but I have to go with Xena."

"Xena wins. Buffy is dead," Jimmy declared, putting his arms up indicating a touchdown. "So now." He paused while Debbie waited. "Who's better looking?"

"Hmm. Who's hotter?" Debbie said low to herself.

Jimmy laid it out. "Xena, Warrior Princess or Buffy the Vampire Slayer?"

Debbie thought long. "I have to go with, and it's nothing against Buffy. You know I love the Buff. But again, I have to go with Xena."

Jimmy said, "Okay, moving on."

"Wait, Jimmy. What's your verdict?"

"It was your question, not mine."

"Wait. That means you think Buffy is better looking than Xena?"

"I didn't say that." He could smell trouble coming.

"But you're not denying it either. I thought you liked women with some meat on them. You know, shapely."

"I do. I love meat. The bigger the better."

"So what are you saying? I'm big?" she asked accusingly.

He saw no clean exit and went all in. "You're the most beautiful and perfect woman who ever lived." He waited nervously.

Debbie laughed and said, "I'm just fucking with you."

Jimmy sighed with relief and said, "You might be in trouble now. Don't make me come over there."

"What exactly would I have to do?" she shot back and winked. "Okay, I have one for you. Who wins the fight? Chuck Norris or Jet Li?"

"All right, a couple of questions first."

"Shoot."

"I'm assuming they're both in their prime, and is it a fight to the death?"

"The first part isn't a question and yes, always to the death," was her retort.

"Look, everybody likes a little ass, but nobody likes a smart ass," Jimmy said back.

"Don't start your Deep Creek sweet talking on me," she said.

"Chuck Norris," Jimmy decided.

"Why?"

"Because he's Chuck Norris. He won the Full Contact Karate Championships like six or seven years in a row. He's a real fighter."

"Okay. It's your turn."

But Jimmy changed the subject. "What if she's still out or doesn't want to talk to us?"

"Her life is gone, and we saved her ass. Why wouldn't she talk to us? We'll find out soon enough."

"Okay then," said Jimmy. "Who's the best actress..."

"Meryl Streep," Debbie said immediately.

"No, no, wait. I wasn't finished. Who's the best actress under fifty?"

Debbie said quickly, "Cate Blanchett."

"No good. She's fifty."

"You said fifty."

"I said under fifty."

"All right. Reese Witherspoon. Final answer."

"Good choice," said Jimmy. "I forgot about her. She has what, a dozen Oscars?"

Debbie laughed. With a Southern drawl and to Jimmy's delight, Debbie quoted Jimmy's favorite line to the serial killer from the one of Reese's earlier movies. "Fuck you and your skipper wife, Bob. Who is *your* pick for best actress under fifty?"

"I was thinking Sandra Bullock."

"She's definitely over fifty, Baby," Debbie corrected.

"Really? She doesn't look it. Okay then, Chloe Grace Moretz." For whatever reason, Debbie seemed unhappy with that choice. He quickly changed to Reese and moved on. Normally he enjoyed debating her, but this wasn't the time. "Hey, back to the other subject. Do you think Enoch Erran is dead?"

"I don't know. I think there's a good chance he is, don't you?"

"Hell," said Jimmy, "for all we know, the Lizard man was Enoch Erran."

"How's that?" asked Debbie.

"Well, it's generally accepted that Reptilians can shape shift to look like anybody they want."

"Accepted by who?"

"Accepted by whom," he said and then went on despite her contrary reaction to being corrected. "UFO people. People that believe in alien mythology."

"I hesitate to call it mythology at this point. I still can't believe we killed that thing."

"I know," said Jimmy. "You were badass, Babe."

"Yeah?" she fished.

"Oh yeah. He was fast, but he couldn't touch you. And then when I thought I was done, there you were hacking his head off." Jimmy remembered it like it just happened.

"She told me to," admitted Debbie.

"Who told you what?"

"From the table…I heard her say, 'Not the chest. The throat.'"

"I guess we should thank her for that."

They drove for a while in silence, listening to Eliane Elias sing jazzy songs in Portuguese. "Yeah, I have many questions for her," said Debbie, contemplative and sort of to herself.

"Like, why didn't our pistols fire? That one sticks in my craw."

"That's another one," said Debbie, her voice trailing off.

Riverside Hospital was a vast complex. One six-story anchor building in front, with many other wings and structures to the left, right, and in the rear. Jimmy remembered it being just a three-story single building thirty years earlier when he had his first knee surgery. Despite its size the parking lot was packed, and they ended up finding a space way off to the side where the forest bordered the property. There was a shuttle driving around but they opted to walk. At the front entrance, Jimmy stopped and asked, "So, what's the plan?"

"Simple. We go in, we find her, we dress her, we bring her out," again showing him the bag of clothes.

"You packing?"

".22 semi in my pocket. You?"

"Yeah, I got my Ruger. Okay. Let's do it."

They went through two layers of double glass doors past a huge gift store, a front desk, and rows of check-in booths. It was even bigger than it looked on the outside. Jimmy spotted two security guards, both armed with nines and tasers. They stopped in the middle of the enormous lobby. "Where now?" Jimmy asked.

"Elevators," said Deb.

"You know where they are?"

"Over by the sign that says elevators."

"Don't make me," Jimmy said, smiling. She punched him on the shoulder.

Room 341 was easy enough to find. It was a double room with only one bed behind a blue curtain. Debbie pulled the curtain around the semi-circular track and there she lay, covered up to her neck by a sheet. Her head was turned away and her previously long black hair was cropped to about one-half inch. The were two nasty gashes on her skull. One above her left ear and another at the crown. Both heavily sutured. The left side of her face was puffy and purple and black. Both eyes were swollen almost completely shut. She looked much worse than Debbie had imagined. Debbie leaned in close and said, "Miss."

The woman opened her eyes as much as she could, and recognition emerged. "I've been waiting for you," she said hoarsely. She freed her left arm and started trying to pull back the sheet. The arm was also covered with yellow, black, and purple bruises. Especially the bicep. Three fingers had metal braces on them. She groaned softly and asked Debbie for help. When Debbie pulled the sheet down, she and Jimmy were shocked by her condition. She was naked. The upper body was covered with large vivid bruises. The right arm was in a sling. There were multiple cuts on her. Three diagonals were spaced across her chest. It looked like a claw mark. Another followed the contour of the base of her throat almost halfway around her neck, and there were two slices, one above and one below the naval, both more than six inches long. From her lower hips all the way down to her ankles, she was wrapped in ace bandages. Only her swollen blue feet stuck out.

"Oh my God. Oh, Honey, you need to stay right here."

"No." She could hardly speak. Taking Debbie's hand in hers, she said, "We need to go. It's not safe here."

Debbie was torn. She looked at Jimmy for his opinion. "She looks really bad, Debs."

The woman painfully turned her head so she could look into Debbie's eyes. "You remember yesterday?" Debbie nodded. "It's not safe," she repeated.

Debbie made her decision. "Jim, get the truck and pull it up to the front doors. Find a wheelchair and get back up here. I'm going to get her dressed."

"I'll be right back," he said, and took off.

"And bring a hat," Debbie called after him.

"Ten-four," she heard him say.

About twenty minutes later, Jimmy entered the room pushing a wheelchair. He gave Debbie a Redskins cap that he kept in the truck along with an emergency change of clothes.

The woman was sitting up on the side of the bed. Through winces and groans, Debbie gingerly put the cap on her head. It stood out against the blue sundress she was now wearing. Debbie didn't even try to put on the flip flops. Amid grunts and gasps of pain, Debbie and Jimmy pretty much lifted her into the wheelchair.

"Sorry," the woman said. "It's the broken ribs."

Debbie pushed her to the elevator while the woman devoured the granola bar. On the way down, Jimmy said, "What's your name?"

"I'm Shewuma. Kachina of the Hopi tribe." She shoved the rest of the bar into her mouth.

"Kachina?" Jimmy recognized the term from the *Ancient Aliens* show. "You mean..."

Debbie cut him off as the door opened. "Save it for later, Babe. Let's get out of here."

As they approached the exit, a security guard confronted them. "Excuse me," he directed to Shewuma. "Are you sure you should be leaving? Where's the discharge nurse?"

Deb thought fast. She did her best flirty giggle and said, "She's not being discharged, sir. We've been visiting our mom. You see, Wu and my mom were in a car accident last week. Wu got out only two days ago, but Mom is still here. We were just visiting her."

Shewuma added, "Yes, Officer, but thank you for your concern."

The guard seemed on the fence, so Debbie took a deep breath and let it out slow. Before he could stop himself, his eyes went to her breasts that were pulling against the tight T-shirt. A bit embarrassed, he sent them on their way. "Nice one, Babe," said Jim.

"I knew he'd look," said Debbie.

Smiling, Jimmy said, "I'm still looking."

Shewuma caught them both by surprise by saying, "So am I."

They put Shewuma into the passenger seat as gently as possible. Almost as an afterthought, Jimmy broke down the wheelchair and threw it in the back. "You never know," he said to Debbie.

Shewuma slept all the way home and they didn't bother her. Once home, Jimmy went in first and put the animals outside. Taking their time, they finally got Shewuma into the spare bedroom. It was sparse. A double bed, night table, and an empty dresser by the window.

"Do you have to use the bathroom?" Debbie asked her.

"Not right now," she said apologetically.

"That's okay, Sweetie. Don't you worry about anything. Just rest and get well." She leaned toward Jimmy and said quietly, "Get one of those poopy pads we used for Mom. They're right there in the linen closet. We'll just change her until she can get around better."

Jimmy nodded and was back in seconds. After they had her situated in the bed, Debbie closed the blinds and curtains. They were about to slip out of the room when Shewuma said dreamily, "Thank you. I just need a little time."

Debbie ran her finger down the side of Shewuma's face lightly, barely a touch. "You sleep as long as you want, Honey. We'll be here." She left the room feeling oddly drawn to this strange woman.

CHAPTER 12

CHANGES

It had been more than two days since Debbie and Jimmy put Shewuma in the spare bedroom. They were coming into the house after a hard morning workout together. There was nothing like being soaked, tired, and content. The dogs wanted to stay outside, so they left them in the backyard.

Jimmy headed straight for Debbie's walk-in shower that she had custom built for herself. He entered through the staggered glass panels that overlapped. No door. Debbie's own design actually. There were showerheads on each end and a high-pressure overhead rain nozzle in the center. It was in Jimmy's mind the best money she'd ever spent. And that was saying something. As well as she saved money, she could spend it just as hard.

Debbie veered off to check on their houseguest. No change. Shewuma was still sleeping. Tippycat lay on top of the dresser, watching her as he had for most of the last two days. Debbie checked her pulse and took a quick glance under the blanket, then joined Jimmy in the shower. He was washing her back with his hands when he asked, "How does she look?"

"Well, her face looks pretty good. It's crazy how fast the swelling and the bruising went away. And her hair is growing out really fast. I've never seen anybody grow hair like that before."

"Has she eaten or drank anything?"

"No. She's been completely out the whole time."

Jimmy laughed. "You said hole." He moved down to washing her legs and said, "Should we wake her up and give her some water?"

"Let's see how today goes."

He went to work washing her butt. It was shapely, pretty much a bubble butt. But also hard, solid.

He kept on it so long that she said, "I think it's clean, Jimsy."

"Good," he said. "Now I can start on the front. Arms up." He washed her pits, then went up and down her arms. "We need to change her, right?" He cheerfully went to work on her breathtaking breasts.

"No, she's good."

"Doesn't seem possible," he said. "We used to change your mom twice a day."

"I looked under. No poop, no pee, nothing." She looked down at his fingers tweaking her erect nipples and stifled a laugh. "What are you doing? Tuning a radio?"

"Time to wash possible." Debbie squealed as he went in low. They always enjoyed their showers together.

While they dressed, Jimmy asked another question that had been on his mind. "How are we with money?"

"We're okay for a while. You know I've been stashing cash since that fucking nightmare of a real estate crash. But we still need to prioritize an income stream sooner than later. Hey, didn't you wear those pants yesterday?"

He held them up and sniffed them. "Yeah, and I'll wear them again tomorrow if I want to," he said nonchalantly.

"Who do you think your talking to Willis?" she said back.

"What T-shirt are you going to wear?" he asked.

"I'm wearing the one that shows three dogs walking toward you in cowboy hats on the front and their tails walking away wearing cowboy boots in back. What are you wearing?"

He took the black one on top of the T-shirt drawer and held it up. On the front it read, "When I Get Weak In The Hips, I Get Strong In The Lips." On the back was a picture of Richard Pryor. "Are we going out today?"

"No, not to my knowledge. Why?"

"How about wearing that white mini skirt?"

"Okay. Hey, it's 10:30. Are we eating breakfast or lunch?"

Jim wanted breakfast. "How about fried eggs, cheese grits, and biscuits? I want some scrapple." Debbie made a yuck face. "You want some bacon or ham?" He picked up his keys, wallet, and Old Timer lock blade and headed towards the kitchen.

"Yum. Ham" she called after him while picking out jewelry. "Throw some tater tots in the oven too. I'm starving."

"I'm on it," he answered back.

When her jewelry was perfect, Debbie went down to the den and put on a Natalie Cole CD. The smell of fresh biscuits wafted from the kitchen. On her way to get some silverware, she stopped by the stove and slapped Jimmy on the ass. He was cooking in his apron that read, "Eat me."

"Do you want to eat on the island or the table?" Debbie asked.

"I don't care. Wait! The table. It's easier to look up your skirt."

"You're a nut," she said.

"I'm serious and you know it."

Debbie set the table and then put two glasses in the freezer to get them cold for the milk. She took butter and jelly out of the refrigerator and then asked, "Do you want honey or ketchup?"

From the kitchen doorway, wide awake, and naked as a jaybird, Shewuma said, "Both sound good to me." Most of the bruising and swelling on her whole body was gone. The small cuts looked almost healed. The more critical large cuts were closed and the skin was barely red. And her hair. It had already grown what should have taken a month. Jimmy watched as Debbie ushered her down the hall to get some clothes.

"Lord, girl," Debbie said to her. "You can't just go around showing everything you got to grown men."

"Why not?" Shewuma asked. She sounded sincere.

"Because it's just not in women's best interest over the long haul. Keep some mystery. Come on, let's get you dressed. Hey, when did you have time to shave your hooch?" asked Debbie.

"I don't have to shave it."

"I wish you could teach me that. Save me a lot of time."

"You're on," said Shewuma. Debbie assumed she was joking and chuckled.

In the spare bedroom, Tippycat was wallowing on his back all over Shewuma's pillow. "That's Tippycat," said Debbie. She gave Shewuma the same blue sundress and flip flops from the other day. "Tippy has been watching over you since you got here."

"Yes, we've met. I understand he has some brothers and sisters too."

Debbie shot her a sideways glance for knowing that but let it go. "We consider them our children. You'll meet them soon."

"Any human children?"

"Nope."

She surprised Debbie by asking, "Are one of you infertile?"

The question was not only unexpected, but to many people could have been perceived as a smidge insensitive. "Boundaries, boundaries," admonished Debbie. "But no. We don't have any children by choice."

Back in the kitchen, Debbie sat Shewuma on a stool and gave her a big glass of water. Shewuma downed the water while Debbie went for a glass of orange juice. She drank the orange juice straight down as well. "Coffee?" asked Debbie.

"I would love some... black. And another glass of that water would be great too."

While Shewuma was drinking water and sipping coffee, Debbie went over to Jimmy and whispered in his ear, "Did you see how she looks?"

"Yes," Jimmy whispered back. "She looks great for having such small titties."

Debbie slapped his arm. "I meant how she healed up so fast."

"I know. I was joking. Her titties aren't really that small. I'm just so used to yours. You know?"

"You better stop it," said Debbie, very serious.

Shewuma said from across the room, "Thanks for the compliment. You two aren't bad yourselves."

Debbie took a breath to answer but stopped and whispered again in Jimmy's ear, "Is it possible she can hear us?"

Shewuma answered Debbie's question. "It is possible."

Debbie was nonplussed. Taking it in stride, Jimmy told Debbie, "See how many eggs she wants."

"Hey, Wu, do you like fried eggs?"

"Did you call me Wu?"

"Sorry, it just came out that way."

"No, I like it. I haven't been called Wu since I was a child. Yes, I love fried eggs."

"How many do you want?" asked Debbie.

"Can I have six?" Wu asked tentatively.

"Six it is," said Jim. "Three for me, two for Debbie, and six for the budding High Priest of Miserability." He broke one egg after another onto the grill until there were eleven cooking. "Put everything on the table, Dibs. These will be off directly."

Debbie sat where she always did at the head of the table. Jimmy sat to her right and Shewuma sat across from him to her left. They ate in silence, except for Shewuma's occasional oohs and aahs for the scrumptious meal. Jimmy was finished and that was no surprise. He was a fast eater. But Debbie, dubbed the world's slowest eater by friends and family, was also finished. Meanwhile, Shewuma kept eating. They watched her eat the six eggs, five biscuits, all the cheese grits and tater tots, and at least a pound of ham. So much for the kids getting some leftovers. After she swallowed her last bite, she burped, said, "Excuse me," and began taking dishes to the sink.

"Whoa," said Debbie. She sat Wu down, taking the dirty dishes and handing them to Jimmy. He put them in the sink and came back to the table.

Shewuma let out an unexpected burst of laughter that startled them both. "Sorry." She pointed to Jimmy's apron. "Eat me. It struck me funny." Debbie and Jimmy smiled. He took off the apron and laid it over the chair's back.

"Shewuma, did you get enough to eat?" he asked. The question was more joking than serious.

"Oh yeah. Thank you. It was fantastic. I can't remember the last time I ate that well."

Jimmy said to Debbie, "I understand the refrigerator at 22nd Street now."

Shewuma began to giggle as she read his T-shirt. "Strong in the lips," she said out loud.

"This is what we say about Jimmy," Debbie told her. "Not rude, not crude, just nasty." They all laughed, but then Debbie's demeanor turned deliberate. "Look Wu…Shewuma."

"No, I like it when you call me Wu."

"Okay, Wu. I hate to get serious, but I have tons of questions. We have." She motioned to Jimmy, who was nodding. "We don't even know who you are. And that fucking Reptilian thing. And our best friend Bo is dead. And Enoch Erran is AWOL. And…you know." Debbie threw her hands up in the air.

"Why wouldn't our weapons fire?" Jimmy added.

"Yeah, that too," said Debbie.

Shewuma finished her last bit of milk and set the glass on the table. She said solemnly, "I am so very sorry for the loss of your friend. And I swear to you both I will never forget his sacrifice for me." She paused and then said, "Enoch is dead."

"Were ya'll married?" asked Jimmy.

"We were what is called Crevetch in the Erran tongue. It's sort of married by human standards but different. It's hard to explain."

"Erran?" asked Debbie.

"Enoch's language from his home world."

"Holy shit," said Jimmy and slapped his forehead. "You're saying Enoch Erran was an alien?"

"Yes. Here, let me explain. Enoch was from a planet called Erran in the Pleiades constellation. Erran wasn't really his last name. Errans don't have last names. And Enoch was his Earth name. You couldn't pronounce his given name."

Debbie was confused. "Is he Pleiadian or Erran?"

"He's actually both. Over the millennia, they have become interchangeable terms. Some also call them Nordics or Nords. But I don't like that name."

"Why?" Debbie asked.

Jimmy took the answer. "I know this, Debs. I saw it on *Ancient Aliens*. In the past, people thought the Pleiadeans were the Nordic/Viking Gods like Thor and Odin. But Nord took on a bad connotation like Chink or Spic. Right?"

"Pretty much," agreed Wu. "I'm impressed that you know that."

"You'll find that Jimmy is a dichotomy of obscure knowledge while still being innocently dense at times. So, what exactly does Crevetch mean in English?" Debbie asked.

"In English, it has more than simply one precise meaning. And some of them wouldn't make sense to you."

"I don't understand," said Jimmy. "Is it a language or not?"

"This is how Enoch would explain it to you. The discrepancies of translating words in the Erran language to words in a human language have different meanings based on the inflection, context, and intent because of the fluid algorithmic nature of the diagraming of their sentences." Then she shrugged.

Debbie said, "What the fuck does that mean?"

"Let's call it married and move on. I'm getting a headache," said Jimmy.

"No wait," said Debbie, determined. "So did you two have a ceremony or make vows to each other or something?"

"Yes. He made the required Erran orthodox demands, and I gave the accepted Erran orthodox response." She was trying to explain better. "Think of it as being drafted to live and train together. To mate and protect..." She stopped.

"Protect what?" they both asked.

"No," she said shaking her head. "You two have been wonderful. You saved my life, you brought me into your home, you've shown me nothing but kindness. I don't want to tell you something that could endanger you. Actually, I shouldn't have told you anything."

Jimmy asked his next question. "We know you were raped and tortured by that Lizard man. But why?"

Debbie winced at his bluntness. "Sorry, Wu. Jimmy can be harsh. But I have the same question. Why?"

Wu hesitated, so Debbie stood up and began to pace. "Look, Wu, I think your wanting to protect us is admirable, but it's misguided."

"Explain," said Wu.

"We killed that thing to save you at great personal risk. We lost Bo doing it. That should count for something right there. But if there are any repercussions from any of this, it's coming right back to this house. We took you to the hospital. The police know who we are. Anyone looking for you could easily find out we brought you here. Leaving the hospital with you is on camera. I think you owe it to us to tell us what's going on."

"Come on, Wu. Who are you?" Jimmy practically pleaded for the answer.

Wu thought for a moment and agreed. "Okay, you're right. I'll tell you everything."

"From the beginning," said Jimmy.

She gathered her thoughts. "Let me formally introduce myself. I am a Kachina of the Hopi Nation. I am a Star Child of the Realm of Man. I am Crevetch to Enoch Erran, Keeper of the Sanctum."

Debbie sat back down. Tippy jumped into her lap and she stroked his head. "That's quite an intro," she said to Jimmy. He shushed her, eager to hear more.

"My full name is Shewuma Ashwiyaa Hopitu. In English, Shewuma means White Bird and Ashwiyaa means Warrior."

"White Bird," said Debbie. "That's so beautiful."

"A dove flew in the window of our pueblo while I was coming out of my mother. It was a big deal because there are no doves in the Arizona desert. Hence, White Bird."

"What is the Sanctum?" asked Jimmy.

"Wow. The Sanctum is a long and complicated story. Think of it for now as Enoch carrying the nuclear football for the president and I'll come back to it later." They nodded acceptance. "According to the histories of my people, Star Children are direct descendants of the original Gods."

"Aliens," Jimmy whispered to Debbie.

"Stop. Be quiet," she whispered back.

Shewuma continued. "In the Hopi tradition and in many other cultures around the world, children are tested at a young age for the sacred lineage."

"Tested how?" asked Jimmy, as Debbie rolled her eyes at the interruption.

"The Elders perform a ritual that releases our hidden DNA. But I'm not really supposed to talk about it. So, my lineage was confirmed and my destiny unveiled. Crevetch to Enoch, guardian of the Sanctum and protector of man from the desecrated evil. The Elders trained me until I was sixteen in the ways of survival, spirituality, responsibilities of the Kachina, and knowledge of our histories and traditions. The next thirty years were spent under Tiwak and Agoge, training while fighting alongside other Star Children. Tiwak and Agoge brought me to the peak of my capabilities in spiritual, psychic, and physical combat."

"What are those training words you said?"

"I know this," said Jimmy.

Debbie dismissed him. "Jim, stop."

"Tiwak is Apache training to fight and survive harsh environments. And what is Agoge, Jimmy?"

"It's how the Spartans trained their children to become soldiers." He shot Deb a look.

"Bingo," said Wu and continued. "I was Crevetched to Enoch around 1911 and we came to Newport News. Occasionally I would be called away on a mission, but mostly Enoch and I lived next to the wondrous Chesapeake Bay, protecting the Sanctum and enjoying life."

"You expect me to believe you're over one hundred years old?" asked Debbie, still wrapping her mind around it.

"One hundred and fifty-seven. It's nice of you to say I look younger."

"Okay, we'll come back to that," said Deb. "Go on."

"A few months ago, Enoch changed. I had never seen him this way before. Errans are positive, straightforward, and contented people. He became withdrawn and sullen. He left for two days without a word to me. He had gone away in the past on many occasions, sometimes for weeks, but I always knew where he was. And he always stayed in contact with me up here." She touched her finger to her head. When Jim and Deb both looked puzzled, she explained, "Errans are telepathic. They won't talk at all unless they have to. Last Thursday we were ambushed by the Drachonians. They must have come from underground. Drachs usually work alone but there was definitely a group of them. They had come to take the Sanctum. Which we still need to discuss. I killed two before I was taken and I'm sure Enoch must have done some damage as well. But when I came around where you found me, there was only the one Drach there." Shewuma's eyes became a blank stare. "He had Enoch staked to the wall with spikes. His hands and feet had been removed. He tortured Enoch and told me if I gave up the Sanctum, he would stop. But I didn't know where it was. I never have. Then he told me that when Enoch was done, we would have our own special time together. Enoch suffered so much for so long. It seemed like an eternity. Early on the morning that you three arrived, the Drach finally decided there was no chance Enoch would break and decapitated him, chopped him into pieces, and took his remains away in trash bags." Her face clouded and she held back tears. "Then he started on me in earnest."

"Oh, Sweetie, I'm so sorry," Debbie said, taking her hand.

"Wait," said Jimmy. "You said this started on Thursday. Bo and I were there Friday morning, and we came back on Sunday. Are you saying Enoch, in that condition, survived for over three days?"

"Jesus, Jim!" Debbie said.

Shewuma went on, speaking mechanically, emotionless. "No, it's okay, Debbie. That is what I'm saying. Errans are extremely hard to kill. They heal incredibly fast, much faster than I. Their blood clots immediately, literally. Their internal organs all have multiple functions. If one fails, another will take over. And it's nearly impossible to suffocate them. Even with no oxygen, their body will shut down, like a coma, and their brain will split body fluids into hydrogen and oxygen. It's just enough oxygen to keep them alive for years. So anyway, when I had lost hope, I asked the Gods for help, and they sent you to save me."

She looked at Debbie and then at Jimmy. Tippy jumped into her lap and she sat silently, rubbing under his chin.

"Damn!" said Jimmy. "That's one hell of a story."

"Are you okay if I ask you some specific questions?" said Debbie.

Shewuma took a napkin and wiped her face. "Sure. Ask away."

"So, you couldn't have told him where the Sanctum was no matter what he did?"

"That's right. I know now. Enoch never told me so I would live long enough for you to come. The Drach assumed I was lying and knew where it was. He would hurt me for a while and then take a break and rape me. Eventually he would have killed me too."

"You say that like Enoch knew we were coming," said Jimmy.

"Oh, he did. Enoch had the Sight. Many Errans do." She said it with such certainty that Jimmy didn't have a response.

Debbie asked her, "He raped you more than once?"

Shewuma nodded. "Yes, several times."

Very concerned, Debbie asked, "What if you're pregnant?"

"No, I'm not," Wu replied.

"So these Drachs can't impregnate women?"

"Oh yes," Wu assured her. "Drachs very much enjoy sex with other species and can impregnate just about anything. Although their clans do have strict seeding protocols."

"So what is the Sanctum?" Jimmy asked again.

"Wait, Babe. But you're sure you're not pregnant. How?"

"I would have to enable the fertilization of my egg."

"I don't understand," said Debbie.

"Kachinas and often Hybrids in general have much more control over their bodies than humans. We can do many things you would consider amazing or even impossible."

"What can you do that we can't?" Jim asked.

"Well, I can hold my breath for a long time with no problem."

"You could do that right now?" asked Debbie.

"Sure," said Shewuma. She took a deep breath and held it.

Jimmy saw 11:45 on the stove clock. Debbie scooted her chair up next to Wu and put her hand up by her nose and mouth to prevent cheating.

At 11:51, Jimmy called it. "That's six minutes. I believe her."

Shewuma let out the air and went on breathing normally.

"Man," said Deb, and let out a low whistle.

Shewuma laughed at their sudden childlike fascination with her. "Let's see. It has to be awfully extreme for me to get cold or hot. Um, I can control the growth of my hair and fingernails.

"That explains the hair and the no carpet," Jimmy said to Debbie, and she nodded back.

"Anything else?" Debbie asked.

"I'm very strong."

"Aha," said Jimmy. He came around to her side and put his right arm on the table. "This one I can verify. Let's pull arms."

Shewuma was delighted. "Arm wrestling? Let's do it."

Debbie said go, and Shewuma slammed Jimmy's knuckles to the table.

"Jesus, Deb, I think she's probably stronger than that monster we killed."

Wu picked up a biscuit and began to eat it casually. "So is show and tell over?"

"Hell no," said Debbie, intoxicated with her new toy. "How can you eat so much?"

"I eat constantly, and I've never gained weight." She took another bite of biscuit.

"Now you're just bragging," said Debbie.

Shewuma produced a modest smile and said, "In the interest of full disclosure and because you two have been so nice, I should tell you this. I'll be aware of anything that's going on in the house…Like this morning." She stopped to let it sink in.

Jimmy said, "Oh, like earlier when you could hear us whispering?"

"Yes."

Then he caught on. "Jesus. She's talking about us having sex earlier," he said to Debbie.

"I get it," Debbie replied. "So you have really good hearing?"

"Hearing, smelling, feeling. I can see in the dark just like it's daytime."

"No way. Come on, Debs. Let's test her," Jimmy said excitedly.

"It's the middle of the day, Jim."

"Your walk-in closet. No windows." And he was off.

Debbie's eyes went wide. "Okay, let's go do it." She grabbed Wu's hand and pulled her laughing down the hall to the bedroom.

Shewuma stopped at the closet door, checking the place out. "This bedroom is huge. I love it."

"I'll take you on a tour later," said Deb. "But come in here first."

Wu gushed over the closet while Jimmy closed the door and put a sweater at the bottom to block out any possible light.

From across the closet, Shewuma said, "Okay, what are we doing?"

"How many fingers do I have up?" asked Jimmy in total darkness.

"Two. Well, now three, now two. Stop changing them."

"Okay, what am I doing now?" He put his hand on Debbie's breast, prompting a startled snort from her.

"Ooh," said Wu, "that's pretty hot."

"That's enough," said Debbie. She pushed his hand away and flipped on the light.

With Debbie and Jimmy in complete awe, they went to the den. Jimmy sat on the end of the couch, while Debbie and Wu each took a recliner. The dogs were at the back door scratching the glass and whining for the new meat.

"Oh my goodness," said Wu, struck by the enthusiastic kids just outside.

She started to get up, but Debbie said, "Hold it a minute."

"Sorry," said Wu. "I love animals."

"I can see," said Debbie. "But I have another question. From what you said earlier, are you expecting someone or some…thing to come looking for you?"

"Probably," she answered honestly. "But I would never let anything happen to you two."

"Praemonitus, Praemunitus," said Jimmy.

"Forewarned is forearmed," translated Wu.

"You speak Latin?" Jimmy was surprised.

"Modicum," Wu said, smiling.

"You're full of surprises. But we can take care of ourselves. We just like to be ready," Debbie assured her.

"Oh, I know full well what you guys can do. And I can never repay you for what you've already done. That's why I hate to ask you this one last favor."

"Shoot," said Debbie.

"Enoch told me that if anything ever happened to him, go see the man at this address. Wu cupped her hand and passed it over the Sun God tattoo on her forearm while saying a word in Hopi. There was a flash of light and Debbie and Jimmy watched fascinated as she flipped her hand to reveal a small piece of blue glass in her palm. She held it between her thumb and forefinger and said something else in her native language. A large holograph appeared floating in the center of the den. A face appeared, classically handsome with perfectly symmetrical features, long white hair, and emerald green eyes. Debbie was struck by how gorgeous he was. She glanced at Jim and he was oblivious.

"Wow, that's Enoch, isn't it?" Debbie asked Wu, unable to hide her admiration.

"Yes." Wu saw the look in Debbie's eyes and said, "I know, right?"

The face faded and directions appeared that read, "Find the old man at the end of River Road, Covington, Virginia, in Alleghany County." Debbie grabbed a pen and jotted the information down. Shewuma reversed her previous actions and the object disappeared under the tattoo once more.

"That's so cool," said Jimmy. "It's like Star Wars shit. What was that thing?"

"Most call it a Cric. It belonged to Enoch. It's their version of a computer. The Errans carry them inside their bodies. They are supposedly organically programed to each individual."

"Cric?" asked Debbie.

"Crystalline Integrated Circuit. Enoch didn't have it in because he was transcending." Their expressions called for more information. "Transcending is a holy time for them. Like Yom Kippur or Passover. Anyway, Enoch gave it to me to hide when the Drachs were coming. It's why your weapons wouldn't fire. I never saw a gun that would work anywhere near Enoch."

"So you want us to help you find this old guy," Debbie said, and looked at Jimmy.

"Please," said Wu.

Jimmy threw up his hands, shrugged, and said, "We're in it now."

"Okay," said Debbie. "We'll do it. But today, young lady, we need to get you some clothes and underwear. You need to know, though, that money is tight right now."

Shewuma looked at her as if she'd just remembered something important. "Take me to the Wells Fargo bank in Newport News at Newmarket Shoals. There's a safety deposit box there. It should have money." She was quite pleased with herself.

"You have the key?" asked Debbie.

"I know where it is."

"Okay," said Debbie. "But first you need to put some drawers on."

"Hold on," said Jimmy, heading for the crazy sounds of the dogs at the back door. "First you meet the kids before they bust the door down." He opened the door and stood back as the animals, yelping with joy, rushed the new girl in the recliner.

A little later, Debbie and Shewuma were ready to go shopping. Deb looked all over the house but couldn't find Jimmy. "Nicky!" Debbie called out for the beagle. He came down the hallway full speed and slid to a stop on the kitchen's tiled floor. Debbie ruffled his ears and said, "Where's your daddy? Where's your daddy?" Nicky ran to the back door with a whine that was seconds from becoming a beagle howl. Debbie opened the door and he was off like a shot. Outside, Debbie just barely saw Nicky disappear around the back side of the shop. When she got there, she found Jimmy fixing some rotten boards on the back gate.

They had built the entire fence themselves when they first moved in. It had three gates total, but Jimmy was especially proud of this one. It was actually a set of two gates in one. On one side, a three and a half-foot normal opening. On the other side was a six-foot gate. Both were latched to a four by six post set in a concrete formed hole. If needed, both gates could be opened and the anchor post removed, leaving a near ten-foot opening large enough to accommodate any size vehicle entering the backyard.

"Hey, you," said Debbie while admiring his shirtless, hairy chested, glistening physique. "I couldn't find you."

"That's why I told Nicky where I would be."

Debbie laughed. "He loves his daddy. We're leaving to go shopping. Don't you want to go?"

"I would, Babe. But Sergeant Dudley Do Right from the hospital called. He's coming over. Said he had some more questions, and he's returning your Beretta since it hasn't been fired. I'm glad we keep them so clean."

"Well, that's a stroke of luck," said Debbie, continuing to look him up and down.

"Are you eyeballing me, Girl?"

"Damn right I am, Creeker Boy. See you later."

As she walked back to the house, Jimmy called after her. "Hey, Dibs, I thought you weren't going to wear that mini skirt out and about?"

"I never said that," she answered, waving bye. Then she began to exaggerate the movement of her ass as she walked up the deck steps.

"Ahh, she is so hot," Jimmy said to himself and sighed. Nicky followed her. "Nickaa!" he called, and the beagle ran back to him, howling.

Deb took the Muscle for the bank run. She figured Wu would enjoy riding in the Trans Am and she didn't get to drive it that often anyway. She turned right out of the driveway and to Wu's delight, burned some rubber just for fun. Both girls waved to a shirtless, old, gray-haired man in gym shorts and wearing knee braces. He was painfully thin, ribs jutting out, a little hunched over and running. You couldn't really call what he was doing jogging. It was more trudging. His head hung down and he didn't acknowledge them at all.

"Mr. Rawlings, our neighbor," said Debbie, rolling her eyes. "He always looks like he's about to keel over."

"This is a really nice car," Wu said, stroking the seats and the dashboard.

"This is Jim's baby. He may love it more than me." She put in an Ella Fitzgerald CD.

Wu shook her head. "Not possible. Not in that skirt anyway." Debbie felt Wu checking her out and got a bit flushed. Wu kept talking. "A 1975 Pontiac Trans Am. Very iconic. First year for T-tops in them."

"You know cars?"

"I know a lot of things. I'm not as simple-minded as you probably think," she said playfully.

"Hold on a second," said Debbie. She merged onto I-64. Surprisingly, there was very little traffic. She pulled a radar detector from under the seat, put it on the dash, and turned it on. "Want to see what this baby can do?" Debbie asked.

"Hit it."

Debbie down shifted and mashed the pedal. As the back tires popped a long squeal, the front end raised up from the incredible acceleration.

"Fucking A!" hollered Shewuma.

Debbie shifted to fourth gear and turned down Ella. She started singing a song that Shewuma had never heard before.

> *"Flying down the highway, driving it my way,*
>
> *Headlights blazing a trail.*
>
> *Well, a siren splits the air, and from out of nowhere,*
>
> *A cop is on my tail.*
>
> *Yeah, I went through his camera at a hundred and five,*
>
> *But there ain't no way he's gonna take me alive.*
>
> *When he gets back home, he'll have something to tell,*
>
> *He'll be telling all his friends about the Firebird from Hell!*

Wu was impressed. "That's a cool song. I've never heard it before. Kind of Southern rock," said Wu.

"It's Jim's song. He wrote it."

"No shit? He's full of surprises."

"Oh yeah. He and his cousin Corrine grew up playing the guitar together. They've both written lots of songs. Matter of fact, Corrine and her husband Daniel have a band out in Oklahoma. They play for a living."

"I haven't heard Jimmy play since I've been here."

"He kinda stopped playing after she moved away. They were really close." Her voice trailed off.

"Is that the whole song?"

"Oh no. There are two more verses. And you said hole."

Wu snorted. "*Beavis and Butthead*, right? I used to love those guys."

"Jimmy and I quote them a lot. Want me to sing more?"

"Hell yeah," said Wu. "I want you to teach it to me."

Debbie sang on.

"Sitting at the go with a GTO, getting ready for the kill.

Then Me and Spunky D, yeah, we blow him away, like the man was standing still.

Well, she's not just a car, she's a living machine.

And there ain't nobody touch her when she's feeling mean.

If you see bolt of lightning and it gives you a thrill,

Then you may have caught a glimpse of the Firebird from Hell."

Deb looked at Wu and said, "More?"

"Keep going," Wu insisted.

Debbie looked at the speedometer and they were doing 96 mph. She rolled down all the windows and the wind rushed in loud and strong. Debbie's long blonde hair began blowing about wildly. She sang at the top of her lungs.

"Pull out on a two lane, six cars to pass.

1000 feet straight at us is a semi hauling gas.

I say pull it on back and get out of the way,

But Dibsi looks at me and says not today.

(No, she's crazy)

Well, she puts it to the floor and the engine screams.

She says this is the race that she saw in a dream.

Then she hollers come on Baby! And I rebel yell.

And we'll make it, or we won't in the Firebird from Hell."

Shewuma put her seat all the way back and hung her bare feet out of the window, her blue sundress blowing up under her neck. Debbie passed a semi on the right, ignoring the double yellow lines. The trucker looked in the car, waving and yelling out his window. His blaring horn faded as they raced away. "You're a nut!" Debbie yelled above the din. "You didn't put any underwear on."

"I don't have any," countered Shewuma with a big smile. "Do you think he noticed?"

They both burst into laughter. "Sing it again," yelled Wu. "I want to learn it."

"Okay," Debbie yelled back. "Sing with me." And they sang all the way to Newport News.

Jimmy was driving his last eight penny galvanized nail when Nick began to beagle howl from the driveway at the front of the shop. It was either a rabbit or the cop, Jimmy thought. Rounding the corner, Jimmy saw an unmarked Ford Taurus coming up the driveway. Detective Sergeant Reubens sat in his car while Nicky stood by the door barking.

"Nicky, heel," commanded Jimmy. Nicky ran back and sat by Jimmy's legs, calm but alert. Only then did the detective exit his vehicle, warily eyeing the dog. As he approached, Jimmy could hear the other dogs barking from inside the house in response to Nicky's alarm. Jimmy held out his hand. "Sergeant Reubens," he said, and they shook, "would you like to go in the house? Want some coffee or a beer or something?"

The sergeant could hear the other dogs as well and declined the offer. "Here, Mr. Archer." He handed Jim a Ziplock bag containing Debbie's Beretta and clip.

"Where's the ammo?" Jimmy asked, holding up the bag for examination.

"I apologize for that. There's a form you can fill out and I can submit a request to replace it."

"Just forget it," said Jimmy, annoyed.

The sergeant said, "So, your friend, Bocephus Dean. You and your wife said he went to…" He consulted his little notebook. "Mr. Johnson's house across the street. That would be Tillman Johnson. Old fella. Been living there all his life."

"That would be," echoed Jimmy.

"And you never saw him again? Haven't seen him since?"

"No sir."

"I haven't caught up with him yet, but I still need to confirm that." He paused.

Jimmy said, "Yeah, so?"

"Mr. Dean's mother filed a missing person's report."

"I know," said Jimmy. "We've been in contact with her. Debbie was going to do it, but Miss Dora insisted she do it. We've known each other a long time. We're close. You know?'

"Does Mr. Dean have any issues or enemies? A girlfriend perhaps?"

"Well, no particular girlfriend, though he slept with a lot of women generally speaking. He had lots of issues and enemies, which I'm sure you know if you've been checking up on him."

Reubens ignored the bit of attitude. "Yes, court in two weeks for a three-strike case. With a criminal record that would curl your hair," the Sergeant said, then waited. Jimmy said nothing, and the Sergeant went on. "You posted bond for him?"

"Like you don't know?" Jimmy said with more attitude.

"You don't seem very concerned about it. You stand to lose a lot of money if he doesn't show up for court."

"Well, we already paid $6,000 to the bail bondsman and he owns Bo's car now. We already lost our money. It's the bail bondsman who stands to lose a lot more."

Reubens was growing tired of Jimmy's answers verging on sarcasm and it was pissing him off. "One more question. Why did you refer to him just now in the past tense?"

Jimmy felt cornered and all he could think of to answer was, "Did I? I don't know." It quickly changed to vexation. Jimmy felt the urge to tell the truth, that Bo was a hero and they saved the girl from a monster. But he and Debbie had discussed it over and over. No bodies, no proof of the crazy story. Jimmy blurted out, "Who the fuck are you? Colombo?" He instantly realized that was probably not the best response.

"Look, you." Reubens pointed his finger at Jimmy angrily. Nicky released a low growl. The Sergeant took a breath and reverted back to the calm policeman. "Mr. Archer, we found many things in that basement. Ropes, blood, a 9mm pistol with Mr. Dean's fingerprints no less. What we didn't find was a big man with funny eyes. You and your wife are holding back. And I promise you I'm going to find out what happened that morning."

Jimmy couldn't stop himself and said, "Good luck."

Reubens started to speak but just went to his car. As he got in, Jimmy asked, "What about the woman who was raped?"

Reubens stuck his head out of the window and said, "Apparently the Feds took her. She is no longer our concern. Don't leave town," he added and backed out quickly.

"Come on, Nicky," Jimmy said, scratching the dog's head. "Let's go get a beer."

Debbie took the first Newport News exit from I-64 and then pulled into a massive service station. Before getting out, she asked Shewuma, "Do you want anything? A drink or something?"

"Sure," said Wu.

"Tea, Pepsi, water?" Deb inquired further.

"Okay."

Debbie got out but leaned back in and said, "You want anything else?"

"Like what?"

'Well, they have corndogs, doughnuts, chips."

"Okay," Wu repeated.

"You're an odd girl," said Debbie, and went into the store. She needed to pay cash for the gas. Alicia had told them not to use the credit cards this close to the bankruptcy filing. They pulled out of the gas station with thirty dollars of gas, a sixteen-ounce root beer, a bottle of water, and a large bag of cheesy Chex mix. Shewuma drank most of the root beer straight down and then steadily scarfed handfuls of the Chex mix.

"Where do you put it?" asked Debbie.

Shewuma laughed and offered her some. Debbie declined and Wu went back to eating.

"Where do we go for the key to the box?" Debbie asked her.

"The bank," said Shewuma, chewing a mouthful.

Puzzled, Debbie asked, "The bank has the key?"

"Sort of. I'll show you when we get there."

As always, Debbie parked in the back of the parking lot to avoid dings to the car. As they approached the bank, Debbie wondered how this would work. She had a safety deposit box and knew you had to have the key. They wouldn't just give it to you. From the edge of the parking lot, a covered walkway went about forty feet back to the bank entrance. Shewuma stopped with a hand on Debbie's shoulder and said, "I'll be right back."

Debbie watched with amazement as Shewuma shimmied up the corner support pole, reached around to the top edge of the roof and with one hand swung up onto it. Seconds later, she swung back down and landed lightly on the sidewalk. In the process her sundress blew up, exposing all her personal business, much to the disgust of a middle-aged mom and the fascination of her two adolescent boys. Wu showed Debbie a fake rock she'd retrieved from the roof. From it, she produced a key.

"How long has it been up there?" asked Debbie

"A while," said Shewuma.

Thinking there was always a chance they would need a quick getaway, Debbie said, "Maybe I should wait in the car."

"Sure," said Wu. "I'll be right out."

It only took two songs by Ella and Shewuma was back carrying a paper grocery bag. Debbie's curiosity was peaked now. Out of the bag, Wu pulled stacks of banded hundred-dollar bills. "One, two, three… six. That's $12,000!" exclaimed Debbie. Without hesitation, Wu handed Debbie two stacks of bills. "Oh no, Honey," Debbie began.

Wu said, "Stop, Debbie. Just hold onto it for me."

"Well, okay," said Debbie. "But you can have it back whenever you want it."

Next, Wu pulled out two passports, two driver's licenses, no doubt expired, and what appeared to be a credit card. There were also several multi-colored headbands. Lastly, she removed two sheath knives. Debbie caught her breath sharply. They were obviously Native American and custom made. "Oh, Wu, you haven't seen Jimmy's knife collection yet. He's going to die when he sees those knives. Where did you get them?"

"I made them," Wu said proudly.

"They're gorgeous," said Debbie. "Is that blade made of bone?"

"Yes. Elk bone blade and elk antler handle." She handed one to Debbie for inspection.

"Wow!" said Debbie, turning it over in her hand. "He's going to love these. Do you mind if I run a couple errands while we're down here before we go shopping?"

"Cool beans," said Shewuma. Debbie pulled out onto the highway while Shewuma put everything back in the bag except the $4,000, which remained on the console. Shewuma refused to touch it, so Debbie put it under the seat and pulled the radar detector back out.

"Now you're talking, Doodle," Wu said.

"Where did hear Doodle?"

"I heard Jimmy call you that a few times yesterday. Plus, it's in the song. Debbie Doodle, Dibsi. I think I even heard a Spunky D."

"I thought you were asleep."

"More like meditating."

Debbie downshifted and popped a wheel through the yellow light. Shewuma said, "I love watching you drive a stick shift in that skirt."

Debbie was a little confounded and asked, "Are you flirting with me?"

"Maybe a little."

"Well, I'm straight," Debbie declared bluntly while feeling quite flattered.

"I know," said Wu.

"And I love my husband," she added, ignoring a tingle in her stomach.

"Who wouldn't? He's super-hot." Then she touched Debbie's arm.

Debbie pulled her arm away and said, "Why do you keep touching my arm?"

Wu said, "Sorry, Dibs. I haven't told you. I'm also an empath."

"An empath?"

"When I make contact with someone, I feel what they feel."

"That's weird. I'll have to think about that one."

Shewuma kicked back the seat and rolled down the window. "Come on. Let's sing."

Debbie rolled down her window too. They accelerated up the entrance to I-64 and belted out in unison, "Driving down the highway."

It was early evening when Debbie and Shewuma pulled into the driveway at home. Shewuma inhaled deeply. "Boy, that chicken smells good," she said, apparently gripped by hunger.

"I don't smell anything," said Debbie.

Once in the house, the aroma of roasted chicken was thick in the air. "You really do have one hell of a smeller," Deb said.

Shewuma went up to Jimmy at the stove and put her arm around his shoulders. Debbie watched her with mixed feelings. Was she flirting with both of them?

"What are we having?" Wu asked Jimmy excitedly.

Jimmy took a quick look in the oven and said, "Baked chicken, roasted carrots, brussel sprouts, and some wild rice."

"What's this?" she asked, pointing at the big, covered frying pan.

Jimmy pulled the lid off and set it aside. "It's onions, peppers, celery, mushrooms, cabbage, and peas. They're cooked with curry, garlic, and Worcestershire sauce. You put it on the chicken and rice."

Wu jumped up and down with her hands together, sort of yelping.

"Man, you really love to eat, don't you?" said Jim. "You might well be the new High Priest."

"The what?" asked Wu.

"Never mind," said Debbie. "I'll tell you about it later. Jimmy, look at this," she said, holding out one of Shewuma's knives.

He dropped the spatula and took it from her. "Oh Lord. Is this bone and antler?"

Wu nodded. "Yes sir. It is."

"She made it herself," Debbie added.

"Oh shit, Shewuma. You have to teach me how to do this."

"You bet," she agreed.

Jimmy held it up under the cabinet light and examined it closely while Debbie picked up the spatula and turned the vegetables.

Over dinner to the background saxophone of Sonny Rollins, Jimmy told them about his conversation with Reubens. The revelation that the police no longer cared about Wu was odd. He was also going to confirm the story that Bocephus went to see Mr. Johnson before he disappeared. That was troubling. It could be a problem. A big problem.

They made a plan to visit Enoch's mystery man. Covington was three hours heading into the Blue Ridge Mountains. Why not travel Skyline Drive and see the sights on the way? Take the kids. Take a cooler of beer. Did Shewuma like beer? Of course she liked beer. Make sandwiches. Make a day of it. They were full of anticipation as they made plans. After doing the dishes, everyone went outside to play with the dogs and throw the frisbee. Debbie told Jimmy about Wu's theatrics at the bank, and he didn't seem very impressed. So, Debbie told Shewuma to show him something. Shewuma scampered up the down spout to the shop roof. Then diving, grabbing, swinging, and jumping, she went through the trees in their backyard and the surrounding woods. The dogs followed her on the ground, trying to keep up. She circled around and ended up on the roof of the house. After scaling the chimney, she danced a little on top and wasn't even out of breath. Jimmy looked at her and then at Debbie. "She just doesn't like underwear, does she?"

Debbie elbowed him in the ribs and yelled to Wu, "Come on down, show off! It's getting dark." Relaxing later inside, they had a pitcher of Jimmy's own creation: vodka, red wine, orange juice, and cherry juice. He called it the Deep Creek Special. They caught a buzz and watched reruns of *Ancient Aliens* on Prime. Jim and Deb asked Wu questions while she critiqued the information being presented. It got very late. Jimmy and Debbie were leaning against each other on the couch, holding hands. Wu sat beside Debbie, her legs curled up, drinking the last of the third batch of Deep Creek Specials. It had been many years since she had a high of any kind. She stroked Tippy, lying beside her purring. The dogs played with their toys on the floor. Debbie had turned off the TV and put on a CD of Jimmy's cousin Corrine and her husband. Wu sighed with utter contentment. It was probably the best day of her whole life. She touched Debbie on the arm to tell her just that and almost fainted. The depth and range of emotion between Debbie and Jimmy was overwhelming. Shewuma stood up, "I should go to bed so you guys can spend some time together."

"Are you sure?" asked Debbie.

"Yes, I'm sure," she answered, a bit embarrassed by the intrusion into their personal feelings.

"Well, come on. Let's get you out of that spare bedroom and into the luxury suite on the other side. You'll have your own bath and kitchen and TV. Come on, I'll show it to you." Debbie headed over, pulling Wu behind her. At the end of the hall past the kitchen and utility room were two exterior looking doors. The one on the left came in from the double garage into a small mud room, with a bench, umbrella stand packed full, and several coat hooks lining the wall. Debbie opened the door on the right, and they entered a fair-sized kitchen. There was a square table against the side wall with three chairs around it. "This is a mother-in-law suite. My mom lived over here." Debbie had been a licensed realtor for years and fell into the house tour easily. She pointed out the stove, refrigerator, and microwave. She highlighted the large pantry with the bifold doors on the right. On the left was a good-sized bathroom with ample cabinet space and a tub/shower combo. Straight ahead were two doors. On the left was a bedroom with a closet, two chests of drawers, and a mirrored dresser. The double bed had a nightstand on the far side, and a giant wooden rocking horse hung from the ceiling in the corner of the room.

Shewuma pointed at it and said, "What's the deal with that?"

Debbie chuckled. "A lesbian girl who used to work for us for a while had a crush on me and made it as a gift."

"It's really nice," said Wu.

"Yeah, she was always trying to get me to go with her to the Hershey bar in Norfolk. Get the name?"

"I get it. Her, she, lesbian. It's clever. Did you go?"

"No," said Debbie. She pushed Wu's shoulder playfully. "If not for Jim, who knows?"

"What did Jimmy think about her hitting on you?"

"Oh, you know guys. He thought it was kind of hot."

"Yeah, I know guys." Wu brushed Debbie's hair behind her ear with two fingers. "I think you're a bad girl deep down."

Debbie realized she was blushing and turned awkwardly to move on from what had just happened and continue the tour. "Here's the living room. A big screen TV with cable and DVD player. And you will soon see that we have a shitload of DVDs. There's a couch, a recliner, and your own separate front door. If you look through the peephole, you can see our front door at the other end of the porch. Debbie was avoiding Shewuma's eyes. Wu touched her arm and said, "I didn't mean to make you uncomfortable, but you're so damn sexy."

Debbie looked her in the eyes. "I love Jimmy."

"I know. You told me," said Shewuma, and kissed her on the cheek. "I'm just fucking with you. So what's in the locked room we passed back at the beginning?"

Debbie took the key from on top of the door jamb and opened it. Wu was fascinated. "We call this the library," said Debbie, gesturing around the fifteen by fifteen-foot room. To the immediate left were two side-by-side, floor to ceiling bookcases. Continuing around the rest of the room, the walls were covered with do-it-yourself shelving, the adjustable kind, with removable brackets and prefabricated shelving boards. In the center of the room was a three and a half by five-foot table, half covered with stacks of DVDs. The bookcases were packed with a myriad of different books that were apparently grouped by subject. Under the table were many more books and DVDs in milk crates.

Shewuma saw lots of Science Fiction: the *Dune* series, *Potter*, *Lord of the Rings*, the *Twilight* series, Asimov, Heinlein, Ray Bradbury, Lieber, Poe, Jules Verne, even a row of *Remo the Destroyer*. There was a large paranormal section, from Sylvia Brown to Evelyn Paglini. Then there were F. Scott, Twain, Hemingway, Joyce, a set of cookbooks by Bobby Flay and another by Julia Child. There was even a set of the *Encyclopedia Britannica* from the sixties. Every kind of book she could imagine. Even a section of old comic books, probably worth a fortune now. The next wall was games. Board games, chess, checkers, Life, Monopoly, Yahtzee, trivia games, and all the classics. But there were also many games Wu had never heard of: Small World, Shogun, Dead of Winter, Above and Below, Axis and Allies. There was even a Donald Trump game from the nineties.

"Do you like playing board games?" Debbie asked.

"I love them," said Shewuma.

The shelves on the opposite wall were completely filled with horses. Lots of high-end figurines. Breyers, Treadwell, Woodall. There were also dozens of horses in plastic, wood, and ceramic, as well as knickknack horses and pictures of horses.

"I'm going out on a limb and say Debbie Archer is a horse person."

Debbie smiled. "Yeah, I've had two horses in my life, States and Windy. And I worked at Shamrock Stables for years."

"I love horses too," said Shewuma. "And your collection is magnificent."

The last wall was a free-for-all. In the very center was a Pocahontas doll flanked on either side by effigies of the Japanese people from their daily life to the Shinto gods. Above and below was a hodgepodge of mugs, platters, steins, dragons, and several busts of African women. But what struck Shewuma the most was a makeshift shrine that sat behind the door.

"An altar?" asked Shewuma

"Yes, I guess so," said Debbie.

The base was a console table, possibly antique, Wu thought. She studied the items on it. A large knife with a wolf's head handle and ceramic sheath depicting packs of wolves running through the forest. A mirror leaned against the wall in the center. Taped all over it were family pictures. Debbie pointed out everyone. Jim and Debbie's parents, Jimmy's sisters, his grandfather, Cap'n Dick. cousin Corrine, Bo, Debbie's aunts and uncles, and many transitioned pets. Also on the alter were an incense burner, candles, and several pieces of jewelry.

"What is that?" asked Wu, pointing to a tall antique bottle filled with water.

"It's holy water," said Debbie,

"Really?"

"Really. It's actual holy water. It's been here eighteen years and has never evaporated or gotten moldy or anything."

"What's it for?"

"Jimmy likes having it. He has a lot of weird shit. He kind of studies stuff. The supernatural, religions, aliens. Once," said Debbie like it was a secret, "Jimmy did a cleansing of an office. He used prayers and the holy water."

"What was he cleansing the office of exactly?"

Debbie was wide-eyed and serious. "Well, things were breaking down, lights flickering, clients getting freaked, and then…" Debbie moved in closer. "A secretary would keep her baby in a spare office. It started screaming and when they went in, it was out of the crib and across the room. It had a discoloration on its forehead that never went away. Jimmy cleansed the place and everything went back to normal."

Wu pointed to a handwritten composition encased in a wooden frame with gold beading lining the interior that was hanging above the mirror. "What's that?"

"That's my Ode to a Tooth. I wrote it to Jimmy to thank him for helping me over a really bad weekend."

Shewuma read the poem aloud.

Ode To a Tooth

Not long ago I was feeling bad.
A toothache was the cause.
The pain was severe and hard to endure
And never gave me a pause.
Oil of cloves, aspirin paste,
And Excedrin by the ton.
I had subdued the dreadful suffering awhile
But alas the pain had won.
The battle was fought both long and hard.
All the remedies were at hand.
Till I slumped into the arms of defeat
The pain I could no longer stand.
An appointment was made to cure the ill
A dentist I was to see.
The tooth was pulled and put to rest.

The ache was history.
Pain relievers were prescribed
So the agony would be defeated.
I took them morning, noon and night
Until they were depleted.
Throughout the ache and dreadful pain
There was comfort to be found.
Through all the never-ending care
And love that did surround.
The care received was special indeed.
It put a nurse to shame.
Surely you wonder who is so kind
And want to know their name.
The person in question is the love of my life.
The best friend I've ever known.
His name is Jimmy…Archer that is
And his love for me is always shown.
So, tip your hat and give him a hand
I'm very proud to say.
He's one in a million this man of my dreams.
And here he is to stay.
Love,
Debbie

"Wow," said Wu. "You draw, you write poetry, you ride, you fight, and you're super-hot. Anything else I should know?"

Debbie self-consciously pointed back to the photos. "Look at Jim's parents. He looks like both of them, doesn't he?"

"Uh huh," said Wu, and moved on to the next picture. "Are these your parents looking so very happy here?"

"Yes."

"Do you mind telling me about them?"

"That's my dad. He died in 1994. And that's my mom. She passed in 2013."

"Can I ask how your father died?" Wu sensed hesitation and said, "If you don't want to talk about him, I understand."

"No, it's okay," she said wistfully and remembered her father. "Dad was a guy's guy, you know? Workmen always liked to hang out with him. He would strike up a conversation with a stranger and you would think they'd known each other for years. He fought in Korea and Vietnam. Purple Heart and a Bronze Star. I'm very proud of that. After he left the service, he went to work as an insurance investigator. The way Mom told me, he had to go to another state to investigate a fire at some plant. He and the Fire Marshall were at the scene when a wall collapsed, killing them both. Mom didn't want to live alone, so we built this house and the three of us moved in together."

"Do you mind if I ask about your mother?"

Deb paused, then said, "Of course not. She had a stroke. Seemed like she was going to be all right. But then she had another one. Worse this time. She was an invalid after that and we took care of her until she died."

"We? Jim helped?" Wu seemed surprised.

"Oh yeah, we had a system cuz you know, we had to feed her, change her, and turn her regularly. We had to run the business too. Toward the end, she called Jim Frank and I was the lady who worked here. The last couple of months, hospice would come and help. It sounds bad but it was almost a relief when she passed. For her too, I think." Debbie looked at Wu's face for a reaction.

Wu took her hand. "It doesn't sound bad, Dibs. You stuck by her and took care of her. And she loves you for it."

Debbie pushed back the memories. "Well, anyway, this is your side now."

Shewuma hugged Debbie and said, "I've never known people like you before. Thank you."

At a loss for words, Debbie just nodded and said, "Tomorrow I'll show you our war room, which contains our weapons collection."

"Excellent!"

"Come on," said Deb. "Let's get your stuff."

CHAPTER 13

David E.

Jimmy and the kids woke Debbie up at 6:00 am to get an early start. She wasn't very happy about getting up an hour early, so Jimmy promised her a face massage when they came home. That lit her up a bit. After showering in a cap, Debbie braided her hair in anticipation of a long busy day. She had already decided to wear jeans, her boppers, and a light jacket to conceal her Beretta. "What about the T-shirt, Jimmy?" she yelled from the walk-in. "What T-shirt are you wearing today?"

He ran into the walk-in, wanting to show her. "My travel shirt. Gas, Food, Lodging, Fucking, and Dodging."

She started laughing. "I know what I want to wear."

"Wait," said Jim as she started to put it on.

After a moment she said, "I'm waiting. What am I waiting for?"

"Nothing, I'm just enjoying the sights. Why don't you leave it off for a while?"

"No, I can't just walk around the house in my bra. Especially this bra. It shows too much cleavage."

"Exactly," said Jimmy. "And don't think I'm asking this for me. I consider myself a connoisseur of underwear, so this is more like work for me."

"You're crazy. Besides, Shewuma looks at me kind of funny sometimes. She touches my arm a lot. She told me she's an empath. Do you know what that is?"

"Yes. It comes from her Mantis DNA."

"Where did you come up with that?"

"I talk to her too, you know. She has a crush on you."

"Which is a little weird."

"No, it isn't. To know you is to have a crush on you."

"You're sweet," she said holding up her T-shirt for him see. Across the chest it read, "This is not eye contact."

Jimmy put his arms around her waist. She pulled in her hands and arms, holding him off. "Go finish getting ready and make breakfast and lunch and all that preparation shit you do." She said it halfheartedly and giggling.

"It's done. I've been up since 4:00 am."

She relented and slid her arms around him.

Walking down the hall to say good morning, Shewuma changed her mind when she became aware of the musky scents and rhythmic sounds coming from the bedroom. Instead, she took the animals outside. Lying on the dew-soaked grass, she hollered, "Come get me!" And boy did they.

An hour later Debbie walked into the den in the middle of a tug of war free-for-all. Shewuma had a knotted rope in each hand. Petey was pulling one and Nicky the other. Across the room, Molly was dragging Connor around by a rawhide bone. Even Tippy was in. He sat behind Petey, periodically swiping at his wagging tail. The most prominent thing about the scene to Debbie was that Shewuma was buck naked. Hanging on the back doorknob was Wu's new green, satiny V-neck mini dress that she bought specifically to adjust into a manta. On the coffee table were a pair of white panties, a tan leather belt, and both bone knives. Debbie took the opportunity to really scrutinize Wu's body for the first time. Her muscles were well defined, but she wasn't muscular like Debbie, more toned. Debbie found her breasts oddly intriguing. They were average size, but the nipples were a bit large and the areolas darker than she'd ever seen. Even just playing with the dogs, her movements were graceful and effortless. Romping with the kids seemed to give her a childlike joy. Her open, infectious smile made Debbie smile as well. The only thing she had on were the moccasins they found at the Shoe Warehouse. Beaded on top with fringe around the side. Wu was very taken with them, so taken that Wu bought every one they had in her size, seven pairs. Debbie opened the back door and commanded, "Outside." All the kids were gone in an instant but Tippy. He came to Debbie, circling her legs and wanting attention. Wu stood up still in her pet-playing afterglow. Debbie noticed how hard and tight her butt was. It was almost out of place with such shapely legs.

Wu said, "They're great, aren't they? I love those guys. When I figure out what I'm going to do and get settled, I'm going to get me some."

"You know you can stay here as long as you want," said Debbie. "But you can't keep running around naked. Why aren't you wearing your clothes?"

With a calculating look, Shewuma said, "Everything got wet playing in the grass and I'm letting them dry. But I promise I'll go put something on as soon as you stop checking me out."

Debbie suddenly felt awkwardly aroused, like an adolescent caught while unexpectedly seeing a naked neighbor through a window. Flustered, she quickly turned and walked out of the room. Shewuma heard Jimmy leaving the bedroom so she grabbed up her things and quickly ran over to her side of the house.

A short time later, Jimmy called out, "Let's eat," from the kitchen.

Debbie and Shewuma sat next to each other at the table facing butter, syrup, whipped cream, a bowl of scrambled eggs, and two pounds of crispy bacon. Debbie was relieved to see Wu wearing a dress and hoped she was wearing underwear as well.

"How many do ya'll want?" asked Jimmy, ladling pancake batter on the grill.

"Two," answered Debbie.

"How many can I have?" asked Shewuma.

He laughed and said, "You are truly the new High Priest of Miserability. Let's start with ten and go from there."

"Oh God, I love this place," Wu told Debbie.

Deciding to take Miss Interceptor over the other two vans, they were on the road by 8:30 am. Debbie drove as usual. Jimmy generously offered Wu shotgun, which she accepted. He sat in one of the back bucket seats. Everyone settled in. Wu reclined her seat back two notches and put her feet on the dashboard. Debbie pointed to her lap, exposed up to her panties and said, "I'm going to need you to keep that thing covered."

"Nobody is looking anyway," said Shewuma.

"Oh, I snuck a peek," said Jimmy.

Debbie leaned over to Wu and said, "See what I mean? He loves underwear."

Surprised, Jimmy said, "I can't believe you let me get away with that comment."

It surprised Debbie too. "I guess I'm getting soft."

Jimmy took his .45 caliber Glock, extra clip, and Debbie's .40 caliber Baretta, in holsters, and slid them under the seat within reach. He leaned forward with his elbows on the high back of the front seats. The kids found their own comfy spots. Molly liked to spread out in the back. Nicky lay in the seat behind Debbie smacking his lips. He really didn't care much for riding. Connor went to his regular spot on Debbie's left thigh and was looking out the window. Petey was more of a nomad. He roamed from one lap to another and one spot to another. Tippycat opted to curl up in a ball beside Molly in the back. They hit the road waving, with no response from neighbor Rawlings as he neared his own driveway. His feet barely moving, Jimmy said, "One day he's just going to fall out."

"But he keeps going," said Deb.

Jim handed Shewuma a case with about fifteen CDs in it. Then he opened the cooler and passed out bottles of Millers. "Be sure and give me your bottle top," he told Wu.

She handed it back to him and asked Debbie, "Why?"

"He shoots them," she explained, snapping her fingers. "It's pretty cool. You'll love it."

Jimmy held his bottle up front and they all clinked. Then he recited the Deep Creek variation of a well-known beer toast.

"I think that I shall never hear a poem as lovely as a beer.
That relaxing drink they have on tap with golden base and snowy cap.
That ice cold brew I drink all day, until my memories fade away.
Poems are made by fools I fear, but only Miller can make a beer."

Wu held her hand back for a high five. "That was great," she said.

"Wait until you hear it a thousand times," Debbie snarked.

With true hurt in his voice, Jimmy said, "Doodle."

She knew it was mean and immediately regretted saying it. "I'm sorry, Babe. I think I actually snapped at you for looking up Wu's dress earlier."

"I forgive you. I know how you can hold a grudge." He leaned up and pointed to the CD case. "Wu, pick one."

Shewuma fingered through the choices and held up *Allman Brothers at the Fillmore East.*

"Excellent choice," said Debbie. "Best live band ever."

Wu popped it in and Debbie paused it. "But first. You ready, Wu? We have a surprise for you, Jim."

Shewuma put her thumb up and they broke into the first verse of "Firebird from Hell." By the time they finished, Jimmy was clapping and hooting. He was very pleased. Then Debbie hit play and "Whipping Post" began its twenty-three-minute chronicle.

"If I was ever in a position to need walk-on music, "Whipping Post" would be it," said Jim.

Two hours later and well past Richmond, they stopped at a rest area. Everybody grabbed an animal and took them out until they all did their business. Then the girls went, followed by Jim. Back on the road and to Wu's delight, Jimmy opened two bags of Fritos. He handed one to Wu and kept one for him and Debbie. Jim opened a beer for himself and asked, "Water or beer, Babe?"

"Water."

"Water or beer, Wu?"

"Both."

"I should have known that. Both for the High Priest."

Debbie put on a Chris Botti CD and they settled in. After a while, Debbie turned the music down and said, "Birds gotta eat, same as worms. Who said it?"

"I know this," said Jim.

Shewuma looked perplexed.

"What movie is it from," Debbie explained.

"Oh, okay."

But before she could say anything, Jimmy leaned up and said, "*The Outlaw Josey Wales*."

"That's it," said Deb.

"I knew that," said Wu, sounding a bit cheated.

"You need to speak up, girl," said Jim, then, "Here's another one. Don't write checks with your mouth. You can't cash with your ass."

Debbie was blank. Shewuma thought for a moment and said almost arrogantly, "*Sucker Punch*. That was Scott Glen."

"That was pretty obscure," said Debbie, annoyed.

"No, that was impressive," countered Jimmy, then to Wu, "She really hates to lose. You're up."

Wu very precisely and in a stern voice said, "Fasten your seatbelt. It's going to be a bumpy night."

"I don't know the movie," said Jim. "But you sound just like Betty Davis."

"It's *All About Eve*," said Debbie. "And you did. You sounded exactly like her."

"One of my many talents," said Wu. "I'm good with voices."

"Do Katherine Hepburn," insisted Jim. "I love her."

"Okay," said Wu. With a quivering voice, she did her best Katie. "We would carve our days like a piece of sculpture, then suddenly last summer."

Debbie and Jimmy laughed and clapped. "That was wonderful," said Jim. "I would swear that was Kate sitting there with her underwear showing."

Debbie laughed. "Rein it in, Oscar lady," she said, reaching over and pulling Wu's dress back down.

"You two seem to have fun no matter what you're doing," noted Shewuma.

"Well, what's the point if you're not enjoying life? We really like each other too. That helps," said Debbie.

"Well at the risk of sounding corny, I really like you guys too."

Jimmy leaned up and said, "To know us is to love us."

"I caught you," said Debbie. "Stop looking at her legs."

"I could say the same thing to you," Jim challenged. "You've been checking her out all morning."

"I'm just checking the mirror over there. That's all," said Debbie and moved on to another game question.

Jimmy leaned his face between the seats, holding his phone. "Dibs, this says it costs $20 to drive on Skyline Drive."

Debbie frowned. "Fuck that."

"I'll pay for it," Wu offered cheerfully.

"No, Sweetie. It's the principle," said Deb. "Hell, look around. There are mountains everywhere anyway." Doing *Scarface*, she added, "We don't need no stinking Skyline Drive."

Jim said, "I guess we might as well go on and find the mystery man."

Debbie checked the GPS and said, "We're only twenty minutes away from Covington."

"Sounds good," said Jimmy. "Anybody want a sandwich? I have ham and cheese, bologna and cheese, and turkey and cheese."

"Hell yes," Shewuma said enthusiastically.

"Sure," said Deb.

Jim said, "How about lettuce and onions on it? I have some that I wrapped separately to keep them nice and crunchy." He set a bowl of green olives on the console as well.

They both answered affirmatively. Wu said to Debbie, "He's like having our own little Rachel Ray."

Jimmy made a face. "Or how about Wolfgang Puck?"

"Bobby Flay," said Debbie.

"As long as I don't have a uterus," Jimmy replied, and they all laughed.

He passed out the food. Between bites they speculated aloud about Enoch's mystery man, who he was, and what was going on. All the while, they were each covertly slipping bits of people food to the kids.

Covington was easy to find, but there was no River Road on the GPS. There was a West River Road. That led to a high-end neighborhood. Probably not it. There was a river, the Jackson River. It ran through the middle of town. Jimmy was mockingly calling it Jackson Creek. Where he grew up in Deep Creek, the James River was five miles wide. He could throw a baseball across this one. It didn't take long for Jimmy to insist they stop and ask for directions, which Debbie never liked to do. But since they'd been on the road for a while, she relented by calling it a pee stop. They pulled into a Wawa with gas pumps and did a full pit stop. After gas and bathroom breaks for the kids and humans, Jim went in search of directions. A heavy-set, redheaded woman behind the counter smiled as Jimmy approached her. He asked her about River Road. She thought about it and shook her head. Then, in a startling move, she yelled across the store in a loud, crackly voice, "Anybody know River Road?"

Four people appeared at the counter looking very serious. There were two grown men who looked like construction workers. A teenage girl with glasses sporting a bulging backpack. And a sharply dressed biker chick. She wore studded and strapped black boots, jeans with worn-out knees, an expensive-looking leather jacket covered with zippered pockets, and black and yellow gloves right out of a motor bike league. Maybe in her fifties with long brown hair, her face was odd. Jimmy couldn't put his finger on it. No matter. They all began discussing the location of River Road. Only in a small town. Shewuma edged in with three packs of Hostess Ho Hos. They all finally came to the consensus that there was no River Road.

Shewuma stood next to Jimmy, already eating the first HoHo. Mouth full, she said, "We'll never find that old man."

"Oh," said the biker lady as she turned toward them, "You probably mean old David E. that lives back in the woods. His road isn't River Road, but it is a dirt road by the river."

"That's probably who we're looking for. Thanks, ma'am," said Jim. He held out his hand. She was holding an orange soda with both hands and ignored the gesture. Then she leaned in and said, "You and her together?"

The best answer he could come up with was, "Yeah, but not like that."

"Hmm. You should come see me later," she offered.

"Thanks anyway, but I'm married," he replied.

"No, I didn't mean it like that…never mind. Okay, so here are the directions. Go west through the light and a little ways past the Wendy's billboard, you'll see a chain across a dirt road going into the woods. About a mile down that road lies a house. A shack really. David E. lives there. He's kind of a hermit. Not real outgoing, but he's really nice… and cute too."

"How is it you know him so well?" asked Jim, curious about the sudden flood of information.

"He comes to see me sometimes. You see, I'm a psychic. And I'm the only one between here and Charlottesville. I have a shop just up the street there on East Gray. You got his package?"

"Huh?"

"His package. Just a week or so ago, he came to me asking if I knew when his package would come. And I says no. Go ask the post office. I don't know nothing about no package."

Wu had been silent up to that point. To her, it looked like this woman was hitting on Jimmy, which peeved her. She decided to weigh in. "Your constant use of double negatives notwithstanding, you didn't know about the package and you didn't know Jimmy was married. You're not much of a psychic, are you?"

The biker, clearly offended, looked at Wu's HoHo and said, "Those are gonna make you hippy, girl." She turned and walked toward the exit. Suddenly, she whirled around—eyes glazed—and said, "They're coming for you." Then she shook it off and hurried out of the store.

"That's our crazy Chloe," said the lady behind the counter.

Back in the truck Debbie was concerned. "Where have ya'll been?"

"Did you see that slutty biker chick all in leather leave the store?" Wu asked Debbie in a bit of a huff.

"Yeah, I saw her," Debbie said, not particularly interested.

Jimmy thought the slutty comment was heavy-handed coming from someone who wore short dresses and no underwear. But Wu was visibly pissed. "She tried to pick Jimmy up just as blatant as you please."

"Well," Debbie said as she kind of sloughed it off, "it happens a lot with him and biker chicks. And Black women seem to be drawn to him too."

"I hate to break up the girl talk," said Jimmy, "but the hussy (he used air quotes) gave us directions to the old man's place. She called him David E."

Shewuma cut in, giving Debbie the directions to David E.'s house, as well as a play-by-play of what happened in the store.

"I don't really think she was hitting on me. I didn't get that vibe," said Jim.

"Yeah, right," said Debbie. "You wouldn't know the vibe if it sat on your face." That made all three laugh wildly.

"And she says that I'm nasty," he could barely articulate to Wu as he gave her a fist bump.

The directions turned out to be sound. Debbie pulled on the dirt road and stopped Miss Interceptor at the chain barricade hanging between two metal posts that were blocking the entrance. It was a stretch to even call it a dirt road.

"We walk?' asked Wu.

"No way," said Debbie. "Jim?"

"I got it, Babe," he said as he got out. The back hatch raised and he firmly said, "Stay!" to the animals. From the spare tire compartment he produced a large pair of bolt cutters. After popping the chain, he got back in the truck and said, "Let's rock."

Wu looked at Debbie, impressed. Debbie said, "We're property managers. We always have a master key."

The road was tight and the trees were so thick that Debbie turned on the lights. The sound of branches scraping Miss Interceptor elicited a few obscenities from Debbie as she drove through the encroaching boscage. There was even a hostile "This is bullshit!"

About a half a mile more and the trail opened into a field of wild tall grass. Thirty yards farther sat what property managers Jim and Debbie used to call a depreciating asset.

"Stop!" said Wu, and Debbie hit the brake. Shewuma opened her door. "Just a precaution. Don't give me away." She winked and disappeared into the green landscape.

"Where do you think she's going?" Debbie asked Jimmy.

"She can pull my arm. I'm gonna give her the benefit of the doubt."

They pulled up within feet of the small square shack. The roof was rusted tin. Weathered cedar shakes covered the sides, with the occasional one missing. The windows on either side of the rotten front door were falling apart. Jimmy put a bullet in the chamber of his .45 Glock and clipped it onto his belt. He handed Debbie her .40 caliber Beretta and she did the same. The dogs were restless but they would be okay. Oddly, Tippy stood on his hind legs, looking out the back window and bristling. Jimmy and Debbie both took a breath, let it out, nodded to each other, and got out of the truck. There was no sound, no movement anywhere. They approached the decaying front door with their hands on their pistols. The door opened and a man appeared in the entrance leveling a sawed off double barrel shotgun. He was old, maybe seventy. But he was handsome in spite of it. About 5' 8" with a gray beard and a head full of thick white hair. He wore an old stained tan suit and a shirt that was most certainly white at some point in the past. They stopped cold and waited. With their peripheral vision, they could see Wu coming silently across the dicey roof from the rear of the shack.

The old man spoke. "I don't know or care who you people are. Just turn around and leave or I'll shoot you dead."

Shewuma dropped down onto the rotting planks of the porch, snatched the shotgun from his hands, and threw it to Debbie, who instinctively caught it. The old man was surprised but still reacted. He pulled a sidearm from his belt and Wu slapped it away. He backed in and slammed the front door. Wu stopped the door from closing with her foot. The old man pushed the door with all he had, but it wouldn't budge. He peeked through the three-inch gap, holding his last defense, a tree branch that doubled as his cane. The woman at the door was both incredibly fast and strong. The other two had his guns. Quickly calculating his options, he opted for a different strategy. "Who are you?"

With both hands, Shewuma made the symbol of her people. "I am Shewuma, Kachina of the Hopi nation, Crevetch to Enoch of Erran, Star child of the Realm. I am not your enemy, David E."

Surprised that she knew his name, he said, "So you're married to Enoch?"

"I was," she said, correcting him. "He has transitioned."

"Anybody could say they were married to him. Especially a Hybrid," he responded, still wary.

Shewuma produced the Cric and held it up. The hologram of Enoch's face and then David E.'s address appeared. That did it. "Come on in," said David E., opening the front door and gesturing them to enter.

Debbie cracked the twelve-gauge and removed the one shell in it. Jimmy walked in, inspecting the pistol. It was a 1911, .45 caliber semi-automatic. The loyal sidearm of the U.S. military for more than a century. It was old and worn out, like everything else in this shack he'd seen so far. He popped the clip and it was empty. But there was one bullet in the chamber. Putting the bullet back in the clip, he slapped it back into the handle. If possible, the condition of the inside of the house was worse than the outside. It was one open room, about twenty by twenty feet. In the center was a two-by-three-foot partial sheet of warped plywood sitting on cinderblocks that served as a makeshift table. In fact, cinderblocks made up most of the furniture in the place. Seats at the table, supports for a cot on one wall, a cinderblock nightstand, and the legs for a wood stove. The stove's stack was improvised from terra cotta sewer pipe that went through a hole in the roof sealed by duct tape. Jimmy spied a small gas heater with two propane tanks beside it. Realizing how cold it must get in the mountains, he still questioned the setup in such a confined area.

David E. saw Jimmy studying the heater. "Beats freezing to death," he said.

"I get it," Jimmy answered.

There were three cardboard boxes against the wall. The first contained some clothes, towels, and blankets. The second was a catchall with hand tools, silverware, scissors, duct tape, and such. The last was food. Mostly dried food like beans and rice. There were some canned goods, several boxes of assorted crackers, and four jars of peanut butter.

"This could be our retirement house," Jimmy joked to Debbie.

"Stop it," Debbie said while trying to keep a straight face.

"It's not much but it's home," said David E. "I've been living here for about six years. I'm off the grid completely. I'm a ghost."

"What is that?" asked Jim, pointing to something in the center of the table. A computer tower, keyboard, and screen were all hooked up to what resembled a waffle iron.

"It's a standalone," said David E. "All I can do is play some games, make calculations, and read whatever was already on it."

"They call it an air gap now," said Debbie.

"Really?" asked Jim.

"Yeah."

"How do you run it? There's no power here," asked Jimmy.

"It's all hooked up to that." David E. pointed to the waffle maker. "It's called a Rexon battery. It could run a whole house for a year."

"There's no such thing," said Debbie.

"No, not for another thirty or forty years," said David E. with a hint of a smile.

Debbie chalked it up to dementia and moved on with the introductions. They gave David E. his weapons back on the condition that he promised not to shoot at them. He, in turn, offered them peanut butter crackers, told them how to get fresh water from the well, and explained the toilet procedures. There was a clearing behind the tall bushes to the east. There were plenty of leaves and a shovel leaning against the sapling. David E. laid his cane on the floor and motioned for everyone to sit down. Shewuma told him in great detail what had happened to them over the last couple of weeks. Debbie and Jimmy jumped in with supplemental information whenever they felt it necessary. When they were done, David E. sat up straight and said, "That's quite a story. Explains all those stiches."

Shewuma touched the exposed part of her chest and neck, revealing sutures. She'd forgotten about them. Debbie and Jimmy had as well. They just stopped seeing them.

"We'll get them out tonight, Honey," said Deb, sensing Wu's sudden awkwardness.

"So bottom line," said David E., "what can I do for you?"

"I'm not sure," said Shewuma. "Enoch said to find you, so we did."

"I get why you're here," he said to Wu. Then he looked at Debbie and Jimmy. "I'm wondering why you two are still involved at this point."

"Well, we managed the house that Wu and Enoch lived in," Debbie began. But Shewuma interrupted her.

"I called them."

David E. leaned in, interested. "You called them?"

"No," said Debbie. "We were the property managers, and..."

David E. put his hand up. "Hold on, Debbie." Turning to Wu, he said, "Explain what you mean when you say you called them."

"When I saw that we were lost, I said the words and asked the Gods for help. They sent Debbie, Jimmy, and Bo to save me. I was weak when I was in the hospital. I called on the Gods again, and Debbie and Jimmy came and took me away."

David E. slammed his fist on the table. "It all makes sense. One of you has been sent for the Sanctum."

Incredulous, Shewuma asked, "You have it?"

"Yes. Enoch brought it to me months ago and said to hold it until a Pleiadian came for it."

"None of us are Pleiadian," pointed out Wu.

"I'm not so sure," said David E. "Produce the Cric, Shewuma," and she did. "Can you manipulate it at all?"

"Just what I did earlier, and I can hide it here in my arm. That's it. It's an artifact of Erran. I have no control of it."

"Well, let's make sure. Do me a favor, Shewuma. Move it around your head, face, and all over your body." She did, and nothing happened. "Now give it to Jim." Jim took it. "Do the same thing. Move it around your head and by your ears."

Jimmy did it while saying, "This is silly."

"Do you feel anything?" He didn't. "Okay, give it to Debbie. Do the same thing, Debbie."

"Why? What's the point?"

"Maybe nothing. Just indulge me please."

Deb nonchalantly began moving it around this way and that, expecting nothing. As she went over her left ear, it disappeared. She looked at her empty hand and became frightened. "Where is it?" she asked with alarm.

Jimmy stood up and said, "What the fuck!"

Shewuma put her hands to her open mouth and squealed, "Oh my God!"

She seemed to understand what was happening. "What? What is it, Wu?" Jimmy said to her. Debbie was acting confused and disoriented and he said, "Debbie, what's happening? Talk to me."

Debbie stood up and said, "I think it's in my head. I can feel it in my fucking...head."

Jimmy took her shoulders, but she pulled free and ran outside, dry heaving and squeezing her skull. The three followed her as she went to her knees and started to throw up. The dogs were going crazy in the van. Jimmy was at a loss. Not unlike what he would've done in high school if they drank too much, he simply held her braid up while she puked.

"She's okay. She'll be okay," David E. was repeating.

Shewuma rubbed her back, telling her in a soothing voice, "Relax, Debbie. Clear your mind."

Debbie stopped heaving and stood up slowly. David E. produced a handkerchief. Jimmy took it and wiped her mouth. "You okay, Babe?"

"I feel really weird," she said, moving her head back and forth. "That thing is in my head. I can feel it. Like it's alive or something." Debbie dropped back to her knees and looked up to the sky. Her eyes rolled back in her head, exposing just the whites. "Oh, Jesus Christ!" she said and began to shudder.

Jimmy went to his knees beside her and held her. "Wu, call 911."

Shewuma put her hands on his shoulders and took his feelings. His fear of losing her was almost manic. "She's okay, Jim. I swear. She's just turning."

It made no sense to him. "Turning what?"

"Of course," said David E. "She has Erran DNA. She's who Enoch was talking about."

"What?" said Jimmy in disbelief.

"Erran DNA in her genes. The Cric has activated it. She's processing, adapting. She's a Hybrid," he exclaimed as Wu nodded in agreement.

"No, she's not," Jimmy shouted.

"Jimmy. Jimsy!" shouted Wu. That got his attention. "Let me have her. Trust me."

Uncomprehending and feeling helpless, Jimmy backed off and let Wu take her. Shewuma held Debbie's face and looked into her eyes. "Breathe, Debbie, breathe." Debbie closed her eyes and began to breathe deeply. She opened her eyes and looked cognizant but confused. "Put your hand over your ear where the Cric went."

Debbie passed her hand back and forth over her ear and frantically said to Wu, "Nothing. Nothing is happening. I can still feel it in there, like a whirlwind."

Looking into Debbie's eyes again, Wu said, "Debbie, relax. Clear your mind. Breathe. Come on, Debbie. Slow it all down." Debbie was breathing normally now. "You're my Dibsi. Jimmy is here. You're good."

Awareness seemed to dawn as Debbie opened her eyes and smiled a little. "You called me Dibsi."

"That's it," said Wu. "It's all you, girl. Put your hand back over it. See it," Wu coached. "See it in your mind. Then see it in your hand."

Debbie pulled her hand away and there it was. She handed the Cric to Wu and tried to stand. Jimmy helped her up and she smiled at him. She kissed him on the mouth and then turned and kissed Wu on the mouth as well. Debbie's shoulders slumped with exhaustion and they each took an arm. She looked at Wu and they both began to laugh.

Jimmy said, "What's so fucking funny?"

The comment made them laugh even harder. Debbie was becoming steady on her feet and opened the side door to Miss Interceptor. The animals poured out. Tippy took off across the field toward the woods and Molly bolted past them toward the back of the shack. The other three went straight to Debbie and she loved them up. Debbie suddenly appeared happy and energetic. David E. was taking it all in, fascinated. Wu asked Debbie, "You ready to try again?"

"Give me a few more minutes."

Jimmy said, "Try it again? Are ya'll crazy?"

Seeing the anger and confusion in his face, Debbie took his hand and pulled him close. In his ear she said, "It's all good, Baby. I get it now." Then he heard her voice—literally inside his head—saying, "It's all good."

A calm swept over him. He looked into her eyes and said, "Did you really just do that?"

She gave him a crooked smile and turned to the others. "Wow!" she said and spun around twice, her arms outstretched like a ballerina. Then she called out, "Molly, come here, girl." Molly was running hard toward them and she had something in her mouth. She was carrying a tiny white chihuahua by the scruff of its neck. "Drop it," said Debbie and Molly released it into her hands. She gave the pup to David E., who kissed it right on her licking mouth.

He held her close and introduced her. "This is my girl Bridget."

"Bridget the midget," said Wu and even Jimmy laughed. Jimmy made sure the dogs peed and then put them back in Miss Interceptor. David E. cuddled Bridget the whole time. Shewuma touched his hand while he held her and realized Bridget was probably his last real link to humanity.

"Where's Tippy?" asked Jim, remembering he'd taken off earlier.

"He's good. He's keeping watch," said Wu. Debbie nodded.

Jimmy was still watching Debbie with trepidation. Something happened to her with that blue rock, and he was the only one that seemed to be concerned.

"Let's go back inside," Debbie said. They all went in and sat back down around the table on cinderblocks. David E. produced a bottle of Absolut Vodka. He waved it around, saying, "I've been saving this for a special occasion." He opened it, took a swig, and passed it to Wu.

She took a long, hard hit, gave it to Jimmy, and motioned for him to drink. "It's a toast," she said.

Jimmy took a swallow and asked, "What are we toasting?"

"Me," said Debbie.

Jimmy gave her the bottle and it continued around the table. "So why are we toasting you?" he asked Debbie.

David E. held up his hand and said, "Hold on a minute." While the bottle went around once more, David E. went fishing under his cot. He came back and sat an old, worn, black bowling ball bag on the table. "Enoch brought this to me about five months ago," he said as he unzipped it and reached inside. "He told me to keep it until the true Pleiadian came for it." He pulled a life-sized blue Skull out of the bag and set it on the table in front of Debbie.

Wu tossed the Cric to Debbie. She snatched it from the air and laid it on the table next to the Skull.

"Be careful with that thing," Jim said, remembering what happened earlier.

Debbie held the Cric in one hand and touched the Skull with the other. "This is what it's all about."

"It's a Skull made of blue glass," Jimmy said apathetically.

"No. Crystal, not glass," said David E.

"Quartz Crystal," added Wu. "The Sanctum." She respectfully made the sign of her people.

"Oh, you're not serious," said Jim as all the *Ancient Alien* shows he'd watched for years came flooding back.

Debbie took a long slow breath and closed her eyes. The Skull began to emit a florescent blue light.

Jimmy was startled. Wu tried to put him at ease. "It's safe, Jim. She's just talking to it."

"What do you mean? One of you tell me what the fuck is going on or that thing is going under the left rear tire." He stood up, obviously very serious. David E. began tapping on his keyboard.

Wu put her hand on his clenched fist. "Debbie's a Hybrid. She is of the Erran bloodline. She's a Star Child."

"No, she isn't. I've known her since we were kids," insisted Jim.

David E. spun the computer screen around to face Jimmy. He saw many pictures of Crystal Skulls with captions labeling them as alien in origin. "I've seen this shit on TV," said Jimmy. "All these are fakes. And how are you running that computer? There isn't even a meter outside."

"The Rexon battery there. I told you about it when you got here."

"I thought you were making that up," said Jimmy, getting very exasperated.

"Well, what do you want to know about first? Debbie or the Sanctum?"

He looked at Debbie's eyes. They had become dazzling points of blue light. It was freaking him out. "I'm fine, Babe," came her voice in his mind. He was watching her and was sure she hadn't spoken.

Jimmy tore his attention from Debbie back to David E. "Debbie has alien DNA in her. A lot of people do. Most of the time, it's so diluted that it's inconsequential. But some people like Debbie have a strong lineage. After a certain point in the genealogy, even a strong lineage will become dormant and stay dormant. Through a lifetime. Through generations of lifetimes." He leaned forward intensely. "But sometimes it can be activated."

Jimmy saw what he was getting at. "You're saying this Cric brought her alien DNA to life."

"In a manner of speaking, yes." said David E.

"And Enoch knew it would," added Wu.

"Oh come on, Wu. How could he know that? You talk like he planned all this." He was a long way from convinced.

Wu was sincere as she said, "Errans have the sight. They know what's going to happen. They've been manipulating the affairs of man for millennia."

"You say you're both Star Children," said Jimmy. "Will she do all the crazy shit you can do?"

"There's no way to know yet what will happen."

"Wu, this sounds so ridiculous. I'm trying to decide if I should just pick Debbie up and get out of here right now."

"Read this," said David E. as he spun the screen around again. Jimmy read about the Hopi Tribe and their Star Children. Their centuries old histories of Serpent people and Insectoid beings. The training of Kachinas to help and protect mankind.

Jimmy turned to Shewuma. "So you have all of this Reptilian and Mantis DNA in you?" Shewuma nodded yes. "The same Reptilians that killed Enoch and tortured and raped you? That's your DNA? Help me out here, Wu."

David E. said, "There are many different factions of Drachonians. They call themselves clans. Most just live in the Bloworld and mind their own business. A few help mankind. But there is a sizable group that have been working with governments and organizations to manipulate man and control the world for centuries. They are the ones who killed Enoch and hurt Wu. They want the Sanctum."

"You mean the Skull," said Jim. "Why?"

"You want to hear all of this now? It's kind of a long story."

"Hell yeah! It looks like Debbie and I have stepped into the middle of a big pile of shit. I want all the information I can get."

"Stepped in what, slid how far," Debbie said playfully. The blue lights were gone, and she sat with a big smile on her face. "Where's the vodka?" Wu leaned forward and handed her the bottle.

David E cleared his throat and kept talking. "Think of quartz Skulls as computers. But to keep it in perspective, that computer on the table is to this blue Skull like a slide rule to artificial intelligence."

"I get it," said Jimmy. "They're smarter than us."

"Yes, but it's more than that," David E. explained. "Their technology is based on power sources, scientific principles, and mechanics that we not only can't duplicate, but we also don't even comprehend. They can fold time and space. They have propulsion systems that defy gravity and rival the speed of light. They can make themselves and their ships invisible. And they have destructive power that dwarfs our nuclear weapons."

Jim posed an obvious question. "Then why work undercover? Why abduct people? Why torture her? (pointing to Wu). Why not just take over?"

David E leaned forward, animated. "That was the plan at one time in the past. A big war, winner take all. After destroying Mars and Peyton."

"Wait," interrupted Jimmy. "What's Peyton?"

"The fifth planet," said Shewuma. "We called it Ceres."

"No," said Jimmy, smiling. "The fifth planet is Jupiter."

"It is now," said David E., dead serious. "That asteroid belt between Mars and Jupiter used to be the fifth planet from the sun. Until the aliens obliterated it." The vodka had come back around to David E. all but empty. He tilted it up and finished it off.

"Are you buying any of this?" Jimmy asked Debbie.

He did a double take when he heard Debbie's voice in his head say, "Yes, Jimsy." Then she winked at him.

"How are you feeling, Dibs?" asked Shewuma.

"Great," said Debbie. "Like, healthy great. Really, really…uh… vigorous."

"No surprises there," said David E. "Errans have a life span of many hundreds of thousands of years." He had produced another bottle of liquor. Bourbon this time and only half full.

Debbie was staring at the Cric in her hand. "Are you ready to try it again?" asked Wu.

"Not just yet," said Debbie, feeling a bit giddy. "I want to, but it gives off so much information and this buzz of …" She couldn't come up with a word to describe the sensation.

"Power?" offered Wu.

"Maybe. Sort of."

Jimmy barked, "Don't be crazy, Debs. Keep that thing away from your head."

Wu looked at him and back to Deb. He didn't understand and needed convincing. "Take your time, Debbie. Errans take years to learn how to manage those things." She took the Jack Daniels from David E. and hit it hard.

Against his better judgement, Jimmy was beginning to believe them. "Okay, they had a big war. And you, little lady," he said to Wu, "need to slow down on the alcohol."

Debbie, Wu, and David E. started laughing. "She might look dainty," said David E., "but she's as strong as an ox."

"Yeah, little is the wrong adjective," said Jimmy. "I carried her up some stairs and she's heavy. At least two hundred pounds."

Wu stopped laughing. "No way," she said, sounding miffed. She passed Jimmy the bourbon. He was getting drunk. He passed the bottle to Debbie.

"Well," said David E., eyeing Wu, "she has denser bones and muscles. I could see her weighing two hundred."

"You can see this this too, right?" said Shewuma, flipping them both off at the same time. That broke Debbie up even more.

Jimmy gestured to David E. to continue. "So, the war."

David E. was getting pretty tipsy as well. "So, to keep from blowing up the earth, hell the entire Solar System, all the aliens came together and made a deal. But…" He lost his train of thought and then said, "Aha!" as he remembered where he was. "So that peace lasted for a very long time. But the Anunnaki broke the treaty. They tried a sneak attack. Ended up causing the great flood and nearly wiped out mankind. But they failed because the Errans had come up with a counteroffensive."

After a pause, Jimmy asked, "What was their counteroffensive?"

David E. pointed to the Skull. Wu pointed at the Skull. Debbie pointed down at the Skull with both hands.

"You mean this Skull?" said Jimmy.

"The Crystal Skull," said Debbie.

"The Sanctum," said Shewuma.

"Remember," said David E. as he took the bourbon, "it's a supercomputer." He held up the bourbon. "I'm done," he said to Wu. "Do you want it?" She took it eagerly.

Mostly as a joke, Jim said, "So I could get the internet on this thing?"

"No, you can't compare the Crystal Skull to that thing," David E. said, pointing to the Dell tower on the table. "Crystals are a big part of that advanced technology we were talking about."

"So how is it that the Skull here was the solution to the big sneak attack?" He looked at Debbie and said, "I've got a buzz."

She ran her finger down his cheek and smiled at him.

David E. continued. "The Errans built thirteen supercomputers and called them the Sancti. They magnify and manipulate the earth's electromagnetic radiation and use it to create a dampening field. This field projects up from the earth and out through the Solar System. Alien technology runs off what is called celestial energy."

"What is it?" asked Jim.

"We don't know. We can't comprehend it."

"Tesla knew," said Wu.

"I've heard that," said David E. "Anyway, the dampening fields created by the Sancti restrict celestial energy. Like pulling the plug on a toaster. No power, no alien tech. And without it they have to live in our world. That one is the Sanctum. The thirteenth Skull. It connects, controls, and programs the other twelve, or so I'm told." David E sat up straight and folded his arms.

"Everything in this book could be wrong." Jimmy sighed.

Sounded familiar to Wu but David E. said, "What?"

"It's a quote from one of his favorite books," said Debbie.

"Oh yeah," remembered Wu. "*Adventures of a Reluctant Messiah*. That is a good book."

"I think I get what you're saying," said David E. "Perhaps a demonstration? Debbie, are you up for it?"

"Sure," said Debbie. Before Jimmy could stop her, Debbie passed the Cric over her left ear and it disappeared into her head.

"Dammit, Deb," said Jimmy.

She twitched involuntarily and a "Gaack!" escaped from her throat. Except for some goosebumps, she seemed good.

"That was much smoother than the first time," said Wu.

"Yeah, just give me a second," said Debbie, with her hands on the back of her head. "There's a lot going on up here." After a moment, she relaxed and rolled her shoulders. A hologram of a computer board appeared, hovering over the center of the table. "This is David E.'s Dell tower." One after another, each major component of the computer would detach and enlarge for identification. Debbie dismantled and explained each one as they filed by holographically. "There's the hard drive. There's the SSD. The memory module. The video case." The hologram shifted to a panoramic vista of the Blue Ridge Mountains through a driver's side window. Then it shifted front through a windshield, looking at the highway, like POV driving in a video game.

"What is this?" asked Jim.

"These are my exact memories of us driving up here," said Debbie. The view shifted over and down to the right, showing Wu's legs. Then back up through the windshield.

"I knew you were looking at Wu's legs," said Jim.

"I was checking the mirrors," Debbie shot back, and the hologram disappeared. Debbie looked at Shewuma and began quoting Shakespeare in Wu's native language.

"What's she saying?" Jimmy asked Wu.

Wu was delighted. "She's reciting *Hamlet* in Hopi."

Debbie switched to Spanish and then Japanese for a few lines before she stopped.

"Dibsi," said Wu, "where is Tippycat right now?"

Debbie scanned the room. "In the woods. There." She pointed at the northeast corner of the shack.

"How can you see him?" Jim asked.

"I don't know," she answered.

"Probably a heat signature," said David E. "Thermal and through the wall no less. I didn't think that was possible."

Debbie's eyes were bloodshot, and she looked tired.

Jimmy was concerned. "You all right, Babe?"

"Yeah," said Debbie. "This puppy in my head is going to take some getting used to." That statement worried Jim more than he cared to admit.

Shewuma was there behind her, rubbing her shoulders. "You're doing incredibly well, Debs. Just take your time with it."

Debbie was soaking up the massage and Jimmy said, "You should leave that thing out. You don't know what could happen."

Debbie smiled at him. "Mother Hen Mother Hen. There's a loose duckling in the pond."

"Hey, that's my line," he protested.

"I know, but it's the first time I've ever gotten to use it on you. I'm usually the worrywart. But for you, I'll take it out." She passed her hand over her ear and removed the Cric easily this time. She set it on the table.

Jim backed off. "Okay, I get it. Just be careful. So, what else will this Cric do?"

Deb said, "Wu?"

Wu went back and sat down with the bourbon. "Well. Enoch could remember everything he ever heard or saw verbatim. He had the infrared vision but also night vision. He could magnify his sight to see really far away or up close—like microscopic. It enhanced his hearing too. And he could patch into electronic things and control them. Cell phones, TVs, even satellites. It also made him stronger and faster by manipulating his hormones. And he could do EMP and LCS.

"I know what an electromagnetic pulse is," said Jimmy. "But what is an LCS?"

"It's what kept your gun from firing at the Drach back at the house. I forget what it stands for."

Pretty drunk by this point, David E. said, "Lens. No. Lemon. No. Limited Combustion Suppression," he proudly said.

"But listen," continued Wu, "even without the Cric, the Erran DNA has a lot going on. David E. mentioned their lifespan. But Errans are also healers and telepaths, and they have the sight."

"Do you think Debbie will be able to do all that?" asked Jim.

"We'll just have to wait and see," said Wu, excited by the possibilities. She hit the bourbon again. Jimmy was pretty buzzed and had an insightful thought. He looked at David E. accusingly and said, "There's something here that doesn't make any sense." Everyone waited for his revelation. "If these Skulls keep aliens from using their technology, then why are there UFOs?"

"And crop circles," added Wu.

Suddenly Wu stood up, tipping over her cinderblock, alarmed. "Hear that?" she said. Nobody else heard anything. The Sanctum began to glow. Then Bridget, lying on the floor next to David E.'s feet, raised and cocked her head, listening.

Outside, Tippycat screeched an alarm. "Shit!" yelled Shewuma. She hit Jimmy and David E. in the chest simultaneously with her outstretched hands, knocking them both to opposite walls. Then she dove at an angle across the table, grabbing Debbie's T-shirt and pulling her along as she went by. At that instant, at the far end of the shack, a beam of sizzling red light cut through the roof, side wall and floor and kept going deep into the earth below. It followed a burning path that left the house, table and woodstove cut cleanly, almost perfectly in half. "It's a plasma rifle. Get out of here!" yelled Wu. Right after that, strafing fire from a .50 caliber machine gun turned the roof to Swiss cheese. The shack began to fall apart. Jimmy with the Skull and Debbie holding the Cric—both glowing bright blue—ran outside. Shewuma saw David E. on his knees, sobbing over Bridget, her little white body sliced into two pieces. The skin at the diagonal cut from the plasma stream was still smoking. "David E., let's go," she commanded. But he ignored her. With no time for grief, she scooped him up under her arm like a roll of carpet and ran out of the crumbling shack. Jim and Debbie were already outside, so she dropped David E. and let her breath out slowly. She took her consciousness inward. Using the techniques she had been taught since childhood, Wu slowed her time sense to a crawl. Life was now moving at a snail's pace. Surveying the scene revealed a dire situation. A black helicopter had attacked them. High in the north sky, it was floating slowly through time in a banking turn for another strafing run. This time there would be no cover. Jimmy was pulling his .45 Glock in slow motion. It was all but useless at that distance, but it was a good sign of his mettle. Not hiding or backing down but fighting. Debbie stood frozen, looking at the Cric in her hand. It was glowing blue, as was the Sanctum at Jimmy's feet. Debbie had no clue that the Men in Black were no match for her. Shewuma knew if she grabbed Debbie and ran now, they could make it to the woods and a probable escape. But the others would surely die. Enoch had brought them all here together for a reason.

So be it. Wu snapped back to real time and hollered as loud as she could, "Debbie!" right into her face. Debbie looked at her, eyes wooden and vacant. Shewuma slapped her hard. Jimmy knew he was out of range but began firing repeatedly. Shewuma went to strike Debbie again, but Debbie caught her wrist. Debbie's eyes came to life. "You can stop them with an EMP, Debbie…Say it!" said Wu. There were only seconds now.

Debbie looked up at the chopper descending like a black angel of death. She passed the Cric over her head and doubled over with clenched fists, then screamed at the chopper as if her voice were a weapon, "EMP!" Then she dropped to the ground on her knees and elbows. The chopper didn't fire but kept coming. The tail wavered and the engine died. As it got closer, Wu could see the two Men in Black in suits and sunglasses desperately manipulating the controls.

Jimmy's clip was empty, and he looked at Wu. "Get Debbie behind the truck," she said. She too headed to the truck for cover, grabbing David E. by the ankle and pulling him along with her. She tossed David E. toward the back and told Jimmy to stay put. The helicopter was coming down fast and crooked but controlled. It definitely had no power but the pilots were well trained, and they were going to land it. "It's not going to crash," Wu said to Jimmy, who was putting a spare clip in his .45. "I'll be right back," said Wu.

"You want my Glock?" he offered.

"No," she said, dashing off and pulling her bone knife from its sheath.

Debbie groaned; she was coming around. Jimmy helped her into the passenger seat. Then he opened the rear hatch and ordered the panicky dogs to stay while he helped David E. lie down in back. He picked up the Skull and looked around for Shewuma. "Wu," he called out.

"I'm here," came from what was left of David E.'s home for so long. Going to the shack, Jimmy could see inside the chopper. It had landed safely just as Wu thought it would. He saw two Men in Black suits awkwardly in the seats, their slit throats gurgling blood. They hadn't even removed their seatbelts. Shewuma was the real deal. Jimmy went in and Shewuma was picking through the rubble. She saw he was holding the Skull and held open the dusty bowling bag. Jimmy dropped the Sanctum in and zipped it up. The Rexon battery was destroyed. Wu scooped up David E.'s spare clothes and the sawed-off shotgun and piled it into Jimmy's arms. "I couldn't find the pistol," said Wu. "We need to go. There could be more coming. You drive the truck out to the highway and I'll meet you there. I have to find Tippy."

"I'll wait for you at the chain," said Jimmy.

"You won't have to. Come on. You're going to need a push start. Debbie's EMP will have fried the battery."

Jimmy was about halfway back to the highway, plowing through the branches, when he was startled by the opening of the side door. Shewuma appeared in the back passenger seat holding Tippycat. She slammed the door, chopping off some branches in the process. Jimmy reached back and she squeezed his hand. "We're good now," she said.

"Is Tippy bleeding?" asked Jimmy, concerned.

"Yeah," said Wu. "His leg. It's not that bad, but I need to wrap it."

"Under your seat is a first aid kit," Jim told her. "What happened to him?"

Jim could tell by her voice that she was impressed when she said, "He got himself a Scout."

"What's that?"

"I'll tell you later." After applying antibiotic and gauze, she asked Jimmy, "How's Debbie?"

"She seems okay. A little groggy maybe."

Shewuma took a bottle of water out of the cooler and helped Debbie take a drink while telling her, "That was a big deal. You downed that chopper with no experience."

"So you really think Debbie did that?"

"I know she did it." She kissed Debbie on the forehead and said, "You did good, Debs." Then to Jimmy, "She's gonna be fine. Here, Jim, you drink some." Then she went back to check on David E. He was sitting up against the back door petting Molly, curled up beside him. Remembering his reaction to Bridget, she felt bad for him. "Come on,

David E. Let's get you in the passenger seat." While helping him, their hands touched, and she was inundated with his feelings of grief and self-loathing. Once settled in, she told him, "You didn't do anything wrong, David E."

"I've never done anything right either," he mumbled.

"Do you want a pain pill for that knee?"

"No." They drove past the chain, and he told Jim, "Go left."

"I-64 is to the right," said Jimmy.

"No, go left. We need to get Chloe. If they've seen me with her, she's in danger."

Wu touched his hand and said, "Let's go check on her. Okay, Jim?"

"You got it." If Shewuma wanted to, that was good enough for him.

Following David E.'s prompts, they pulled up in front of what once was a 7-11. Now it was two separate addresses. One side looked empty. The other side had PSYCHIC painted on the glass windowpane in big white letters. David E. was fighting with his knee to get out of the truck when Wu put a hand on his arm. "I'll go get her, David E. You wait here."

Feeling all but useless, he gave her a resigned nod. Jimmy jumped out of the truck to go with her. Wu stopped him and said, "I think you should stay here with Debbie. Just in case."

"You're right," he said. He pulled the Glock from the holster and climbed back in the truck.

"Are we home yet?" asked Debbie, still sounding woozy.

"Not yet, Babe. You just rest."

"Okay. Love you."

It occurred to him that she still had that thing in her head. He considered the options and decided to let it go for the time being.

Shewuma was back in a minute, alone. She climbed in and said, "She's gone. Looks like she left in a hurry."

"Damn," David E. said, and he hit his thigh with his fist.

Wu pursued it. "Why is that? Why did she take off right now? We just saw her this morning."

"Are you trying to say she's part of what happened back there?" he asked, sounding a little riled.

"No," Shewuma lied. "Relax. I'm sure she's fine. And with her new resources, I think Debbie will be able to find her with no problem." That seemed to pacify him.

Passing the dirt road to David E.'s place as they drove out of town, Jimmy said, "Holy shit, guys. The chain I cut is back up."

David E. said, "I guess I'm back on the grid."

Something caught Shewuma's eye through the windshield. A black dot in the distant sky. "Shit's about to get real," she said. Jimmy gave her a questioning look in the rearview mirror. She faked a smile and asked, "What movie is that from?"

"*Bad Boys II*," Debbie murmured.

When they were finally back on I-64 heading east, Jimmy breathed a sigh of relief. It was like being in the real world again. The dash clock was blinking 12:00. It was still afternoon. Good. They should be home before dark. The mood in the truck was silent and pensive. "Who wants a beer?" asked Jimmy, trying to lighten things up.

"I'm on it," said Wu. As she handed Jimmy a beer, he handed her his phone.

"Wu, find me the nearest O'Reilly Auto Parts. I need to get a new battery."

Wu checked his cell, then said, "That EMP fried the phones."

In a sleepy stupor, Debbie said, "715 Richmond Street in Staunton. Not far from the Interstate. About an hour and twenty minutes away."

Wu leaned up front. She patted Debbie on the leg and handed Jimmy his phone, saying, "How about that, Jims?"

"Okay, Staunton it is," said Jimmy impressed and put in a Little Feat CD.

By the time they were halfway home, the pervasive creepy and uneasy feelings of earlier had faded. Debbie had come around and seemed relatively normal. She decided to leave the Cric in her head—at least for a while. Jimmy wasn't happy about that. Shewuma appeared to have pulled David E. out of his dark mood. Jimmy felt a little restless and announced, "Hey, I have a question. What's the most annoying thing about Hollywood movies?"

"Do they actually have to be made in Hollywood?" asked Wu.

"No, any movies," said Jimmy. "Anybody. Go."

"Eating," said Shewuma. "They always sit down to these wonderful spreads with plates full of food and they don't eat anything. Or worse, they take these ridiculous, tiny, fake bites of a cookie or doughnut. And don't get me started on chopsticks. Apparently there's some law in Hollywood against eating Oriental food on camera with a fork. I guess the chopsticks are supposed to be chic or cool, but it's just annoying."

"Asian food. Not Oriental," corrected Debbie.

"No way," Wu said adamantly. "I've been watching samurai and kung fu movies since before you guys were born. I like Oriental and I'm saying Oriental."

"I'm not surprised that's the main gripe of the High Priest of Miserability," said Jimmy.

"What does that mean?" exclaimed Wu. She leaned up beside Debbie and asked her, "Why does he keep calling me the High Priest thing?"

Silently, Debbie spoke directly into Wu's mind. "I'll tell you later."

Shewuma slapped Debbie's arm and said, "Debbie Doodle, that was awesome."

"Is she taking in your head?' asked Jim.

"Yeah, just like Enoch used to do."

"That's nuts. How does that work?"

Before Wu could answer, Debbie said, "Enough of that. It's my turn. It's movie phone calls. They rarely say hi, but they never say bye. They never say who it is. Don't you guys always say hi, this is me, and bye when you're done? It's just normal and polite."

"I do," said Jimmy.

"Me too," agreed Wu. "I see your point."

Even David E. nodded yes.

"David E., would you like to go next?" asked Jimmy.

"No, you go ahead," he said.

"Preaching," said Jim. "I don't give a flying fuck about the director's ideology. I don't want to hear politics or social bullshit. I want to see a good movie. Period."

"Amen, brother," was David E.'s first foray into the conversation.

"I'm with you, Jims," said Wu.

"Right on," said Debbie.

"I have one," offered David E.

"Go," said Debbie, excited that he was participating.

"Every few years movies always get remade. Everything in Hollywood is a rehash. I don't think an original plot has been written for a movie since I was a child."

"They probably get written and nobody's interested," said Jim.

"Well, there's the next question," said Shewuma. "Name movies in the last, let's say fifty years, that have original plots. And I'm starting with one of my favorites, *The Matrix*."

"No way," said David E. "Besides the book *Necromancer*, it's also been done in a *Twilight Zone* and an *Outer Limits* episode. Metaphorically, of course."

"Really?" said Jimmy.

"Ah, a fellow movie connoisseur," said Debbie. "I have one for you. *Terminator*."

"Nope," said David E. again. "Jumping from the future to the past and doing things in the past that forces you to come from the future in the first place. It's been done dozens of times."

"You're tough," said Jimmy. "I'm almost afraid to say it, but *Memento*."

"I'm sorry. I'm not familiar with that movie," said David E. Then he looked at Debbie, a bit startled at first. A slight grin materialized on his face, and he shook his head slightly. "Yes, I'll concede that one, Jim. And I look forward to watching it, Miss Debbie."

"I have a new one," declared Shewuma. "Who's the best-looking actor ever?"

At the same time, Debbie and Jimmy said, "Brad Pitt."

"I hate to disagree, but Errol Flynn," said David E.

"Oh," said Jimmy. "I'm in. I'm changing mine to Errol Flynn."

Debbie pounced on it. "Jimmy, you know you can't change your pick."

"Nobody told me that rule," said Wu.

But Jimmy interrupted them with a statement from left field. "Wait, guys. David E., you never answered my question."

"Refresh me," said David E.

"If alien technology won't work here, why are there UFOs?"

"And crop circles," added Wu.

"And anal probing," said Debbie, prompting snorts from Jimmy and Wu.

"I can't speak for crop circles and the other thing."

Debbie turned in her seat and sniffed her finger, causing Wu and Jimmy to erupt in laughter. David E. waited until they settled down and then continued. "The UFOs belong to us." There was stunned silence.

"If you want me to believe that, then you need to keep talking, Buddy," said Jim.

"Of course," said Debbie. "It makes sense."

Jimmy held up his hand. "I want to hear it from him, not the Skull."

Debbie didn't take his comment too well but said nothing.

David E. shifted forward in his seat. "All right. Everything is made of atoms. Atoms have electrons."

Groans came from Jimmy and Shewuma.

"The world is simply moving electrons. Electricity."

"Pick it up," said Wu as she rolled her eyes.

"I quit college for a reason, David E.," said Jimmy.

"No, listen. Moving electrons are electricity. And electricity creates magnetic fields. That is the basis of our technology here on Earth. From fire to hot air balloons to air conditioning to space stations. It's all about moving electrons. Now, we haven't even come close yet to achieving the most advanced level of this electromagnetic technology. But the aliens have. They passed that level long ago. When their tech was shut down, they reverted to the highest levels of our own technology."

Jimmy said, "So, you're saying the flying saucers…"

"And the crop circles," threw in Wu.

"I swear I won't forget the crop circles anymore, Wu," Jim assured her and went on. "So the aliens are using more advanced forms of our own technology?"

"Yes," confirmed David E. as Debbie nodded in agreement.

"So in theory, we'll have those same flying saucers someday?"

"Not just someday," said David E. "And not just flying saucers. Genetics, science, communications, energy."

"You're saying we have all this tech now?"

"Not humanity as a whole," said Debbie, "but factions of it. Remember the Rexon battery?"

"The waffle maker," said Jim. And then, "Hey, you said hole."

Everyone laughed but David E. He was sincere when he asked, "What are you guys laughing about?'

"*Beavis and Butt-Head*," said Jimmy, a little surprised he had to explain the reference.

"Keep going about the technology, David E.," said Wu, who was turned facing him now.

"It's hidden from the public at large."

"What's the point of hiding it?" Jimmy asked.

David E. sighed and ran his hand through his hair. "Different reasons for different people. Control, power, fear of public reaction, personal gain. The aliens would rather we didn't have it at all and work hard to suppress it.

"So they're trying to stop us from advancing our own technology," concluded Wu.

"Well, they were until it all went to hell. You heard of the Roswell crash?"

Jimmy said, "You're going to say everything was back engineered from flying saucers? I saw this stuff on TV."

"Think about it," said David E. "First there's fire. A half million years later there's the wheel. Ten thousand years later there's electricity. Logical progressions, right? But only seventy years later, just after the Roswell crash, we're working on nuclear power and artificial intelligence."

Debbie added, "Don't forget Kevlar, fiber optics, lasers, stealth, integrated circuits."

"Exactly," said David E.

"Ya'll sound like the *Ancient Alien* reruns," said Jimmy, still skeptical.

"Hey, you asked," said David E. "Think about this. In 1949, we used vacuum tubes. Twenty years later, we landed on the moon. Do the math."

Shewuma cut in. "I hate to change the subject, but I have to pee and we're coming up on a rest area. At the word pee, Connor stood up on Debbie's lap and wagged his tail. Tippy jumped into Wu's lap from the back seat. Molly's big hound dog head appeared between the bucket seats, sniffing and licking her face.

"Looks like the kids need to pee too," said Jimmy. Petey jumped into his lap. With both paws on Jimmy's chest, Petey stared him right in the eyes. "Especially Petey Petitey."

The pit stop at the rest area went smoothly and Debbie stubbornly insisted on driving. Everyone was already back in Miss Interceptor except for Shewuma. Then they saw her running full speed back to the truck. The automatic side door started to open. Jimmy saw the key fob in the ignition switch and said, "How did that happen?"

"I opened it," said Debbie.

He didn't know what to say. Shewuma got in, looking miffed. "I smelled one of those black-suited motherfuckers out by the tree line," she snarled.

"You think they're watching us from the woods?" asked Jimmy.

"Maybe Wu just gave *him* some wood," Debbie said and laughed out loud.

Wu leaned toward Jimmy in the passenger seat and said, "Is she okay to drive?"

"Like it's my decision."

"I'm fine to drive, Wu," Debbie said, still laughing at her own joke. It began to rub off and everyone else smiled too.

"No one can make Debbie laugh like Debbie can," Jimmy said.

As they merged onto I-64 east, everyone scanned the highway and the sky for anything black. They saw nothing. Jimmy cracked his window and snapped a beer bottle cap he'd been saving. The wind hooked it backward and it bounced off the windshield of a tan Jeep Wagoneer two vehicles back. At the wheel sat a tall pale man wearing a black suit, hat, and sunglasses. His mirror image sat across from him in the passenger seat. "Heading east on I-64," he said out loud. "Copy," came the reply from their earbuds.

As they passed Richmond, Jimmy picked up the leather case to find a CD. "How about Joni Mitchell?" Debbie suggested.

"Or maybe Stevie Ray Vaughn," said Wu.

"Nope," said Jimmy. "Rikki Lee Jones is right here in front." And he popped it in. "Any beer left?"

"One," said Wu.

"You drink it," he said.

"Okay." She took a long hit on it and gave Jimmy the bottle cap. She turned in her seat toward David E. and asked him a question that had been on her mind. "David E., how do you know Enoch?"

"I worked with him at Edgewood Arsenal a couple of times."

"You were Army?" asked Deb.

"CSM retired."

"My dad retired out of Edgewood Arsenal. Aberdeen Proving Grounds. Command sergeant major."

"Was he in one of the alien programs?"

"I don't know," said Debbie. "I never thought about what he did there."

"When was he there?" asked David E., intrigued.

"Let's see," she said, thinking. "He came back from Nam and then went to Fort Eustis. He went to Edgewood in 1975, I think. He stayed there until he retired in 1990 while Mom and I lived in Newport News."

"I just missed him," said David E., slapping his knee. "I left Edgewood in early '75. It's a small world."

"I remember that," said Shewuma. "Enoch spent time there in '67, again in '69, then '75 and '76.

"You have good memory," said David E. "And you're just as pretty as he used to say." It was unexpected and Wu thanked him with genuine appreciation.

"Wait," said David E. "It just occurred to me. If you were with Enoch in '67, that makes you at least sixty-five years old?"

Shewuma winked at him. "Or I could be a lot older than that."

Debbie painfully accessed the latent memories of her Cric. "Wu hooked up with Enoch in 1910."

"That's right," confirmed Wu.

"No way. You Kachinas are something else," said David E.

"Gives you a whole new appreciation for older women," said Jimmy.

"David E., back up a minute," said Debbie. "The military had you working with Errans?"

"Actually, I only worked with two Nords. I mostly worked with Greys and on other programs."

Shewuma broke in sternly. "I don't like that word, David E. Prefer you don't use it."

"Sorry, Honey. Old habits. Back then we called them all…uh…that N word."

"I'm sorry, David E., but its usage has become so derogatory. Nowadays it's only used by debunkers, naysayers, Drachs, and the military," Wu said.

David E. was surprised at how personal Wu was taking it. "I'm sorry, Shewuma. I won't ever say it again. I promise." He put his hand out and they shook. He sounded much better than earlier. But she still saw dark spots in his aura. And his touch oozed regret, loss, and—unexpectedly—lust. It threw her a little.

She said, "Forget it. I guess I just miss him. It never occurred to me that he could die until it happened."

Debbie took the exit for Williamsburg. The dogs became restless knowing they were almost home.

Petey jumped in Jimmy's lap to see out the window. "This conversation is far from over," said Jimmy. He cracked the window so Petey could stick his head out into the wind. Molly startled David E. by laying her ample front paws on him and looking out his side window as well. Tippy went into Shewuma's lap from over the back of the seat.

Debbie turned from the two-lane state highway onto a heavily wooded, residential road. She surprised David E. by saying directly into his mind, "This is our neighborhood." Nicky realized where they were and stood up, circling and whining. David E. wasn't expecting where they lived to be so isolated. There were no power lines. *They must be buried.* The occasional driveway went by, but he saw no houses from the road. The driveways disappeared into the trees, indicating multiple acres for the lots. Debbie spoke in his mind again, "Almost there." This time he wasn't spooked. He wondered if she were communicating with all of them or just him. They stopped at a wide driveway entrance made of aggregate and flanked by two brick columns topped with rustic lamps. She was waiting for an old jogger to cross the space. He was thin, wearing black gym shorts and no shirt. Debbie waved to him and he waved back as he went by. He heard Debbie's voice say, "That's our neighbor, Mr. Rawlings." Did she say it out loud? He wasn't sure. About three tenths of a mile down the driveway, the trees opened into a typical grassy front yard and a very large, red brick rancher. A wide sidewalk starting at the driveway followed beside the front porch to the front steps. They continued to the side, where the double garage door was opening automatically. Parked there were two vans and a pickup truck, and there was a turnaround near the tree line. He caught a glimpse of a two-story detached building a little farther down. They entered the garage and parked next to a mint, late model Trans Am.

"David E., I don't think you've been introduced to the vehicles," said Jimmy. "We've been traveling in Debbie's darling Miss Interceptor, and next to us is my baby, the Muscle."

They clamored out of the SUV. Debbie opened the side garage door and let the enthusiastic kids into the backyard. Limping heavily without his makeshift cane, David E. circled the Muscle, checking it out. Shewuma stayed with him, giving him the particulars on the engine and special features. "This looks like the one Burt Reynolds drove in a movie," said David E.

"You're probably thinking of *Smokey and the Bandit*, and you're close," said Wu. "But Reynolds actually drove this particular car in a movie called *Hooper*."

Jimmy heard her and was extremely pleased and impressed. "How do you know all that?"

Wu said, "I looked it up."

Debbie unlocked the door to the house and went in. "Come on in, ya'll."

Jimmy and Wu went on through but Debbie stopped David E. there in the mudroom. From an umbrella stand she pulled an adjustable black metal cane and gave it to him. "A present. It belonged to my mom."

The knee had been giving him a fit and he said earnestly, "I appreciate it."

They joined Jimmy and Wu in the kitchen and Debbie took charge. "Wu, show David E. the spare bedroom and the guest bathroom. Then you guys can freshen up. I'm going to feed the kids and then change clothes. Jimmy is going to make some supper, aren't you, sweet lips?"

"Yes, dear. Whatever you say, dear."

"I'll unload Miss Interceptor first," said Shewuma.

"Thanks, WuWu," said Debbie.

"I'll help you," offered David E.

"Are you sure? I know your knee is hurting," said Wu.

He held up his newly acquired cane. "No, I'm good. Besides, I never thanked you for today. I owe you."

"Forget it. Come on." But then she stopped so suddenly that he ran into her. "Jim, what's for supper?"

"Lasagna and garlic bread. You want anything else?"

"Yeah," was all she said.

"How about corn on the cob?"

"Yummy."

"As you command, High Priest."

As they went back to the garage, David E. asked her, "What's the High Priest thing?"

"I don't know," said Wu. "Nobody will tell me."

CHAPTER 14

Things Aren't Always What They Seem

They sat at the dinner table and ate silently for a spell. Jimmy was exhausted to his bones. No wonder after the day they had. He looked around at everyone. To his right, David E. was visibly whipped and smelled kind of funky. Across the table, Shewuma demolished a cob of corn, looking fresh as always. Debbie, to his left, who he thought had the worst day, seemed fine. "How you feeling, Babe?" he asked her.

"Good, Jims. I'm good."

"Wu?"

"Yes, sir?" She looked at him with her mouth full, not slowing her attack on the corn.

"Don't you ever get tired?"

She shook her head and then shrugged her shoulders, still eating.

"Is it good?"

"Umm," she responded.

"You're mowing it down like a beaver," he said.

Debbie and Wu both looked at him funny. "Are you being dirty?" asked Debbie.

"Na, you know. A beaver cutting down trees with his teeth."

Both women said, "Oh." Then Debbie said to Wu, "You never know with him."

Shewuma said, "Uh huh," and kept eating. When she finished her fourth cob of corn, she helped herself to more lasagna. "Jimbo?"

"Yes, Wu?"

"This is absolutely delicious. And so cheesy."

"Thanks, High Priest," he said, accepting her praise.

"You made this yourself?" asked David E.

"Yes," said Jimmy. "I made it last week and froze half. So all I had to do was nuke it and make the bread. And the corn, of course."

"It really is very good," David E. agreed.

"Jimmy's a great cook," said Debbie as she sent the garlic toast around again.

"I second that," said Wu. And took two more pieces.

"You should open up a restaurant," David E. said.

"We actually had one for about a year," said Debbie. "Called it the Cross Roads."

Shewuma sat up straight. "No way. Down on Harpersville?"

"Yeah, that was it," said Debbie, tickled that she remembered it. "Did you ever eat there?'

"No, I wish I had now. I remember seeing it, though." She went back to her lasagna.

"Why did you give it up?" asked David E.

"It nearly killed us," said Debbie, thinking back. "We would go in at 5:00 am. Jim worked the back; I worked the front. We closed at 10:00 pm. Got to bed about 1:00 am. Then up at 5:00 am again. After six months, we would sing "I'm Free" by The Who on the way home, exhausted. We even tried closing on Mondays for a while. But after eleven months, we sold it. We had to get out while we were still sane."

"The restaurant business is not for the faint of heart," said David E. "Even under the best circumstances, it's hard to make a profit."

"Sounds like experience talking," said Jim.

"My grandparents had one," said David E. "I worked there when I was a teenager. It was brutal." They laughed. "So what's the secret to the iced tea? It's the best I've ever had."

"Oh, that's Debbie," said Jim. "She adds the sugar while the tea is hot. People rave about it."

"I'm raving," said Wu through a mouthful of food.

"What did you do after you left the service?" Jimmy asked David E.

"I became a Ufologist," he said, then waited for the usual dismissive reactions. When they didn't scoff, he went on. "I worked for a company called UUAGS." He said it as a word.

"Ufologists United Against Government Secrets," Wu said with her mouth full.

"No shit," said Jimmy. "I've heard of them."

Using the access to her new, boundless knowledge, Debbie said, "Over four thousand members, been around for fifty years. Mocked by the media and detested by the power elites."

When David E. didn't say anymore, Jimmy pursued it. "How long were you there and what did you do?"

David E. wiped his mouth and put the napkin on his empty plate. Debbie offered him more lasagna, but he declined. He poured himself another glass of tea and set the pitcher on the table before turning to Jim. Jimmy wasn't sure if he was going to speak, so he said, "I guess I'm really asking how you ended up like you were today?"

Debbie rebuked him. "Jesus Christ, Jim. Be nice."

David E. held up his hand. "It's okay, Debbie." He still seemed reluctant but started talking. "After everything I had seen in the Army, I wanted to expose it when I retired. But I couldn't. When I left, they told me straight up that the survival of my reputation, my friends, and my family all depended on my discretion. And I knew they were serious. But I still had to do something. So, I went to work for UUAGS. They welcomed me with open arms. I was put with an experienced investigator named Jerry Satchell. He was just supposed to show me the ropes, but we worked so well together that they made us a team. We worked a lot of cases and had a great track record. Sightings, abductions, whistleblowers, even some paranormal incidents. We became their go-to guys. After a few years, we thought we could do more on our own. We started our own private investigation company that specialized in ufology and the paranormal." He paused. But everyone was hanging on his words, so he went on. "We made a little money, spent lots of time with our families, and helped people who had nowhere else to go for help. It was great. In 2006, we acquired a client. I'm not going to say his name, but he'd been working in a secret underground government complex in New Mexico for a few years."

"Dulce?" said Debbie and Wu together.

"Yes, Dulce," he acknowledged. "You guys know your stuff. Anyway, he wanted to write an expose. He had all the information. Alien tech, government coverups, and he was going to name names. Jerry and I really liked him too. He wanted us to help him verify as many facts as possible so it would be harder to discredit him. Which they would definitely try to do when the book came out."

"How do you do that?" asked Wu.

"Verify the locations and work done there. Place people when and where he said they were. Match documented military tests with sightings or incidents. You'd be surprised how much you can get from a privacy act request, even when most of it is redacted. Then Jerry and I found a smoking gun of sorts. He was staying at a motel in Illinois. Men in Black came to his room, beat him, and threatened his life if he didn't walk away from the expose. He went public with the attack. Figured it would be safer for him. The NSA called him out as a fraud. And the media went after him, of course. But the motel had hidden cameras in the parking lot, and we found film footage of the Men in Black coming to his door, forcing their way in, and leaving twenty minutes later. Bruised and bleeding, he left right after them and drove himself to the emergency room. All documented. We had them. We called our client to give him the news, but he didn't answer. We were worried and went to his house. We found him dead, front door wide open. The EMTs said he had a heart attack. But that wasn't true. We knew he'd been murdered."

"How?" asked Jimmy.

"He was thirty-nine years old and his hobby was triathlons. Then one day later, even before his funeral, his manuscript and flash drive backup disappeared from the publishing house. There was a break-in and that was the only thing missing. So we went back to search his apartment and it was empty. The landlord said two FBI men in black suits showed up with a civil forfeiture warrant for drug-related crimes. Then he said a moving company and a cleaning crew emptied the place out in four and a half hours." David E. paused and sipped his tea, watching for the signs of skepticism he'd come to expect over the years.

Molly came up and put her head on the table next to Jimmy. He rubbed the valley between her eyes and said, "So what did you do?"

"I got mad. I had kept silent protecting those sorry bastards most of my life. And for what?" He was becoming visibly angry. "Jerry and I went back to Karnak and sat down with our wives. Betsy was my wife." He sighed and looked up. "We'd been together forty-three years, and we had a young son we'd adopted recently." Speaking of his family seemed to calm him down. He saw Wu's question about the young son coming and addressed it before she asked. "My son is a long story. Anyway, what the powers that be didn't know was that I had a copy of the book. I explained to them that I was going to put the book out myself. Against Jerry's objections, I made it very clear that none of them would have any involvement at all. But they must not tell anyone anything. I would add the information about the circumstances surrounding his mysterious death in an epilogue and self-publish the book anonymously. I figured I could get UUAGs to help me. I just wanted to get em back or something. You know?" He paused. They could see it was becoming hard for him to continue.

Shewuma stood up. "How about a drink?"

"Okay," said David E.

"Bourbon, everybody?"

Approval came from around the table. Wu came back from the den's wet bar with a bottle of Knob's Creek and four shot glasses from Debbie's shot glass collection. Debbie filled the glasses with Daffy Duck, Bugs Bunny, Porky Pig, and Yogi Bear etched into the sides. They were a little too full and spilled as they were passed around the table. Jimmy raised his glass and said, "Huzzah." They all followed suit and drank. Debbie refilled hers and passed the bottle.

"You guys like your liquor," said David E. He took a sip of his second shot and wistfully commented, "Betsy and I used to drink pina coladas while we watched *Perry Mason* reruns." He took another sip and went on. "The next day, I was heading to meet Jerry for lunch at the diner when I got a call from the sheriff of Karnak. It's a small town and we all knew each other. He told me that Jerry and his family were in a car accident and were taken to the hospital. I went straight there. I was informed that Jerry, his wife, and daughter all died in the crash. A terrifying thought came to me. I called my wife's cell, but no answer. Driving home felt surreal, like a dream. I pulled up and my house was gone, a pile of ashes. The one body they found was burned beyond identification, but I recognized the engagement ring I had bought Betsy when I was nineteen. Mr. Rory sold it to me on credit because he knew my dad. My son's body was never found." His shoulders slumped and he stared at his bourbon. Wu had to know and touched his hand. His soul cried out with such pain that she had to pull back. As though she had somehow eased his suffering, he sipped the bourbon and continued. "I sat in my truck in shock till I fell asleep from exhaustion. When I woke up, I knew I was going to die. At first I was resigned to it, but then I got angry. I decided to run, to live. Years before when I worked with Enoch, he had pushed a sliver of rock up under my thumbnail. He said when I needed him, he would know. It made no sense at the time and freaked me out a little. I tried to get it out, but I couldn't. I meant to go to the doctor, but it didn't hurt and I eventually forgot about it. Turns out it was some type of tracker. A week after my wife and son's deaths, I pulled into a rest stop in Kentucky and there he was. He helped me disappear, gave me money. He told me to stay alive. A couple of years later in West Virginia, he showed up out of the blue. He gave me a copy of the police report on the death of Jerry Satchell."

"I remember that," said Shewuma. "Enoch went to West Virginia for a week in 2009. That was for you?"

"Yes," said David E. "The report said Jerry died of suicide. Said he strangled himself with his own IV tube in ICU."

"That's fucking crazy," said Jimmy. "They killed him. And a hell of a coincidence that he chipped you all those years before."

"Not a coincidence," said Shewuma. "He had the sight. Everything he did was for a reason."

"Wu," said Jimmy, "don't get mad, but this Enoch being the Wizard of Oz is starting to wear thin."

"Wait," said Debbie. "I see what she's saying."

"What do you mean?" Jimmy scoffed.

"Follow me. After Dad was wounded in Nam, out of the whole world, they stationed him at Fort Eustis. The DOD helped him get a house in the first subdivision ever built across the street from Deep Creek. Coincidence? That put you and I in the same homeroom of the same school for how many years?"

Jimmy started counting on his fingers but then just said, "All of them."

"Random chance?" said Debbie. "I was born in January of 1976. Dad went to Edgewood Arsenal in March of 1975. Wu said that Enoch went to Edgewood Arsenal in 1975 and I have his DNA."

"Yeah, spring of '75," Wu added.

"More coincidence?" said Debbie. "Shewuma and Enoch rented from us. We saved her life and took her to David E., and he was holding the Skull for me. Stop me when you think coincidence has gone to hell in a handbasket."

"So what would I have to do with any of this?" asked Jimmy.

"I couldn't have killed that Drach without you. And maybe there's more. We don't even know yet." Debbie's eyes went blank, then she blurted out, "You will find the strength to subdue great evil."

"What?" said Jimmy, getting vexed.

"It just popped out," said Debbie.

"I knew it. I knew it," said Wu, all excited. "You have the sight."

"You're just making shit up now, Wu," said Jim.

"Where were you born?" David E. asked Jimmy.

"Deep Creek."

"Where were your parents from?"

"Well, Daddy was a Creeker, but Mom was from Carolina."

"How did they meet?" asked Wu.

"That's kind of a weird story," said Jimmy. Then he exploded. "Fuck this! I am done!" The day had caught up with him and he'd had enough.

Debbie came up behind his chair and began rubbing circles around his temples. "Easy, Babe." She motioned Shewuma to come and take over. While Wu was massaging, Debbie put pressure between his eyebrows and pinched the nerve between his thumb and forefinger. Within seconds, he was relaxed and almost asleep. "Okay," she whispered to Wu and they returned to their seats.

Jimmy suddenly felt calm and refreshed. "Where did that come from?" He sighed.

Debbie looked at Wu and David E. and shrugged. "I don't know. Just seemed right."

Wu patted Deb's hand. "You're Erran now. You're a healer."

Jimmy sat up and said, "I'm sorry, guys. Everything you're saying kind of makes sense. It's just been a long day."

Debbie refilled his shot glass and said to David E., "These people need to be stopped."

"There is no stopping," he said. "Better to stay away or stay out of it."

"Well, we're safe here, right?" asked Jimmy.

"Oh, they know we're here," countered David E. "I'm guessing they followed you to me, and they probably know everything. I wouldn't be surprised if they're waiting for us right now."

Debbie and Jimmy shifted uneasily, and Wu's eyes grew wide with revelation. "Holy shit!" she exclaimed.

"What?" asked Debbie.

"Your neighbor we waved at earlier. I've seen him twice before. He doesn't run. He plods. He wears two knee braces and he doesn't wave or even look up."

"You're right," said Jimmy. "Rawlings always jogs, or plods, in the morning. Never in the evening."

Debbie stated the obvious. "You're saying it's not Mr. Rawlings?"

"He's a Drach," said David E.

"He has to be," said Shewuma. To Jimmy shaking his head no, she said, "They can shapeshift. They can look like anyone they want."

"Oh, come on," said Jimmy. "I don't really believe that."

Debbie took his hand and telepathically said to his mind, "Jims, after all that's happened this last week, this is where you draw the line?" She smiled and he realized that the world would never be the same again.

"What about the Rawlings? Should we call the cops?" asked Jimmy.

"No point," said David E. "They're out. They have no idea what's going on and the police wouldn't know the difference. They'd think we're crazy."

"Yeah," added Wu. "The Rawlings will wake up after it's all over wondering how they lost so much time."

"Like abductees," said Jimmy.

"Exactly like abductees," confirmed Shewuma.

Debbie went to the kitchen island and pulled a Colt .32 caliber six shooter from the drawer. Handing it to Jimmy, she said, "Take the kids out and lock up real good."

Jimmy made sure it was loaded and called the kids. "Outside."

David E. was surprised they had a pistol in the kitchen. "Boy, you guys are always ready," he remarked facetiously.

"You better believe it," said Wu. "They don't make many like these two."

"You ain't seen nothing yet," said Debbie. "Come on. I'll show you what we affectionately call the war room."

It was actually an average spare bedroom. But because it housed Jimmy and Debbie's weapons collection, it had been dubbed the war room. Debbie entered and stepped aside, waiting for David E. and Wu's reactions. "I've never seen any private collection like this before," said David E. as he looked around.

Shewuma had already picked out her favorite spot. She was inspecting and stroking Debbie's Black Bear compound bow hanging next to two quivers of arrows. "May I?" Wu asked Debbie. Her hand gently rubbed the stabilizer like it was her lover.

Debbie said, "Knock yourself out."

Wu took it off the wall gently, handling it with pronounced respect. She raised it up and down several times, testing the feel and the weight. Then she pulled it up, drew the bow string all the way back, and released it delicately. "Forty-seven pounds," she said. "I think it can set to a hundred."

"That's what I was told," said Debbie.

"Knowing you, I'm guessing it has a name," said Wu.

"I call her Lightning," said Debbie. "I see you know bows."

Wu raised her left eyebrow slightly and said, "Hopi Indian."

"It looks good on you," said Deb, realizing as she spoke that it sounded a bit provocative.

Shewuma held Lightning straight out in front, puckered her lips, and poked out her ass, Betty Boop style. Debbie laughed uncomfortably and turned quickly to see what David E. was doing, mostly so Shewuma wouldn't see the rosy glow traveling up her neck to her face.

David E. was examining an antique musket from the Civil War. He turned it back and forth and then pulled it to his shoulder, aiming down the barrel. "We cleaned it as best we could," said Debbie. "But I don't think it's safe to fire."

He was enthralled with the weapon. "That doesn't matter. This is a Springfield 1861. Do you know how hard it is to find one of these?"

Debbie laughed at the question. "Oh yeah," she said. But he was rambling more to himself than to her.

"One of the first rifled barrels ever," he said. "Probably accurate to four hundred yards. Used percussion caps instead of flintlocks. You even have the bayonet. Really exceptional."

Debbie was enjoying his appreciation for the rifle. Few people understood its significance. "Thanks," said Debbie. "Jimmy and I drove across country to pick it up." David E. recognized his overexuberance and put it back slowly. Debbie asked them, "Do you guys want to just look around or would you rather have the grand tour?"

"Oh, the tour," they both agreed. The walls were lined with three-foot tables all the way around the room. There was the occasional gap for access or storage or some item on the floor.

Debbie first explained that there were two large suitcases full of more knives and these were just Jimmy's favorites. Then she started to the right of the door. "Jimmy's been collecting knives since he was a young child. Creekers love knives. They treat them better than they treat most people."

"Creekers?" said Wu.

"Yeah, people from Deep Creek where Jimmy is from. They call themselves Creekers."

"That is so familiar," said Wu.

Debbie continued. "After getting married, we started to branch out into swords and then anything edged or different. The guns and projectile stuff were mostly me." She pointed out the swords hanging on the walls around over half the room as she talked about them. There were machetes, claymores, rapiers, sabers, a cutlass, samurais, falchions, and more. "We have three *Lord of the Rings* replicas, but my favorite of all is this gradius."

"Like the Roman soldiers used?" said David E.

"Yes," said Debbie. "Anyway, most of what is on this first table are his nicer knives. Lots of high-end stuff. Mostly fixed blades. Only a few specialty or first edition folders." From under the table Debbie pulled out latex gloves and handed them out. "Keeps body oils off the metal of whatever you handle. Jim is a little funny about it."

"Of course," said David E. "The oils can make them tarnish."

Shewuma seemed taken by a special edition blade called the King of Hearts. "That's one of my favorites too," said Debbie. David E was more interested in the straightforward Bowie and boot knives. He seemed especially partial to the Bucks. Debbie continued the tour. "These are mostly grouped by name brand: Hibben, Buck, Cold Steel, Case, and so on. Farther down there are ones from other countries: Germany, Switzerland, China."

David E. picked up a curved blade from India. "A kukri," he said.

"I thought it was called a Gurkha," said Shewuma.

"They have at least four different pronunciations, and they're all spelled differently," said Debbie. "I guess the rest of this table and the first part of that next table, you could call other. I mean, there are all kinds of sheath knives, daggers, and stilettos, but they aren't particularly noteworthy. Jimmy found many or bought them at garage sales. He never saw a knife he wouldn't buy or steal. Now back here," she said as she stepped into a gap between the tables, "We have ammo cases. David E., the bottom one has twelve-gauge shells. Help yourself for your scattergun. I'm sorry, Wu couldn't find your .45."

"It didn't shoot anyway," he said.

"And you pulled that thing on me?" Wu said, slapping his shoulder. "I could have hurt you, boy."

"Promises, promises," he replied, realizing it was the first time he'd teased a woman in many, many years.

"Careful what you wish for," Wu said back to him.

Debbie wasn't sure, but she felt like they were flirting. She continued. "As you can see, these containers against the wall have flags in one and umbrellas in the other. Two of these umbrellas have hidden swords in them." She seemed especially proud of that.

David E. went through the many different flags. American, British, Virginia, Kansas, Army, but he singled out two in particular. "Confederate and Union flags," he said sounding surprised.

"Yeah," said Debbie. "Some people get disturbed about those real easy."

"Who is the flag person?" he asked.

"That would be Jim. The umbrellas are me." She moved on. "These are all folding knives. We have tons of them. There's another suitcase full in Jim's closet. We have lock blades, assisted openers, straight razors, big ones, small ones, single blades, multiple blades, utility knives. These are all Swiss Army knives and," she said as she put her finger to her lips and made a shhh sound, "three switchblades. They're not legal in Virginia."

Shewuma picked up a butterfly knife. With three quick flips, it was open. "Nice technique," said Debbie. "Jimmy doesn't really care for them, but he wanted one in the collection. Now this next section is just unusual items. We have blackjacks, batons, brass knuckles, two bullwhips, and even a lunge whip."

"Lunge whip?" said David E.

"It's for training horses," said Wu. "Debbie is a horse person."

"Are you a horse person too?" he asked her.

"Hopi Indian," she said again, raising her eyebrows.

"Of course," he said.

Debbie moved on. "This is the cane section. We had to get a cane for my mom and Jimmy became interested in them. Here's one that is very special." She picked up a metal cane with a black matte finish. There was a sleeve of metal strips near the center that went around it. Debbie held it straight out. With her thumb she flipped down a hidden trigger. "Watch this," she said—her eyes shining—and pulled it. A load of popping and crackling electricity burst from the metal shards, causing David E. and Shewuma to instinctively pull back, spooked.

"Stun gun," said David E., impressed.

"One million volts," said Debbie. "And that's not all." She pushed the trigger back into hiding and using both hands, pushed down and turned the handle. Out came twenty-four inches of surgical steel. "Jimmy keeps it razor sharp." She gave it to David E. for inspection.

Captivated, he examined it, feeling the weight and checking the edge on the blade. He showed it to Shewuma. "Nice," said Wu. "Where do you get something like that?"

"Some company in Arkansas made it," said Debbie.

"Bagford and Sparks," said David E.

"Yeah, that's it," said Debbie, surprised he knew it.

"I know who they are," explained David E. "The Army used to have contracts with them for, uh, unusual small arms. This cane is really something."

Debbie handed him the shaft and he slid the sword back in. He held it up to her, but she wouldn't take it.

"David E., Jimmy and I discussed it, and we want you to have it."

"No. Thanks, but I couldn't," he insisted.

Jimmy's voice came from the doorway. "Take it, David E."

Only Wu had heard him come in. "You should have heard him coming down the hall, Debs."

"I guess I need to turn up the hearing on this thing," she half joked. But she then asked the Cric mentally to increase her ability to hear. A voice in her head confirmed auditory was now set at maximum. "I think I turned it up," she said to Wu's mind. Wu just smiled and winked.

Jimmy walked over to David E. and pushed back the cane as David E. offered it. "If what I think is going to happen happens, we all need to be ready for it. Unless you would rather carry that double barreled sawed off twelve-gauge instead."

David E. smiled and nodded. He kissed Debbie on the cheek and shook Jimmy's hand. "I'll take good care of it," he promised.

Shewuma couldn't help it and sneaked a touch on everyone. Feeling full of the moment, Wu said, "Come on, Dibs. Let's see the rest of this stuff."

Deb clapped her hands. "Let's do it. Here in the corner, we have axes, hatchets, and tomahawks."

Shewuma picked up a full-sized battle ax and tested its heft. She was impressed and said to Debbie, "This is really sharp. You could take a head off just like that."

Her childlike appreciation of a deadly weapon made Debbie smile. "I bet you could at that, Shewuma."

But Shewuma was already checking out the tomahawks. "Jimmy," she said, "these are mostly replicas and knockoffs. But this one on the end is the real deal. It's a beauty. Where did you get it? I'm guessing it's Chickasaw or maybe Choctaw."

"Good eye," said Jim. "My cousin Corrine had it made for me. It's from a Choctaw reservation."

"Sweet," said Wu.

"Well, it's yours," said Jimmy.

"What?" She was stunned.

"You lost yours when the house burned, right? You need a new one. Or maybe you prefer this." David E. was checking out a piece with a curved axe blade on one side and a wedged, sharp spike on the other. "Can I see that, David E.?" Jimmy took it and handed it to Wu, who was still reeling from Jimmy's gift. "Maybe you prefer this. It's a little big for a tomahawk, but I'm sure you could handle it. They call it a zombie axe."

"Handle it?" said Wu. She took it and flourished the axe through several figure eights as the others moved back cautiously.

Serious, Debbie asked, "You guys haven't run into any zombies, have you?"

Wu and David E. shook their heads and laughed.

Wu was still deciding between the two when Jimmy said, quite to Debbie's surprise, "Take both, Wu. You never know. You might have to throw one. Then where would you be?"

She set them down and gave Jimmy a big hug. Then she hugged Debbie and the hint of jealousy she picked up was unexpected.

"This next table," said Debbie, "is full of things that go bonk on the head." There was a mace, a morning star, and a bat with nails driven through it. Clubs with and without spikes. Nunchucks. Three different staffs leaning against the wall and a war hammer. But Wu was taken by the flail with two spiked balls attached by chains.

"Is this an antique?" she asked Debbie.

"Not really, but it's real."

They backed up as Wu made it spin like helicopter blades.

"You know," said David E., "I read that flails weren't practical and were rarely used in warfare."

"That's true," said Wu. "But it's only because it takes so much practice to master them."

"How do you know so much about them?" asked Debbie.

"Full metal jousting tournaments in Maryland," said Wu, as serious as she could be.

"We need to talk later," said Debbie.

Acting demure and pressing her finger to her cheek, Wu said, "I hope so."

Debbie said to Wu's mind, "You are bad."

Jimmy left to get ready for bed and Debbie moved on. "I'm very proud of this: my projectile section. Besides my compound bow and different sized crossbows, we have throwing knives, throwing stars, a blow gun, throwing axes, boomerangs, several types of slingshots, a mega dart gun, a lance, two spears, bolas, a miniature functioning catapult, and even a rabbit stick." While David E. went from one to the next with equal interest, Wu was fixated on a particular set of throwing knives. There were three twelve-inch flat bar throwers, all in the same case, one behind the other, and stepped up for ease and speed of drawing. "Those are really nice," said Debbie. "Solingen steel from Germany."

Wu flipped one in the air and caught it. Then checked the balance on the side of her finger. "You mind?" Wu asked, indicating the cork dart board hanging on the far wall.

"As long as you don't miss the target," said Debbie. "Jimmy loves those knives."

Shewuma threw the knife so hard that it went through the dart board and buried deep into the wall behind it.

Deb whistled low. "Nice shot," said David E.

Wu quickly retrieved it and sheepishly apologized as she wiped the sheetrock dust from the blade with her dress.

"I'm glad Jimmy didn't see that," said Debbie.

Jimmy's head popped inside the door. "Everything all right? I thought I heard something."

"Everything is fine, Babe," said Debbie.

"Okay," and he was gone again.

"Yikes," said Wu.

"Whew," said Debbie, pretending to wipe her brow. "Next is just a miscellaneous table." And it was David E.'s favorite so far. Lots of camping and hunting gear. And just plain interesting items. There were compasses, survival knives, fire starting kits, thermal blankets, animal calls for deer, turkey, and duck. Also, gas masks and spare filters. A grappling hook, keychains, and handcuffs. Novelty knives with blades in ink pens, belt buckles, combs, and brushes. Even a ceramic knife that could go right through a metal detector. There were fake credit cards and playing cards made of metal with sharpened edges. Shewuma and David E. were amazed by the host of ingenious ways to hide a blade.

Shewuma picked up two items on the table tied together with a piece of string, intrigued. "Are these rubber knives?"

"Yes," said Debbie. "Jimmy got them for practicing."

"What a great idea," said Shewuma.

"Probably," answered Deb. "But I never had much interest in knife fighting. I can take a knife from you pretty quick. But that's as far as it goes. If I can't beat you down, then I'll just shoot you."

"Like you did with the Drach?" Wu asked. "We'll start working with these tomorrow."

"Why? I did okay with him." Debbie wasn't really interested.

"Because you'll be throwing around your EMP and LCS. That only leaves hand to hand. And Drachs, Ebones, Men in Black, they all carry machete folders as backups."

"Really?"

"It's true," said David E. He pulled up his left pant leg far enough to reveal a nasty scar across the shin. "That's from a Drach machete."

"We start tomorrow," said Wu.

"You talked me into it, you silver tongued devil," said Debbie.

Jimmy rejoined them in sweatpants and a T-shirt that read on the front, "I never argue." And on the back, "I just explain why I am right." Shewuma could smell that he was freshly scrubbed and took it in deeply.

The last section was firearms. Two rifle racks hung side by side on the wall. Starting top left of the first column, Debbie called them out. Two twelve-gauge shotguns, a Remington 870, and a Beretta A400. Debbie was particularly fond of her. Next, a Remington 30-06 bolt action—Jimmy's favorite—then a levered Winchester 30-30, and finally a Marlin 336 classic. The next column was serious firepower. An AK-47, an M-16, an M-4 carbine, an M-249 light machine gun, or saw. David E. knew it was technically illegal for a private citizen to own one but didn't pursue it. Lastly, a .30 caliber M1 carbine used by her dad in the Korean War and left to her when he died.

"That carbine looks pristine," noted David E.

"That's Debbie's favorite. She can put one in your eye at three hundred yards with that thing."

"Except they only hold eight in a clip," said David E.

Debbie chimed in. "I have two thirty-round clips for it that I bought online."

"Sweet," said David E. "This is one hell of a group of rifles."

Thinking back to the destructive power she'd witnessed earlier that day, she said, "Thanks. But now I know the thing we're missing is a plasma rifle."

"Good luck," said Shewuma. "Those are few and far between. I've only seen three in my whole life. Enoch had one, but it's gone with the house I guess."

"Really?" said Jim. "I thought the military had them now. Or at least prototypes."

"What the government has is nothing like what you saw today," said David E. "They have plasma cannons and rail guns, but they still shoot ammo. What you saw today is a combination of light and ionized gases. That is way beyond anything we can do."

"Yeah," said Wu. "And they have to be charged with celestial energy."

Jim was confused. "You said there is no more alien energy."

"Right," she answered. "So, when they're empty, that's it." She looked at David E. for confirmation.

"Yes, she's right. That one they used on us today would have been something they were saving for a long time. It would have to be at least, what?"

"Fourteen thousand years old," interjected Debbie. "Gives you an idea of how bad they want that Skull. I can't find a reference, David E. Does my EMP fry a plasma rifle?"

"You bet, Debbie. Plasma rifles, blue lights, lasers."

"They got nothing on you, Babe" said Wu, smiling proudly.

"Blue lights?" questioned Jimmy.

"There are a lot of things we need to tell you guys, but I'm exhausted." David E. did look weary.

"Me too," said Jim.

Debbie realized she wasn't the least bit tired. Wu looked fresh as well. But then, the guys were still human. "Okay, let's finish up the tour so you pussies can go to bed."

"Oh, man," said Jim and laughed.

David E. said, "The mouth on you."

"Yes," Wu barely whispered from across the room, "the mouth on you."

Debbie heard her clearly. The hearing had improved markedly. She brushed the comment aside and spoke. "You two should know that there's a Henry single shot, twelve gauge behind the front door and a Savage eight shot, twelve gauge behind Wu's front door. Both loaded. You know, just in case."

"I saw them," said Wu.

"Good to know," said David E.

"The Christmas tree," Jim said to Deb.

"Oh yeah," remembered Debbie. "There's a Mossberg pistol grip twelve gauge under the Christmas tree by the back door."

"I noticed you have a Christmas tree up in the middle of summer," said David E.

"We leave it up all year," Debbie said a little defensively.

"Why?" asked David E.

"Because we like it. That's why," Debbie answered a little harshly.

"I do too," said Shewuma. "Have you seen those ornaments? Kristi Yamaguchi, Princess Leia, Captain Kirk, Troy Polamalu."

"Okay, okay," David E. said, putting his hands up. "I was just asking."

Debbie gave him a slightly dirty look. Shewuma warned, "Southern girls are very funny about their Christmas lights."

"I get it," he said, and changed the subject. "Debbie, let's do the rest of these on the table before I collapse."

She addressed the last table sitting under the rifle racks. "Well, we have these two antiques. The musket and the flintlock pistol. We have quite an array of different sidearms." The table was mostly full of at least twenty-five pistols of different brands, types, and calibers. "But this one is special to me." She picked up an over and under .38 derringer with a pearl white handle. "I have hollow points in it. Fire the one, cock it, fire the other. I like to take it out and shoot it on New Year's Eve because it leaves a nice trail of fire."

"It's gorgeous," David E. said admiringly.

"Everything else is BB guns and squirt guns, which I also collect. Oh, and I have one more thing." She closed the bedroom door. Hanging on the back were two flak jackets, two camouflage jackets, and several rolls of regular and thick nylon rope, along with a couple of homemade snares, a roll of thin wire, and two binoculars. Leaning in the corner was a telescope with a tripod and an honest to goodness halberd from the Middle Ages. Molly roamed in and sat by Jimmy's feet. Tippycat came in behind her and jumped into Debbie's arms.

"Jim," said David E., "this war room is extraordinary."

"I want to move in here," said Shewuma sort of seriously.

"Well," said Jimmy, "Debbie and I discussed it. And if the shit hits the fan…"

"When the shit hits the fan," corrected Wu.

"Exactly. When. We want you guys to be ready." He looked over to Debbie and she took over.

"You two outfit yourselves with whatever you think you might need. Take it. Use it."

"Except for these knives here." Jimmy swept his hand over the jewels of his collection. Take any sword but the blue Samurai set over the door."

"Jimmy, I couldn't," David E. started.

Jimmy cut him off. "No. When these motherfuckers come for us, we all have to be armed and ready. Come on, David E. Which gun do you like? How about the AK-47?"

"No, I have my shotgun," he said, thinking. "But I really have my eye on that .38 derringer." He picked it up and examined it lovingly.

Debbie went rummaging through a box under a table and found something. She said, "Here, David E. It's one of those pocket holsters. The derringer fits real nice." David E. was speechless. "You know where the ammo is and get whatever else you want. A knife, brass knucks maybe?" Debbie saw Wu looking at her funny. "What, WuWu? What is it?"

Wu looked down at the floor, self-conscious, and said, "Can I use your bow?"

"My bow!"

"I'll take good care of it, I swear. In fact…Never mind. I understand. I should just make a new one."

Debbie stopped her. "No, no. I just meant are you sure you wouldn't rather have a gun?"

"Oh, I'm sure," said Wu.

"Okay, Honey. If that's what you want, it's yours. I have lots of arrows but only four hunting tips. All the rest are bullet heads for practicing."

"That's fine," said Wu. "I can take care of that. She took Lightning and the two quivers of arrows down and slung them over her left shoulder. Then she sidled up to Jimmy, acting demure and looking down.

"Oh lord," said Jimmy. "What are you up to?"

"Can I please have a big favor? Can I use this one please?" She was pointing to a twelve-inch, Case fixed blade with a beautiful wooden handle. It was extra special to Jimmy. Hand-etched into the blade was a picture of an Indian chief in full headdress, with the word Arapaho underneath. That made it one of a kind. And there was another catch.

Jimmy hesitated and said, "That is the first knife Debbie ever bought me as a present. You better ask her."

Wu put her head on Debbie's shoulder and said, "Please?"

Jimmy was taken aback when Debbie said, "Okay, go ahead."

Wu picked up the blade, hugged Jimmy, then Debbie. In a surprise move, she took one bone knife and put it back in the open spot. "And one more thing," Wu said to him.

"Only one?"

"I would also like to use the triple set of throwers from Germany."

"You know how to throw?"

Debbie stole a glance at the dart board and said, "Believe me, she knows."

Jimmy pretended to think about it before making a stipulation. "You can have all of it on one condition. From now on you have to wear underwear."

Wu said, "I don't think I could agree to that in good conscience."

"Pretty good answer," said Jimmy. Debbie punched him in the shoulder.

Shewuma didn't miss the look on David E.'s face from her comment and addressed it. She threw her hands up and said, "What can I say? A woman my age is bound to have quirks."

Debbie left the room—pulling Jimmy behind her—and called out, "How old are you, Wu?"

"Like you don't know," said Wu, admiring her new toys.

David E. watched her as she put both knives on her belt. "Seriously, Wu, how old are you?"

"Older than you, sweet lips," she said with a wink. "Come on, let's get you settled in."

CHAPTER 15

GETTING ACQUAINTED

David E. hadn't had a hot shower in years, so he took a long one. Afterward, looking at himself in the steamy mirror, he considered a full shave of the beard. Naw, he'd just trim it up. Debbie had left him well equipped. A shaving kit, deodorant, aftershave and cologne, toothbrush, underwear, pajamas, and a red terrycloth robe. He opted for the white boxers and the robe. Having been in the bathroom for some time, David E. was surprised to see Shewuma still sitting on the edge of the bed where he'd left her earlier. Her white mini dress wasn't covering much, and she smiled when she noticed him checking her out. He knew he was caught and quickly looked away, fiddling with his new cane. "Thought you would be in bed by now, Shewuma."

"So did I," she said coyly.

He turned and faced her matter-of-factly. "Look, I don't know what's going on here."

"I think you do," she said.

"I'm old, Shewuma."

"So am I."

"You're Enoch's wife." He was still looking away.

She put a finger under his chin and gently guided his face up to meet hers. "Enoch is gone and so is your wife."

Feeling torn, confused, and exhausted, David E. said, "There is someone."

"I know,' said Wu. "Neither of us is looking for a commitment. But I think we could both use some attention." She stood up, moved in close, and said, "I can't believe I'm working so hard at this. I must be losing my touch." She took off her knife belt, pulled the white dress over her head, and dropped them to the floor.

David E. looked her taut, bare body up and down and then looked back at her face. Her copper skin was glistening, and her brown oval eyes looked back provocatively. "Are you sure about this, Wu?"

"Don't worry. You don't have to respect me in the morning." She untied the cloth belt, slipped the robe off his shoulders, and let it fall. She reached down and felt his erection pushing out against the boxers. "I see you made up your mind."

"You're hard to resist," he said heavily.

"Now you're talking. Lights off or on?"

"Are you kidding? Have you ever seen yourself naked? Definitely on."

Wu shut the door and lay back on the bed, pulling him with her by his thick, hard penis. Incredibly aroused, he ignored the pain in his knee as he climbed up between her legs. With no pretext of foreplay, he entered her quickly. The thrusting was harder than he intended but he couldn't help it. He had lost control. He wasn't going to last very long, and he didn't care. His obsession—his life for that moment—was to release his seed into this incredible woman. Shewuma cupped his buttocks and pulled him in with each thrust.

With a breathy whisper in his ear, she said, "Give it to me, David E. Let it go." As she felt him begin to come, she used her empathic abilities to let his frenzied climax wash through her. Unlike women, men's orgasms always seemed so abrupt and acute to her, like a punch to the gut.

He withdrew and rolled on his back. "Shewuma, I'm sorry I…"

"Hey," she cut in, "look at me." As he did, all he saw was a blue light before slipping into unconsciousness.

Shewuma sat up on him, straddling his stomach. She brushed her finger across his gray beard and smiled. Firmly but in a normal tone, she said, "David E., can you hear me?"

"Yesshh," he slurred.

"Tomorrow you will remember that we became close. We had fun. We bonded. You will feel relieved and happy. Your burdens will lessen. You will remember everything about tonight but the sex. Everything but the actual sex," she repeated. "Now go to sleep, you dear man, and be free."

When Jimmy and Debbie went into their bedroom, she locked the deadbolt out of habit. All the doors in the house except the closets had at least two locks. Jimmy also had two holes drilled in each window. They could be secured in place by a nail, six inches open or completely shut. Security was always Debbie's obsession, but he agreed that you couldn't be too careful. She saw Jimmy already lying on his side on the bed watching her. Connor and Petey were settled comfortably into their doggy beds. Molly was nestled on the recliner. Nicky was on the bed, snuggled into the crook of Jimmy's bent knees. And Tippy was curled up beside the bedroom door instead of his usual perch on top of the armoire. Debbie went into her usual bedtime routine. Hair down and brushed, makeup removed, teeth brushed, and a cool shower. Jimmy attentively watched her walk naked from the bathroom to her walk-in closet. After setting out her clothes and jewelry for the next day, she wondered what to wear to bed. For reasons she didn't understand, the day had left her feeling quite horny. She put on a short, low-cut, pink satin nighty and a pair of pink fluffy slippers. Jim would like it. He had a thing for sexy outfits. She left the walk-in and spun around to show it off. Then she approached the bed, exaggerating her hip movements and pushing her chest out. It was to no avail. Jimmy was sound asleep. It had been a long day so she decided not to wake him. She sat down on the side of the bed and kicked off her slippers. Looking around the room brought the realization that she wasn't the least bit tired, let alone sleepy. Putting her slippers back on, she and Tippy quietly went to find something to do. With the colt .32 in hand, she ended up reading at the kitchen table. Tippy lay in the center of the table watching her, behavior that wasn't allowed when Jimmy was around. Debbie had been reading for a short time when Tippy's ears went up. She increased her auditory perception times four and heard the toilet flushing in the guest bathroom. Then she and Tippy heard someone coming down the hall. Her first thought was that it was Jimmy. But they weren't his footsteps. Shewuma emerged wearing only her moccasins and carrying everything else. While trying to pretend she didn't notice that Shewuma was naked, Debbie turned her chair to face her and asked, "What are you doing up?"

Shewuma tried to sidestep the question by taking Debbie's book and examining the cover. "*Chapterhouse: Dune*, huh? What is old Duncan Idaho up to?" She handed it back to Debbie and said, "Doing a little light reading, I see."

"Couldn't sleep," said Debbie, still curious why Wu was there.

Shewuma laughed. "You're Erran now. Your sleeping days are over. Enoch would go for months without sleeping at all."

Stealing furtive glances at Wu's state of undress, Debbie asked, "Have you been with David E.?"

"Maybe."

Debbie put her book down. "Oh my God. Did you sleep with him?"

"Maybe," Wu said again as a shit-eating grin spread across her face.

"Wu, a woman like you? He'll fall in love with you and it would just become a mess."

"No, I blue lighted him. He won't remember the sex, just that he feels better."

Debbie closed her eyes and spoke as if she were reading. "Xena Blues, organic nanobots that enter the brain through the optic nerve and delete memories." She opened her eyes and saw Shewuma scrutinizing her generous cleavage. It made her a bit self-conscious, and she felt the need to explain the sexy nightgown. "I put this on for Jimmy."

"It's hot," said Wu.

"He was already asleep, though."

"His loss." Wu could sense that Debbie was uncomfortable and changed the subject. "You're really coming along with that Cric."

"Where did you get the Xena Blue nanobots?"

"I found it on one of the MIB in the black helicopter. I don't know if I told you, but that was so impressive. You bringing down that chopper first time, no experience."

Debbie caught herself eyeing Wu's long legs and snapped her gaze back up to the half-smile on Wu's face. "I know you could have gotten away. If I couldn't have produced that EMP, you would have died too."

"Oh, I had faith in you. Besides, you're not getting rid of me that easy."

Still finding no direct reference in the boundless database of the Cric, Debbie said, "So, Wu, you said the EMP does affect the Xena Blue nanobots."

"Call them blue lights, Sweetie. You sound like a nerd. And yes, it will knock them right out for a while. But it doesn't fry them or anything. It's like they are alive…sort of. Tech stuff. I don't know."

"So why?"

"Why what?" Wu was lost.

"Why did you blue light David E.?"

"He was hurting, Dibs. His aura was fucked and he felt like he had failed everyone and everything. He needed help. I found that cleaning the pipes with no baggage does wonders for a man in his frame of mind. Plus, I got to ride his orgasm. It was intense too, believe me."

Wu's empathic faculties were intriguing. Trying to be discreet, Debbie said, "You seem awfully promiscuous."

"I prefer open-minded," contended Wu.

"You're admitting you slept with him, but he just won't remember it."

"Yes," confessed Wu.

"Aha. So, you two did the nasty?"

"You caught me," said Wu. "We fucked."

"He boinked you," Deb countered, smiling.

"I rode the baloney pony."

"Buttered the biscuit." Wu chuckled and Debbie gestured for her to come on.

Wu came back with, "Slapped little Johnny behind the ear."

"Glazed the doughnut."

Both were getting quite tickled. "Pressure washed the porpoise."

But Wu saying, "Taking Grandma to Applebee's," made Debbie bust out laughing.

"You got me. I've never heard that one," Deb could barely say.

"That's because I'm sluttier than you," said Shewuma, dancing with her shoulders.

"Oh, you think so," said Debbie as she pulled up her nightgown for a full flash. Wu got a little too quiet and looked for too long. Debbie jumped to her feet and pulled the nightie down. Somewhat embarrassed, Debbie said, "Sorry. I went too far."

Wu noticed that Debbie's nipples were hard and well defined through the satin material. "I'm not complaining."

"You're so bad," said Debbie and changed the subject. "You heal so fast. When did you take out the stiches? I was going to do it for you." Debbie touched the fading discoloration where Wu's throat had been cut. She felt Debbie's sexual curiosity with such force that she no longer trusted her own judgement and stepped back. Wu suddenly felt like she was in an old movie from the forties, the one where two people meet in the wrong place at the wrong time. She was starting to develop feelings for this woman and it had to stop.

"Are you okay Honey?" asked Debbie.

At a loss for words, Wu pointed her left thumb over her shoulder and cocked her head in the same direction. "I need to head off to bed," she lied, and turned toward her side of the house.

Debbie said, "Don't you want to hang out for a while?"

"Yes," said Wu, giving herself a stinging slap on her own ass. "But I won't. Good night, beautiful." Shewuma walked away.

Debbie was amazed that she could still hear Shewuma puttering around her side like being right there. She turned down her hearing and there was silence. The book had lost her interest; all she could think about was Shewuma. Something happened between them that was palpable and left her feeling flustered and uneasy. She was wondering whether to go tell Jimmy about it when she thought she saw movement through the crack in the blinds. Tippy also turned his head in reaction to something. She picked up the .32 pistol, turned the hearing back up, and peeked between the blinds. Nothing. She rushed to the foyer, turning off all the lights on the way. Through the crack in the front door she could tell it was quiet outside. Deciding against turning on the porch light, she slipped by the storm door and held it open for Tippy to follow. If anyone were skulking, he would know. There was no moon, and the front yard was pitch dark. She remembered they had a motion sensor for the floodlight on the gable. If someone had come around there, it would be on. Still, she had this odd feeling. "Damn," she said to herself, "I wish I could see in the dark." Instantly, her field of vision went from blackness to the appearance of looking through a viewfinder. Tippy growled under his breath. Looking down, Debbie saw him as a yellowish, slightly distorted version of himself. She realized she had not yet scratched the surface of what this Cric could do. Tippy's ears turned like radar, and he looked to the left side of the yard at the tree line. She'd heard something there too. She followed his gaze and saw the heat signature of what had to be an opossum. Was she seeing with night vision or infrared? Either way, she was excited about her newfound ability. The opossum scurried deeper into the woods. Tippy reacted but stopped when Debbie said, "Leave it, Tippy." An owl called out into the night for a mate. Debbie followed the sound and saw his image about thirty feet off the ground just past the tree line. She scanned the perimeter several times and saw and heard nothing. Wondering again about the floodlight, she went down the porch steps and onto the sidewalk. It picked up her movement and light filled the yard. Her special sight was gone as quickly as it came. Tippy seemed satisfied too and with a, "Let's go in," they both bounded up the steps to the porch. Had she said that out loud? She wasn't sure. The telepathic communication had quickly become natural to her. "I need to be more aware in the moment whether I am actually talking or not," she mumbled. She wondered if she would ever be able to receive thoughts as well as send them. And were there limits? Could she send thoughts to multiple people? What about distance or strangers? Were they factors? She didn't know. So much to learn and work on. Back inside sitting at the table, Tippy put his paws on her legs. "Come on up, Tipster," She intentionally said out loud. He jumped in her lap and purred. She stroked him while several things nagged at her thoughts. The Men in Black, Mr. Rawlings, and the thing with Wu. What was that? Jimmy would tell her not to worry about things that haven't happened yet. In Deep Creek, that's just making up shit. After a few deep breaths, she tried to go back to reading *Dune*. After one page, she put the book down. There was no way around it. She was way too pumped to read and still horny. Reading about giant worms wasn't helping any. She stood up and went straight to the bedroom.

In the darkness, she could now see Jimmy plainly. He was sleeping soundly on his back. There, just as she expected, was a sleepy time boner making a circus tent of the sheet. She shoved Nicky off the bed and Jimmy reacted a little. She slid under the sheet and scooted her back up against him. As usual, in a sleepy stupor, he turned and spooned her, pushing his hardness against her thigh. "Jim. Jim, wake up." He came around enough to feel her grasping his cock. "Put it in me," she beseeched. He entered her and began to thrust, only just becoming consciously aware of what was happening. He felt her thighs and hips trembling and knew she was holding her breath. Was it possible she was coming after only a few seconds? She pulled away from him and before he could react, she threw off the sheet and roughly pushed him onto his back. He had never seen her like this before and he liked it. She climbed on top of him, put him inside her and began to pound up and down hard. He felt for her breasts and met her thrusts. Tomorrow was going to be a good day.

CHAPTER 16

CURVEBALLS ARE TOUGH

The next five weeks went by quickly and an early fall was threatening. Jimmy stood on the deck in his boxers and a Space Ghost T-shirt, holding his Taurus .357 caliber revolver. To his left, Molly sat beside him while Tippycat lay curled on the deck railing. All three heads moved back and forth in unison as they watched the two terriers and the beagle chase each other around the yard. It was still dark enough for the backyard floodlights to be on. Jimmy shined his atomic beam flashlight around the base of the fence and into the bushes, looking for the gleaming eyes of trespassing critters. He rubbed his hand over a huge black bell, acquired in his youth from an idle and neglected train station in Lee Hall. The bell was now mounted on the railing. The bumpy, rough coolness of the cast iron metal felt good on his palm. He was tempted to ring it. But it was too early and the clang could be heard for miles. A developing rust spot caught his eye, and he made a mental note to sand and paint the bell before winter. The thermometer that hung from it by a piece of wire read forty-nine degrees. He was pretty sure it was the first time the temperature had dropped below fifty since May. Debbie walked up and stood beside him wearing leggings and a sweatshirt, her usual workout garb. She handed him a Captain America mug of steaming black coffee and kept the Pittsburg Steelers cup of java for herself.

"I didn't hear you get up," she said.

"That doesn't seem possible."

She took a sip and put her head against his shoulder. "I was in the front woods watching the deer."

Jimmy was having trouble getting used to her not sleeping. For so many years, he would be up by 5:00 am and Debbie never rose before 7:00. That time in the morning was his private time and he cherished it. Now she never slept. And she could see and hear everything that went on in the house. It still didn't seem possible. And then there was Shewuma. She was something special, but she was also a pain in the ass. She could see in the dark, hear better than Tippy, and out-smell the beagle. Sometimes, the smell factor became creepy. Like when she knew if you were horny, pissed off, or had to use the bathroom. And she was always flipping up her dress flirtatiously. He and David E. were fine with it, but it made Debbie mad sometimes. Unless, of course, Wu was flirting with her. Then Debbie got tongued tied and turned into Bocephus. Yes, his private time was a thing of the past. Debbie was talking to him, and he snapped back to attention.

She was pointing to the back left corner of the privacy fence. "There are some deer there in the woods." Confirmation came when Molly and Tippy stood up on alert as the other three dogs ran to where she was pointing, sniffing the air and barking.

"How did you know?" asked Jimmy.

"I can hear them. Also, you smell that musky smell?"

He took a deep breath of the morning air. "Are they in heat?" Jimmy wondered out loud.

"No, they won't rut until October."

There was also that, Jimmy thought. Since hooking up with the Cric, she knew pretty much everything. Not necessarily a bad thing, just annoying at times. Just two days earlier he had asked her when the last time was that she took the Cric out of her head. Completely dumbfounded by the question, she replied, "Why would I take it out?"

He was also pretty sure she was stronger than him now. Shewuma had explained to him how Debbie could manipulate her hormones and body chemistry to increase the potential of her physical capabilities, ward off cold and heat, and do other things too. He missed some of what she said because she happened to be pulling one of her naked stunts at the time. Being stronger didn't bother him, though. He had always enjoyed the fact that Debbie was a badass. He thought back to when they first met. Only ten years old, he and his cousin Ronnie were walking behind the Deep Creek Inn, taking a shortcut home. As they rounded the corner of the building, they saw a young girl with long blonde hair being teased and harassed by three older boys. Jimmy then witnessed the most perfect act he would ever see in his life. The girl gut punched the middle boy and dropped him to his knees. The other two descended on her ruthlessly. The boys were much older, and Ronnie said, "Let it go, Reg." But he had to follow when Jimmy rushed in. As would become the signature of their reputations in the future, pocket knives turned the tide. The older boys fled. Jimmy looked at the blonde girl lying in the gravel, clothes torn, nose and knees bleeding, and fell hopelessly in love. They helped her up and Jimmy introduced himself. "Hi, I'm Jimmy. You okay?"

Looking straight at Jimmy, she said, "Thank you. I'm Debbie."

"I know. We're in the same homeroom."

Feeling a bit left out, Ronnie said, "Hey, I was there too."

"Yes, you were," said Jimmy and slapped him on the shoulder. Turning back to Debbie, he said, "That's my cousin Ronnie. Come on, we'll walk you home." On the way, she ranted about the mean boys and swore she would never be treated that way again. Just a month later, Jimmy gave her three dollars for her first karate lesson at the YMCA. And six years after that, she was dubbed an honorary Creeker when she choked out Raymond Burland on a dare. The memories made him feel more like everything was going to be all right. Things could change so quickly. And for the first time in his life, he was troubled about the future and where it might take them.

"Yeah," sighed Debbie.

"Yeah what?" asked Jimmy.

"I thought you said something."

And that was another thing. The telepathy stuff. He didn't think that was going to work out. Especially if she started reading *his* mind. "I guess I'll go cook breakfast."

"Okay, Babe. I'll bring in the kids."

She started down the steps, and he said, "Love you."

"Love you back."

In the kitchen, Jimmy pulled several items out of the refrigerator. Ham steaks, cheddar cheese, eggs, and a sweet onion. He put a box of Bisquik and some bowls on another counter. Debbie came in while the kids ran down to Shewuma's door.

Debbie was surprised to see the Bisquik. "Biscuits not from scratch?"

"Naw, don't feel it this morning."

"I'm going to change clothes."

"Hey," he caught her, "before you go, will you get me the ham steaks from the fridge?"

"Sure, Babe," she said happily. She opened the door, bent over and looked around, moving everything with no success. "I don't see them, Jim. There's no ham." She looked back and saw Jimmy holding the ham and just watching her ass, a big smile on his face. She threw her arms around his neck and kissed him. "Don't ever stop looking at my ass," she said.

"Don't ever stop looking for the ham," he countered.

"You're still in your boxers," she pointed out.

"I have some sweats in the dryer."

"Well, be sure and put them on. We have guests."

"Yes, ma'am." He put on his pizza face apron and started the biscuits. Within seconds he had forgotten about the sweatpants. It wasn't long before he heard the kids stampeding down the hall and Shewuma's voice praising them. She was out and about. When she entered the kitchen, Jimmy did a double take. She was wearing only a bra, panties, and moccasins. Trying not to be obvious about checking her out, he made a joke. "Wu, who dresses you?"

"You guys are always telling me to wear underwear," she answered with a smart aleck tone. Then she beamed a smile.

"You're just bad," Jimmy said.

"So I'm told by your hot wife every day. Up here." She pointed to her forehead.

"That psychic stuff is fucked up," he said.

"You get used to it. It's actually quite convenient in a lot of situations. Enoch could be a thousand miles away and we could still talk like he was right here."

"Do you think she'll get that good at it?" Jimmy asked, sounding concerned.

"Hard to say." She looked over his shoulder and said in her girly voice, "Whatcha making?"

"Sunday breakfast. Biscuits and gravy, eggs, ham, and grits. You like biscuits and white gravy, right?"

"You know I do."

"Of course. You're the High Priest," he said in mock reverence.

"Please tell me. What's the High Priest of Miserability story?"

"Well," he started, then suddenly remembered. "Oh shit. I'm in my boxer shorts."

Looking him up and down, she said, "So I noticed."

"Wu, will you get me the pair of sweatpants out of the dryer?"

"No."

"Come on, Wu. I can't be in here with you in my underwear," he said thinking of what Debbie's reaction would be.

"I'm not complaining." She was smiling.

He gave her the biscuit ring. "Keep cutting these out and I'll be right back." A moment later he was back and saw Debbie at the other door holding a pen and paper. She was wearing—of all things—a low cut, backless mini dress. Wistfully watching Wu make biscuits in her underwear, she noticed Jimmy observing her. She quickly went to the kitchen table, sat down, and began drawing. The whole situation felt odd. Like he had caught her or something. He went up beside Wu and started placing the biscuits on the sheet pan. He leaned over and whispered, "Debbie was eyeballing you."

"I know," she whispered back.

Still whispering, he said, "She talks about you a lot. I think she may have a crush on you."

"I think I have a crush on her too," Wu joked.

"Seriously," he said softly, "you know everyone either fears her or is enamored of her. There's no middle ground."

"You guys know I can hear you, right?"

"Yes, Debbie," said Wu.

"Shit," said Jimmy under his breath. He had momentarily forgotten about the super hearing.

Shewuma left the biscuits and sidled up behind Debbie. She put her hands on Debbie's shoulders. Massaging them, she gently moved in close so their cheeks were almost touching. "Whatcha doing?"

"I'm making Daniel a birthday card. I need to get it in the mail today to get it there in time."

"Who's Daniel?"

"Our cousin-in-law. Jimmy's cousin Corrine's husband. Remember? I told you about him."

"You made all this by hand?" Wu seemed skeptical. The front read "rock, paper, scissors," but "scissors" was crossed out. Penciled in next to it was "gun." There was a picture of each object next to the words. On the inside, it read, *"I WIN."* To the side, a Rambo looking rabbit with a headband, scars, and firing a machine gun. Then it read *"HAPPY BIRTHDAY DANIEL"* in loopy scripted letters. There was scrollwork around the whole thing. "You drew all this? It's wonderful. It looks so professional. Hallmark couldn't do any better." Her massage was gradually creeping over Debbie's collarbone and getting perilously close to her breasts.

"Stop messing around," Debbie said to Wu's thoughts.

"Okay," said Wu. "I guess I'll go help your husband cook and keep bumping into him, pretending it's an accident."

"You are exceptionally bad today," Debbie said to her mind.

"So I keep hearing," she said over her shoulder as she headed back to the stove. "All right, Jimbo, what are we doing now?"

"Making white gravy."

"I always wanted to learn that. Show me," she said, cutting her eyes back at Debbie.

Debbie left and came back with a purple silk kimono. She was just putting it on Shewuma when David E. entered the kitchen in his red terrycloth robe, alert and smiling. He sat down and Debbie gave him coffee in a mug shaped like a human skull.

"That's unusual," he said as he inspected it.

"Found it online. Thought you'd like it. Have a good night's sleep?"

"The best," he replied. He was a different man than the one they'd found hiding out in Covington, Virginia. Considering their backgrounds and the fact that they hardly left the house, Debbie was surprised they all got along so well.

"Let's eat," Jimmy announced as he and Wu brought the food to the table. Everyone dug in eagerly. With a mouthful, Wu said, "Biscuits and gravy is my new favorite food."

"Why are these scrambled eggs so ridiculously good?" David E. wondered out loud.

Debbie answered him. "Jim puts American and Cheddar cheeses, ham chunks, and onions in them."

"Onions. Really?" said David E. "I wouldn't have thought I would like that."

"He minces the onions and fries them first. Then he adds the eggs and other stuff," explained Debbie.

"Jimmy," said David E., wagging his fork. "As my daddy would say, you're a cooking sombitch."

"I heard that!" concurred Wu, reaching for the gravy bowl.

Later they sat around the table drinking their coffee in the afterglow of a great meal. Jimmy realized it had been a long time since anyone had mentioned their situation. Looking around the table he said, "So, what's the plan?" There was no response. "You know, the aliens, the Skull, and all that shit."

"I think we should be proactive," said Debbie.

"So do I," agreed Wu.

"I don't know," countered David E. "Your house is very secure, we have the animals on guard, and we're well armed. Hell, they may leave us alone."

"You don't believe that," said Wu. "You even told us they would come for you at some point."

"No matter," he said, "because I'm leaving. I could never repay you for what you've done. But I think it's time I moved on and you'll have one less problem to deal with."

"No, you're not," said Jimmy. "One thing for sure is we're in this together now."

After a few minutes of silence, Debbie stood up. "I have an idea," she said, and dashed off. They bounced ideas off each other, trying to figure out what Debbie was up to. They were surprised when she returned with a bunch of board games. Clue, Game of Thrones, Trivial Pursuit, and Small World. "Let's have a game day."

"You want to play board games?" said David E.

"Hell yeah," said Jimmy.

David E. and Shewuma looked at each other. "Why not?" said David E.

"Why the hell not," said Wu.

David E. and Wu cleared the dishes and wiped off the table before going to get dressed. Jimmy and Debbie put the dishes in the dishwasher and let the kids out. David E. returned quickly in his standard tan suit and white shirt. "Thanks for always washing my clothes, Debbie. You know I would do it."

"You have no idea how much time I have to kill every night, David E. Trust me. I don't mind."

They were setting up Clue when Shewuma walked in. She turned slowly to show off her pleated mini dress, a black and white print that buttoned all the way up the front. Her hair had grown to shoulder length and hung free. She turned, leaned forward slightly, and flipped up the back of her dress, exposing her panties.

It took Deb by surprise and her face flushed with heat. "Wu, what are you doing?"

"I just wanted you guys to see that I'm wearing underwear," she said flirtatiously. "Nice, huh?"

"Not bad for a White girl," said David E.

"Technically," said Wu, "I'm not sure I am considered White by the U.S. of A. Census Bureau."

Debbie realized she was staring at Wu and looked over at Jimmy. He was studying her intently. The whole flirty thing was beginning to make her feel uneasy. For some reason that she couldn't pin down, Wu was really getting to her lately. Turning to David E., she changed the subject. "David E., I've been looking for Chloe and have only found one piece of information about her."

"The psychic in Covington?" asked Jim.

"Yes. David E. is still obsessed with her."

"Easy, Deb," said David E.

"Sorry, David E. Overstepped a bit," she said.

"Well since we're on the subject," he shrugged, "what did you find out?"

Debbie leaned in on her elbows. "The only evidence I could find that she ever existed was a temporary business license from the city of Covington. Nothing else. No property ownership, no credit, no IDs, no history, no birth certificate. And I checked the databases of every state."

"Really?" asked Jim. "You can do that?"

"I know, right?" said Wu.

David E. deadpanned, "Okay, let's play Clue."

Shewuma touched his hand and spent several minutes shaking off the feelings of guilt welling up in him. After Debbie won three games in a row, Jimmy stood up and made a confession. "I should have told you guys hours ago. Debbie always wins at board games. Except for chess. I can beat her at chess sometimes."

"Well, let's play something else then," said David E., stretching his bad knee.

"No, that's bullshit," said Shewuma. "Let's play again. I'll beat her." She gave Debbie a competitive stare.

Speaking directly into Wu's mind, Debbie said, "Aren't you cocky?"

"I love it when you talk dirty," Wu said out loud.

"Are ya'll talking up here?" asked Jimmy, pointing to his forehead. "What did you say to her, Debbie?"

Debbie's eyes were locked on Wu's as she fibbed. "I asked her if we should take the kids out before it rains."

"Yes," said Shewuma, not breaking eye contact. "If she waits too long, she could get very wet. Right, Dibs?" Wu smiled and waited for Debbie's reprimand. Instead, Debbie just smiled back.

Jimmy knew they were messing with him, but something else had stolen his attention. "It's afternoon. Anyone hungry?"

"No," said David E. "I'm still full of breakfast. And if I know you guys, we'll be drinking soon and I think I'll save room."

Jimmy asked, "Debs, are you hungry?" The girls were still staring at each other. It had become a contest. "Wu. Do you want something to eat?"

Wu broke the stare with Debbie, looked at Jimmy, and laughed. The setup was almost too easy. In her head, she heard Debbie's voice say, "Don't you dare."

She looked back at Debbie, a big smile on her face and said, "Yes, Jimmy. Thank you."

Debbie followed it with another mental message. "I won the staring contest."

"Cheaters never win," said Wu.

Jimmy thought she was still talking to him and replied, "My granddaddy would disagree with that. Do you want food or snacks, High Priest?" He bowed slightly.

"All right, you," Wu taunted, "explain the High Priest thing or we go, right now."

Jimmy sprang from his chair into his favorite wrestling stance with a wide grin on his face. Wu stood up, flipping her chair back onto the floor.

"Stop it!" Debbie demanded. "Stop it right now. You children can take it outside or to the mat. But you are not wrestling in the house."

"You're lucky," Wu said teasingly to Jimmy.

"I'm here every day," he shot back.

Debbie stood up. "I'm taking the dogs out. You two heard what I said." Then she hollered, "Outside!" There was a mad dash by the kids for the back door.

Wu righted her chair and sat back down, wagging her finger at Jimmy. "You really think you can take me, don't you?" she challenged.

"I'm a Creeker," was his answer. Then, "What about the food?"

"I'll eat what you eat."

"Snacks it is," said Jimmy, and he went to work.

With Jimmy banging around the kitchen and Debbie outside, Shewuma took the opportunity to surprise David E. with a kiss on his cheek. "You're a sweetheart and a hell of a guy," she said. "So what do I have to do to get you to help me beat Debbie in a game of Clue?"

David E. smiled and said, "Have you ever heard the saying, don't write checks with your mouth that you can't cash with your ass?"

"As a matter of fact, I have. And my checkbook is rocking." She touched his arm as they both laughed out loud. It would be great if they could beat Debbie. But she had achieved her main goal and that was to get his mind off Chloe and lighten him up.

Hearing the laughter, Jimmy said from the kitchen, "Hey, did I miss something good?"

"Yes," said David E. "But it was dirty and you're too young."

Jimmy came back with a bag of peanut butter pretzel nuggets, salsa cheese dip, tostado chips, and leftover heated biscuits cut in half, topped with butter, ham, and provolone cheese. He handed everything to Wu except the pretzel nuggets. She took the snacks with delight and said, "You da man."

Debbie won the fourth game of Clue despite Shewuma and David E.'s obvious collusion. "Can we play Small World now?" David E. asked Wu.

"I guess," she said begrudgingly. With all her snacks gone, she motioned to Jimmy to give her his bag. With a big smile on his face, he took out the last pretzel nugget, sat it on the table, and crushed the bag. Shewuma gave him a pouty face and said, "You so mean."

He tossed her a bag of Fritos he'd hidden and said, "I got your back, High Priest."

"You ate that whole bag of pretzels, Jim?" Debbie asked him.

"You said hole," pointed out David E., quite pleased with himself.

"You said hole," Jimmy repeated.

"Hole," said Wu. And they all laughed.

"Jimmy," said Wu, waving her hands for everyone's attention, "Won't you please explain to me about the High Priest?" She gave him an exaggerated, pleading, soulful look.

Debbie stood up and said, "Jimmy, why don't you tell her the story while I go to the bathroom, get some booze and set up the new game?"

"Now you're talking," said David E. "I'll go inventory the wet bar."

Shewuma munched her Fritos and waited patiently for the long overdue story. Jim leaned back and gathered his thoughts. "It all started back in high school. My cousin Ronnie and I both wrestled, so we spent about five months out of the year eating practically nothing."

"Why?"

"Well, you lose as much weight as you can so you wrestle in a lower weight class. That makes you bigger and stronger than most of your opponents right off the bat. Debbie did it too. In any sport with weight classes, that's what you do."

"Wait, what sport was Debbie in?"

"She never told you?" asked Jim and Wu shook her head. "Debbie competed in full contact karate and kickboxing tournaments for years. Look at all those trophies in the library. Lots of them are hers. She even fought MMA for a little while. She was really good too."

"That is so hot," Wu said. She felt a rush, and a tingle went from the back of her throat down between her legs, causing her body to shudder. She cleared her throat. "Why did she quit?"

"Well," said Jim, "she was in her third match. There were only about forty seconds left and she was behind on points. She took the girl down with an armbar. The ref wouldn't call it and the girl wouldn't tap. Debbie ended up dislocating her radius and snapping the ulna bone right through the skin. She stopped competing after that. Said it wasn't fun anymore. It's hard to get her to talk about it."

Wu made a mental note to pursue it further with Debbie. "So back to the High Priest," she said.

"Oh yeah," said Jimmy. "After wrestling season and months of no eating, we went crazy. Our favorite thing was to go to Fass Brothers fish house for their all you could eat special. Fish, shrimp, fries, and pups."

"Pups?"

"Hush puppies."

"Oh, yum."

"We would ask what the record was and then tell them to keep bringing food until we beat it. It didn't take long for the eating to become competitive between us. So, one night we decided to see who could eat more. First, we went to Dino's. We each got a large pizza and a thirty-two ounce soda.

"Wow," said Wu, smacking her lips. "You're making me hungry."

"After Dino's, we each ate a Quarter Pounder on the way to Burger King, where we each had a Whopper with cheese, fries, and a drink. On the way home, we stopped at 7-11 and got some Suzy Qs and two quarts of chocolate milk."

"No way," said Wu, eyes wide.

"I swear. When we finished, we were so full we had to undo our pants. We couldn't lay on our stomachs and our breathing was labored. I said I was miserable, and Ronnie said he was beyond miserable. So, we called it Miserability. Not a feeling, but a state of being."

Wu was laughing. "You are so crazy."

"Well, we were leaning back on the couch moaning and groaning and I realized that no one had won yet. I took out a small bag of M&M Peanuts. I offered him some and he refused. He was done, toast. He watched me eat them one by one until they were gone. At that moment, he bowed his head and christened me the High Priest of Miserability."

Shewuma was loving it. "That's wonderful," she said.

"Yeah, it was for its day. Compared to you, it's meager." He handed her the last peanut butter pretzel nugget and said, "I hereby bequeath the title of High Priest of Miserability to you."

Shewuma popped the nugget in her mouth and said, "I am honored to accept."

Everyone was back by then and started clapping. Wu stood up and did a Queen of England wave around the table. In all her long years of being alive, she could never remember a time when she enjoyed life so much as now—in this house—with these people. "I am the High Priest," she declared proudly.

"You truly are," said Debbie and offered her hand. Wu took it and Debbie twirled her across the kitchen floor.

David E. started pouring the scotch and said, "Let's play."

Two games of Small World and one bottle of scotch took them into the early evening. They agreed that the second game of Small World was it for the day. Shewuma had won the first game and Jimmy was on the brink of winning the second. "I can't believe I'm going to beat you," Jimmy said proudly.

"Good job, Babe," said Debbie distractedly.

"You never take losing this well."

"You won fair and square," she said, sounding far away.

Under the table, Wu had slipped off her moccasin and hooked her foot around Debbie's ankle. Debbie found herself greedily latching onto it with her other foot. Wu soaked up Debbie's feeling of anxiousness and sexual attraction. Earlier in the afternoon, Wu had made a suggestive comment. And something happened between them for the first time. Instead of a joke, a light brushoff, or even a curt rebuff, Debbie simply smiled. As Shewuma kept raising the bar with her flirtations, Debbie was responding in kind. Wu hadn't meant for it to go this far, but their fleeting remarks and risqué touches had avalanched into wanton innuendos and reckless contact. Wu had felt an intense emotional connection to Debbie from their very first touch in the hospital. She had a strong physical attraction to her as well. But look at Debbie. Who wouldn't? Her feelings for Debbie had been growing ever since. She couldn't stop them, so she buried them. Debbie was unavailable. Period. But not today. Just the contact of their feet made Shewuma woozy with desire. She had to pull back and pretend she wanted a glass of water. Standing at the sink, she tried to clear her head. How long before the men recognized what was going on? The guys were experiencing a day of fun and comradery. The reality for Debbie and Shewuma was a day of intense feelings and lustful intentions. At this point the veil was becoming thin. "I should probably back off," Shewuma thought, "but I don't want to."

With a scotch buzz and a game win under his belt, Jimmy stood up and stretched. "Ya'll come with me. I want to show you something."

"Okay," said Debbie. "But first you feed the kids and take them out while I put up the game."

The animals responded to the words feed and out immediately. "I'll do the kids," said Shewuma, wanting some fresh air.

"I'm going to the head," said David E.

"Me too," said Debbie.

"Good," said Jimmy. "Everybody come back and meet me in the den."

Ten minutes later, David E. was relaxed in a recliner. Jimmy and Wu sat on the couch with Debbie between them. Debbie snuck a forlorn glance at Wu. She wanted to make intimate declarations to Wu's mind but couldn't bring herself to do it. It made no sense, but she was feeling a real desire for this woman she knew so well but was darkly mysterious and compelling at the same time. A crazy, silly, but absolutely real attraction was becoming overwhelming. Debbie spread her knees so they touched the knees of both Jimmy and Wu. She felt her face getting red hot and pulled them back together.

Wu had never felt such desire for a woman. It was new and exciting. The knee touch was like an electric shock, revealing that Debbie wanted her too. She tried to focus her attention on what Jimmy was saying.

"Ya'll are going to enjoy this," said Jimmy, pointing the remote at the TV. "It's some of Debbie's competitive fighting I recorded over the years." Debbie's smiling face filled the screen while Jimmy's voice talked about her upcoming karate match. It switched to a mat in the center of an auditorium. Debbie and a bulky redhead, each in their Gi, bowed and started the match.

"They aren't wearing gloves," Wu said right off.

"It's the Seidokaikan style. It allows everything but low kicks with no protective gear at all." He skipped ahead to Debbie fighting an Asian girl. This time she was in some skimpy gold shorts and a black tank top. "Here she is a few years later in a kickboxing match. See how they wear the gloves? Similar to boxing gloves but different."

Wu and David E. both watched, impressed, as Debbie took the Asian girl apart steadily until knocking her out in the third round. After two more matches, Jimmy went on to an MMA match. Wearing just shy of a black bikini, Debbie was squaring off with a muscular brunette.

"Damn, you look hot," said Jim.

"Super-hot," added Wu.

David E. and Wu both commented on how dominating Debbie was in the ring. The opponent rarely made contact while Debbie punished her with her fists, elbows, knees, and feet. Shewuma watched fascinated, moving and jerking with the action. "This is great, Jim," said Wu. "Oh, a spinning back kick. That's so Buffy and Angel. Debbie has the most incredible reflexes, Jim."

"I know," said Jimmy. "She's crazy fast."

They each grabbed one of Debbie's thighs. "Easy, cowboys," said Debbie, removing both hands. She wondered what that could be like, Jimmy and Wu both together. With a twinge of guilt, she shook it off.

Jimmy paused the DVD and stood up. "I need to go to the store. Or better yet, get pizza. We don't have anything to eat here."

"Now?" said Debbie.

"Aren't you hungry?"

"Not me," said Debbie.

"I've been grazing all day, but I'm peckish," said David E.

"I'm ravenously hungry, Jimmy," said Wu, looking directly at Debbie with all the innocence of a street urchin about to pick her pocket.

"The High Priest has spoken. I'm going," said Jim.

"Make one a meat lovers with no sauce. You have a piece?" asked Debbie.

"I'll get my .380 Ruger. Meat lovers with no sauce. That's a first."

"You and David E. should go together," suggested Shewuma.

Debbie shot her a look but said nothing.

"Yeah, I'll go with you," said David E, getting up. "More eyes and all that. Besides, I might get lucky and have to use my new cane on some lowlife."

Debbie was torn. She wanted to stay with Wu, but should she? She kissed Jimmy goodbye, and as the men left, she suddenly felt very exposed. Trying to act casually, she said, "Okay, Wu. I'm going to show you some wrestling tapes of Jimmy."

"That sounds kinda sexy."

"Everything sounds sexy to you."

"Hey, come on," said Wu. "Sweaty, scantily clad, muscular men groping each other, right?"

Debbie laughed as she sat back down on the opposite end of the couch from Wu. With the men gone, they both were nervous, because also gone was the safety of not being able to act on what they were both thinking about all day. Minds racing, they were seeing the wrestling but not watching it. Shewuma slid to the middle of the couch and Debbie's body went rigid. She felt Wu's presence like an approaching storm. Unpredictable, unstoppable. Shewuma had always been open about her attraction to Debbie. Debbie both loved and dreaded the teasing and flirting. But it was never an palpable option…until now. Had she gone too far? Her breaths intensified in quiet anticipation that wavered between fear and intoxication.

Shewuma studied Debbie sitting on the edge of the cushion in her little black dress, back perfectly straight, hands clasped between her legs, staring at the TV as if it held the secrets to the universe. Shewuma knew Debbie had spent her whole life with only Jimmy. For her, a situation like this would be confusing, maybe agonizing. And with a woman no less. Wu could only imagine how nervous she must be. How conflicted. Wu wanted so badly to reach out but held back. She wondered why. They both felt it. They both wanted it. She wanted Debbie's body, sure. What person wouldn't? But she also wanted her love, her soul. Oh God, how had she let herself fall into this? At first, being with Debbie was fun. Then it became necessary. And now? "Stop!" she told herself. "Don't think it and for God's sake, don't say it!" How could this possibly even work? For most people, sex was the solution, the goal. For them, it would be the problem, an obstacle. Their many long talks had revealed deeply personal things to her about Debbie. For Debbie, making love was about commitment, spirituality, and monogamy. She took her marriage vows to heart. And in her own way, she was deeply religious. Debbie wasn't going to throw all that out with the bathwater because some woman who ran around naked got her hot and bothered once. She could debate the theory of desire with herself all day. But in the end, it still had to be dealt with. Desire was its own entity, alive and conscious. Demanding release. Wu swallowed hard and put her hand on Debbie's bare leg.

"No," said Debbie softly, looking straight ahead.

"Why?" asked Wu.

"Because I don't want to."

"I'm touching you. I know that's not true."

Very deliberately, Debbie lifted Wu's hand and placed it on the couch. She pulled her dress down as far as she could and said, "It's not going to happen, WuWu."

"You called me WuWu." Wu scooted closer and put her left knee up on the couch. She had Debbie's attention now. Slowly, Wu undid all the buttons on her dress except the middle one. "That one is yours if you want it."

"I'm not gay," said Debbie.

"Neither am I." Wu sighed. As she pulled the dress down from her shoulders, exposing the silken, see-through bra, she said, "Sometimes people just need each other, Dibs."

"I'm married and I'm in love with Jimmy," Debbie said, feeling out of body. She started to reach for Wu but somehow managed to pull herself back.

"I believe you. All of that and he can cook too." She spread the bottom of her dress until she was exposed up to her belly button. Looking at Wu's navel and against her better judgement, Debbie whispered, "Oh, Wu, I love that it's an outie." Drunk with seduction, Debbie sighed. "Jesus, you're so sexy."

Abandoning reason, Shewuma swung her leg over and straddled Debbie's lap. They began rubbing their hands over each other, squeezing and touching, just wanting contact like a couple teenagers losing control for the first time. Shewuma's hand moved inside of Debbie's V-neck and invaded her bra, tracing the texture of Debbie's hard nipple with her fingers. With a rush of adrenaline, Debbie flipped Wu onto her back. Feeling Wu's legs wrapped around her, Debbie began kissing her fiercely, finally releasing what had been building since they met. Their tongues probed and tasted while their groins struggled to make contact. Wu slid one of her legs between Debbie's legs and moved her body so they could press their privates against each other. Debbie felt Wu's undulating hips and pulled back to look at her face. She was darkly beautiful and so completely in the moment. Wu opened her mouth and pulled Debbie's lips to hers. She pushed her hand under Debbie's dress across her hard belly and into her panties, where her fingers sent Debbie's pleasure to new heights. In the throes of passion, Debbie involuntarily put her hand around Wu's throat, yearning for total possession of her. She slid her hand down inside Wu's bra and clutched at her breast. It was all too much and went straight to her head. "I'm going to come," Debbie cried out into Wu's thoughts. A moan escaped Debbie's throat and her hips and legs began to tremble. Shewuma slowed the movements of her fingers and slid her other hand down to the back of Debbie's panties, pushing just inside the tight ring of Debbie's anus. Debbie fell into wave after wave of an almost unbearable orgasm. Shewuma rode the waves with her.

As the euphoria subsided, Debbie looked down at Shewuma and saw her neck arched and her face tensed in ecstasy. "Did you come, WuWu?" she asked, still breathless.

"No, but you did," said Wu, looking radiant.

"You felt my orgasm?" Wu nodded yes, still recovering.

"That is so fucking hot," said Debbie.

"It ain't just whistling Dixie," said Wu, gently pushing Debbie's hair back from her face.

Debbie lightly kissed Wu's neck while pulling down her bra straps and freeing her breasts. She tongued her way down across the nipple to the sensitive underside. Then Wu yelped, "Ow! Are you biting me?"

Debbie met her gaze and said, "I'm gonna do a lot more than that." She pulled off Wu's panties and began to slide her pursed lips down across Wu's quivering stomach.

Suddenly Wu raised up in alarm. Debbie heard it too. "Oh damn," Debbie said, struggling to get up. They had completely forgotten about the men. And the men were back. It was a mad scramble to get dressed.

David E. entered on his cane, carrying three Walmart bags in his free hand. He walked by them and into the kitchen. "Hello, guys. Nothing exciting happened." The girls both greeted him awkwardly.

Jimmy followed closely behind David E. and was carrying multiple bags in one hand and three pizzas in the other. He stopped and examined the odd scene. Debbie and Wu were sitting on opposite ends of the couch, both breathing hard, their faces flushed. "Hi, Dibs. High Priest. Ya'll enjoying the wrestling?"

They had forgotten the wrestling DVD was running and their answers were barely audible. Debbie realized that Wu's panties were still in her hand and stuffed them under her thigh. Jimmy leaned down over the back of the couch and kissed Debbie on top of her head. "Everything good?" he asked, feeling a weird tension in the room. "What have you two been up to?" They both felt caught with no response. Jimmy started laughing. "You two were wrestling, weren't you?"

"You got us." Debbie could barely say it.

"No wrestling in the house, huh?" he murmured and walked into the kitchen.

Debbie and Wu looked at each other in disbelief. "Let's go in the kitchen," said Debbie.

"My panties," Wu whispered.

"Of course," mouthed Debbie and dropped them in Wu's lap on her way out.

Wu quickly put them on and followed her. Debbie helped put the groceries away silently. Her thoughts swirled around what had just happened on the couch. She heard little of the guys' saga about the Walmart crusade and the pizza jaunt to Harris Teeter. That was when Wu walked up to Jimmy, grabbed his T-shirt, and said, "You and me. The mat. Now!"

"Let's go," said Jimmy, without hesitation.

"Go get her, Jim," yelled David E., laughing. "We need one for the guys."

Debbie watched them go, wondering what the hell Wu was up to.

Shewuma and Jimmy went to the gym in the shop. As they climbed the stairs, Jimmy said, "And yes, I am looking up your dress."

"Your charm can't help you now."

They faced off on the mat. Jimmy was loose but Wu was very focused. "Do you want to stretch first?" asked Jimmy.

"No."

"Well, give me a minute."

"Take all the time you need, pussy."

"Okay, bitch. Let's do it."

Jimmy was completely blown away when Wu pulled off her button up dress and tossed it aside. He looked at her, saying, "Wu, you're uh…" he pointed to his own chest. Shewuma looked down and saw her bra strap hanging and one titty exposed. "Wrestling you in your underwear is bad enough, but that's just not fair."

She ignored his humor, tucked it in, and came at him incredibly fast, reaching for his throat. He slapped the arm into the lunge at the elbow and ducked under it and away easily. Wu faced him again with surprise on her face. "Just to make sure here," Jimmy said. "Are there any rules?"

"Your balls are safe. Otherwise, no rules." She lunged in low for his legs.

Jimmy sprawled back. Countering her with a three-quarter nelson that negated her incredible strength, he pulled away. She faced him again, not believing he'd turned her away twice. He *was*, after all, only a human. She came at him again with more caution. They locked up and with an underhook and brute strength, she attempted to throw him to the mat. He nimbly spun out of it and got away again. After two more aborted takedowns, Jimmy could see that Wu was getting pissed and he was getting tired. He was amazed at how strong she was. Much stronger than Bocephus. Strong like that scaly Lizard man. With a combination of skill and luck, he'd managed to avoid her. But he wanted to win. He needed to attack and take her down while he still had the umph to do it.

He faked to the left and went low to the right. She bought it and he came up holding her foot tucked in both arms. He thought he had her, but she was too strong and merely twisted and snatched her foot free. He was out of gas now and needed to stop. One more try. He slapped her hard across the face and shot in low. She came forward as he planned, and he was in deep with perfect double leg penetration. He picked her up high on his shoulder, tweaking his left knee in the process, but he finally had her. As he slammed her toward the mat, something impossible happened. He landed on his right side across the mat from her. He instinctively rolled through it and came up on his knee. Wu stood with her hands out, waiting. With all his years of wrestling—and fighting too, for that matter—he couldn't figure out what the hell she just did. He rolled over on his back, arms stretched out, and said, "Enough. I'm tired and I'm hungry." He reached for Wu's outstretched hand and she pulled him to his feet.

"Me too," she said.

"You don't look tired."

She smiled and hugged him. "Let's go in."

"Okay, since you insist," said Jimmy. He limped for the stairs, his left knee hurting and his back not happy. Wu slid up under his arm and put her arm around his waist, taking the weight off his knee, prompting a sigh of relief. "I never wrestled anyone like you before," he said humbly.

"Same here," said Wu, which made him feel a little better.

When they got to the den, Wu helped him to the couch. Debbie's first response was unexpected. Not what happened or who won but, "You wrestled Jimmy in your underwear?"

"We didn't wrestle. She kicked my ass," said Jimmy.

"That's bullshit," said Wu. "This guy isn't a wrestler. He's a monster."

"I'm the one crashed on the couch," he told Debbie. "She's like wrestling a tree trunk."

"His knee," Wu said to Debbie. "You may be able to help him."

Debbie put her hand on it and her eyes rolled back, searching the Cric for advice. Then she said, "Yeah, I think I can." She straightened the leg by putting his heel on the coffee table. Clearing her mind, she dug her fingers into the tissue surrounding the knee. "Ow!" he said but then relaxed into it.

Shewuma kicked back in the recliner, listening to Carole King on the stereo. It had been a long time since she'd felt any kind of muscle fatigue. With no real expectations, Debbie had been massaging Jim's knee for several minutes as per the instructions in her head. Suddenly the knee seemed to respond to her touch. It was as if it had become animated in her mind. She could feel the damaged cartilage on both sides. The patella called for help and the ACL ligament was crying. "Jimmy's knee is talking to me," she said to Shewuma with skepticism.

"Of course," said Wu. "You're Erran. You're a healer now. Heal him."

Debbie went back in. She assured the meniscus that they could heal themselves and they believed her. The scar tissue in the ligament had healed against the flow of the muscle. She massaged it in the right direction while explaining why to his knee. Just the beginning of a process, she realized. It would take regular treatment for a time to get it right. Jimmy looked asleep. "Jim? Babe?"

He opened his eyes and began flexing his knee. "It feels good," he said.

"I think we can make it better. We'll work on it every day. Okay?"

"Sure," said Jimmy getting up.

Debbie kissed him and said, "Go get a shower and we'll eat some pizza."

"You go ahead and have some," said Jimmy. "I need to lay down."

"Okay. Love you."

Wu watched him walk down the hall. The limp was almost imperceptible now. When Jimmy was out of sight, Debbie offered her hand to Wu, pulled her up out of the recliner and held her close. "Where is David E.?" asked Wu.

"He ate some pizza and went to bed," said Debbie. "What was that about with Jim?"

"I don't know. Maybe I was jealous or something. But I see now. He's something special."

"I know," said Debbie. They held each other and began to slow dance to Carole King's song, "Will you Still Love Me Tomorrow." The song ended. "Everything has changed," Debbie whispered softly.

"Yes...I love you. Shit," said Wu. "I swore I wouldn't say it."

"I love Jimmy," said Deb, stunned by the unforeseen revelation.

"I know," said Wu. And echoed again, but softer, "I know."

"I only see one option," Debbie confessed and kissed Wu passionately.

Wu kissed her back deeply, understanding it to be their last.

After a shower, Jimmy put on his boxers and climbed into bed. He heard Debbie in her closet. A few minutes later, she came out carrying a plate with a slice of pizza and wearing her baby blue robe that went to the floor. As she came around to his side of the bed, he asked her if she was going to take her shower. "Not just yet." She set the pizza on the end table. Pulling her robe to the side, she put her right foot up on the edge of the mattress, exposing her leg. He saw she was wearing tan stockings. He started reaching up for her, but her hands to his chest stopped him and pushed him back flat onto the bed. "I know how much you like outfits," she said seductively. With a step back she opened her robe and dropped it to the floor. She was wearing a blue bra and garter belt set he'd bought her when they first got married. He was pretty sure it was the first time she'd ever worn it. His breathing became shallow just looking at her.

"What's the occasion, Babe?"

"Shhh!" She pulled off his boxer shorts, causing his already firm cock to slap against his belly. She took hold of him and felt how incredibly hard he was. He reached for her, but she stopped him again. She took a dark wash towel from the end table drawer and dangled it in front of him. "I have a surprise for you," she said and placed it over his eyes. He lay in the dark for about a minute, speechless and eager. Just when he thought he couldn't wait any longer, he felt movement on the bed. She straddled him and guided his cock inside her. She felt heavier and smelled different. Subtle, like the difference between brown sugar and honey. The blindfold was snatched away, and he was shocked to see Shewuma on top of him, slowly gyrating her hips. She was naked except for a headband with a single hanging feather. Debbie lay to his side propped up on an elbow. He looked at her, confused and overwhelmed at the same time. Debbie leaned in and gave him a lingering kiss, saying, "It's okay, Baby. We're gonna do this." With his cock deep inside her, Jimmy could see Wu rocking rhythmically while still maintaining as much body contact as possible. She looked at him with her dreamy brown eyes and moaned softly. He looked at Debbie's angelic face and generous breasts, barely contained by the tight lacy bra. He saw Debbie and Wu holding hands farther down, their fingers intertwined. But when Debbie stroked Wu's calf with her nylon foot, that did it. It was too much for him. Jimmy's body shuddered and he exploded inside Wu. He grasped her thighs, trying to stay as deep in her as possible. He wanted to keep his eyes open, but the intensity wouldn't allow it. Even after he'd given her all his seed, his body kept surging, pushing and moving as deeply inside of her as he could. When he opened his eyes, he saw Debbie on her knees with Wu's head cradled in her bosom.

Wu looked into Debbie's face. "That was incredible," Wu said hoarsely.

"You felt what he felt?"

Wu merely nodded. Debbie went in, brushing their lips at first and then kissing her fully. Wu raised her pelvis up and then pushed back down, her eyes wide with surprise. "He's still hard," she said.

"Welcome to Deep Creek," said Debbie.

Jimmy began apologizing to Debbie for coming so quickly. "I'm sorry. You looking like this and her…"

Wu put a finger to his lips and Debbie whispered to him, "It's good we got that first one out of the way, Babe. Now we can get serious and rock this woman's world."

CHAPTER 17

A NEW LIFE

Lying uncovered, Jimmy woke up and saw a naked female on her stomach next to him. Moonlight intruding through the partially open blinds revealed Shewuma's tight athletic ass. Jimmy admired her for a moment while thinking about last night. Still reeling from their sex marathon, he felt he should hug her or thank her or something. Taken by the sight of her relaxed and breathing, he decided to let her sleep. He left the bed—moving the blankets and sheets on the floor with his foot—and exited the bedroom as quietly as he could, grabbing his flannel robe on the way out. No lights were on in the house. Neither Debbie nor Shewuma bothered with them anymore. As he walked down the dark hallway, he could make out Debbie sitting at the kitchen table still in her baby blue robe. She was surrounded by a glowing blue bubble. As he came closer, details formed. The Skull sat on the table. Debbie's hands were on it, fingers spread far apart. The blue light was darker and shimmering wherever she made contact. Curiously, Tippycat also lay on the table. Jimmy wasn't pleased about that. Molly's eighty-five pounds were curled up beside Debbie's chair. Both terriers were in her lap, intertwined into one furry ball. And next to her in a separate chair that she would have put there specifically for him, Nicky lay still but awake and alert. Tails set to wagging as he approached. Debbie ignored the terriers as they jumped down to greet their daddy. She was either unaware or unconcerned with the sudden influx of animal commotion prompted by Jimmy's arrival. He petted the kids and waited. He still wasn't comfortable with her obsession over the Skull, but it was her life now and he was trying to accept it. The blue aura faded and she stood up, flipping on the kitchen light as an afterthought. The new overhead LED was disturbingly bright, and Jimmy shielded his eyes until they could adjust. Debbie felt no discomfort as her pupils contracted instantly in the flood of light. She waited for his full attention.

As she came into Jimmy's focus, her face was unreadable as she asked him, "Wu still asleep?"

"Yep."

"Did you enjoy yourself last night?"

He caught an odd tone and thought it best to answer with the same question. "Did you?"

"Of course," she said flatly.

"So did I," he said, not knowing yet where this was going.

"You two really seemed to hit it off," she said with some condescension.

Jimmy suddenly felt defensive for something he hadn't done, and it hit him wrong. "We didn't hit it off nearly as much as you two did. I've never seen you that into sex…well, except for that time we were high in the elevator."

Debbie's eyes were intense. "Do you love her?"

"Jesus, Deb, think about what you're saying. If anybody loves her, it's you. Don't think I don't know you guys were making out while we were at the store. I'm not stupid." Debbie wanted to speak but he stopped her. "No, I'm not done yet. You set this whole thing up last night. I would never have done anything like that and you know it. I don't understand where you're going here. You just want *her* now. Maybe you want to break up and blame me. Maybe you don't want her anymore. Maybe you feel guilty. Whatever you've got going on, don't put that bullshit on me." He had worked himself up into a frenzy. "Fuck this. I'm going to hit the bag for a while."

"In your robe at 5:00 am?" He didn't care and turned to leave. In his mind, she said, "Jim, please don't go. I'm sorry."

He stopped. With a stern look, he said, "If you want to talk to me then say it, Goddammit!"

"I'm sorry," she said out loud, pulling him back to her.

He put his arms around her and could tell she was trying not to cry. The fight went out of him. "What's is it, Babe? Tell me."

"It's so fucked up, Jim. I'm jealous. Jealous of her, jealous of you. I shouldn't have done it. It was stupid. It was impulsive. It was weak. It was wrong."

He held her tighter. "Debbie, it happened. You didn't break any laws. You didn't hurt anybody. You're overthinking it or maybe over feeling it. I don't know. But if you're trying to explain it, quantify it, you're just pissing in the wind. It's done. It's over."

She pulled back and looked at him squarely. The resolve in her voice was significant. She was serious when she responded. "Yes, it's done. It's definitely over."

"Whatever you say, Dibs. Just try to back it down a notch and let yourself work it out."

"She told me she loves me," Debbie revealed.

That was unexpected and Jimmy said, "And that scares you." When she didn't answer, he tried some levity. "Hey, everybody loves you. Even Gladys the Battleaxe."

She hit his chest, partly in jest. "I'm serious, Jim."

"I know, and apparently so is she. So take it easy on her. I get the feeling she hasn't had a lot of uh…let's say, real relationship experience with humans."

"No," Debbie insisted. "I need to get it out there and set things straight right away."

Debbie was so hardheaded when she had her mind set. But he tried again. "Why not slow it down, play it by ear, for her and for you both. You're not going to kick her out, are you?"

"No…Wait. Why are you asking that?" Jealousy was creeping back into her voice.

"Cut it out, Deb. You do what you gotta do. Ya'll work it out. I'm out of it."

Acting annoyed now, she turned and put the Sanctum back in the old bowling bag. "I'm not really a take it slow and play it by ear kind of girl."

"No, you most certainly are not," Jim answered affectionately. He wondered what they'd started. One thing was for sure. Those two were on their own. It was a lose-lose for him to be involved. Debbie set the bowling bag in the corner of the dining area next to the China cabinet. Before his eyes, the bag and the Skull became an extra dining room chair setting against the wall. He touched it and it felt like a chair. He was floored and asked, "What is this?"

Shewuma's voice said, "It's a physical hologram." She stood at the kitchen entrance wrapped in a white sheet.

"Wu," Debbie said, startled. Then she asked, "You heard everything?"

Low and nodding, Shewuma answered, "Yes."

Calmly and with an air of detachment, Debbie said, "We need to talk about last night. But right now, there's important information I need to tell all three of you about the Sancti."

"I'll get David E.," said Jimmy. His and Wu's eyes met. His aura was all over the place, so she grazed his arm as he passed her. He was confused and tense. But she also felt his support and affection. It helped her feel hopeful.

"Jim, I already called David E.," said Debbie, kicking into boss mode.

Commenting, "I see," he turned and went to the back door and shouted, "Outside!"

Alone in the kitchen, Debbie and Shewuma stood looking at each other in awkward silence. Debbie's aura was full of brown streaks. Not a good omen for her frame of mind.

Not knowing how to begin, Debbie said, "Jimmy thought you were asleep."

Wu simply told the truth. "It was the most incredible night of my life. I couldn't sleep." Wu thought Debbie looked radiant with her tousled hair and still stockinged feet peeking out from under the robe. She started toward her.

For a second, Debbie felt the weight of indecision bearing down. But then her resolve roared back. She held up her hands for Wu to stop. Her lips became a thin line across her face. Very pointedly she said, "It was a mistake, Wu."

Wu said quickly, "It was my fault. I'm sorry. I pushed too hard."

"No," said Debbie. "I blame myself. I let it go too far."

"Debs!" Wu pleaded.

"Stop it, Wu," snapped Debbie. "There's no talking it out, no soul searching. It's done. We move on."

Wu felt as though the air had been sucked from her lungs. Seeing no crack in Debbie's hard veneer, Wu made a request. "Can I touch your arm?"

"No," said Debbie firmly. "I'm going to get dressed. You should do the same." She left briskly, afraid if she looked Wu in the eyes, it might undo everything she'd just said.

As David E. left his room in the uniform of tan suit and weaponized cane, he heard Debbie's bedroom door slam shut. He saw Shewuma in the kitchen wrapped in a sheet and leaning into the refrigerator. He said a cheery good morning to her and headed straight for the coffee maker. He didn't see the single tear about to drop off the end of her nose.

Fifteen minutes later after watching one news cycle on cable, David E. went to the kitchen window and turned the blinds up to let in the light of the breaking dawn. Shewuma sat silently to Debbie's left, her long black hair unbrushed and still wearing the sheet. In his robe, Jimmy was setting up a cold breakfast. Along with a gallon of milk, the choices were Cap'n Crunch, Rice Krispies or Cheerios. There was also buttered toast and a plate of hard boiled eggs. He thought it odd when Debbie pushed her bowl aside and only took four eggs. As she peeled them, Jimmy listened with amusement as David E. explained how the arson deaths of two dozen people in a Mexican bar was the work of aliens. Jimmy had come to understand that in David E.'s mind, everything was the work of aliens. Jimmy stood by his chair and watched everyone digging in. "Anything else we need before I sit down?"

Wu spoke up. "Can I have some chocolate for my milk?"

"For the High Priest." He returned with Nesquik and Hershey's Chocolate Syrup.

"Thanks, Babe," said Wu as she took both.

He was worried about her. Debbie could be hard on people. It was a gift and a curse. But Wu seemed okay.

Once they were eating, Debbie began speaking. "Communication with the Sanctum is an ongoing process. But I've recently learned some important facts. Now you all know there are thirteen Skulls. Twelve do the work. The thirteenth is the Sanctum. It programs and oversees the other twelve." Wu and David E. nodded. Jimmy looked lost and shook his head. Debbie patted his hand and said, "You sweet, sweet man. So, each Skull is locked into its own Cric. The Crics are organically programed to a Sentinel. The Sentinels are Errans who specialize in the duties and responsibilities of each Skull. The Sentinels protect and maintain the Sancti. Did Enoch tell you any of this, Wu?"

"No. Getting information from him was like pulling teeth. But it makes sense."

Debbie went on. "Of the thirteen Sancti, eleven of the Sentinels are dead and the Skulls and Crics are missing."

"What?" said Wu, rising in her seat. "How is that possible?"

"There were always rumors," said David E. "The Errans would never confirm or deny it, but if they could kill Enoch, why not the others?" Realizing what he'd said, he looked at Wu. "I'm sorry, Honey."

"It's okay, D.E." Not knowing why, Debbie was slightly annoyed at Wu saying D.E.

Jimmy spoke up. "So, what your saying is that someone is stealing all the Skulls, right?"

"Yes," said Debbie, her face intense. "And the Drachs are working for them."

"Probably the MIB too," added Wu.

"That indicates influence from the government," said David E.

Jimmy tried to slow them down. "This is all conjecture. We're just making shit up, right?"

"I don't think so," said Debbie. "The Sanctum should be in constant communication with the other Sentinels and Skulls. But the eleven are silent. The twelfth one seems to be out there, but I can't talk to it. I don't know why. And my Sanctum is convinced that the twelfth Sentinel is alive. All I know for sure is that the twelfth Skull's name is Naro."

It wasn't lost on Jimmy that Debbie called the Sanctum *mine*.

"They have names?" asked Jimmy.

"It's Latin for tell," said Wu.

"Probably deals with some type of communications," said David E. Wu gave him a thumbs-up.

"Makes sense," said Deb. "But I can't reach it. Maybe I'm being blocked somehow."

"But they're still functioning, right?" asked Jimmy.

"Yes," said Debbie. "As far as I can tell, you need my Sanctum to change the programing of the others. And it hasn't changed the primary directives."

There it was again. *My Sanctum*. It was disturbing.

"For the most part," said Debbie, "deciphering the Sanctum has been straightforward. But some parts seem impossible to interpret."

"No," said Wu, taking her hand. "You're doing great."

Debbie squeezed back. Seeing Wu in the sheet eating a boiled egg almost made her smile. But she caught herself and pulled her hand away. "So," Debbie summed up, "based on the information I can glean, there's a statistical probability of 92.7 percent that the Drachs and/or their silent partners have most if not all the missing Skulls. Probably the Crics too."

"Hmm," said Jimmy. "Then they will definitely be coming here."

"Definitely," agreed Debbie, with Wu and David E. nodding their consensus.

"We should expect a coordinated attack by a group of Drachonians," said Wu.

"Or MIB," said David E.

"I'm afraid so," sighed Debbie.

"Do you know where the missing Skulls could be?" asked Jimmy.

"No idea."

"Had any premonitions?" asked Wu. Deb gave her a questioning look. "Enoch had the sight, so I figured you have it too. He always knew what was going to happen. Until that last day anyway."

"No," Debbie said. "The best I can do is keep trying to figure out where the one missing Sentinel and the rest of the Sancti are."

"That's not much of a plan," said Jim. "Plus, we have to go to the bankruptcy hearing today."

"Oh shit," said Deb. "I forgot."

"You're kidding," said Jimmy. "With your new computer mind, you forgot?" Deb shot him a dirty look. He put his hands up defensively. "We have to go. It's at 2:00. We should be home by 4:00 or so."

"All right." Debbie pointed at David E. and Wu. "But you two be really careful. When we get back, we'll come up with a better plan. In the meantime, the animals are here, the AK-47 and the SAW are loaded, and I had Cox Cable turn the security alarm back on."

Jimmy said, "We weren't supposed to be doing anything new until after the hearing. Credit cards, etc. Remember?"

"Technically," said Debbie, tapping her left ear, "I turned it on myself."

"So we're not paying for it? Cool," said Jimmy.

"Awesome," said Wu.

"Quite impressive," said David E.

Debbie smiled, a bit pleased with herself. "I'll give you guys the alarm code before we leave."

"We'll be fine," said David E, looking at Wu.

"I have a long day planned anyway," said Wu. "Jimmy, can I please use your shop and tools?"

"Of course, WuWu." Taking offense at Debbie's frown, Jimmy added, "You use whatever you want, Wu. But now we have a serious issue to discuss." He stood and curiosity drew everyone in. "What are we going to have for lunch today after this crappy breakfast," he said to minor objections. "I think we deserve a treat. High Priest?"

"I defer to your judgement, High Priest Emeritus," she said, smiling.

Jimmy turned to David E. "You're ex-military, David E. How do you feel about SOS?"

"I love SOS," he said dreamily. "I haven't had it in years."

"You probably eat it with hamburger, right?" asked Jimmy.

"Of course."

"Well, I make it with dried beef. It's better."

"Oh no, I don't think so," disagreed David E.

"I thought you would say that." Deep Creek kicked in. "How about a bet on which is better?" Jimmy proposed.

Debbie was interested. "How's that?' said David E.

"We each make it. I use dried beef and you use hamburger. We let the girls decide which is better."

David E. looked at Wu and Debbie to get their reactions to the odd challenge.

"I am the High Priest now," said Wu. "I definitely feel qualified."

For the first time that morning, Debbie began to loosen up and smiled. "I'm in."

"What is SOS?" asked Wu.

"Oh, you're going to love it," said Debbie. "It's High Priest food for sure."

"All right," said Jim. "I'm going to get dressed and work on the fence gate. David E., I'll meet you back here at 11:00 for the big cook-off."

David E. followed Jimmy down the hall, asking him about his recipe. Debbie and Shewuma were left looking at each other. "I'm going to go work out," said Debbie with a noncommittal air.

"You're going to work out in your sexy clothes and robe?" asked Wu.

Debbie looked down at her clothes. "No. I guess I need to change."

"You'll never change," said Wu, and Debbie couldn't help but smile. "Mind if I work out with you?"

"I guess it's okay," Debbie lied. "But put on some actual workout clothes. Don't be wearing a skimpy one-piece or something."

Wu was off, saying, "Wouldn't trust yourself, right?"

When Debbie came up the shop stairs to the gym in her black yoga pants and matching crop top, she suddenly felt exposed and wished she'd worn sweats. The animals had followed Wu and she was playing with them on the wrestling mat. Debbie started to feel pangs of jealousy about the kids' affection for Wu but shook it off. It was silly. She liked her. Jim liked her. Why shouldn't they like her? Besides, Debbie swore Wu could talk to them. Then she noticed Wu checking her out and realized there was no way around it. She really did enjoy her company.

"Hey, Dibs," said Wu, "you look good. I'm going to start lifting." Wu set the bench press to its maximum, six hundred pounds. She lay on her back on the small bench and arched her body up from her neck to the balls of her feet. Jimmy would call it a hyper press. The position helped to bench an excessive amount of weight. Wu did ten reps and clanged the weights down. The caramel-colored mini dress she was wearing was almost up to her waist. She sat up and looked at Debbie. "Did I impress you?"

"Well, Jimmy would certainly be impressed. He benches about two hundred fifty. What impressed me is that you're wearing underwear."

"I do that for Jimmy and David E. Not you. Seeing my hooch makes them nervous. Besides, men like a little mystery. You know that. You're the queen of mystery." She threw all that out at once, then waited for a response.

Debbie said, "I guess I just don't understand why you feel the need to expose yourself."

"There is no *need* to do it. I enjoy it. I think I look pretty good. Besides, I don't have much else going for me."

Debbie's reaction was sharp. "That's not true, Wu. You're pretty and sexy, sure. But you're also funny and smart and strong and badass. You're like a superhero for Christ's sake. You don't need to flaunt your hoohah to impress people.

Shewuma was truly touched. "So, you still like me?"

Debbie had to stop herself from going in for a hug. "Of course I like you, Honey. We're family now. I'm just not going to have sex with you." The words just slipped out, but Debbie felt better having said it.

Wu stood up and adjusted her dress. "I can live with that, Dibs. I just don't want to lose the fun, the bond we have. Our time together. You know?"

Debbie did know and felt the same way. "Me either, WuWu." Debbie took to hitting the heavy bag but stopped. She noticed something while Wu was setting up the military press. "Why are you wearing your belt out here?"

Shewuma called it her battle belt. It was black leather. The Arapaho blade was on the left side, cross draw style. The three German throwers were on her right hip. The tomahawk was stuffed in the front, and the zombie axe hung skewed in the back from a homemade leather loop. The buckle was an oval shape with a silver matte finish and a blue-green stone in the center. She wondered if it was genuine turquoise. "Are you kidding?" said Wu. "I work out in it. I sleep in it. I live in it. If I need it and don't have it, then all the times I had it before were pointless."

"That sounds awfully Deep Creek. You're a natural Creeker."

"Thank you." Looking pensive, Wu said, "Dibs, we still haven't discussed the elephant in the room, and I think we should."

Knowing full well what she meant, Debbie said, "What elephant?" She had hoped they were done talking.

"We had a three-way with your husband."

With a sigh, Debbie removed her practice mitts and tossed them on the shelf, then said, "Wu, what happened last night was wrong."

"Why?"

"Well, you just said it. We had a three-way with my husband."

Wu persisted. "I understand that you wish you hadn't done it or maybe even didn't like it. But I ask again. Why was it wrong?"

"Wu, I love him."

"Of course you love him," Wu said sincerely. "Any fool could see that. Why does that make it wrong?" Debbie and her aura were hard to read. "Would it have been okay if it was just us and Jim wasn't involved?"

"I didn't mean that. Hold it. Why? You didn't like him being there?"

"Of course I did. I told you. It was the most amazing night of my life."

"Exactly," said Debbie accusingly.

It hit Wu out of left field. "Are you jealous he might have feelings for me?" Debbie's non-answer was Wu's answer. "Debbie, I would never try to come between you and Jimmy. No pun intended," she joked. But Debbie wasn't amused. "Debbie, he loves you more than life. Trust me. I saw it. I felt it. I was there."

Debbie's reaction was harsh. "So was I and I saw how you made him come." There. She said it.

"Oh, Debbie Doodle, that was no big deal. He's a guy. He got some strange. Guys aren't like us. They can't help overreacting to getting laid by someone different. Look, I came. You came. He came. It was just sex." Wu saw Debbie's face tense and her aura darken, and she had a small epiphany. "Dibs, you're jealous of both me and him."

"No," Debbie insisted. But then she backed off. "I don't know." Shrugging her shoulders, she said, "It has to be a sin or something." The debate wasn't going the way Debbie expected. But it didn't change the way she felt. Hell, she wasn't even sure how she felt.

"Debbie," Wu said softly, "I was raised in very disciplined, moral, and spiritual confines. I'm one hundred and fifty-seven years old. I spent my whole life training and then with a man I hardly knew. I know a truckload of extraordinary shit has been coming at you sideways lately. You lost your business, Bocephus is dead, then you find yourself attracted to a Hybrid woman, and bam! You're in a threesome." Wu stopped, watching Debbie's aura go crazy. It prompted a realization that staggered her.

"Wu?" Debbie asked as Wu paused.

"Debbie, you should have told me you've never been with anyone but Jimmy."

"How could you know that?"

"Your aura gave you away, Sweetie." Wu reached her hand out. But Debbie—taken completely by surprise—refused it, confirming Wu's statement. "You said you love me, and we barely know each other," Debbie said.

"Dibsi, stop. Listen to me. Please." Shewuma held out her hand again, her face imploring. Debbie took it reluctantly. "Dibs, you think it's about sex. And for you, maybe it is, I guess. But to me, sex is more like a hobby. I spent a life of duty, purpose, and responsibility as a Star Child. And yes, I've had a ridiculous amount of sex with many different people. It's been the only real diversion from my life's obligations. But I've never had unconditional love. I'm a Hopi. I'm a Kachina. We value community, commitment, and family. I never truly had those things until you. Debs, you came for me. Then you came back for me. You saved me. You opened your home, your children, and your husband to me. All unconditional. For the first time since I was a child, I'm not living in the moment. I'm excited about what's ahead. I love my life now and it's because of you. And you're right. We are family now. You, me, Jimmy, David E., the kids. Whatever happens, I will always be grateful. I will always be here for you. And that's why I love you. Though you being exceptionally hot doesn't hurt." She let go of Debbie's hand and sat down on the bench. She looked up at Debbie and waited for her to reply.

Holding out her arms and tearing up, Debbie said, "Can you really see auras?"

"Yes," said Wu, and rose into Debbie's waiting hug. And for only the second time in her life, Wu felt a tear form in her eye.

They pulled back and Debbie said, "So you're kind of a slut?"

It was all Wu could do not to jump up and down. Her Debbie was back. "I have stories that would curl your hair."

"Would you teach me to throw knives like you?" Debbie asked.

"Only if you get Jimmy to teach me how to make his chicken and dumplings. But seriously. there is something important I need to teach you first."

"What?"

"It's about controlling your sense of time."

Debbie cocked her head for some quick research. "That's real? I'm just getting theory and wives' tales."

"Oh, it's real all right. Now come on. Let's get to work on you, Ho."

Debbie laughed and said, "Let's do it, Slut."

When the clock on the microwave in the kitchen turned to 11:00 am, Debbie and Shewuma turned to the boys and said, "Go!" To be fair, Jimmy made both pots of rue for the SOS contest. He knew for sure that David E. was no chef when he had to stop him from dumping the raw hamburger into the thickened sauce. "Fry it up first, David E."

"You're a good man," David E. responded. "You could have won this contest twice already."

"Toast or biscuits?" Jimmy asked to the room.

David E. gave a resounding toast and Wu declared, "Both."

Jimmy told David E., "I also made some potato cakes and sausage."

David E. inhaled deeply. "Smoked sausage? I haven't had smoked sausage for thirty years."

"Good," said Jim. "Want some eggs with it?"

"That's an awful lot of food, Jim," said David E.

Jim answered with one word. "Shewuma."

"Yeah, I know what you mean."

From across the other room, Shewuma said, "Careful, boys. You're on thin ice. But I'm glad you're watching out for me." She leaned over the CD player to change out the discs. From her vantage point on the couch where she was folding clothes, Debbie caught herself watching Wu's dress ride up her backside and quickly looked away. "Caught ya," Wu said devilishly.

"You did that on purpose," said Debbie.

"Nobody made you look." Wu chuckled.

"What are you putting in?" asked Debbie.

"Bruno Mars, Big and Rich, Tedeschi and Trucks, and I want to try this Kandace Springs. I like the picture of her on the front."

"You'll like her. You like jazz. And I listened to her the first time because I liked that picture too. Great minds."

"I need one more CD."

"Put in that one there on the right. It has no label. It's Jimmy's cousin Corrine."

"Perfect," said Wu and hit All Repeat. "Uptown Funk" filled the room as Jimmy yelled, "Let's eat?" from the kitchen.

Each place setting at the table was given two monkey dishes containing one each of the SOS recipes. Jimmy stood and tapped his tea glass with a fork. "Before we eat, everyone has to taste both SOS and pick your favorite." Tasting happened amid the sound of oohhs and aahhs coming from around the table. Jimmy stood back up. "Okay, we need a consensus."

"Wait, wait," David E. said. "Let me nip this contest in the bud. I want to concede. I've already tasted yours and it's spectacular. You're the master chef." The girls clapped. "Jimmy went through this same thing with my dad years ago," said Debbie, smiling. Jimmy was heartened to hear her sounding more like her old self.

"Yours is yummy too, David E.," said Wu.

David E. pretended he was revealing a secret. "Truth be told, Jimmy pretty much made them both."

"So, someone tell me what the hell SOS means," demanded Wu.

"Shit on a Shingle," the other three said, almost in unison. Wu still looked puzzled.

"You put it on toast," Jimmy explained, pointing to his toast corners peeking out from under the mass of creamy, beef-filled sauce.

Wu did a *Sting* acknowledgement and brushed her finger alongside of her nose. After they were finished, Wu went on and on about how delicious the SOS tasted. She was sure she must have eaten it before but couldn't remember when. And since no one else wanted the fried eggs, she ate all four. David E. twice mentioned the need to start exercising if he was going to keep eating Jimmy's cooking.

Debbie commanded everyone's attention. "We need to do these dishes so Jim and I can get dressed for the bankruptcy hearing."

"I'm ready," said Jimmy.

"No, you aren't," corrected Deb. "You're not going to court in a shirt that reads, 'There is no gravity. The earth sucks.' Understand?"

"Yes, dear," he mocked.

"No," said Wu, with David E. nodding in agreement. "We'll take care of the dishes and the kids. You two just get ready. Go on."

Jim and Debbie happily left the dishes and went to their bedroom. Once there, Jimmy said tentatively, "You seem like you feel better."

"I do," said Deb. "I guess I got a little weird. You were right. Wu and I talked. Everything is okay. But no more sex."

Jimmy said in mock horror, "Ever?"

"You know what I mean."

"Whatever you say, Gorgeous." He slapped her ass as she waked by.

Shewuma and David E. had just finished the dishes when Jimmy and Debbie appeared. They were so gussied up that David E. and Wu let go with whistles and catcalls. Jimmy was in a shimmering gray suit with a blue and white striped tie. His tie pin was an old-style clip-on replica of a muzzle loading long rifle. Debbie wore black heels and a white blouse with a navy blue suit that had the skirt stopping at least two inches above her knee. David E. was taken by the musket pin and said so.

"Hubba, hubba," Wu said, complimenting their classy, conservative appearance.

"Yeah," agreed Jim. "She's hot, isn't she?"

Debbie stuck out her right leg and turned it seductively. "He's just excited because I'm showing some leg."

Wu laughed and said, "I would've thought he was a boob man."

"Jesus," said David E. "You guys will say anything."

"Different generations," said Jimmy.

"Oh really," said David E. "And what generation would Wu be exactly?"

"She's a sweet young thing," Deb said pointedly. "And that's all you need to know." She held up her fist and Wu bumped it.

David E. said, "If you don't mind, Debbie, I'm going to use your computer and do some research."

"Help yourself," said Debbie.

Wu winked at her and said, "Porn?"

"Porn," returned Debbie, nodding.

David E. just shook his head. "You two are bad."

"So, we might be back a little later than we thought," said Debbie.

"It's the clothes, right?" said Wu. "You going to find an elevator afterward?"

Jimmy was surprised. "You told her about the elevator?"

"See what I mean?" said David E. "You two just go enjoy your legalities and whatever else you plan to do. I don't need to hear the details."

"Wait. There's one more thing," said Jim.

Wu was expecting a joke. "What's up?"

"I received a text from Detective Sergeant Reubens. He said our story about Bocephus was confirmed by Mr. Johnson across the street."

"I never met him," said Wu. "But Enoch said he was a great guy."

"The problem is," said Jimmy, "what Mr. Johnson confirmed to the cops was a story that Debbie made up." He left it open.

"Drachs," said Wu.

"Yes, definitely Drachs. I need to research this," said David E.

"So that's why we might be late. We thought we would check him out after the hearing."

"No," Wu insisted. "Let's go together tomorrow. It could be a trap. Who knows what's there?"

They looked back and forth and agreed. "Okay," said Debbie. "Tomorrow then. Safety in numbers. You two make yourselves at home."

Wu said, "You know we will."

As Jimmy and Debbie drove out of the neighborhood in the Muscle, they passed a jogging, waving, smiling Mr. Rawlings. They both waved back, knowing he was fake. "What the fuck have we gotten ourselves into?" mumbled Jimmy.

Jimmy and Debbie arrived a half hour early at the building in City Center designated for the bankruptcy hearing. They waited outside until Alicia showed up two minutes after the hearing start time. They hugged and hustled in to find a seat. Debbie and Jimmy were expecting a long and arduous process. Happily, they were wrong. Except for the hour waiting to be called, it was a snap. The court officer talked to them for about ten minutes. He asked some random but easily answered financial questions and that was it. In the parking lot afterward, Alicia explained what would happen next. In about two months, she would go before the judge. If there were no issues, they would get a letter. The bankruptcy was done. Debts discharged. They hugged their goodbyes and left. At Debbie's insistence, they stopped by Jim's mom's house for a visit. Then they headed home while discussing dinner.

Tippy wasn't there, but the rest of the children went nuts when Jimmy and Debbie entered the house. It took a good ten minutes of petting and cooing to settle them down. David E. was delighted to see them arrive with two buckets and two bags from Kentucky Fried Chicken.

"Where is Tippycat?" asked Deb.

"He's been outside with Shewuma since you left," he realized.

Jimmy began unpacking dinner with David E.'s happy cooperation. Debbie headed out to the shop, maybe a tad concerned. She entered the side door of the shop and Tippy leapt into her arms. "Hey, Baby," she said, scratching between his ears.

Hunched over the workbench, her back to the door, Wu responded without looking, "Hi, Honey."

"I was talking to the Tipster," Debbie corrected her.

"I know." Wu turned, excited or nervous. Debbie wasn't sure which.

"Okay, Debbie. I took care of the arrow tips," she said and waved her hand at the table. The work shelf was lined with at least three dozen fiberglass arrows and many more that Shewuma must have made herself. The first four had Debbie's broadhead hunting tips on them. After those, the rest were attached to homemade Native American-looking arrowheads. "I'll finish them up tomorrow." Wu went back to winding fishing line around the one she was working on.

Debbie picked one up and turned it back and forth, observing the work. "They look like authentic, classic warheads. Where did you get these?" Debbie asked, stumped.

"I made them," said Wu, very focused on her work.

"From what?" Debbie was completely at a loss.

"I used those slate steps you have going from the back deck to the sidewalk. Don't be mad."

"Mad? Are you kidding? That is fucking amazing." She inspected them one after another.

"Well, good," said Wu. "Then you should be okay with ahh…the other thing."

"What other thing?" Just then she spied Lightning propped up on blocks of wood sans bowstring. Visibly disturbed, Debbie asked, "What did you do to my Lightning bow?"

"Okay," said Wu. "Don't overreact. But I could only get the bow to draw to ninety-five pounds."

"You say that like it's a problem. Who would want to draw a ninety-five-pound bow anyway?"

"I took the fiberglass oar from the kayak and used it to make the bow limbs stronger. The draw should be a little over two hundred pounds now. Don't hate me." Wu cringed and waited.

Debbie looked at her with a whole new level of respect. "You really do make all this stuff like you said. Come here. Get over here."

Debbie hugged her. "It's wonderful, Wu. Jimmy will die when he sees what you've done. Can I try it?" Debbie pointed at the bow.

"It should set until tomorrow," said Wu.

"Let's go eat. We brought fried chicken home."

"I'm right behind you."

"That's what scares me," said Deb, and they both laughed.

When Debbie and Wu entered the kitchen, the men had set the table and put out the food. Grouped in the center were KFC original recipe, mashed potatoes, gravy, coleslaw, baked beans, and biscuits.

"Oh, sweet Jesus," Wu exclaimed.

"Are you a Christian?" David E. asked seriously.

"No," said Wu. "But sweet Angwusnasomtaka in this context just isn't the same."

They were laughing but Jimmy stopped because he recognized the name and said, "Wuya, the Crow Mother of Kachinas."

"Yes," said Wu, enchantedly surprised. "Thank you. You've been checking up on me."

Jim made the sign of the Hopi and said, "Wuya blesses you and watches over you and yours."

Wu's face went mushy. She went around the table to Jim, made the symbol of the Hopi, and kissed him on the lips. When she got back to her chair, she heard Debbie's voice in her mind saying, "We're all here for you."

After dinner, Jimmy noticed that Debbie hadn't eaten any mashed potatoes. "Don't you want some of these sides, Babe?"

"No, I'm good," said Debbie.

As had become the custom, they worked together to clean the table and do the dishes. Then they sat back down. Debbie gave everyone a wine glass, saying each time, "Pretend it's a snifter." She went around again, filling the snifters with Mouquin Brandy. They killed the bottle while talking about their respective days. Everyone enjoyed Wu's tale of deconstructing the property to enhance her weapons. Debbie and Jim recounted their uneventful legal dealings, their visit to Mom, and another sighting of the faux Mr. Rawlings from next door. But David E.'s research online piqued the most interest. "First," he said, "before I forget. Three black choppers flew over the house today."

"As it happens, there were four," corrected Wu. "Three regular and one that made no sound."

"Four then," said David E.

Jim pointed out that they lived less than five miles from Camp Perry and saw their fair share of choppers.

"Yeah, but never four black ones in a day," said Deb.

"That is excessive," Jimmy agreed.

David E. said, "I didn't realize we're that close to the Farm. That's interesting."

"The Farm?" said Wu.

"It's a CIA training base," said Debbie. "Camp Perry. The Farm is a nickname."

"That is kind of cool," said Wu. "So, tell us the big news, David E."

"Okay. What I found out today is that in the East End, which the media calls South East, Newport News, by the way." Debbie and Jimmy both pshawed the statement. "The crime rate in the last quarter was down by fifty-four percent almost exclusively because of the inactivity of a local gang called KIC."

"What does that stand for?" asked Jimmy.

David E. shrugged and Debbie said, "Killers in Crime."

"They put some thought into it," said Jim. "Wu, did you ever run into them?"

"Just once and they never came to our house again."

"Are you going to let me tell this or not?" David E. was getting testy. They snickered as he continued. "So, this gang pretty much ran the area of East End where you and Enoch lived and where our friend Mr. Johnson, the fake Mr. Johnson, apparently still lives."

"Of course," said Wu.

"It makes perfect sense," said Debbie.

"My thoughts exactly," said David E.

"What?" questioned Jim. "Ya'll haven't said anything yet."

"Think," said David E. "The Drachs killed off the KIC gang. Took over Mr. Johnson's house and used it to go after Enoch and the Sanctum."

"Probably dug under the street to get to our chamber," said Wu. "I barely went down there, and Enoch was transcending and didn't have his Cric in. He wouldn't have heard them coming."

Jimmy understood. "Pretty obvious now that you say it. Maybe they're still at Mr. Johnson's house because they didn't find the Sanctum yet."

"Makes sense," said David E. "And when the cop talked to him, he would have no idea that it wasn't the real Mr. Johnson."

Wu stood up. "I say we go there tomorrow and take out that son of a bitch."

"I'm with you," said Jim. "That fucker is dead."

Debbie agreed too.

David E. looked at Debbie quizzically. "What? Revenge?"

"Yes. Revenge."

"Revenge it is," said David E. "We'll do it for Wu."

"And for Enoch," Wu added.

"In anticipation of this possibility, I've come up with a plan," said David E. "Let's go over it quickly so Debbie can change it." They laughed but then turned serious.

The next morning, the group was on the road heading to Newport News by 9:00 am. After a breakfast of ham and cheese omelets, grits, and biscuits, everyone was in a pretty good mood. The kids were at home. Debbie was relatively sure that that no one, alien or human, would invade a house full of hunting dogs and a giant cat. Besides, if the alarm went off, the sheriff's office would respond within minutes. The sky was cloudy, and she tapped into the weather channel to see if it was calling for rain. Every day the Cric opened up to her a little bit more with the systems and signals it could access, the ways it could manipulate and enhance her physical characteristics, and the vast knowledge at her disposal. She was beginning to wonder if the Cric's only limitation was her.

Debbie was driving Miss Interceptor as always. Wu joined her in the front seat, which automatically put her in charge of the tunes. Jimmy and David E. relaxed in the back. The temperature was in the low fifties. After a long hot summer, the chilly air was kind of nice. Debbie fidgeted, pulling at her blue coveralls. Her blond hair was on top of her head in a wide flat bun. A brown leather belt carried her .40 caliber Beretta on the right and a four-inch Buck folder in a leather case behind it. David E. wore a long, dark brown Macintosh raincoat. Hidden underneath, his double barreled sawed-off shotgun was hanging from a makeshift hook that went over his shoulder. Jimmy wore jeans and a black, oversized hoodie. He was packing his .45 Glock and as always, carried in his pocket the Old Timer lock blade. But just in case, he had a short, fat belly flayer in his boot. Shewuma was fetching in her usual green manta and moccasins. Her black hair was a single braid, and she wore a headband that Debbie remembered came from the bank deposit box. It was green and blue with eagle feathers and beads hanging down around it. A quick mental search revealed it to be a type of war bonnet. The items attached were given for acts of bravery in battle and not given lightly. When she told Jimmy about it later, he was impressed but not surprised. "Lord only knows what that girl has been through in her life, Dibsi," he said.

They questioned her lack of disguise, but she wouldn't be swayed. Since she had more combat experience than all of them combined, they let it go. As far as weapons, Wu was loaded for bear. The Arapaho hunting knife, three German throwers, tomahawk, and zombie axe were in place. And now she had Lightning. Her remastered bow that drew at two hundred plus pounds, enough force to penetrate even thick plywood. Wu was exhilarated about the upcoming task. And she was more than a little impressed—after touching each comrade—that they were relaxed and not nervous.

"I've been wondering about something," brought up Jimmy. "What if we come up against more of those plasma guns? The bastard in Covington cut the house in half."

"Not likely," said Wu. "They're few and far between. I've only seen three fired in my life and one of those belonged to me and Enoch."

"Why?"

"Pretty simple really. You need alien technology to charge them. About three minutes of firing time or one of Debbie's infamous EMPs." She motioned to Debbie, who tilted her head in acknowledgement. "And they become scrap metal."

Jimmy was nodding his head with a new understanding. "So, the blue lights? Same thing?"

"Yes," said Wu and looked at Debbie.

Debbie explained. "Each Xinite used in a blue light has to be grown individually. And one tab contains trillions of them. The Greys can grow them without alien tech. But it needs a nuclear reactor and takes a very long time. So, they're very time intensive and costly. Coveted really. They just don't use them willy-nilly."

"Wow," said Wu. "They used them willy-nilly on us. 22nd Street, the chopper in Covington, your neighbor Rawlings. They want the Sanctum something fierce."

"Yeah, they do," sighed Debbie.

"One more question, Debs," said Jimmy.

"Shoot."

"Who is this willy-nilly and why is he saying these terrible things about us?"

It struck everyone's funny bone. The laughter faded and that still left thirty minutes of driving to kill. Shewuma put in a CD and the truck filled with the sounds of the bossa nova. "What is this lovely voice?" David E. asked Jimmy.

"Her name is Eliane Elias. She's a Brazilian jazz singer. Plays the hell out of the piano too. She is a…" He couldn't remember the word. "What is that word, Debs?" He smiled. "It just popped into my head. Prodigy."

"She sings like an angel," said David E.

Courtesy of Debbie, a floating hologram appeared between the seats of Eliane Elias on her piano in a slinky black dress, playing, singing, and swinging her long blonde hair. David E. was captivated. "I think David E. is smitten," said Wu.

"She's good looking too, huh?" Jimmy said. "Hey, I have one. Sexiest woman ever, not including spouses."

Pointing back at Jimmy, Wu said to Debbie, "Vanessa Williams, right?"

"Oh no. Not so, onion breath," Debbie replied.

"What? Onion breath?" The comment disturbed Wu and she cupped her hand over her mouth and sniffed.

"Oh, Honey, I'm kidding," said Deb. "It's just something Johnny Carson used to say. Jimmy only says Vanessa Williams for best looking. For the sexiest, it'll be one of two others, depending on his mood."

"Okay," said Wu. "You're up, David E."

"Hmmm." David E. couldn't decide. "It's between Ava Gardner and Elizabeth Taylor."

"I would definitely go Liz over Ava," said Jim.

"Me too," agreed Debbie. "Liz."

Shewuma jumped in. "I say nay. I'm all in on Dolly Parton."

"That's one of Jimmy's choices," Debbie said. "Dolly Parton or Kimberly Guilfoyle."

"Really?" Wu chirped. Looking directly at Debbie's considerable breasts she said, "You've spoiled him. You know, Kimberly Guilfoyle used to be a Victoria's Secret model and I saw her naked once."

Jimmy reacted. "I want to hear that story in detail."

Debbie stopped them cold. "Easy, children. Get back to the game."

Wu pretended to whisper back to Jim beside the seat. "I'll tell you later."

Jimmy gave Wu a thumbs-up and said, "Normally Debbie would be right about my picks. But today I'm feeling nostalgic because I watched *Rio Bravo* last night. I'm going with Angie Dickinson."

"Good choice," said David E. "I didn't think about her."

Jim's answer surprised Debbie. "You can't change your pick, David E.," she declared.

"It's okay. I'm good. I'll stay with Liz."

That created a three-way tie. Debbie said, "How about I break the tie? Whomever I pick is the winner." Assuming she meant that she would side with one of them, they agreed. "Good. Then I pick Elvira, Mistress of the Dark."

Wu pointed at her accusingly. "Misleading the witness. You cheated."

"No, I'm good with her," said Jimmy.

David E. was also okay with Elvira.

Wu hung in there. "Really? With all the black, heavy makeup, and bad sexual innuendoes?"

"Sure," said Debbie.

"You bet," said David E.

"Hell yes," said Jimmy.

"This is classified, Wu." said Debbie "But I learned to twirl tassels with my breasts from watching an Elvira movie."

Wu put up her hand. "Just stop. I have to stay focused."

Debbie laughed and said, "You make up a question."

"I will," said Wu. "My question is…the best male singer of all time."

"Any genre or style?"

"Yes," said Wu.

"Which one?"

"No, I meant any genre."

"Who's on first?" said Debbie, while poking Wu in the side.

"Dead or alive?" asked Jimmy.

"Yes."

"Which?"

"Either one."

"What's on second?" Debbie said, laughing.

"Stop," said Wu and slapped at her arm.

"It's a slam dunk," said David E. "Frank."

"George Michael," Debbie quickly countered.

"That was unexpected, Dibs," said Wu. "I pick Nat King Cole."

"Nat is a good choice, but I have to go with Frank Sinatra," Jimmy declared.

Debbie said, "Okay. Guys against girls. I change my answer to Nat King Cole."

"Wait," said David E. "You said you can't change an answer."

"She just did," said Wu.

"Okay, forget it," said Jimmy. "We'll call it a tie."

"We have time for one more," said Debbie. She kicked Miss Interceptor up to eighty as the construction ended and the highway opened into three lanes. She held up one finger. "Best female jazz singer ever."

"Diana Krall," Jimmy said immediately.

"Yesterday, I would have said Sarah Vaughn," said David E. "But after this morning, I have to say Elaine Elias."

Wu laughed. "Miss Elias has beguiled you, David E. I present the underrated Miss Cyrille Aimee."

Debbie turned bossy. "I'm claiming jurisdiction here. The answer is Ella Fitzgerald. I cannot believe nobody picked her."

"Well, you just keep cheating on your own rules," said David E. "First, you change your answer and then you just say you automatically win? You can't just…"

Wu put in an Ella CD in David E.'s mid-sentence and cranked it, drowning him out.

Debbie looked over at her with a mischievous smile and said to her mind, "Girls against guys." Wu winked at her and turned it up louder.

Once in East End, Jimmy wondered out loud if they should go by and see Miss Dora.

"What would I say to her, Jimmy? I'm not good at lying," said Debbie.

"No, you're not," he agreed.

"Who's Miss Dora?" asked David E.

"She's Bo's mom, our friend who was killed when we found Shewuma," said Jimmy.

"Well, think about this," said David E. "If you're being followed and tracked, you could be putting anyone you visit in jeopardy."

"Never mind," Jimmy conceded.

As they drove the bustling main artery of East End, Wu turned off the CD playing Ella Fitzgerald and the truck became eerily silent. Shewuma took a tube of lipstick from the glove box and applied two red hash marks tilting down on each cheek and a row of red dots above her eyebrows sloping downward meeting at the bridge of her nose. Debbie looked over at Wu's warpaint and the hairs on her arm stood up. "Look at Wu," she said in Jimmy's mind.

He leaned up enough in the back seat to see her warrior face in the rearview mirror. Her eyes were empty. He thought back to the MIB with slit throats in the chopper and goosebumps appeared all over his body. "Wow, you look badass, Wu" he said.

Wu's eyes met his in the mirror and she said in her native language, "Today I am death."

Debbie backed into the driveway of an abandoned house near the corner of Chestnut and 22nd Street, a short distance from Mr. Johnson's residence and the charred remains of Enoch and Wu's house across the street. Everyone but Debbie hopped out of Miss Interceptor. Jimmy removed the license plates with an electric screwdriver. Wu opened the back hatch, took out her bow, quiver of arrows, and tomahawks, then literally seemed to disappear. David E. went around and got in the passenger seat next to Debbie. Debbie rolled down her window and Jim—now wearing a baseball cap—handed her the plates, screwdriver, and two baseball caps, one each for her and David E. He squeezed Debbie's hand. "Love you. Be careful. Take care of my girl," he said to David E.

David E. gave a thumbs-up and Debbie said, "Love you back," as Jimmy turned and walked toward Mr. Johnson's house. It struck him how downtown, the main roads were always so busy, while the side roads remained relatively empty.

Debbie parked Miss Interceptor in front of the gate to Mr. Johnson's sidewalk. She got out with an ID hanging around her neck. It was just an old college ID taped to some ribbon. With the cap and coveralls, she looked convincing enough. With her peripheral vision, she saw a

Knucklehead two houses down on her right and Jimmy two houses down on her left, casually walking towards her. After she heard David E. exit the truck, she approached the front door. Debbie rang the doorbell twice in quick succession announcing loudly, "Codes and Compliance."

When Mr. Johnson opened the door, he looked a little fuzzy around the edges. It gave her a chill. She had known Mr. Johnson informally for a few years through Bocephus. Would he know her? They stood silently long enough that he asked, "Can I help you?"

So, it was true. Any reservations about aliens still lurking in the remnants of her humanity vanished. This wasn't a man. It was a shape shifting Drachonian. Bizarre. The living room, dining area, and kitchen were one large room. She wondered what to say next when he spied her sidearm. An ultra-high frequency sound was emitted from the base of his throat. An alarm? It made Debbie wince and the neighborhood erupted with dogs barking. She delivered a powerful, adrenaline-fueled front kick that caught him full in the chest. The momentum took her into the house as he flew across the room and slammed into the sheetrock in a puff of dust, wedged between two wall studs. Wrenching free in a panic, he rushed her with his claws extending through scaly fingers. As Debbie drew her pistol, she heard glass break. Before she could fire, the Drachonian Mr. Johnson hit the floor face first. An arrow was buried in the back of his skull. Green blood spurted from around the shaft. Debbie looked up and saw Shewuma disappear from the backyard through the broken kitchen window. Shewuma dropped down from the roof to the front porch and moved up beside Debbie, startling her.

"I smell more," Wu said to Debbie. "Let's clear the house." With a wet popping noise, she pulled the arrow from the Drach's head and wiped the green blood on the fake Mr. Johnson's shirt. They nodded ready. Shewuma went left down the hall toward the bedrooms. Debbie went right to the garage.

Outside, three sentries reacted to Mr. Johnsons high-pitched signal. Two Knuckleheads with bright yellow eyes came running from across the street. Jimmy fired two hollow points from his Glock and they both went down, gaping holes in their heads. The last sentry was using the front of Miss Interceptor as cover and leveled a 9mm at Jimmy. David E. fired both barrels of the shotgun and removed his head.

Debbie stepped onto a garage floor covered with pieces of broken cement, rocks, and dirt. In the center of the room, a five-foot diameter hole went straight down. She peered over the edge and saw two yellow snake eyes staring back. Without hesitation, she put a hollow point squarely between them. She whirled to fire at a figure in the doorway but recognized Shewuma. "Stop sneaking up on me, girl," she said.

Wu was all business and said, "The house is clear. Let's collect the Drach's weapons and go check on the boys."

"Collect their weapons?"

"Debbie. Big rule. Never turn down free ordinance."

Outside the four quickly piled into the truck and Debbie burned rubber. Prying eyes from yards, porches, and windows watched them head for the Hampton City line. Three blocks away, Debbie pulled over. She and Jimmy jumped out and put the license plates back on. Shewuma stashed her weapons in the back under a blanket. Jimmy got back in and helped David E. in his struggle to remove the Macintosh while still sitting in the bucket seat. He noticed Wu staring out at Debbie's still open driver's side door and leaned up to check it out. After freeing her hair from the barrettes and shaking it out, Debbie removed her coveralls, exposing a very short and engagingly flirty black sundress. A hint of cleavage from the scoop neck became more revealing as she leaned over to stuff the coveralls under the driver's seat. Between Jimmy's first aid kit and spare shoes, the coveralls wouldn't fit. With a huff, Debbie simply dropped them on the road and hopped in the driver's seat. Feigning ignorance to Jimmy and Shewuma's ogling stares, she said playfully, "What? It's my getaway outfit. You know in case I get pulled over or something." With both hands, she adjusted her breasts and pulled her dress down.

"Damn, she's hot," Wu said under her breath.

David E. commented, "Debbie, you look very pretty and distracting. Which I assume is what you're going for."

She found his face in the mirror as she drove off and said, "Thank you, David E."

"Those were my only pair of coveralls," Jimmy complained.

Debbie pulled the side of her hem up to her hip and pushed it back quickly. "I'll make it up to you, big boy."

Wu put her open hand behind the seat toward Jimmy and repeated louder, "Damn!"

Jimmy said, "I can live with that." And gave Wu a low five.

Less than fifteen minutes after entering the East End, they were heading back to Williamsburg on I-64, mission accomplished. Jimmy snapped out of Debbie's spell. "Is everybody okay? Anyone hurt?"

They were all good. "That went about as well as it could have," said Debbie.

"Thanks, David E.," said Jim.

"Anytime, Buddy," he replied.

"What? What happened?" Debbie asked.

"He had my back. Took that fucker's head clean off." Jimmy's Deep Creek was coming out.

"Hey," said David E., tapping Debbie's shoulder. "Jimmy popped two of them on a dead run."

"Nice work, guys," said Debbie. "But Wu, Jesus, how many did you get?"

"Four."

Jimmy reached around the seat and squeezed her bicep. "You're bad, Wu. You're a natural born Creeker."

Shewuma put her hand over Jimmy's and said, "I just want to thank you guys. This means a lot to me, and I won't forget it. I know Enoch rests easier now."

"We're always here for you, Honey," said Deb. And then proudly, "That's eight of those bastards we put down."

"What about witnesses?" said David E. "Do we need to create an alibi?"

"Naw," said Wu. "By the time the police get there, they'll find nothing."

David E. remembered. "Oh yeah. The Drach's poison will disintegrate them into dust."

Jimmy asked Wu to put in a Diana Krall CD. Instead, she started to sing his song. "Flying down the highway. Driving it my way." Debbie and Jimmy joined in. "Headlights blazing a trail." They were pumped. It was a good day. It was a win.

Because David E. wanted to learn it, they ended up singing "Firebird from Hell" four times total. Eventually, things calmed down and Diana Krall played and sang them the rest of the way home.

CHAPTER 18

MISTER PORTIS

Mr. Portis locked up his gray Prius in the vast parking lot and started the long walk to the NASA building attached to Langley Air Force Base in Hampton, Virginia. Portis headed through the front doors of the main building holding up his NASA II ID card. The security guard acknowledged him with a nod but didn't speak. Portis had been the director of NASA II for many years. It was a peripheral agency and was considered irrelevant by all except for the highest-ranking officers on base. He walked with purpose, looking straight ahead and avoiding the pleasantries, greetings, and even eye contact normally common in a workplace. To see Portis was to remember him. His presence was pedestrian, his appearance average. Unforgettable was the raised, jagged scar that started on the right side of his mouth and went around and across his jaw and straight down his neck. Most were happy to avoid him and those who did approach would be summarily dismissed. In the rear of the building right before the emergency fire exit, a lone door had a sign over it reading, "NASA II Do Not Enter." Portis ran his finger around the raised edge of the sign, checking for dust. There was none. Good. Inside the sparse office were three desks to the left. Each had a laptop, a landline phone, and assorted office supplies. The middle desk belonged to Portis. The other two belonged to his only employees—two assistants he called Will and

Grace. On the far wall were two file cabinets. Looking out of place on the opposite wall was a massive antique barrister bookcase made of mahogany. Portis was partial to mahogany furniture. The bookcase contained twelve volumes of the history of the Midde East, a *USAF Personnel Directory*, and a *Merriam-Webster* dictionary. The rest of the shelves were empty. Portis sat down at his desk and opened the laptop. He saw a small blinking red light on the bottom corner of the screen. His first alert in months. Funny. He didn't feel the alert. He mentally checked the receptor in his neck. Of course. He'd shut it off last night. Being distracted during his leisure time was unacceptable. He had so little fun anymore. Mental note: Have Will pick up more Krud Kutter. Nothing like it for taking out blood stains. He moved over to the bookcase and said softly, "Portis 4271." As if floating, the jumbo barrister bookcase smoothly moved to the left, revealing an oversized freight elevator door. Once inside, he pushed the only button on the panel. Seconds later he was nine stories underground. How many sublevels there were and who used them were very top secret, but the ninth floor was his. Passing through a small office with three waiting room chairs and a closed, locked rolltop desk, he entered a twenty-five by twenty-five-foot conference room. The walls were covered with blank screens that resembled plexiglass. In the center was a boat-shaped conference table made of gray metal with a matte finish. The room looked simple and gave little indication of its capacity to obtain and analyze every available scrap of digital and analog electronics in the world. In stark contrast to the simple table, the boardroom chairs were made of mahogany with tufted Italian leather and brass trim. Portis settled into one of the scrumptious, high-backed leather seats and looked across the table at one of his two assistants, an attractive black woman in her early forties. She wore simple pumps, a conservative navy blue skirt, a crisp white button-up shirt, and her hair was in a tight bun. She sat motionless. Portis watched her for a moment as if waiting. It made her uncomfortable, but she knew better than to speak first.

Finally, he smiled and spoke. "Hello, Grace. Show me what you've got."

"It will just be a minute, Sir." Now she could go to work. Her hands opened over the table and a virtual keyboard appeared. Portis watched her type with incredible speed.

"Typing was the first thing about you that impressed me," he said.

"Thank you, Sir," Grace replied, staying focused.

He kept on. "Also, there was your exceptional IQ. What is it…184?"

"Yes, Sir," she replied.

"And, of course, your perfectly shaped ass." He watched her reaction intently. Grace missed a key, but she kept going. He was obviously in one of his moods.

"Thank you, Sir," she said, hoping to assuage the comment but not encourage him.

It suddenly occurred to him. "Grace, where's Will?" A three-dimensional hologram appeared floating over the table. It showed a street in East End of Newport News jam-packed with police. A group of locals were watching from behind crime scene tape.

"Will is enroute to this crime scene. It's the same address as the failed Sanctum mission earlier this year."

He cut her off. "I recognize it. What happened?"

"Print," said Grace. A slit appeared in the table and spit out four documents. She stood up and walked them around the table to Portis.

"Sit down here beside me, Grace," he said as he read the documents. Grace sat down, preparing for his usual inappropriate looks, comments, and possible groping. But as he read, his face hardened. Portis stood up and said, "How many?"

"At least eight, Sir," Grace said.

"Why?"

"We're not sure. We're studying the situation. Will is on his way and two agents were dispatched to the Archer house. We suspect it's Sanctum-related and they're somehow involved. But so far, it's inconclusive." Portis crumpled the papers and handed them back to her.

"Two misfires with twelve dead Reptilians on the same project is not acceptable, Grace. There's going to be backlash. I swear, I never had these problems when I ran the teams myself. The one fucking Nord mission that I don't lead, and it goes to shit."

Grace started, "There was the one..." But a hard look from Portis stopped her cold.

"I need to see the brass and get in front of this right now. Grace, look at me." Something about direct eye contact with Portis was frightening, but she had no choice. "Tighten it up, Grace. I want to know everything ASAP."

"Yes, Sir," she replied and looked back down.

He entered the elevator but stopped the closing doors. "Grace. Here," he called.

She hurried in. "Sir?"

"How about that other Nord?"

So, he did know what she was just going to say. The last Portis-led mission to dispatch the Nord and acquire his Skull and Cric wasn't a complete failure, but it was also far from successful. "No change in his status, Sir." He let the doors go and Grace breathed a deep sigh of relief.

Portis went back up to his office and made three uncomfortable phone calls to his superiors. He didn't want this news finding its way to Director Lange. In his gut, he knew who was responsible for the massacre. It had to be that Indian bitch. It was time they put her and those new friends of hers on a short leash and finish this job. The sooner they had the Sanctum, the better.

CHAPTER 19

MIB

After Shewuma's Revenge, as the mission came to be known, Miss Interceptor arrived at home to the cacophony of distressed animals coming from inside the house. They had been too long without their humans. So, out in the backyard they went, people and kids. Running, chasing, wrestling. Even David E. threw the frisbee for Molly. It took a half hour of family attention to satisfy them. Later, Debbie called them inside. Animals, Hybrids, and humans. Everyone was filing in when Debbie spotted Wu and Tippycat having a debate by the back privacy fence. She cranked up her hearing until she could clearly make out Wu's voice. "Come on, Tipster. Debbie wants us to go in." Tippy whined annoyingly in response.

"What's up?" Debbie said directly to Wu's mind.

"He wants to hunt," said Wu, knowing Debbie could hear her from across the yard.

"Tippy, come!" Debbie commanded in a booming, forceful tone. Mom was the boss and Tippy responded by racing Shewuma to the deck steps.

In the den, Jimmy sat on the edge of the couch, still playing with Nicky. David E. was kicked back and relaxed in one of the attached side by side recliners. Everyone pretended not to watch Shewuma flop on to the end of the couch and stick her leg over the arm, swinging her foot. Debbie went to the wet bar, saying, "Jim, turn on the CD player. Wu, cover yourself. It's time for a toast."

Jimmy turned on the music and sat down. The next disc loaded and Billy Kilson's drums joined the party. Wu pulled a blanket that had been folded over the back of the couch over her legs. From her collection, Debbie clinked four of her favorite shot glasses down on the coffee table along with a bottle of the coveted Jefferson Reserve bourbon. "Call out if you want it," she said. She held up the first shot glass. "Jack Palance." On the shot glass was a picture of him wearing a cowboy hat, with his sardonic smile.

Shewuma and David E. both said, "Me." Debbie looked from one to the other, waiting. Shewuma gave David E. her pouty face and he said with resignation, "Give it to Wu."

Wu squealed and took it. "You're a true gentleman, David E."

Debbie checked out the next one and just tossed it to Jimmy. "Hey, what was it?" asked Wu like she was missing out.

"Cap," Debbie said.

"Ah, Captain America," David E. said with reverence.

"Nobody else got the chance for Cap," Wu complained.

"You already have one," Debbie countered.

Wu pulled the blanket to the side and changed her sitting to cross legged. "I didn't know we could only have one," she said, bringing back the pouty face.

"Wu, you're being a brat," said Debbie. "Put the blanket back." Then she wiggled the next shot glass at David E. provocatively. "Frank Sinatra anyone?"

"Nice," said David E. and caught Debbie's toss.

"And I take the unicorn," Debbie said. She opened the Jefferson Reserve and went around the room filling the glasses. From the center of the room, she toasted with her shot and said, "To the most badass family since the Bloody Benders."

Before she could drink, Jimmy said, "The who?"

"The Bloody Benders. You know. Owned a store. Killed people and ate them."

"Never heard of them," said Wu. David E. was shaking his head.

"Okay then, to the most badass family since the Richstensteins." She looked around hopefully.

Jimmy shrugged. He didn't know them either. "Naw" said Wu. David E. was still shaking his head.

She tried again. "The Corleone family?"

"Now you're talking," said Jimmy.

"Family. I like that," said Wu.

David E. raised his glass, and they drank.

Debbie went around and filled their glasses again. Jimmy stood up and held his glass high. "To paraphrase Captain America. The courage and initiative of one man," he said as he directed his drink toward Debbie and then Wu, "or woman can turn the tide of any battle."

"Here, here," said David E. Everyone went to their feet and drank.

Then something caught Wu's attention. She put her glass down and said to Debbie, "Do you hear it?"

"I hear something," said Debbie. The dogs began to growl and whine.

"What is it?" said Jimmy.

"A car coming through the woods," said Wu. Grabbing Lightning and her quiver of arrows, she said, "I'm going up on the roof," and she was gone out the back door. Tippy barely made it out before the door shut behind her.

Debbie told the guys, "Somebody's here. Just in case, I'm going on Wu's side and cover ya'll from her front door. Jim, you go answer our front door. David E., you back him up. Kids, come!" she called, but Molly stayed with Jimmy.

"I got him," said David E.

Jimmy checked the clip in his Glock, then pulled the slide and put one in the chamber. David E. pulled the two-shot derringer from his pocket and said, "Ready." Jim nodded just as the doorbell rang. As they approached the front door, David E. spied the twelve-gauge propped in the corner. He pocketed the derringer as backup and broke open the shotgun to make sure it was loaded. He moved through the opening of the foyer into the dining room and out of sight of the front door. Peeking through the window blinds, he said low to Jimmy, "There's two men in black suits."

"Are you shitting me?" said Jimmy. The doorbell rang again. Jimmy took a breath and let it out slowly. With the Glock behind his back, Jimmy opened the door. There they stood. The one on Jimmy's right held the storm door open with his foot. They were identical. Black suits, hats, shoes, and sunglasses. Both were pale and their hands were inside their coats. "What can I do for you fellas?" Jimmy greeted them as cheerfully as he could manage.

"Mr. Archer?" the one on the left asked as they both removed their sunglasses.

"Maybe. Why?"

The one on the right spoke. "We need to speak to you, your wife Deborah, Command Sergeant Major David E. Major, and the woman called White Bird."

"You need a lot of shit that I don't care about, boys." Jimmy's eyes narrowed and he tightened the grip on the hidden pistol.

"It is in your best interest to cooperate with us, Mr. Archer," said the one on the left.

"You don't want any of your family to get hurt or in trouble," the one on the right finished. Up until then, neither man had shown any kind of emotion or even changed their expression. But when Molly's head appeared beside Jimmy emitting a low warning growl through bared teeth, they both tensed and drew back slightly.

"If you're threating me, it's a piss-poor try," said Jim.

Assault pistol grip twelve-gauge in hand, Debbie watched the scene from Wu's peephole at the other end of the long porch. She saw Jimmy shifting his weight to his left foot. Jimmy was about to kick the right MIB in the balls when Debbie's voice in his head stopped him. "Wait, Jim. See what else they say."

"Okay," he said and held back. The MIB thought he was talking to them.

"Good. Then let us in," said the MIB on the left.

They were startled again by a menacing hiss. Cutting their eyes to the right, they saw thirty pounds of Tippycat perched on the porch railing, ears flat and hair bristling. Jimmy held back a smile and said, "There is no way you two are coming in this house."

Right spoke. "We understand you four were in contact with one Enoch Erran."

Left took over. "And that you may be in possession of his Crystal Skull."

They sounded confident, but it was obvious that Molly and Tippy were making them nervous.

Right MIB spoke again. "We intend to come in with or without your cooperation."

"Well," Jim sighed, "I've enjoyed all I can stand of this conversation with you two."

But Debbie held him back again. "The cops are coming, Babe. Stall them as long as you can," she told him silently.

He wasn't happy about it, but he complied. "I'm ordering you two shmucks off this property."

The left MIB went into another round of what they expected to happen or face the consequences. Debbie sent out a message to all three. "Be ready, guys."

Arrow nocked, Shewuma had been squatting on the edge of the roof over the steps the whole time. She heard, then saw the deputy sheriff's car through the woods. There was no siren, but the lights were flashing. Debbie must have called 911. "Interesting choice," Wu thought.

The patrol car broke from the woods and stopped behind the MIB Chevy van. Both MIB simultaneously responded to the vehicle's sliding stop. When they turned back, MIB on the right was looking at Jim's .45 and the left was staring down the barrel of David E.'s twelve-gauge. Wu landed lightly on the steps behind them, arrow drawn.

Debbie came from the other front door, covering them with her shotgun and warning them not to move.

Right met Jimmy's eyes with surprise. "Yeah, dickhead, you were that close," said Jimmy. Right tensed and Jimmy whispered, "Come on. Do it," prompting a smile from Wu.

While his car sat running with the door open, the deputy was warily moving up the sidewalk with his right hand on his sidearm. Between past combat experience and many years on the police force, he knew this was the real deal. "Everybody, slow up," he said calmly. "Let's just take it easy and put down the weapons." No one moved; no one even blinked. "Come on, folks," the deputy urged.

"We're not backing down until Heckle and Jeckle take their hands out of their coats," Jimmy hollered back to the deputy.

The deputy called out, "Okay, you two in the suits. Turn around and show me your hands."

Left and Right looked at each other, nodded, turned toward the cop, and put their hands out, showing they were empty.

"All right, people! Weapons down!" yelled the deputy, motioning with his free hand.

Everyone stopped brandishing except Wu. She backed onto the grass, keeping a bead on Right. She saw black spots on his aura, and it gave her an intensely bad feeling.

"Officer, we work for the government," Left said as they moved down the steps and approached him.

"Whoa, guys," said the deputy, pulling his 9mm. "I want to see some ID." They obliged. He seemed satisfied and holstered his pistol. "I'm Deputy Raines," he said to the four armed civilians. "What's going on?"

"These men are trespassing," said Jimmy. "They threatened my family and wouldn't leave when I ordered them to."

The deputy and the Men in Black talked for a couple of minutes. They talked low, but Debbie and Wu could both hear them.

"Officer, we've been investigating these people for months," said Left as they approached him on the sidewalk. Left and Right were explaining to him that all four were wanted by Homeland Security for alt-right conspiracies, drugs, and gun violations. The deputy argued that even if what they said was true, these people were well within their rights to protect their property with legal weapons since there were no warrants or even probable cause. With no other choice, the MIB reluctantly agreed to leave. They arrogantly drove the black van through the yard around the police car and sped off through the woods. Only then did Shewuma lower her bow. She thought the cop was cute and could smell that he was attracted to her. "Thank you, Deputy Raines," she cooed as she approached him on the sidewalk.

Wu acting especially appreciative in an up-close sort of way didn't escape Debbie's attention. "Not really Wu's style but a nice touch," thought Debbie.

The deputy had seen Shewuma squatting on the roof and then jumping down. He was struck by this captivating creature—so athletic and confident—wielding a bow in a mini dress. She had to be Indian. Not the local Mattaponi or Pamunkey but definitely Native American. It took all his professional will to stay focused on the situation. Tearing his gaze from her, he looked around at the others and said, "I'm going to have to see some identification from everyone." David E. pulled out his wallet while digging for his fake ID. The cop would never know the difference.

Jimmy responded, "I'll get them, Babe," to Debbie as he went in the house. But Debbie barely heard him. She was engrossed in the show playing out on the sidewalk.

Shewuma had gotten excruciatingly close to the cop and said, "I'm afraid my driver's license has expired, Officer."

"Oh, that should be fine, Miss. You seem ..." Studying her face, he lost his train of thought. "May I ask your tribal affiliation?" he managed to say.

Debbie thought Wu was overdoing the flirty act.

Wu replied, "I'm Hopi."

The deputy was oblivious to everything else at this point and said, "Oh, I've heard of the Hopi. You're a long way from home. How are you liking Virginia?"

Shewuma's response was blatantly provocative. "I love it, especially the public servants."

The deputy cleared his throat nervously and pulled a business card from his shirt pocket.

"Here's my card," he said. "Maybe I could show you around sometime?"

Shewuma slid the card into the top of her dress, smiled, and said, "Maybe."

Debbie, Jimmy, and David E. had come up behind Wu on the sidewalk and were holding their IDs.

"Never mind the IDs," said Deputy Raines. "You people just be careful. You can't go around pulling guns on Federal agents." He began to back up, not really wanting to leave. "So, you call me if those guys come back." He looked directly at Wu and said, "I mean it. Call me." He turned and practically pranced back to the squad car while talking into the radio on his shoulder. Just before getting into the car, he turned suddenly and yelled, "I didn't get your name."

"Shewuma." she called back.

He repeated it slowly as if tasting it. "She wu ma." Then he got in his car, turned it around, and left, waving to her several times in the process. Shewuma turned and saw everyone's fascination with what had just transpired.

"Women," said David E. as he headed back inside.

"Boy, Wu, you clobbered him," said Jimmy.

"Clobbered him?" questioned Wu.

"It's Deep Creek nomenclature," said Debbie. "It means he fell for you all at once. You played him great."

Wu looked at her questioningly. "I didn't play him," she said.

"Yeah, you know. Worked him," Debbie responded.

"No. I liked him," said Wu.

Without wanting to, Debbie suddenly felt awkward and a little put off. "Well in that case, it was quite a spectacle."

"What do you mean?' said Wu. "Are you jealous?"

Debbie got defensive and said, "Of course not. Don't be silly."

Wu was miffed. "You shouldn't chastise me for liking somebody. You made it very clear you're not interested."

Sounding huffy, Debbie said, "You're overreacting. I just don't think you should throw yourself at men you don't know."

Wu puffed up to respond.

Seeing no upside to the conversation, Jim interrupted. "Hang on a second, Wu. Dibs, how did you call 911? Your phone is recharging in the bathroom."

"I called them with the Cric."

"The Cric is a cell phone?" he asked.

"It does so much. I'm learning as I go," said Debbie.

"Was the Cric a cell phone for Enoch?" he asked Shewuma.

"Yeah, I guess so. Davd E. probably knows more about that than I do."

"We should run this by David E.," said Jimmy.

"How about we do it over food? I'm starving," replied Shewuma.

"That's no surprise," Debbie said curtly. "I'm going to go drink some more bourbon with David E."

With a hard look, Wu started after her but Jimmy intervened once more. "Hey, Wu." He got her attention. "How about I make an early dinner?"

The ploy worked. She stopped and asked, "What are you thinking about making?"

"Something worthy of the High Priest of Miserability. Come on. You can help me. We can snack the whole time."

On the way to the kitchen, Wu said, "Your wife is exhausting."

He laughed and said, "I hear you."

An hour and a half later, they sat down at the kitchen table to a huge pot of chicken and dumplings containing two cut up chickens, a pack of eight more thighs, and twenty steaming homemade dumplings covering the top like a blanket of cotton. The pot was flanked with a bowl of lima beans and ham chunks. On the other side was a pan of bubbling stewed tomatoes straight from the stove. Shewuma wasn't inclined to speak; she just ate. David E. only stopped eating long enough to express his new fealty to Southern cooking. Shewuma was smiling and Debbie had a twinkle back in her eye. Nothing like home cooking to smooth over the bumps. He noticed that Debbie was only eating chicken and offered her some sides.

Debbie said into his mind, "No thanks, Babe. Love you."

"Love you too," he said back.

As dinner began to wind down, Wu brought up something that had been troubling her. "I was always taught that the Drachs worked alone or in tight clans related by blood. Drachs in a clan are almost indistinguishable from each other, but the race itself is quite divergent. Yellow, green, reddish, there's round heads, slim heads, all different body sizes. I can tell you for a fact those East End Drachs were not related."

"Well, they've apparently changed tactics," said Jimmy.

She pressed on. "So after five hundred thousand years of not mixing, they just start working in groups?"

"I see your point," said David E. "Complete flip-flop in methodology and strategy implies a change in leadership." He looked at Debbie.

After some quick research, Debbie said, "Could be, David E. Or maybe they're being paid as mercenaries. The assaults on the Sancti and their keepers over the last hundred years, though, have definitely been well coordinated Reptilian group efforts."

Wu sounded grim. "There are Drachs all over the world above and below ground. If they were to unite, it would be a game changer."

"We just need to stay alert," said Jimmy. "You two are impossible to sneak up on. Plus, we have the alarm and the kids. I think they have the hard job."

"Except they know where we are," said David E.

"Maybe I should beef up the doors and windows some more," Jim said.

Debbie wiped her mouth and put the napkin on her plate. "Jims?"

"Debs," he responded.

"Will you do the dishes? I'm going to practice with that ten-inch thrower."

"Sure, Babe," he replied. "But I would recommend the Cold Steel set. They're more accurate and there's two of them." Wu agreed with him.

Deb said to Wu's mind without eye contact, "I'm sorry about my attitude with you and the deputy earlier." She looked up at Wu's now smiling face. "Would you mind coaching me on the throwing?"

"Sure," said Wu. "I'm just getting started making more arrows. I can work on them while you practice."

"How many are you going to make?"

"As many as I can. You can never have enough arrows."

"Great," said Debbie, and went for the knives.

Jimmy pulled Wu aside. "You two okay about the.... uh, you know?"

"I think so. We talked it out."

"Nice job. She's not big on talking things out."

"No shit," said Wu, bumping his fist. Debbie was back and headed outside.

"Hey, Wu," Jimmy called out. Wu stopped and turned. Debbie kept going. "What you did with the bow and the arrows. Spectacular."

Walking backward and pointing at him, she said. "You too. Spectacular job."

"How's that?"

"I think you know," she said slyly, and headed outside with four barking dogs. Jimmy scratched his head. Wu was hard to figure sometimes. She stuck her head back in the door. "Hey, Jimmy. Do me a favor. David E. is smitten with Eliane Elias. Debbie printed me out some pictures of her and I'm hanging them all over his room. How about putting in as many of her CD's as you have. I want to fuck with him and rock his world a little."

Jimmy laughed. "Consider it rocked."

Wu came back in again. "Hey, Jimmy."

He came to the doorway. "What?"

"About the talking it out. Debbie was specific that there is to be no more sex and no being naked around you guys. But I had an idea that doesn't violate either one."

Jimmy had no clue where she was going. "What's that?"

"We all three watch each other masturbate while I'm wearing my underwear."

Jimmy grinned wide. "That's very creative, Wu. But I don't think it will fly with the boss."

Wu put her hand on her hip, acting sassy. "Are you sure you're just not a little too shy or embarrassed to do it in front of somebody else?"

"Are you kidding? In Deep Creek we were circle jerking by middle school. Hell, by the time I was thirteen, I could change hands and gain a stroke."

Wu started smiling. "Not rude, not crude, just nasty. I would put that on your resume under special skills." She started back out of the door, then turned and said, "I look forward to seeing that someday."

Jimmy headed back to the sink, saying to himself, "I'm sure you do. I just hope Debbie didn't hear you."

The next morning, while sitting around the breakfast table waiting for Jimmy to set up his much-anticipated Mexican breakfast, Debbie asked David E., "Have you ever heard of a Dr. Robert Hazer in regard to rocket propulsion?"

They began to eat. "Can't recall the name," David E. replied. Then to Jimmy on the special breakfast, he said, "This is delicious. Lay it out for me."

Jimmy went over each dish. "We have fried corn tortillas piled with tomatoes, onions, green and red chilies, avocados, and salsa. These are called chilaquiles. The sides are eggs scrambled with cheese, refried beans, cilantro lime rice, and chorizo, a kind of Mexican sausage. You take whatever sides you want and pile them on the chilaquiles."

"These sausages and eggs are tasty," said Debbie.

"It's fucking great," said Wu. "Especially this mole sauce. I haven't eaten real Mexican food this good since Guadalajara in '85."

David E. stopped eating and looked at her. "That was you in Guadalajara in 1985?"

Everyone waited while Shewuma paused an inordinately long time. Finally, she just said, "Yes."

"Nahalia?" asked Debbie.

Wu was a little surprised and answered, "Yes, ma'am. You don't miss much anymore, do you?"

David E. pronounced the word he had just heard very slowly. "What is Nahalia?"

Debbie looked at Wu expectantly. "Go ahead and tell them," said Wu. She seemed disinterested in the conversation as she reached for more rice and molc sauce.

Debbie was eager to share her knowledge. "It's an anagram of several Native American words that mean "to avenge," more or less. It is a very old word. The Hopi histories reference it more than two thousand years ago."

"So, what is it?" Jimmy pressed.

"Well, it's like a hit squad of Kachinas formed to exact revenge or mete out punishment."

"Whoa! Whoa!" interrupted Wu. But she then changed her mind. "Yeah, I guess that's about right."

"Tell us about Guadalajara, Wu," said David E. Jim was also wanting to hear the story. Wu stopped her fork in midbite and sighed. "Pretty simple, really," she said reluctantly. "They killed one of our people, so we took them down." Then she finished her bite.

David E. explained to Jimmy, "The Guadalajara Cartel was probably the biggest, most ruthless Mexican cartel ever. When it collapsed in 1985, the resulting drug wars created most of the cartels that still exist today."

Debbie could sense Shewuma's odd mood. With tedious cross referencing, she dredged up a picture of the man that was tortured and killed by the drug lords. His features were unmistakable. It had to be. David E. and Jimmy were excitedly trying to pull more details from Shewuma when Debbie spoke directly to their minds and stopped them with one sentence. "The man they killed was her brother."

David E. went back to eating. Jimmy simply said, "Sorry, Wu."

Wu wrinkled her brow at the change in atmosphere and then realized what had happened. "You told them," she said to Debbie.

"Yes," said Debbie softly.

Shewuma looked down wistfully at her plate. "We were twins. His name was Ojakakuwong. It means Morning Star. They told me that when he was born, Venus sat on the horizon as bright as the moon. When I came out of my mother forty minutes later, a dove flew in the window, and they named me White Bird. No one could tell us apart until we were three years old. I called him Ojey, and he called me WuWu." Debbie reached for her hand and squeezed it. She looked at Debbie with a sad smile and said something to her in Hopi. Everyone went silent.

Sensing the need to change the subject, Jimmy asked Debbie, "So what's with this Hazer guy you talked about earlier?"

Their hands separated and Debbie said, "Dr. Robert Hazer. There's engaging news about him. He and his son came out publicly saying that the U.S. government works with aliens and has access to super technology. He swore he could prove it. Then he disappeared."

David E. was very interested. "Where did you get that info?"

"From a newspaper called *The World View*."

David E. relaxed. "Probably a hoax. That paper is a rag."

"That's what I thought at first," said Debbie. "So I researched him. He sold a patent for a record-breaking rocket car that he invented when he was fifteen. He earned his PhD in Electrical Engineering by the age of twenty from MIT. Now MIT claims he never went there. Said he was hired by the Navy to back-engineer alien propulsion systems. The Navy says he's lying, but I found a Navy contractor ID of his that even has his picture on it. He claims they threatened his life, destroyed his reputation, and framed him for tax evasion and running a brothel in Rachel, Nevada."

David E. interrupted her. "Rachel, Nevada? That's where Area 51 is located. If it's true, he's probably dead already."

Jimmy chimed in, "I'd like to pick this guy's brain."

"I feel sorry for him," said Wu. "He has no chance."

Debbie agreed. "Yeah, I feel for him too. And listen, David E. There was also an article about your new superbug. Says China is getting swamped by a killer virus and they're trying to keep it a secret."

"You see? What did I tell you guys?" said David E.

"So suddenly *The World View* is a news source," Jimmy joked.

David E. challenged him. "Come see me later and I'll show you stuff that will give you the heebie jeebies."

"Okay, you're on, Big Guy," Jimmy replied.

Nobody spoke for a while as they went back to eating breakfast.

Eventually Jimmy said, "We all need to up our workouts." He looked around the table.

"Agreed," said Debbie.

"Definitely," said Wu.

"I'll pass," replied David E.

Jimmy looked at Debbie's plate and said "Babe, don't you want some rice or beans?"

"No thanks, Baby. I'm good with this." Jim appeared puzzled.

Wu said, "You haven't noticed, have you?"

"Noticed what?" asked Jim.

"She only eats meat now. It's because she's Erran. They're meat eaters. Humans call it a carnivore diet."

"That's not technically true," said Debbie. "I also eat eggs and seafood and the occasional onion."

"So, you're more of a ketovore," commented David E.

"You've heard of it?" said Debbie.

"Oh yeah. It's very controversial."

Jim knew nothing about any of it. "Why just eat meat?"

Deb explained, "It's the most nutrient dense food on the planet. Unlike plants, meat, eggs, and seafood have no insulin spikes, oxalates, tannins, phytates, lectins, or any of the negatives associated with carbohydrates. And once my sugar addiction left, I found it had all turned unappealing."

"I didn't know," said Jim. "I'll sit down with you and we'll figure out how to plan the meals."

Debbie felt bad. Jimmy didn't just love cooking. He loved cooking for her. He took great pride in learning new recipes and tweaking old ones to surprise her. Then something occurred to him. "Wow, that explains a whole freezer full of steaks at 22nd Street." Wu just winked at him and went for more chilaquiles.

CHAPTER 20

WATCHING AND WAITING

It had been almost three weeks since the visit by the MIB. There had been no return visits, no suspicious characters, no choppers, no incidents of any kind. Even Mr. Rawlings, the real Mr. Rawlings, was back, trudging along in his knee braces and ignoring everyone. Jimmy had gotten into the habit of doing a daily perimeter check with Nicky and Tippycat. He examined the last of the trip strings he'd installed about twenty feet back from the privacy fence. It was Wu's suggestion. They were tied with slip knots, colored green with markers, and high enough to let critters pass under undisturbed. They weren't booby traps, just evidence of anyone messing around behind the house. Between the wires and the hunting skills of the beagle and the Maine coon, if anything or anyone had been lurking about, he would know. Tippy would even climb the tall trees and survey the area, something Wu had apparently taught him. She was uncanny with the animals. He never said it, but he believed she could communicate with Tippy and probably the other kids as well. Jimmy was Deep Creek raised and that meant something. He also had two survivalist courses under his belt. Still, Wu would come up with home defense tricks he'd never heard of. She was the real McCoy. Thinking of her naturally shifted his thinking to Debbie. They seemed okay now, close again, on an even keel. According to both of them, there was no chance of anything sexual ever happening again and Debbie would never lie to him. But still, they had that vibe or something. He noticed Nicky staring at him, the tip of his white tail pointing straight up and quivering. Beagles were bred that way. The breeder had told him it meant they were in hunting mode. The tails allowed the hunter to keep track of the pack as they chased prey through the brush and tall grass, and the incredibly loud baying howl also alerted the hunter and kept the pack on track.

"What do you think, Nick? Are we clear?" Nicky began to wag his tail. "Do you think Debbie and Shewuma were bred for a purpose like you?" Nicky's responsive whine became a gurgle in his throat and a howl burst out. "Good boy," said Jimmy, while rubbing his head. "Let's go in, buddy." Tippy soon fell into step behind Nicky and Jimmy. A thought occurred to him, and he detoured into the shop. Pulling an old wooden box from under the workbench, he wondered if it was still there. The box was basically filled with junk, broken tools, broken knives, spring rods, and a few old gun parts. Most of it was rusty or worthless. He dug through the rejects looking for something specific and he found it. The action components of an old needle gun breech loader. Could be just what he and David E. had been looking for. Also, to his delight, he found an unopened plastic bottle of BBs and put them in his pocket. After removing his soiled hiking boots in the mudroom, he followed the sound of voices to the den. He arrived just in time to see Deborah shoot Captain LaGuerta.

"Jesus, you guys are already into the seventh season?"

"Shhh," said Shewuma.

Debbie held her hand up to him. "Hold on, Babe. It's almost over."

David E. raised his eyebrows and shrugged. The show was called *Dexter*. It was about a serial killer and was Debbie's favorite show of all time. She watched the entire series at least once a year. Now she had David E. and Wu hooked on it. Debbie must have seen the series at least fifteen times. Still, she sat on the edge of the couch engrossed as though it was her first. Jimmy took the opportunity to sneak a peek at Shewuma. She wore a red, single-shouldered dress and was leaning back on the couch dangling her leg over the arm. Her dress had creeped up, exposing her underwear to the world. The episode ended, and Debbie shot Jimmy an admonishing look. She leaned over and pulled Wu's dress down.

"Can I speak now?" Jim asked sarcastically.

"Sure, Babe," said Debbie, "if you can tear yourself away from Wu."

"Wait a minute. I'm not the one showing my drawers," he countered defensively. "Besides, you told me to shut up."

"Sorry," said Wu insincerely, sitting up and adjusting her dress.

Debbie backed off. "I didn't mean to cut you off, but this finale was a big one."

Jimmy shrugged. "The last season is fucked up anyway."

"Stop," interrupted Deb. "Don't spoil it."

He shook his head and turned to David E., holding up the remnants of the antique pistol. "This might work, David E. It's kind of my last idea."

"Well," said David E., rising from the recliner, "let's check it out. Nothing else has worked." David E. followed Jimmy through the kitchen into the dining room.

"Wait, David E.!" yelled Debbie. "Don't you want to see season eight?"

He answered with reluctance. "I don't think so."

"But it's the final season," insisted Debbie.

"Look," explained David E., "it's bad enough that he's a serial killer and always gets away with it. But now he has his cop/sister, whatever they are, killing people too."

"But he only kills bad people," pointed out Shewuma.

"Captain LaGuerta wasn't bad," snapped David E.

"Ah, but Dexter didn't kill her. Deborah did," argued Debbie, with Shewuma nodding her head in agreement.

David E. brushed them off with, "I've had enough, Dicky."

Debbie was impressed and said to Wu, "Did he just quote *Murder by Death*?"

Wu smiled. "I think he did. You're rubbing off on him." She handed Debbie the remote.

"What about you, WuWu?" asked Debbie, putting the remote on the coffee table. She didn't need it to control the TV anymore.

"Hold off for a little bit, Debs," said Shewuma. "I want to see what the boys are doing in there."

"Okay," said Debbie. "I'll watch some Craig Ferguson reruns until you get back."

"Ten-four," said Wu with a salute as she turned and followed the boys.

The huge oak dining room table was covered with a sheet and littered with old gun parts, bullets, some hand tools, and several drawings on notebook paper. Shewuma stood off to the side, watching and listening for several minutes. But she couldn't figure out what was going on. So, she just came out with it. Not wanting to be shooed away, she asked in her girly voice, "Whatcha doing?"

Jimmy turned to her, looking exasperated, and held up David E.'s cane. Wu's presence calmed him and he said, "We're trying to turn David E.'s cane into the ultimate weapon."

David E. was furiously drawing another sketch as he said, "It has a sword, and it has a stun gun. We're trying to make it a gun too." He showed Shewuma his sketch. She took it and took the cane from Jimmy. Jimmy and David E. watched patiently while she examined them both. She crumpled the sketch and tossed it on the table, then handed the cane back to Jimmy.

"You're doing this all wrong," she stated.

David E. raised his eyebrows and said, "Don't sugar coat it, Wu. What do you really think?"

Jimmy crossed his arms defensively. "Suggestions?"

Spinning a dining room chair around and straddling it, she eagerly said, "Yes." Jimmy laughed out loud while both men tried not to look up her dress.

"What's so funny? "she asked.

"You just remind me of my granddaddy. That's how he sits. Go on," he coaxed.

"Okay," she continued, "you guys are trying to build a gun to put in the cane or attach to it that's hidden, right?" Both nodded. "It won't work."

"We know," said Jimmy. "We've been trying to come up with something for days."

"You're overthinking it. Forget pistols and rifles," Wu said. With her hands out, she pulled and released an imaginary rubber band. "Think zip gun." She paused so they could absorb it, then continued. "Cut off the end of the cane and thread it so it can be screwed on and off. Insert whatever you have for a .38 or a .45 caliber barrel, and Dremel out a slot behind it big enough to create a spring-loaded firing pin."

Jimmy's eyes widened as her plan came together in his head. He said to David E., "Of course. Just screw off the end, load the shell, screw it back on."

"Right," said Wu. "And when you want to shoot, pull back the pin and release it. BAM!"

David E. jumped a little.

"Then unscrew it and reload. Relatively quick and easy." She was finished.

David E. began drawing frantically and mumbling, "We need to disguise the firing pin." He looked to Jimmy. "We need to find something to use for the barrel."

"No problem," said Jimmy excitedly.

Shewuma stood and spun the chair around back under the table.

Jimmy grabbed her face with both hands and kissed her full on the mouth. Eye to eye, he said, "Wu, you're fucking brilliant. Come on, David E. To the bat cave."

"Hold on, Batman," Debbie said from the doorway. "I need to talk to Robin for a minute."

"Okay. I'll be in the shop, David E.," Jimmy said and took off with the cane.

Obviously anxious to join Jimmy, David E. said, "What? What?"

"Settle down for a minute, big boy. I just went to change out the six CDs. You know the unit plays them one after another."

"I know. It's a nice system," he said impatiently.

"David E., all six CDs in the player were by Eliane Elias. I didn't even know we had six." He just looked at her blankly as she continued. "That kind of defeats the purpose of having multiple discs, doesn't it?"

"I thought you liked Elaine Elias," replied David E. as he limped away.

"Of course I like her," she said. "But the whole point is to mix it up." He was already gone. She turned to Shewuma and asked, "So what was the whole kissing thing with Jimmy?"

"You heard him," Shewuma said proudly. "I'm fucking brilliant. Kinda hot, huh?"

Debbie said, "Maybe too hot."

Wu wagged her finger playfully at Debbie. "You liked it."

Debbie slapped her finger down. "Stop being bad. Look, if you're going with them, then I'm going to pay some bills."

"Fuck that," said Wu, taking her hand and pulling her along. "Let's go watch Dexter dismember people."

David E. entered the shop and made his way through the maze of appliances, office furniture, filing cabinets, and tools to the work table in back.

Jimmy was hunched over the workbench intently studying something. He heard David E. and said, "Good. You're here. I need you to see this."

David E. took the cane from the table and asked an unexpected question. "Jim, do you like *Dexter*?"

Jimmy paused and thought, then said, "Yeah, I like it, but I wouldn't watch it twice a year under normal conditions. But it's Debbie's favorite show, so till death do us part and all." He sat up and changed gears. "So, look, Wu was right. We can do this no sweat." He gestured to a collection of galvanized pipe pieces, fittings, caps, springs, and a brand-new looking tap and dye set. He handed David E. his cell phone that was set on a video showing how to make zip guns.

David E. said, "This is pretty awesome," and touched play.

Two days had gone by since Wu's idea about the gun and the cane. Jimmy and David E. had worked in the shop on the cane shot—as it had come to be called—nonstop ever since. Now it was ready. Debbie and Shewuma were working out in the gym above them. Jimmy ran upstairs and peeked around the post, excited to tell them the news.

At breakfast, all the girls had talked about was practicing some type of Kachina hocus pocus involving time, so he was surprised to see them sparring heatedly. No, check that. They were fighting and paying no attention to him. They were both so fucking competitive. He watched and waited. As always, Wu's strength and speed were amazing, but Debbie was moving so fast he couldn't believe it. She was out striking Wu a good four to one. Still, he couldn't help but wonder if Wu even felt it. She was like a super Bocephus. Grappling with her was like hitting or wrestling a big rock. His mind shifted from skills to looks. Debbie was barefoot, wearing black gym shorts and a tight T-shirt that read, "Touch me and your first boxing lesson is free." Shewuma wore a gamble print tennis dress covered with berries and vines in pink, light blue, and green. She also wore matching pink New Balance tennis shoes instead of her standard moccasins. Apparently, Debbie and Wu had been doing some online shopping. Both sported long single braids that whipped around with their maneuvers like swinging balls on a flail. It was a rare chance for Jimmy to admire Wu unabated. It was against the wifely rules to check out Wu no matter how much she flaunted it and whether intentional or not. And she flaunted it often. But Debbie's number one rule was no acknowledgement of the night the three of them had. Watching them spar and grapple was incredibly sexy and wrenched that encounter from his memory into his thoughts.

Without meaning to, Jimmy sighed heavily and whispered to himself, "Damn."

At that instant Debbie shot a hard look at him as though she knew what he was thinking. That split-second lack of focus allowed Shewuma to land a roundhouse right to her jaw, a blow that knocked Debbie across the room and into the shelves, scattering DVDs and small hand weights.

She got up off the floor looking at Jimmy and she was pissed. "Goddammit!" she said, checking her jaw tenderly. Scanning the floor, she found a missing molar, courtesy of the punch.

When he realized what had happened, he ran over to her very concerned. "Dibs, are you okay?" She blew off the tooth and pushed it back into the bloody hole in her gum. "Jesus," said Jimmy.

"It's okay, Babe," she said, now calm.

"We need to get you to the dentist," he insisted.

"No," said Debbie. "It's sore but it'll be fine by tomorrow."

"What are you talking about?" said Jim. "Your fucking tooth was knocked out."

"Erran genes," said Wu, smiling. "I told you how they heal. They're really hard to kill."

"Nice punch, WuWu," said Debbie, rolling her eyes.

Shewuma winked at a still troubled Jimmy and said, "Just got lucky."

"Are you sure you're alright, Dibs?" Jimmy asked again.

"Yes, Baby, I'm fine. Honestly. So, what do we owe the visit to?" she said, rubbing her jaw.

Jimmy flailed his arms and laughed. Debbie chuckled along with him. "What's he doing?" asked Wu.

"Private joke," said Debbie. "He's acknowledging my dangling preposition."

Still apprehensive, Jimmy said, "David E. and I finished his cane. He wants you to see its maiden shot."

"We wouldn't miss it for the world," said Debbie.

Still worried about the tooth, Jimmy was reluctant to leave, but Debbie reassured him. "It's okay, Babe. We'll be right there."

"All right. Backyard," he said as he left.

"Got it," said Wu, while checking Debbie's mouth to see the damage.

In the backyard, Jimmy had stacked three bales of hay against the fence and painted a white circle on the middle. Then he and David E. waited for the girls while Jimmy told him about the fight and the tooth. Eventually they came around the shop. Debbie was soaked with sweat and toweling off. Wu looked fresh as usual.

"Show us what you got, boys," yelled Debbie.

Jimmy did a drumroll on the fence while David E. walked about fifteen yards back from the hay target. First, he pulled out the cane sword and brandished it. He sheathed the sword and then held the cane high over his head, releasing sparks and pops from the million-volt stun gun. "And now," he said, "the final piece to the ultimate weapon." With his right hand holding the handle, he pointed the cane at the target, then put his left index finger and thumb around the cane shaft near the end. After flipping up a trip switch, he pulled it back and released it. A .38 caliber hollow point bullet exploded just inside the white circle. The audience of three clapped, yelled, and jumped up and down. They went over to congratulate him and inspect the cane.

Debbie saw the fragments of burnt rubber around the base and said very seriously, "David E., you need to buy a big box of these rubber tips." She didn't understand why everyone laughed. Debbie and Wu took turns loading the cane shot and trying it out. "This is very impressive, guys," said Debbie. "And it looks so easy to clean."

"Jimmy did most of the work," said David E.

"Yeah, but it was Wu's idea," Jimmy said.

It was a sunny but cool fall day, and their spirits were high. Off the cuff, Jimmy said, "Hey, let's go out for lunch."

"Do you think that's safe?" said David E.

Jimmy waved his finger, pointing at the three of them. "I'm with three ultimate weapons. I feel safe."

David E. enjoyed the comment but wasn't deterred. "What if we're being watched? They'll know the house is empty."

"No way," said Jimmy. "I do perimeter checks every day with Nicky and Tippy, just like Wu taught me. There's no one watching this house unless it's from a satellite."

"There could be a hidden camera planted somewhere. Or they could be sitting out by the highway waiting for us to leave. Then come and break in."

Jimmy shook his head. "Not likely. But even then, they would have their work cut out. I've reinforced all the doors and windows. We can put the Sanctum in our safe room. The only way into the house is to completely smash out the glass and frame of a window with a maul. Debbie and the police would know immediately if the alarm went off." Debbie was intrigued by the idea. But she was hesitant as well and said so. Jimmy wouldn't give up. "The kids will be here. You can talk to the Skull remotely. If anyone is messing around the house, you would know, right?"

"Yes, I guess." Debbie was weakening.

"You have a safe room?" asked David E.

"Oh yeah. And it is a babe," answered Jimmy. He pressed on. "We can go to Longhorn Steakhouse. It's barely ten minutes away. We can ask for Hope as our waitress. We haven't seen her in over a year."

"That would be fun," Debbie admitted.

"Why don't you guys go and I'll stay here?" suggested David E.

Shewuma stepped up. "No, we all go. Show me a map of where Longhorn is located. I'll meet you guys there. No one will even know I left the house. And if it's as close as you say, I'll probably get there first. Drive the Muscle. If we're being watched, they'll see that I'm not with you. Debbie, you call Deputy Raines and use my voice. Make up a reason for him to come by and check the property while we're out."

"You can do that, Dibs?" Jimmy was beginning to realize how little he knew about his wife anymore.

Debbie smiled. To the enjoyment of all and sounding exactly like Shewuma, she said, "Deputy Raines, will you please come over and look up my dress?"

David E. clapped his hands together. "Okay, I'm in."

"Let's do it," said Debbie excitedly.

She put up a hologram of the area, highlighting the house and Longhorn four miles away. She turned to Shewuma and said, "Are you sure you'll be safe going there by yourself?"

"You're sweet," said Wu, and grazed Debbie's cheek lightly with the tip of her finger. "I just have to get my tomahawk and buckskin jacket and I'll meet you there."

"I'm buying," proclaimed David E. as they headed for the back deck.

"How are you buying, David E.?" Jimmy asked.

His reply was vague. "I may have a credit card," was all he said, smiling.

Jimmy said to Debbie, "I don't want to know how he got that," and they laughed.

"I need to change clothes," said Debbie.

"Do I?" Jimmy asked her.

"Yes."

"Okay. I'm on it. Hey, Wu," Jim said. But he looked around and she was gone.

As they approached the doors to the Longhorn Steakhouse, David E. was struck by how deceiving appearances could be. The public witnessed four relatively normal people entering the building. An attractive couple casually dressed and an elderly man with a cane escorting an ethnic woman in a buckskin jacket. The public couldn't know that the man was a wrestler from Deep Creek and was armed with an array of knives and pistols. By his side—and also heavily armed—was a mixed martial arts fighter with enhanced senses and lightning reflexes. The gray-haired man in the tan suit was a combat veteran with a cane that was also the ultimate weapon. He escorted a Kachina. A Star Child. One of the world's deadliest individuals. *Things are seldom what they seem.*

"Tommy," Debbie exclaimed as she hugged the thirtyish host at the front desk in his white shirt, black slacks, and vest. He stayed in the hug until Debbie pulled back. Shewuma smelled Tommy's pheromones exploding and his aura lighting up like a Christmas tree. But then, Debbie always had that effect on men. Most women too, truth be told. "Is Hope working?"

"Oh, yes, Miss Debbie. Four?"

"Yes, Tommy. Can we have our favorite booth?"

He led them to a big round booth in the back while he caught Debbie up on his dog Vincent and his new internet girlfriend that lived in Australia.

"This is perfect. Thanks, Tom," said Jimmy.

"Yes, sir, Mr. Jim." They were all four scootched in and comfortable when a fiftyish, plump waitress with short blonde hair approached the table. She saw Jimmy and Debbie, broke into a big smile, and literally ran the rest of the way. Debbie stood up and hugged her with genuine feeling.

"Hope," said Debbie.

"Debbie. I thought I was going to have to come looking for you guys," Hope said. She held Debbie tightly for another moment. She then leaned in toward Jimmy. He went to kiss her on the cheek. Hope moved so the kiss went full on her mouth. Shewuma was surprised when Debbie just laughed.

Debbie made introductions. "Hope, this is David E. and Shewuma."

Hope reached across the table and shook David E.'s hand. "Shewuma," she said. "You're Indian?" Wu nodded. "We're almost related. My husband is a full-blooded Iroquois. How do you do on payments? Joe gets $12,000 a year."

Shewuma hesitated, not sure how to respond.

"Oh, sorry," said Hope. "I get it. Mum's the word. You're very pretty." She turned her attention back to Jimmy and Debbie. The next few minutes were spent talking about drinking, her new trailer, having sex with her husband, and asking Debbie and Jim about their sex lives. Eventually she settled down and took their orders. Jim ordered water and Long Island Iced Teas all around. "Good choice," replied Hope.

"I'll get some extra liquor in them." She winked and went on. "So Jimmy, I'm thinking parmesan crusted chicken, rice, broccoli and a side of barbeque sauce."

"You got it," said Jim.

"His favorite," she said to Shewuma. "And Miss Debbie?"

"I'll have a porterhouse steak, medium rare, mashed potatoes, and some of those roasted carrots. And bring my sides separately. Give the carrots to Jim and the mashed potatoes to Shewuma."

"Okie dokie." Hope scribbled on her pad. "And Mr. David?"

"That sounds great," said David E. "But I'm going with the baby back ribs."

"Oh, those are really good," said Jimmy.

"And your sides?" Hope asked.

David E. had a thought. "Do you have corn on the cob?"

"Yes, sir."

"Bring me two orders. I'll be using my fingers anyway."

"Perfect," said Hope. "And you, Miss White Bird?"

Shewuma was surprised and asked, "How did you know that?"

"I don't know why I said it," said Hope, throwing up her hands. "It just popped into my head." Shewuma looked at Debbie and they laughed. Hope laughed along with them, not really understanding what was so funny. With one last glance at the menu, Shewuma said, "I'll have what Jimmy is having, High priests have to stick together."

"I understand," said Hope, still writing. "Most of my family is very religious." It got Wu laughing again.

"And Hope," Jimmy said, "bring her a bowl of chili."

"Small?"

"No. Large with lots of crackers."

Hope left the table with assurances of drinks, bread, and a free appetizer sampler with ranch dressing and house mustard dip. The food kept coming and it was delicious. By the end of the meal, even Shewuma admitted to being a bit full. Hope had spent most of their eating time sitting next to Debbie and talking to her. When they got up to leave,

Hope gave everyone a hug and made them all promise to come back real soon.

On the drive home, Debbie asked Shewuma and David E. what they thought of Hope.

"She's a trip," said Shewuma. "And she has the serious hots for you and Jimmy."

"Can't really blame her for that," Jimmy joked.

"I think she's quite interesting," noted David E.

"Oh, right," said Wu. "You like her because she's always talking dirty."

"Well, yeah," he agreed.

"Fair enough," said Wu.

Back at the house after feeding and taking out the kids, Jimmy suggested they shoot some pool. Everybody was in.

Debbie asked Shewuma, "Wu, you're not wearing that dress to shoot pool in, are you?"

"Of course I am," replied Shewuma.

Debbie sighed with resignation. "Of course you are."

Jimmy, Debbie, and David E. were watching Wu bend over to line up the first break when David E. asked, "So you guys just decided one day you wanted a pool table instead of a living room?"

"Yep," Jim answered. After several long practice strokes, Shewuma sent the cue ball into the rack with an incredibly loud crack, and balls scattered all over the table. "Good break, Wu," said Jimmy. "But nothing went in. My choice." Wu joined Debbie and David E. and they watched Jimmy sink one, then another, and another.

Debbie said, "You guys want to hear the pool table story? It's going to be awhile before he misses."

"You bet," said David E.

"Sure," said Wu.

"When Jimmy was wrestling his first year in high school, he blew out his knee. According to the story, insurance from both parents paid off and they ended up with an extra thousand dollars. They told Jimmy he could spend it on anything he wanted. A pool table, he told them. They said okay, so he and his dad met four of his dad's Creeker buddies at a pool hall in Buckroe Beach."

"Buckroe?" questioned David E.

"Past downtown Hampton," said Wu. "It doesn't matter. Go on, Debs."

"Well, Jim's dad gave the manager of the pool hall eight hundred and fifty bucks. The manager told them to pick any table on the floor but not the two on the stage. They were extra nice and used for tournaments. Primo tables, four and a half by nine foot, with an oak base, two and a quarter-inch slate and point counters built into the rails. Anyway, the manager had to go somewhere. Jim's dad farted around looking at tables until the manager left. Then they promptly took apart one of the off-limit tournament tables and hauled it to the truck. It took four men just to carry the slate top. And here it is still to this day."

"It's a beauty," said Wu.

"Yeah, it's the only thing he loves as much as me, except maybe his gas stove," Debbie joked.

"And he shoots like a professional," added Wu.

"I noticed that," said David E. "We're beating the crap out of you enhanced Hybrids and I haven't hit a ball yet."

"Oh yeah," said Deb. "Whenever we go to bars with pay tables, he always wins us free beers and pizzas. He has a trophy in the library for winning a tournament at Virginia Tech."

"Oh good," Deb squealed, and chalked her pool cue. It was finally her turn to shoot.

Jimmy had just run the table and won another game of Eight Ball when Debbie called them over. She had set up a little drinking station on a foldout table in the hallway. "Are jump shots legal?" Shewuma asked Debbie. "Because they're certainly not fair."

"Depends on where you play," said Debbie. "But in this house, yeah, they're legal. Wait until you see him do a curve shot."

"No way," said Wu. "A curve shot? That's awesome. Can you teach me to curve it and jump it, Jimbo?"

"Sure. But it takes a lot of practice in short dresses."

"Easy, Creeker," warned Debbie.

"It was a joke," was Jim's defense. "So we're drinking?"

Debbie seemed serious when she said, "If we're going to even have a chance to win a game, I need to get you drunk." In the middle of the table was a big metal bowl full of cold bottles of Millers on ice. On one end, from Debbie's collection were a bottle of Tequila and four shot glasses that looked like billiard balls and a plate of lime wedges and two salt shakers. On the other end were a couple of sixteen-ounce 7-Ups for chasers and a mason jar filled with clear liquid.

His eyes glistening, David E. gushed, "Is that moonshine?" He looked at Jimmy. "If I drink that, my shooting will go downhill very fast."

"Go for it, buddy," said Jim. "You don't shoot that well anyway. Besides, I have it covered."

David E. took a long chug from the jar. Wincing, he took a big hit of 7-Up. "Woo! Ahh. That tastes just like what my father used to hide in the rain barrel when I was a kid."

Debbie and Shewuma coordinated their efforts as they both licked the salt from the back of their hands, hit a shot of Tequila and sucked the lime. Jimmy opened a beer and drank half.

He held the beer up and recited his Miller poem.

"I think that I shall never hear a poem as lovely as a beer. That relaxing drink they have on tap, with golden base and snowy cap. That ice cold brew I drink all day until my memories fade away. Poems are made by fools I fear, but only Miller can make a beer."

Referencing the ride to Covington, Wu said to Debbie, "That's two for me and one thousand and one for you." Debbie winked at her and poured more Tequila. Jimmy still won every game for the rest of the night. But no one seemed to care as much about winning anymore.

Sitting cross legged on the wrestling mat in the gym over the shop, Debbie saw daylight through the blinds. Between no longer sleeping and Shewuma's time-sense training, her circadian rhythms could become confused and disorient her concept of time in certain situations. She thought she'd been meditating for twenty-five minutes. It had actually been four hours. It was 6:30 am and she was naked. Shewuma had told her it was a very natural state for Errans to be nude and as she consolidated her Erran DNA, clothes would become less and less of an issue. Debbie had made light of the statement when Wu first said it. But she turned out to be right as usual. Debbie hurried towards the house, grateful for the yard's privacy. She called to Wu mentally, "Wu, meet me in the den with something to wear." She entered the den and Wu stood holding a pair of pink furry slippers. Debbie couldn't help but laugh. "What is this supposed to be?"

Shewuma placed them on the floor in front of her and said, "You wanted something to wear, right? These are cute." Her eyes moved down and back up Debbie's body once, taking it all in. She pined a sigh. Then in one quick motion, she pulled her yellow mini dress off over her head and flipped it over to Debbie. It came off somehow in spite of the battle belt. They faced each other. Debbie was naked and holding the pink slippers and Wu was wearing only her weapons, panties, and moccasins.

Debbie put the dress in front of her breasts and put up her other hand resistively. "You need to put your dress back on, Wu," she said warily. "I was meditating in the gym. I lost track of time and I forgot I was naked, okay?"

"Okay," said Wu. "But why do I have to get dressed?"

Debbie put the slippers on while saying, "So I can keep you in control. The less clothes you're wearing, the more dangerous you are."

"Thanks for noticing," said Wu, smiling.

Debbie continued, "And what if Jimmy or David E. came in here? They would get the wrong idea."

"Well, I got you on that one," said Wu. "Jimmy went running on Cherwell and said he would be gone an hour. David E. went for doughnuts in the little pickup. The kids are over on my side, so it's just us girls."

"Well then, David E. will be right back."

"No," said Shewuma. "I told you not to give him those Krispy Kremes."

"Jesus Wu," said Debbie, forgetting their present state. "That's in Newport News. That's an hour there and back and he's alone. That's not safe."

"I told him the same thing," defended Wu. "But he's a grown man."

Debbie sent David E. a psychic message, "David E., for God's sake, be careful. Watch your surroundings and call if you need me." And as an afterthought, "Get some chocolate glazed for Jimmy."

Shewuma noted Debbie's pause and said, "Are you lecturing him right now?"

"No, not lecturing," said Debbie. "I'm just worried. When did Jimmy leave?"

Shewuma glanced at the clock over the wet bar. "About ten minutes ago. I was surprised. I always got the impression he hated to run."

"You're right. It's been several years since he's done any serious running. But I've been working on his knee and it's really improved, so he's been wanting to try it out. Have you eaten?"

"Jimmy said he'd make breakfast when he got back." Shewuma couldn't help looking Debbie over again. She was so curvy yet still firm and athletic. Debbie's bare presence forced Wu to push down her rising lustful feelings.

Debbie noticed Wu's nipples beginning to define themselves and remembered where they were. She went into boss mode. "Okay, Wu, I'm going to get dressed and you need to put this back on." She tossed the dress back to her. "And I would appreciate it if this stayed between us."

"Sounds like we're negotiating," said Wu playfully. "I'll make you an offer. I'll put on my dress and won't mention that we hung out in the buff, and you let me watch you get dressed."

Debbie chuckled. "You're not right, Wu."

"No, listen. It doesn't break any of your house rules and I know it'll get you all wound up. Then you can jump Jimmy's bones when he gets back. I'll be able to hear you two and I can knock one out."

Shewuma's complete lack of filters and boundaries never ceased to amaze Debbie. She was stunned by Wu's proposal but also flattered. Against her better judgment, she agreed. She attempted to seem indifferent by just nonchalantly saying, "Okay," and headed down the long hallway to the bedroom.

With a constrained fist pump, Wu followed her, watching her move. "My goodness gracious," said Wu under her breath.

Debbie was acting indifferent, but pulsing layers of red and light pink in her aura gave away her sexual tension. Wu could also smell her excitement and took it in with slow breaths. She began to make drum sounds that accentuated the motion of Debbie's hips. It made Debbie smile.

"You are so bad," she sent straight to Wu's mind and playfully smacked her own ass.

In the walk-in closet, Debbie pulled up her panties and Wu said, "You even make those granny panties look good."

"They're not granny panties," said Debbie, feigning offense. "They're French cut." And she began to wiggle into her fringed cutoff jeans.

Wu said, "Hey, slow down. What's the rush?"

"You're just a big ole flirt," said Debbie as she slipped on her bra.

Wu caught her breath. "Let me hook your bra." Debbie drew back a little. "Come on," Wu said. "No tricks. I promise."

"No," said Deb firmly. "You just want to touch me and see what I'm thinking."

"Feeling, Babe. Not thinking," said Wu. "Whole different thing."

"You said hole," Debbie pointed out and they both laughed. "You haven't put on your dress."

"I will," said Wu, sounding a little bratty.

While Debbie put on her socklettes and high-top Sheins, she told Wu, "Pick me out a T-shirt from the top dresser drawer." Wu picked out a bright yellow tank top that read, "Silence is Golden, but Duct Tape is Silver." Debbie put it on and turned once for Wu's consideration.

"Killer, you look great," said Wu, "except for those tennis shoes."

"I always work out in these unless I'm barefoot," said Deb.

"I was thinking a nice pair of heels."

"That's crazy," Debbie snickered.

Wu tried to sound serious. "Wait. Hear me out. You never know when you'll be dressed up in heels at a nice function and you have to fight. Practice makes perfect."

"Nice try," said Deb as she put on her battle belt with Beretta and knives. "Are you gonna work out with me?"

"Of course," Wu answered. "Spar?"

"Go pour some pineapple juice for you and water for me. I have to pee, and I'll be right behind you," said Deb.

"Hey," Wu started.

But Deb cut her off. "No, you can't watch me pee."

Wu left, mumbling, "It never hurts to ask."

"And put that dress on," Deb called out to her.

Shewuma filled two glasses as ordered and drank most of the pineapple juice. Then she searched the kitchen for something to eat. Debbie entered with an armful of practice weapons. There were bamboo swords, padded staffs, and two battle axes with foam heads. Shewuma was eating a whole dill pickle with one hand and a hardboiled egg with the other. The dress was still slung over her shoulder. Watching Wu gobble the food while barely chewing, Debbie said with amusement, "I take it you're hungry?"

With a mouthful, Wu said, "I don't like to spar on an empty stomach."

Debbie pointed out, "You don't like to do anything on an empty stomach."

"True enough," agreed Wu. "What's all this stuff you've got?"

"We've been working knives for a while. I thought it would be fun to try something different."

Wu pushed the last of the pickle into her mouth and washed it down with the rest of her pineapple juice. She reached for the practice weapons. "Let me have them. I'll be right back. Drink your water."

When Shewuma came back, she finally had her dress on. Debbie caught the two rubber knives that Wu lobbed at her, one in each hand. "I guess you didn't like my idea," said Debbie.

"The knife lessons aren't done yet. Today you're going to work two knives at one time."

Debbie's face lit up. She spun the knives in her hands the way Jimmy had taught her and said, "What's that in your belt?"

"It's my fake knife," said Wu, pulling it out. "We only had the two. So, I made me one from a flip-flop."

"Of course you did," said Debbie. "Let's go do it."

Walking out onto the upper deck into a light fog, Debbie and Shewuma enjoyed the sensation of chilly droplets in the morning air. Debbie watched Wu do an aerial cartwheel to the bottom deck, then another onto the grass. "Show-off," Debbie shouted and vaulted over the top railing to the ground. She took off her battle belt and laid it on the bottom deck. Holding both rubber knives in the forward position, she faced Shewuma in a standard karate fighting stance. "What's next?" asked Debbie. "Are we counting?"

"Not today," said Wu, standing relaxed and holding her flip-flop knife. "No drills. No practice. Today we freestyle it. Come and get me."

Debbie started off tentatively but quickly picked up the pace. It wasn't going well. Wu seemed to anticipate her every strike and often returned with a slap on the arm, leg, or torso, which would cause serious injury in a real fight. Debbie backed off and came in again. Wu was all over her. Debbie was becoming frustrated. She stopped and said, "Wu, I got nothing. What's going on?"

"Debbie, listen. You're overthinking it and that's causing you to telegraph. Stop trying moves we've taught you. Relax. Empty your head and fight me like you normally would. But use the knives as your fists and feet."

"Okay," said Debbie. She took a deep breath, then let it out slowly while clearing her mind and rolling her shoulders. Spinning the left knife into a reverse grip, Debbie assumed a deep crouch kickboxing position. She set her teeth and attacked. It was better, much better. Debbie wasn't getting in, but neither was Wu. Surprisingly, Debbie threw an awkward double knife roundhouse at Wu's face and neck. By Wu's standards it was sloppy. She saw it coming and deflected it easily. What Wu didn't see coming was the follow-up spinning back kick that caught her full in the chest. It drove her several feet into the air and she landed on the ground. Wu rolled back through it. As she rose, she saw one of Debbie's rubber knives spinning toward her chest. Wu snatched it out of the air and pitched it back to Deb. A big grin spread across her face. "That's my girl," she said, and charged.

David E. was next in line at the Krispy Kreme counter. The smells and sight of row after row of doughnuts on the conveyer belt being drenched in icing was almost intoxicating. Even that early, they were very busy. But then they were always very busy. A smiling, freckled, redheaded young woman said to David E., "Hello, sir. Can I help you?"

The name tag on her chest read Assistant Manager Fiona. "Yes, Fiona. I would like one dozen…" He stopped and cocked his head as if listening to something. Debbie was talking directly to his mind. It occurred to him that the distance between them was apparently not a factor in her telepathic communications. Having been in the military remote viewing program for several years, he anticipated that her mental abilities would eventually have no limits. He would have to pursue that with her.

"Sir? One dozen glazed?" Fiona asked.

"Oh, sorry," said David E. "I'd like half glazed and half chocolate glazed."

"Yes, sir. Right away." Fiona went to work loading the floppy white and green box with glistening doughnuts.

He chuckled to himself. Debbie liked to think she was so tough. But she was a softie on the inside. More of a mother hen than a boss. Still, though, it couldn't hurt to check out the perimeter. He looked around. Nope. Nothing unusual. Just normal people buying doughnuts. In the parking lot, a woman was unstrapping her child from a car seat. A chap on a Honda Super Cub was pulling up next to his pickup. A middle-aged man and his three boys hurried to the front door, anticipation written all over them. It made him smile. Dads and doughnuts. There was a classic pair. It brought back his own family memories of Sunday mornings. He would go out early to the Farm Fresh bakery and bring home bear claws for his wife and son. Even after so many years, the loss of them hurt like a fresh wound.

"Anything else, sir?" Fiona was offering his box of one dozen.

He took it, paid, and smiled sadly. "Thank you, Fiona. You have a wonderful place here."

"Oh, that's sweet." she said, followed by, "Next!"

David E. suddenly felt weary and leaned heavily on his cane as he walked to the exit. While opening the glass door, he noticed that the man on the motorcycle was still sitting there with his helmet on. Seemed very odd, maybe suspicious. Probably nothing. But just the same, he released the exit door and went to the men's room. After closing the stall so it looked occupied, he put his doughnuts on the corner of the sink and stood behind the entrance door. After three minutes, he began to think it was an overreaction. Just then, the door swung open and the leather clad biker went straight for the stall, brandishing a 9mm pistol. From behind, David E. pushed his cane against the intruder's neck and unleashed one million volts into his body. The gun clattered across the tile. It took several seconds of continuous juice to drop him to his knees. Even then, the assassin turned his head to reveal yellow snake eyes as talons ripped through the fingertips of his riding gloves. David E. pulled the trigger again and held it down. It took him to all fours. Incredibly, he still wasn't out and the battery was nearly drained. David E. flipped up the zip gun trigger and fired the hollow point into the creature's spine at the base of his neck. The body fell over motionless, but the eyes still watched him with a mixture of fear and hatred. He had to make sure it would dust. The light in the snake eyes went out as David E. pushed his surgical steel sword through the right nostril and deep into its brain. Outside, he could hear voices. "Is everything all right? What's going on in there?"

Remembering to take the doughnuts, he slipped past the door into the hallway of fearful and confused onlookers. "Run!" yelled David E., pushing through the crowd. "He has a gun!" He made his way to the pickup truck and left amid what was now chaos. Driving away, he realized how close he'd come to death. Debbie's warning probably saved his life. In the distance, he heard police sirens. All they would find was the gun and maybe a belt buckle and a zipper. Reaching for his cell phone, he remembered that it was charging on his dresser. "Damn," he said out loud. Worried about the others at home, his foot mashed the gas pedal of the little pickup as far as it would go.

Debbie stepped back from Wu breathing heavily and put both rubber knives in her waistband. "They want to go out," she said.

"I hear them," said Wu.

"I'll be right back," said Debbie. In one bound, she went up the six side steps to the top deck and into the house.

Stomach growling, Shewuma jumped lightly up onto the top deck railing and squatted on her heels, facing the back door. She was so impressed with Debbie. All the knife training, drills, practice, and sparring had come together that morning. Debbie was fighting and throwing in weeks with skill that took most people years to achieve. And not just that. Debbie's speed and reflexes—already exceptional— were improving steadily. Wu was concerned. If she didn't peak soon, Wu wouldn't be able to handle her anymore. That would suck for her, but Debbie would love it. Wu heard a rumble. The kids were coming. Four dogs struggling to get through the doggie door all at once was like Walmart opening on Black Friday. Debbie walked out stroking Tippycat. Tippy saw Shewuma and meowed affectionately.

Shewuma answered, "Yes, Unangwa. We'll hunt in a little while."

Debbie did a quick calculation in her head. "Jimmy should be back in less than fifteen minutes."

"Good," said Wu. "I'm starving."

Tippy jumped down and took off. Debbie asked, "How am I doing this morning, Wu? Impressed you a couple of times, didn't I?"

"You impress me every day, Koonguya. Every single day."

Debbie knew that Koonguya meant lover. It stuck her deeply and she went into an awkward silence.

Shewuma stood up on the railing. "Forget I said that. Come on, let's melee."

Glad for the reprieve, Debbie pulled her two rubber knives and said, "You're on." But she stopped and they both perked up their ears. "You hear it?" asked Debbie.

"Yes. I think it's Deputy Raines car." Wu leapt over Debbie's head and onto the roof.

Debbie ran down the back sidewalk and hurdled the fence gate. Turning the corner on the driveway, something felt wrong. She slowed her approach to the oncoming police car. Deputy Raines was with three other officers. Debbie magnified her sight. They were blurry around the edges. They were Drachs. The car accelerated straight toward her. Never feeling in any danger, Debbie took a high step onto the hood and then jumped over the rest of the car as it sped underneath. The brakes locked and it slid to a stop. Three exited the car pulling pistols, while the car went into reverse.

"LCS," Debbie whispered. The car and the guns were a threat no more. While the car engine turned over and over in vain, the three attackers dropped the useless guns and machetes appeared in their hands. From above, Shewuma ran down the pitched roof, planning her attack on the fake Cops. Two side by side and the third behind them were charging Debbie. Drachs were hard to drop from the side. Shewuma let two throwers fly in rapid succession. The closest Drach took both. One knife behind the ear, the other in the soft spot just below the jaw line.

He fell screaming but was a long way from dead. The one behind him saw his comrade fall and looked up at Shewuma on the roof's edge. Perfect. Her third thrower went deep into his right eye, and he went down. The fourth Drach killer exited the car with a machete and Wu saw that it was Deputy Raines. Her heart fell. To mount an offensive like this meant he was most likely dead. Wu pulled her Arapaho blade and sprung high into the air. The fake Raines saw two cohorts down and the third fighting Debbie. He spun around looking for Shewuma, not knowing he was already dead. Shewuma saw Debbie easily holding off her attacker with clever knife feints and nimble dodges. But as soon as he figured out that the knives weren't real, she was in serious trouble. Wu took the machete from Raines' dead hand and hurled it. Machetes were notoriously bad throwers, but she just needed to get his attention. The machete bit deep into the Drach just above his waist. He cried out, dropped his weapon and in a desperate, pain-filled panic, tried to reach and dislodge the blade in his back. Debbie picked up the machete he'd dropped and swung through his neck, almost but not quite severing his head. With his muscles still receiving electrical impulses, the body kept lurching while green blood gushed out of him. His head flopped around like a balloon on a string in the wind. It was the most bizarre spectacle Debbie had ever seen. She watched him, transfixed, until he ran at her. Then she finished the job and kicked the body to the ground. She was wild eyed and felt supercharged, but she calmed down as she watched Shewuma methodically making sure the others were dead and collecting their weapons. Then an image of her husband in a coffin appeared to her. "Jimmy!" she shrieked. She sent a word to Jimmy's mind: "Danger!" Then she bolted northwest into the woods. Wu dropped the pistols and machetes and followed her.

When Debbie put the word danger in Jimmy's head, he stopped and scanned the road in both directions. It was deserted. Wait. Someone was coming around the turn. Oh, just old Rawlings. But without his knee pads. Jimmy pulled his Glock. It had just cleared the holster when all he saw was blue.

Knowing Jimmy's route and estimated average speed, Debbie could figure about where he would be on the road. A straight shot cutting through the woods would save time getting to him. He would be armed. But unlike she and Shewuma, he wouldn't know if someone was a shifted Drach. She heard Wu behind her and ran faster. After running full out through the biting bushes and branches, Debbie finally saw two figures up ahead on the road. Jimmy lay on his back. Over him kneeled the Rawlings imposter. A black curved claw protruding from the index finger was slicing very deliberately across Jimmy's wrist.

"No!" screamed Debbie as she hurtled past the last of the forest and into the street a few yards away. The Drach showed her his true eyes and smiled. He taunted her by tasting Jimmy's blood on his talon. He saw the Indian coming behind the blonde and slowed his time sense to look them over. His confederates must not have fared well. No matter. He had one more blue light. They were both very attractive humans. Perhaps he wouldn't kill them right away. With a twist of his wrist, he sent the blue light to take them down, but it just fell to the road and rolled. *How?* The blonde was almost on him. The Indian behind her was throwing three knives at him in succession. Even in slow motion, her hands were moving quickly. He realized that he was out of time. Both hands went defensively in front of his face. Each palm took a knife, but the third found its way deep into the base of his throat.

With a jumping sidekick to the chest, Debbie knocked him well clear of Jimmy. She went to her knees and leaned over his quivering body. The cut on his wrist looked like an incision and was bleeding profusely. She pulled off one shoe and sock, then tied the sock tightly around his wrist to stem the bleeding. Pulling up his T-shirt, she put her hands on his chest. His heart was beating very fast, and his temperature of a hundred and five was way too high. Shewuma had finished off the Drach and knelt behind Jimmy, gently placing his head on her thighs. She lightly slapped his face a few times. Beseechingly, she said, "Jimmy. Jimmy." She looked up at Debbie. "The poison has him. Do something."

Debbie said, "I don't know what to do."

Jimmy's face became ashen as the color drained from him. His eyes and nose began to bleed. All his veins swelled out, looking purple and distended. His skin was drying out and cracking as his breathing became shallow and raspy. "Deb, we're losing him," Wu said frantically. Debbie looked at Wu hopelessly. Tears welled in her eyes. Wu reached over and slapped her hard across the face. Debbie drew back and anger flashed. "Snap out of it," bellowed Wu. "You're a healer. Goddammit! Save your husband!"

Acting purely on instinct, Debbie viscously bit the end of her index finger until the blood flowed freely from it. "Hold him, Wu," she said, and Wu pinned his shoulders down. Finding the soft spot between his rib and sternum, Debbie jabbed the bleeding finger through the skin. Jimmy lurched and groaned, but Wu held him fast. Debbie moved her finger slowly inside his chest until she felt his heart. It was weak but still beating. Snipping the heart wall with her fingernail, she pushed the bleeding finger against the slit, forcing her blood into the heart chamber.

"What are you doing?" asked Wu, a little worried that Debbie was just freaking out.

"I'm not sure," said Debbie. "But I think I'm giving him my antibodies and white blood cells." Made sense. Wu bit her lip and prayed.

Jimmys heart stopped beating. Debbie hit his chest with her fist twice and it started back up. She felt the heartbeat strengthening. She didn't know the consequences of puncturing the heart wall, but at least he was still alive.

"Debbie, look," said Wu. "I think he's coming back." The veins receded. Color crept back in his skin. The raspy chortles smoothed into normal breathing.

Debbie pulled out her finger and put pressure on the chest hole. She looked around, concerned. "Wu, this is crazy."

"No, Dibs. You did it."

"No," said Debbie. "Something's not right."

Just then, Jimmy raised up, released a low reverberating growl from his throat and opened his eyes. Both women pulled back several steps.

His eyes were bright yellow with black slits in the center. Debbie was shocked. Wu pulled her knife. Jimmy closed his eyes and fell back. His head made a resounding thump as it hit the blacktop. Wu tentatively stepped up and touched his leg. "It's okay, Dibs. He's out cold." She sheathed the blade and checked the bleeding scrape where his head hit the pavement.

"What was with the knife just then?" Debbie asked.

Wu was still unsettled. "When he woke up just now, he felt like killing something. Debs, I think he's a Hybrid. I think there's alien DNA waking up in him."

Debbie pointed to Wu's hand. "Is that his blood?"

"Yeah."

Debbie licked some from Wu's fingers and pressed it against the roof of her mouth.

"What are you doing?" asked Wu, a little taken aback.

"I'm analyzing his DNA."

"Really? You can do that?"

"Yeah. There's a combination of three DNAs here." She cocked her head some and touched behind her ear. "Two are Drachonian, I think. And one is human."

"Two are Drachonian?" repeated Wu.

She looked Wu in the eye. "Not a Hybrid. A Combrid like you, Wu."

Shaking her head, Wu said, "That would explain a lot."

"Let's get him home," said Debbie.

"I got him," said Wu, and scooped him up.

"I'll get your knives," said Debbie. She also retrieved the Glock. They set off toward home at a fast jog, talking while they ran.

"We have to do something with the police car," said Wu.

"There's a dirt access road a little ways past where we were. It goes miles into the woods."

"I'll take care of it," said Wu. "What if they have GPS?"

"If there is, it's not on. I picked up no signals from them or the car."

Wu was impressed. "You've come a long way with that Cric."

"I'm learning."

"Do you want to keep their weapons?" asked Wu.

"Well, they tie us to the dead guys, so I guess not."

"Okay," Wu said softly, fully intending on keeping them anyway.

"I'm sorry about Deputy Raines, Wu."

"Forget it," said Wu. "We got Jimmy. It's a win. We move on."

Debbie changed the subject and punched her arm. "You really covered my ass back there. I appreciate it."

"Hey," said Wu, "you jumping that car was sweet." And from left field, "I hope David E. is alive."

"He is. I'm sure of it," said Debbie, and they picked up the pace.

Coming up the driveway, they saw the silver pickup in front of the shop and heard David E. rummaging inside. As they neared the garage, Debbie said, "Wu, put Jimmy to bed. I'll be there after I check on David E."

"Ten-four," said Wu. She put Jimmy under one arm and vaulted over the back gate. Tippy appeared at her side as the other kids came running from different parts of the yard.

Debbie yelled David E.'s name and felt pure relief when he answered.

Shewuma squatted—perfectly still—on Debbie's hope chest at the foot of the king-sized bed in the master. He had been out since she put him there hours before. Except for dumping the police car, peeing once, and changing the music on the big TV from Marshall Tucker to Dianne Reeves, she had been faithfully guarding him from her perch all day. With the revelation of his pending Hybrid status that morning, there was no telling what would happen as the multiple DNAs in his body integrated. Reaching under the bed sheet and touching his foot yielded the same results as every other read. Nothing. Empty. She was confident, though. His aura was full of red and yellow and indicated healing. And the intense white revealed transition. All excellent. She was optimistic. Throughout the day, Shewuma had heard Debbie and David E. debating the statistical anomaly of two Hybrids married and both turning within weeks of each other. Shewuma was mildly amused by their discussion. She knew what they had yet to figure out. Enoch, of course. Very few had a real understanding of the sight of gifted Errans. Of the many species that possessed the ability to foresee future events, including humans, Errans were at the apex of prognosticators. Compared to Enoch, even most other Errans were nothing more than amateur magicians. Once, on a very rare occasion of opening up to Shewuma, Enoch explained to her a little of how he derailed the plot by the Anunnaki and the Nephilim to take over Earth. Most seers see the one most probable future. But the future is never set. Seeing all possible outcomes is what set Enoch above the others. All prophets had agreed that the alien coup would happen, and the great flood could not be abated. They also saw victory in the short term. Only Enoch knew that the most powerful of the Nephilim would ultimately turn that victory into their downfall. Victory meant defeat and Enoch needed a counter maneuver. The Nephilim were also gifted prophets, so Enoch would have had to disguise his plan. Hence, it could have taken many years—even centuries—to unfold. Wu now understood that they were simply carrying out Enoch's vision. Yes, all the recent events. The loss of the Sancti, Enoch's death, Wu, Jimmy, Debbie, and David E. coming together. It had Enoch's fingerprints all over it. The light from the setting sun streamed through the bay windows. Wu could hear that the kids outside were restless and hungry. She sniffed the air. Debbie was coming down the hall with food! Yum.

Debbie set a paper plate down on the chest next to Wu. "Two peanut butter and jelly sandwiches with pretzels on them just like you like it."

Just then realizing that she hadn't eaten anything since that morning, Wu said, "Dibs, you're a lifesaver." She took a sandwich and chomped two successive bites while going, "Mmmm."

"Any changes?" asked Debbie.

Her mouth full, Wu said, "No. He's shut down. Healing, processing."

Debbie nodded. "Makes sense. That Drach poison would have taken quite a toll on his organs. And I punched a hole in his heart." She felt his forehead and cheeks. "Eyes still yellow?"

"They were an hour ago."

With two fingers, Debbie pulled up his eyelids, then quickly pulled away. "Wu, they're white now."

Shewuma touched his foot. "He's coming around."

"And?"

Wu shook her head. "I'm getting nothing weird or aggressive."

Debbie breathed a sigh of relief. She had found many cases on record where activating alien DNA distorted a person's reality. Even drove some mad. Shewuma excitedly scooted up beside Jimmy on her knees, sandwich in hand.

He shifted and murmured intelligibly. His eyes opened and he looked at Debbie and Shewuma with a blank expression. Then he smiled as recognition crept into his face. With serene joy, he said softly, "My girls." Raising up on his elbows, he said, "What's going on? I remember I wanted to shoot old man Rawlings and then everything went blue."

"Not sure where to start," said Debbie. She thought for a few seconds. "Watch and I'll show you." A hologram of Debbie's memory from that morning appeared over the bed. In real time, the three watched as Debbie crashed from the woods and everything that happened until they got back to the house.

"Wow," said Jimmy, taking it all in. "That's pretty wild."

Wu asked him, "How's that hole she put in your chest?"

Jimmy felt his chest and said, "It doesn't hurt."

Debbie leaned over to Jimmy's ear and said, "Wu said hole." All three laughed.

Not sounding impressed, Jimmy said, "So, I died and turned into an alien."

"There's a lot more," said Debbie. "David E. took out a Drach assassin at the Krispy Kreme."

"Yeah," continued Wu. "And four Drachs disguised as cops tried to kill me and Debbie."

Debbie took over eagerly. "Jim, you should have seen Wu. She was so badass."

"Yeah, but Debbie," countered Wu. "She jumped over the police car when they tried to run her down."

He looked from one to the other as they excitedly alternated back and forth, telling him the morning's events. When they were talked out, he said, "Quite a day. Sorry I slept through it."

"So, how are you feeling, Babe?" Debbie asked him, stroking his forehead.

"Great," he said earnestly. "I feel great." He inhaled deeply. "And you two both smell wonderful." He looked at the remainder of the sandwich Wu held. "I'm starving too." Wu handed the sandwich to him. While he stuffed it in his mouth, she leaned over and retrieved the other sandwich from the paper plate on the hope chest.

"Jesus, Wu. You're showing your butt," said Debbie. Jimmy reached out to touch the back of her thigh and Debbie leaned over and slapped his hand back.

"No charge," Wu quipped, shaking her ass playfully. She came back up to her knees. After a big bite, she gave the rest of the second sandwich to Jimmy as well.

He attacked it and said with his mouth full, "Damn. This is so good."

"Dibsi," Wu said sharply to get her attention. She motioned down with her eyes and head and Debbie followed her gaze.

"Oh Lord, Jimmy!" Debbie exclaimed. With Debbie flustered and Wu giggling, they watched the sheet rise. Somewhere between a whisper and an order, Debbie said, "Jimmy. You're getting a hard-on. Stop it."

"I can't help it, Debs. Did I tell you how good ya'll smell?"

Debbie stood up. "Okay. We're done for now. Jimmy, go take a shower and then I'll check you out. I mean I'll check you over."

"Yeah, I bet you will," Wu said and laughed.

"Stop, Wu," sniped Deb. "Go on, Jim."

"Okay, Babe," he said happily and jammed the rest of the sandwich into his mouth. Throwing off the sheet, he exposed a raging purple boner. Shamelessly, he sprung out of bed and walked to the shower, his erection bouncing as it led the way.

The girls watched him go and then looked at each other, astonished and a bit flushed. Wu let out a low whistle. "You got a fine piece of man-beef there, Spunky D."

Debbie agreed wistfully. "He truly is."

Wu rolled forward off the bed to her feet. "Maybe I better keep an eye on him a little longer."

Not sure if she was joking, Debbie replied, "Yeah, right. I don't think so. You need to go help David E. make dinner."

"Oh Lord. You let David E. cook by himself?" She took off.

"Dibs," Jimmy yelled from the shower.

"Yes, Babe."

"I forgot to bring a towel."

Debbie wiggled out of her cutoff jeans. "I'll be right there."

Shewuma was putting the meal of hamburger steaks, fried onions, mashed potatoes, peas, and rolls that she and David E. had prepared—mostly her—on the table with a big smile on her face. While they cooked, she had been tactfully ignoring David E.'s commentary on the latest disease update. Her focus had been on listening to Jimmy and Debbie making love in Debbie's bathroom. Even through the muffling effect of the walls and the water running, she knew that Debbie had orgasmed twice and was pretty sure Jimmy was about to pop too. But suddenly something was wrong. It was off. To David E.'s chagrin, Wu inexplicably bolted from the kitchen. Jimmy lay out cold on the tile floor in the bathroom. Debbie was holding his face and calling his name. Shewuma turned off the shower and a distressed Debbie looked up at her. "He was coming and then he just passed out, Wu."

Wu picked him up and put him back in the bed. After about ten minutes of Debbie and Wu checking him in their own different ways, both agreed he was safe and okay. He was just unconscious. Wu convinced Debbie that it was just more adjustment to the transition. Debbie was worried but settled down a bit as Wu explained. "My own transition lasted five days. There's a lot going on inside him on a subconscious level, Debbie. He'll be okay. If something bad was going to happen, it would have happened already. We need to let him work it out." Wu took Debbie's hand and squeezed it.

"All right," Debbie agreed. "We watch over him and let him sleep as long as he needs to."

CHAPTER 21

SURVIVAL MODE

Jimmy woke up and scrambled to the bathroom. Unaware that over two days had gone by since passing out in the shower, he hoped he could make it. After a ridiculously long pee, he looked in the mirror. It was startling to him that his eyes were yellow. He watched fascinated as they slowly faded back to their original hazel color. There was enough beard stubble to prompt a quick shave with the electric razor. Washing his face and hands felt refreshing and he put on his blue flannel robe hanging behind the door. Serious hunger pains gurgled in his stomach. He wondered how long he'd been asleep. Unplugging the charged cell phone, he saw that the time was 8:40 am and put it in his pocket. Out in the hallway he wondered out loud, "Where the hell is everybody?" His grumbling stomach led him to the kitchen, ready to cook. But his heart fell when the refrigerator was basically empty. "Debbie! Shewuma!" he called out. In less than a minute, the kitchen was stormed by both women in workout clothes and animals. As if rehearsed, they all stopped, watching him and waiting. He looked perplexed and said, "I'm starving and there's no food. We need to go to the store." That broke the spell and the girls were on him, hugging him, kissing him, saying his name, full of joy and relief. The kids were jumping too, barking and whining. "I love you guys too, but we need to make a list."

Everyone calmed down and Shewuma suggested, "We have Bisquik. How about some pancakes first and we shop after?"

"I still need eggs to make the pancakes," said Jimmy.

"I have some on my side. I'll be right back. Are eggs good for you, Debbie?"

"Sure. I'll have an omelette."

Wu went for the eggs, with Connor and Petey on her heels, barking. The front door closed and David E. walked in. "Where were you? You were supposed to be watching Jimmy while we worked out," Debbie scolded.

"Sorry," said David E. "I just went out front for a minute to get some fresh air. Jimmy, how are you feeling Buddy?"

"Hungry," Jim answered.

"That's a good sign."

"Okay," said Debbie. "I'm going to change out of these sweats. We can eat. Then we have much to talk about." She took Jimmy by surprise with a long, lingering, open kiss. "I missed you," she said, and left. "Wow," Jim said to a smiling David E. He opened the cabinet over the stove. "Who the hell moved the Bisquik?" Turned out it was on the top shelf next to the sink. Jimmy also pulled down plates, glasses, and a bowl and whisk to make the batter.

David E. leaned against the door jamb watching him. "So, do you feel any different, Jim? You know, with the turning?"

Jimmy looked at him. "Yes and no." He went to turn on the middle grill. It was dirty with remnants of grease and burnt pieces of some unidentifiable meat. "What the fuck? They didn't clean my grill?"

David E. held up his hands defensively. "Wasn't me."

Jimmy went in the cabinet under the microwave and came up with a twenty-four-inch electric griddle. He put it on the end of the island, plugged it in, and set it to three hundred fifty degrees. Then he turned back to David E. and continued talking. "I can tell you that I know I'm stronger. I mean crazy strong. And I could smell you coming in the front door just now. I can hear both Debbie and Wu changing their clothes."

"Fascinating." David E. heard nothing.

Jim searched for words. "But inside, I still feel like me. You know?"

"Are you stronger than Wu now?"

"Oh yeah," said Jim. "But don't tell her I said it."

"No, you're not stronger than me," came Wu's voice from the other side.

Jimmy mouthed to David E., "Yes I am." Then he said in a normal tone, "Where are the eggs?"

"Be right there," her voice called out again.

"See," Jimmy said to David E. "We could be whispering, and we could still hear each other."

David E. headed for the den. "I know. It's actually kind of annoying. There's no privacy in this house. I'm going to put on some CDs."

Jimmy measured the dry batter, milk, and oil into the mixing bowl. Brazilian jazz filled the kitchen. "It's my fault," said Wu, standing in the kitchen doorway. She wore a red and white striped mini dress and her long black hair fell free past her shoulders. She looked hot as usual. Unaccustomed to his new senses, Jimmy found that she smelled intensely arousing. "What's your fault?"

"David E. is completely obsessed with Eliane Elias now, and it's my fault." She playfully bumped David E. with her shoulder as he passed her on his way to his original perch in the kitchen.

Wu traded Jimmy the eggs for the eating paraphernalia and began setting the table. With Debbie busy, she took the opportunity to tease the guys. She could smell that Jimmy was more than a little aroused. With every utensil, plate, or glass she placed, she leaned over enough to show some underwear. Guys were suckers for that sort of thing. Come in a room naked and you get their attention. Show a hint of panties and it drove them crazy.

"You're wearing underwear," Jimmy uttered unintentionally.

"Thanks for noticing," said Wu, leaning over a little more to adjust a napkin. "One of your wife's new orders. Underwear is mandatory." She looked back at him. "Disappointed?"

"You could never disappoint me," he said, even as he realized Debbie might take that comment wrong.

David E. was admiring the show as well. "Hey, Shewuma. You said orders, plural."

"Yep," said Wu. "There are three new rules. Underwear. Always wear your battle belt. That one is more for her. And no more secrets."

Jimmy said, "I don't get that one."

Wu shrugged. "Me either."

Jimmy ladled sizzling pancake batter on the hot grill, one after another. Wu finished up her show by putting butter, jelly, syrup, milk, and OJ in the center of the table. Jimmy said, "Wu, do you want to flip them? They're ready."

"Hell yeah." She hurried over. After flipping them, she had two long rows of perfectly browned, slightly puffy, steaming hotcakes.

Debbie walked in looking foxy in a short green and white plaid skirt with suspenders that went around the outside of her pronounced breasts, black heels, and a yellow T-shirt that read, "He's My Man Bitches" across the front. The guys' appreciation of Wu's flirting instantly turned to awkward silence. Debbie felt it immediately. She had heard everything, of course, and wanted to play with it. "Hey, what's going on? You guys are acting weird." She suppressed her smile.

Pressing the center of the hotcakes for the spring of doneness, Wu said over her shoulder, "The guys are embarrassed because they were looking up my dress."

Debbie's reaction was unexpected. She began moving to the bossa nova with a sultry rumba. She teased Jimmy with a devilish grin, saying, "You got to see her panties, did ya?" When she traced her tongue around her top lip, it was too much for Jimmy. He rushed to her, grabbed both of her ass cheeks, and lifted her up while holding her tight to his body. She looked down at him, laughing and letting her long hair caress his face. Still holding her, Jimmy went straight for the bedroom. "Thanks, Wu. I got it from here," said Debbie and threw Wu a kiss.

Wu pretended to catch it and said to David E., "They are so fucking hot."

"Are we still going to eat those pancakes?" asked David E.

Wu started flipping them into a pile onto a platter. "You bet your ass we are."

It was well after noon when Jimmy and Debbie entered the den and stood behind the couch, barefoot and wearing sweatpants and matching *Deadwood* T-shirts. Shewuma lay curled up at the end of the couch and David E. was kicked back in his favorite recliner. They were watching the movie *Bad Teacher*, and it was at the car wash scene. David E. paused the DVD and said, "Welcome back to the land of the living."

Jimmy started to speak but Wu discourteously nipped it in the bud. "Save it until this scene is over. Hit it, David E." He acquiesced and hit play.

Debbie said to Jimmy's mind, "It's her favorite Cameron scene. Except, of course, the scene of the dueling bikinis with Demi Moore."

Jimmy thought back to the drawer full of Cameron Diaz movies at 22nd Street. "Understood," he said, and they waited.

When Cameron was done soaping and spraying herself, David E. paused the DVD again. Wu did one of her magical moves and came vaulting over the couch. "You both smell fresh and well-scrubbed. Thank God you didn't wash your hair." She put her face into a handful of Debbie's hair and inhaled deeply. "Wow," she said softly. Reaching out with both hands, she touched their forearms and repeated, "Wow," this time softer. David E. turned the movie back on. "David E.," said Wu, "if you keep watching, you're going to have to watch it again later with me."

It annoyed him but he turned it off and reached for the stereo remote while saying, "I'll play Elaine until you're ready. You really have a thing for Cameron Diaz, don't you?"

"Who doesn't?" said Debbie. Wu held up her fist and Debbie bumped it. Then Debbie corrected him on something. "David E., I notice you call her Elaine. In Brazil, they pronounce it El e anna."

"Really?" he said. "El e an a, Eliane. Thanks. I like that. I got it."

"I'm going to make some sandwiches," said Jimmy.

"I'm in," said Wu.

"Great," said Jim. "I'll show you how to make coleslaw."

"Cool," said Wu. "Let's go."

Debbie leaned over and kissed David E.'s forehead. "What's that for?" he asked.

"For putting up with her."

"I love her in spite of her herself," he replied.

"I heard that," came from the kitchen.

Forty minutes later Jimmy and Shewuma brought out four TV trays with their late lunch. There were three trays of grilled ham, cheese, and tomato sandwiches, fresh coleslaw, and hot tea. Debbie's tray had just one big tomahawk steak on a platter. "Is the tea sweet?" asked Debbie. "I don't drink it sweet anymore."

"It's not sweet. But you are," he said.

Wu stood back up. "Anybody want some chips?" Nobody did, so Wu went for a bag of Cheetos for herself.

They ate and watched the rest of the movie in relative silence. After it was over, Debbie turned off the TV and the stereo and stood in the center of the room.

"Boss mode, boss mode," the other three bantered back and forth. Debbie ignored them.

"We agree this situation is far from over."

"Yes, we do," said Wu. "They won't stop until we're dead and they have the Sanctum."

"No, they won't," agreed David E.

"Can you guys think of anyone we can enlist help from?" Debbie asked.

Wu said, "I can get us more Kachinas."

"That's good," said Deb. "But that's firepower. I was talking more about logistical, operational help. Maybe even just advice. You know, a government agency, political official, a friendly alien, or something like that."

David E. spoke. "I think that kind of approach would at worst backfire and at best get someone else in as much trouble as we're in. And don't forget about the black choppers. They fly over three or four times a day. That's definitely a government operation."

"David E. is right. These guys are very well financed and well connected," said Wu.

Debbie looked back at Jim, who was nodding in agreement. "Well, let's go over our options," said Debbie. "The way I see it, we need a plan in case there's an all-out attack." She looked at each one of them.

"Go on," said David E.

"For the time being, if they come."

"When they come," Wu chimed in.

Debbie glanced at her but kept going. "We play to our strengths. Jimmy and I attack, Wu takes the roof, David E. and the kids take the Sanctum to the panic room and protect it."

"Panic room. That's right. You said you have one," said David E.

"Yes," said Jimmy. "We built it ourselves."

"I'll give you a tour later," Debbie assured them and continued with her plan. "If it all goes south and we need to vamoose, we need to be ready for that too."

"Why would we ever leave?" argued David E. "We couldn't do any better than here. It's so defensible. Plus, we're armed to the teeth. We have alarms and the kids."

"No," disagreed Wu. "What if they bomb us? What if cops show up with warrants and they use legal channels? What if they burn the goddamn house down around us?" Wu was visibly shaken. All the memories of the days of rape and torture that she kept buried broke though. She stood and yelled at Davd E., "Or worse, what if they capture us? We should attack or disappear." An accusing finger shaking as she pointed at David E., she said through gritted teeth, "You have no idea what those motherfuckers are capable of."

Then Debbie was beside her, stroking her hair. Wu looked at Debbie, her eyes swimming in pain. Debbie pulled her head into her shoulder. "It's okay, Sweetie. It's okay."

Wu remembered that David E. had lost his wife and son. She swallowed hard and said, "I'm sorry, David E. Got a little unhinged there."

Reeling inside from Wu's onslaught and his own demons, David E. merely said, "Forget it. I understand."

Wu sat down leaning forward, her shoulders slumped. Jimmy rubbed big slow circles on her back to soothe her. She straightened up and patted his knee. "I'm okay now, Jim."

"Yes, you truly are," he said. She gave him a little smile.

Wu suggested her reservation as a sanctuary. "But we could never be anonymous there," pointed out Debbie. "We need someplace where we can drop off the grid. Be invisible. Like David E. was. On the sly, I've been in touch with Jimmy's cousin Corrine and her husband Daniel."

"Oh, how are they?" asked Jimmy. "Except for a quick text I haven't talked to her since the family picnic."

"Hold that thought, Babe," Debbie said. "They have a ranch in Oklahoma. Isolated, remote. Surrounded on three sides by an Indian reservation."

"Which nation?" asked Wu.

"Choctaw."

"They would be our allies," Wu said optimistically.

"All the better," Debbie continued. "I told Corrine that we might be in trouble and need a place to hide for a while. She said we were welcome anytime for as long as we want."

David E. was skeptical. "I've been on the run for a long time. And believe me, a helping hand is a very rare thing. She's probably just being nice or could well change her mind."

"No way," Jimmy cut in. "We grew up together. I would do the same for her in a heartbeat."

Wu added, "You're forgetting about help from Enoch and these two." She pointed at Jim and Deb.

"Point taken," said David E.

"Anyone have another suggestion?" Debbie put it out and waited. "Okay then. If we have to go."

"When," interjected Shewuma.

Debbie nodded. "When we have to go, that's our destination. Jim," she said as she looked straight at him, "You're a Boy Scout, survivalist, and a Creeker. You're in charge of having us ready to leave on a moment's notice." She paused.

Jimmy stood and rubbed his chin. Then he looked around at their expectant faces. "I say two vehicles. The extended van was originally built to be an ambulance. Has a beefed-up suspension and electrical system. And it's a 5.4L V8. But it still looks relatively ordinary. We'll have the Muscle take point. It can outrun trouble and steer things away from the van."

Wu's face lit up. "Like *Smokey and the Bandit*?"

"Exactly," said Jimmy.

"Perfect," said Debbie. She loved it when he focused on a project. "Go on."

He was into it now. "I'll stock both vehicles with weapons, ammo, food, blankets, cash, and tools. Anything we might need. I'll keep them both ready twenty-four seven. We'll all have keys to both, but there'll also be spare keys hidden in the gas tank flap." The other three's faces displayed the magnitude of their situation. "Am I forgetting anything?"

David E. sat up and leaned forward. "We need a faraday box."

"We have one," said Debbie.

"What about license plates?" asked Wu. "They're a dead giveaway."

Jimmy snapped his fingers. "Every license plate that me, Debbie, and her dad ever had is hanging in the shop. I just need to make them look current."

"I can help you with that," said Wu.

"Good," said Debbie. "So, you're all square on what you have to do. Right, Jims?"

"I give it the Deep Creek guarantee," said Jimmy.

Debbie turned her attention to David E. "You and I, David E., are going to come up with a primary and some alternate routes to Corrine's house. We'll also figure out the logistics to disappear and stay invisible after we leave. Your specialty. Wu, figure out what we each need for a personal suitcase. Then make sure everyone has theirs ready to go. If we leave." She held her hand up at Wu. "I know. When we leave. Wu, you make sure the gas and water are turned off and the heat is set for vacation mode. You'll also be in charge of getting the kids ready and in the van."

"Got it," said Wu.

"So, we know where we're at and what we have to do."

"See you later," said Jim. "I'm going to start on the vehicles right now."

Wu called to him as he left, "Let me know when you get to the plates."

"Sure thing, Sweet Meat," he called back.

Debbie sounded annoyed and asked Wu, "When did he start calling you Sweet Meat? That's what I call you."

"He's just kidding around," said Wu.

David E. said, "I'm curious. What is the Deep Creek guarantee?"

Debbie smiled. "The Deep Creek guarantee is, 'If it ain't right, it's wrong.'"

"Well, that's encouraging," said David E.

"Come on," said Wu. "Show us the panic room."

"Can we call it the safe room instead?" David E. asked.

"Sure," said Debbie. "Let's go." She said into Wu's mind, "Men. I guess panic room is not macho enough."

In the master bedroom, between Jimmy's walk-in closet and her own bathroom, Debbie had a three by six-foot, mirror-backed curio cabinet. Flipping a hidden switch turned on inside lights and brought every shelf to life. "You've shown me this before," said Wu. "All your favorite treasures are in here." Wu pointed out some things to David E. "These are Debbie's favorite pictures, the Swarovski Crystals she loves, and her favorite knife ever."

Debbie jumped in. "A limited edition Gil Hibben Dragon Lord knife."

Wu pointed to a doll. "My personal favorite. A Japanese Kabuki dancer."

David E. was a bit puzzled. "This is great, but I thought we came to see the safe room."

"Ah," said Debbie. With two fingers, she pushed the cabinet. On hidden coasters, it rolled easily to the side, exposing a five by two and a half-foot metal door. The door was secured with both a keyed lock and an electronic keypad mounted beside it.

"Wow," said Wu.

"Nice," said David E. "The way it's set up, you don't even notice the missing space."

Debbie soaked up the praise. "Thanks. It needs a key *and* a code to get in."

David E. was impressed. "You and Jimmy built this yourselves?"

"Yep. Here." Debbie handed him the key. "This opens the deadbolt. There's a spare key in Jimmy's shaving kit in his bathroom and another taped to the bottom of the ironing board in the utility room. The keypad has a backup battery as well."

David E. put the key in and turned it. He looked at Debbie. "What's the code?"

"WuWu."

"Yes, Baby."

"No," chuckled Debbie. "The code Is WuWu. I just changed it yesterday."

He entered WuWu on the keypad and heard a click. "Easy to remember."

Debbie pushed the door and reached in to flip on the light. Turning sideways was the easiest way to enter and her companions followed suit.

Debbie started the tour. "The walls and doors are AR-500 tiles mounted on reinforced concrete walls."

"Bulletproof?" asked David E.

"And fireproof and earthquake resistant," finished Debbie. "The floor and ceiling are also both formed, reinforced cement. There's a state of the art air filtering system that's disguised on the outside as a fake gutter. Jimmy's idea, by the way. And there's a backup over and under line that can allow airflow and act as a drain line if needed that goes into the woods. Electrical supply is not one but two separate feeds. One is fed directly by our transformer. And unknown to them, we have a backup fed directly by our neighbor's transformer."

"That is fucking brilliant," said Wu.

David E. nodded and said, "It's a nice size too."

"Eight by five," said Debbie. She started listing all the particulars. "There's a fireproof safe for the Sanctum, cash, and a spare .38 Smith and Wesson, just in case." She showed them where the safe's combination was written on the edge of the door jamb. On the back wall, four twelve-inch-deep shelves were crammed with supplies. Gallons of water, MREs, two sleeping bags, blankets, towels, toilet paper, a large first aid kit, a halo charger, and a crank radio with a built-in light. On the floor were a faraday cage containing batteries of all kinds, two watches, two burner cell phones, and a spare twelve-volt car battery."

"You really do have a faraday box," said David E., and Debbie smiled.

Hanging on the wall were two military grade gas masks with spare filters. In the middle of the room were two collapsible stools on either side of a small table, with a pack of cards and a muti-game set. Parchisi, checkers, chess, Chinese checkers, and more came in one box. Debbie pulled down the sleeping bags to expose a survival knife, a twelve-gauge shotgun, and two 9mm Rugers. Debbie assured them the firearms were loaded.

"This room is absolutely wonderful," said David E.

"I don't know," said Wu. "The food is a little tight."

Debbie smiled at her. "And that is the potty bucket in the corner. The chemical next to it kills the smell. And that's it."

They left the safe room and David E. had a funny look on his face as Debbie closed it. "What? What is it, David E.?" Debbie asked.

"It just occurred to me that the hidden door was exposed the whole time we were in there. Must be some way to hide it from the inside."

"I never thought about that before," said Debbie. "That's an excellent idea. But how?"

Wu had a thought. "Why not move the curio cabinet and cover the door with a physical hologram like Enoch had at 22nd Street? Can you do that, Debs?"

"Yes, I can, Wu. Piece of cake. It's perfect."

"A what?" asked David E.

"It's like a …" Wu started and stopped. She looked at Debbie, not sure how to describe it.

"It's just *that*, David E. A physical manifestation of a holographic picture. Looks and feels like the real thing. Ideal camouflage unless someone tries to move it." Debbie unexpectedly pulled David E. in for a big kiss on the mouth.

"What the fuck was that?" said a stunned Wu.

"I need to get a sample of his DNA so the Sanctum can identify him and allow him access to the physical hologram."

"Gotcha," said Wu. She closed her eyes and puckered up her lips for a kiss from Debbie. When none came, she opened her eyes and said, "What about my access?"

"I already have your DNA, Sweetie."

For a second, Wu was disappointed. Then a mischievous smile appeared. "Yes, you do have a ton of my DNA, don't you?"

"Easy, girl," Debbie said.

David E. realized he wasn't privy to everything happening in the house. "Any other secrets I should know about?" he asked, only partly joking.

Debbie thought a minute, then said, "Come on. There are a couple of things in the shop I should show you."

"I thought you were kidding," Wu said to David E.

He laughed. "So did I."

That night at dinner, Jimmy served a recipe he'd never tried before while they reflected on the day. "How did it go with the vehicles?" Debbie asked.

"Great. They're ready to go anytime. I even changed the oil and air filters."

"Really? That's impressive," said David E.

"Yeah, Wu and I finished the license plates. We have fourteen that look legit."

"Well, as long as nobody runs them," Wu added.

"That too," said Jimmy. "Other than that, I'll just rotate the food out every now and then."

"So, everybody is good," Debbie said.

"What's the signal if something happens?" David E. asked.

"*When* something happens." Wu always threw that in whenever someone said if.

"Red," said Debbie. "I'll send everyone the color and the word red. If one of you needs to sound the alarm, just yell red and I'll hear it. Or ring the train bell on the deck."

Jimmy pointed out a problem. "What about the kids? I thought dogs and cats were color blind."

"Hmm, not completely," said Deb. "But you're right that they can't see red. Wu?"

"Just send them the word. I'll make sure they understand what to do. We'll practice it tomorrow."

"This is fucking delicious," said Wu.

"It really is, Jimmy," said David E., refilling his plate. "Where do you keep coming up with this stuff?"

"For the High Priest," said Jim, "the noodles are covered with butter and garlic, and the chicken recipe I found pretty much by accident on YouTube. Take slabs of cabbage and layer them with sour cream, chicken, more sour cream, tomato, and cheese. They call it Lecker Schnell."

Debbie translated. "That's German. It just means fast and delicious."

"Well, it's delicious for sure," said David E. "And I'm not a big fan of cabbage."

As she scraped off all the layers until there was just chicken and cheese, Debbie said, "This does taste good."

"All things considered," said Shewuma, raising her can of root beer, "there's no place I'd rather be than here with you guys."

"David E. raised his iced tea glass and said, "To family."

"To family," they all chimed in, then toasted.

CHAPTER 22

GRANDDADDY

It was still dark when Jimmy awoke looking directly at Debbie's face. Her long blonde hair fell around his head and her mouth was mere inches away. He thought for a second that he was dreaming. "Sorry to wake you so early, Babe. I need to talk to you," she said.

Jimmy smiled. He could tell she was naked. Actually, she was naked a lot lately. He brought his hands up, cupped her pendulous breasts, and said, "Then throw that leg over me and say something dirty."

She pecked him on the mouth and said, "Not right now. It's about your Granddaddy."

That alarmed Jimmy. He sat up quickly and they almost bumped heads. "Is he okay?"

"Yeah, he's fine. Just let me tell you."

"Okay but let me go pee first." The stream hitting the toilet water seemed to go on forever, so Debbie just started talking. "I've been researching your DNA ever since you turned. Much of the DNA thing still isn't clear, but this is what I know for sure."

Jimmy walked in and stopped at the end of the bed. Debbie lay casually on her back, her feet crossed, and her fingers laced behind her head. Jimmy said boyishly, "You look scrumptious. Should I get dressed?"

She looked his nakedness up and down and said, "Not on my account."

Kicking his leg up, he threw himself onto the bed, landed next to her, and came up on one elbow. "Go on."

"Okay. You have two distinct Reptilian DNAs in you. That's what is commonly called a Combrid." She felt he wasn't paying attention, so she explained further. "A combination of separate Hybrid DNAs. Theoretically, there could be an infinite number in a person."

Jimmy smiled. "I get it."

"Some common nicknames are Blenders, Mergs, and Junkers."

"So, what is the difference between the two DNAs?" he asked. "Are they apples and oranges?"

"No, they're both subspecies of what the Drachs refer to as Clans. You have one DNA on a Y chromosome and the other on an X chromosome. The Y is definitely your father's side. The X is most likely from your mother, but I'm not positive yet. Like I said, I'm still learning to decipher this stuff."

Jim interrupted. "What if I was abducted and the Greys inserted the DNA with anal probes? Would my butt be sore?"

Debbie laughed hard and they both heard Wu laughing outside on the roof. "Shewuma Hopitu, you get in here," Debbie said. Then she composed herself. "Now stop joking and listen. You guys are from Deep Creek. Now in Hybrid lore, Deep Creek in Newport News is pretty famous."

Jim was surprised by the revelation. "No shit?"

There was a knock at the door and Wu said, "It's me."

"Come on in, Sneaky Pete," said Jimmy lightheartedly. "You're like Samwise. Eavesdropping from the roof, were you?"

Wu came in barefoot wearing a white mini and her battle belt, her favorite multi-colored headband securing a dozen or so braids. Each was intertwined with painted wooden beads. Wu leaned her quiver and bow near the door. She could feel them both checking her out. White was definitely her color. Jimmy said, "You look gorgeous."

Debbie agreed with the comment that normally might have bugged her. "Wu, your hair is stellar. And the white dress..." she trailed off.

Wu stopped short, taking in the scene of them both naked on the bed. Jimmy became aware first, realizing he was getting plump. He reached over Debbie and pulled the sheet across them both.

"Thanks a lot," said Wu sarcastically. She hopped on the end of the bed and sat cross legged.

Debbie pulled her eyes away from Wu and picked up the story. "Anyway, there's a clan of Deep Creek Hybrids that go way back. My calculations figure that there is an 87.4 percent chance that your Granddaddy is a Drachonian Hybrid."

"You're kidding!" said Jimmy, now reinvested in the story. "Why do you think that?"

"His health for his age. His strength. His ability to drink ridiculous amounts of alcohol and have no apparent effects. And, of course, you two have the same bloodline. On that side anyway. We need to pursue this and go talk to him."

Wu agreed. "Debbie's right. We need to visit Granddaddy Dick."

"Cap'n Dick," corrected Jim.

"He was military?"

"No," said Debbie, chuckling. "It's not Captain Dick. It's Cap'n Dick. More of a title of respect from the locals."

"Regardless," said Wu, "let's go see him. I heard of the Deep Creek Callans when I was a young girl. But it hadn't occurred to me that it was your Deep Creek," she said, pointing at Jimmy. "Funny that Enoch never mentioned it."

"Wait," said Jimmy. "I thought it was way too dangerous to go out and about."

"It is," said Deb. "But this is important. I think it takes priority."

"I agree with your lovely wife," said Wu.

Jimmy was discreetly trying to hide what had become a full-blown erection. They both smelled so yummy. He took one more lingering look at Wu and said, "Okay then. We'll go today. Uh, Shewuma, could you excuse us please?"

Shewuma rolled backward off the bed to her feet. "What about breakfast?"

To Jimmy's dismay, Debbie got up and went toward her walk-in closet. "I'm hungry. Let's get dressed and eat."

Unaware of the self-satisfied smile on Debbie's face, Jimmy and Wu watched her walk until the door closed behind her. They looked at each other. "Damn!" said Wu.

"Fuckin A," said Jim. "Being around you two is…uh…challenging." As Wu walked out, Jimmy stopped her. "Wu, you messed me up there. Can you help a Creeker out?"

Wu smiled. She blew him a kiss and flipped up the back of her dress as she left. "Hey, Wu." She stopped again. "For the High Priest, in honor of Granddaddy, how about a traditional Deep Creek breakfast?"

"Sounds intriguing."

Forgetting his state of excitement, Jimmy jumped up and went to his dresser. "I'll be there in a few minutes." Wu stayed at the door watching him get dressed and felt desire begin to stir. Debbie suddenly appeared and flipped her hand at Wu, saying, "Shoo!"

Wu wasn't expecting so much work for the Deep Creek breakfast. Fresh fish fried in bacon grease that Jimmy kept in the stainless steel cannister on the counter. Scrapple cooked dark and crispy on one side, fried green tomatoes, fried corn, cheesy grits, biscuits, and brown gravy. Jimmy placed the feast on the table while Shewuma called Debbie and David E. Debbie, Jimmy, and Shewuma were waiting in their seats when David E. trudged in on his cane wearing a red robe. It was rare to see him in anything but his tan suits. He sat down, seeming a little grumpy. "Why are we up so early? It's still dark."

"After breakfast, Jimmy's going to see his granddaddy," said Debbie.

David E. was eyeing the breakfast food suspiciously. "I thought we weren't going out now, just staying home. Hey, what's up? That looks like fish and corn. And I don't know what those are," he said, pointing to the scrapple and the fried tomatoes. "I think I'll just have some biscuits and gravy," he decided.

Shewuma burst out with, "The hell you say. We spent an hour making this and you're going to try every single thing on this table."

David E. handed Wu his plate, saying, "Yes, ma'am. Load it up. I don't understand how you guys don't weigh four hundred pounds."

"It's a Deep Creek breakfast," Wu said out loud to no one in particular and they dug in.

The food was so good no one spoke for a while. Eventually David E. pushed his plate away, finished his milk, and said, "I should never doubt you, Jim. This meal was unbelievable. I've never had anything like it. Which I seem to say about your cooking a lot. So, what's up with your grandfather?"

Jimmy offered more biscuits around the table and Wu took two. "Debbie thinks we should talk to him. She thinks Deep Creek is the secret hub of a Drachonian Hybrid clan."

"Oh Lord," said David E., slapping his forehead. "The Deep Creek Callans?"

"You know them?" asked Jimmy.

"I've heard of them, It just never occurred to me it was your Deep Creek."

Wu pointed at Jimmy with her mouth full and said, "See? I told you."

"So how are we going to work it?" David E. asked Debbie.

Debbie was ready. "I figure you and I will stay here with the kids. Jim, you take Shewuma with you. She would enjoy meeting Granddaddy anyway."

"Sounds good," said Wu.

"But listen, Wu," Debbie continued. "He's…how can I put it?"

"Got no filters," offered Jimmy.

"Yeah," agreed Debbie. "He's wide open. So don't take offense at anything he says."

"I won't," said Wu. "He sounds fun. Does it matter what I wear?"

It seemed like an odd question to Debbie. "What do you mean?"

"Well, I could dress really sexy and light him up."

"Good idea," Jimmy said a little too quickly.

Debbie put the brakes on. "You dress sexy enough as it is. You'll light him up regardless, believe me." Giving Jimmy the skunk eye, she said, "You guys be careful and be alert."

"Yeah, the world needs more lerts," said Jimmy. It was always funny, and everyone laughed. "Okay, we go at 9:00 am. Nanny, my grandmother, will be at church and we should have Granddaddy to ourselves."

"What are you going to say to him?" asked Debbie.

"Nothing," said Jimmy. "I'm going to pull his arm."

Jimmy and Shewuma took the Muscle. As they merged on to I-64, he checked Waze for cops and traffic while Shewuma put on a Boney James CD and turned the volume down. "So, Jim, you never suspected anything unusual about Captain Dick your whole life?"

"Cap'n Dick," he corrected. "Sure. There were always stories about how strong he is. Most people don't even believe them. There are stories like that about other Creekers too. Everybody knows them and everybody thinks they're bullshit or exaggeration. Now they make sense." He set the cruise control on ninety-five and pulled out the radar detector.

"Like what?"

Jimmy smiled and said, "You don't want to get me started."

"Yes, I do. Tell me some stories," Wu insisted and wriggled in her seat to get comfortable.

"Okay. Pappy Sam. His wife shot him off Deep Creek pier for fooling around with another woman. He swam across the creek to get away from her with two bullets in his chest." He clutched her forearm to stress his point. "He was a hundred and three years old, Wu."

His touch revealed his profound reverence for the Deep Creek folklore. "Tell me another one," she said, as if she could've stopped him anyway.

"Uncle Odell. A lumberjack. They say he could chop down a tree with an axe using just one arm faster than a man with a chain saw. And my papa. Granddaddy's father. He could knock out his mule with one punch."

Wu goaded him. "Is that all you got?"

"Hell no. The Nelsons left for a vacation. They forgot something and had to come back an hour later. Abbott Roman was walking down Deep Creek Road carrying their refrigerator on his back. He was robbing them and had already cleaned out most of the house."

Wu ate it up as Jimmy told her yarn after Deep Creek yarn. When he took a pause, she said, "Tell me one about your Granddad."

"Wow. There are so many. Alright, here's a favorite that my Grandma Mal told me. When my dad was a teenager, he was one of the, let's say, leaders of the Deep Creek gang. They got into it with the downtown boys on Mesmer's beach. A couple of guys got cut pretty good. Anyway, the sheriff, two deputies, and four more city cops in a paddy wagon showed up at Granddaddy's house."

"Paddy wagon," Wu cut in. "I haven't heard that for a long time."

Jim smiled. "It's great, isn't it? So, they came to arrest Daddy, Junior, and Charles. For assault or whatever. Granddaddy told the sheriff he could take the others but not J.R."

"That's your dad?"

"Yes. He was big trouble back in the day. Still is for that matter."

"What happened?"

"All the cops ended up in the hospital and Daddy never went to jail. Hey, we're turning on Deep Creek Road and then we're going to Archer Avenue."

"Really? Archer Avenue? Named after your family. That's pretty cool."

They parked in the driveway of a modest, siding covered, three bedroom, one bath rancher. Shewuma was taken with the late model car under the carport. "What year is that?"

"That is Granddaddy's pride and joy. A 1964 Chrysler Newport. It has a pushbutton transmission."

"I've never heard of that."

"Yeah. They were rare, even back then."

"You Creekers and your cars."

"Come on, Wu." Jimmy was excited for her to meet Granddaddy. Going up the front stoop, Jimmy told her some basics. "He never calls anybody by their name. Girls are Becky or Lucy. Guys are John Henry or just Boy.

Before Jimmy could ring the doorbell, the front door opened. Cap'n Dick's massive frame and enormous belly filled the doorway. "Hey, John Henry, I heard you drive up. That Trans Am still purrs like a kitten." Jimmy kissed his stubbly cheek and went for a hug. Cap'n Dick saw Shewuma behind Jimmy and broke into a rare smile. "And who is this pretty little thing?"

Shewuma held out her hand to shake. "Hi, I'm Shewuma."

Cap'n Dick sniffed twice, then took her hand and pulled her into a smothering bear hug. Wu and Jimmy both smelled his eruption of pheromones. And Wu didn't need to be an empath to know that he was pretty excited to meet her. Though enjoying the attention, Wu said, "Easy, big fella."

Cap'n Dick let her go and backed into the house, allowing them to enter. Granddaddy was flushed and said, "Sorry, Becky. I haven't met a woman like you in a long time."

"I'm flattered, Cap'n Dick."

Jimmy was seeing this side of Granddaddy for the first time and was fascinated. "Call me Granddaddy," Cap'n Dick said. "It'll help me keep my head straight around you. You're Indian?"

"Yes, Granddaddy. Hopi."

"Oh. That explains it," he said, apparently understanding something that Jimmy did not. "You kids come on in. Eva's at church, but I can find you something to eat."

"We aren't hungry, Granddaddy," said Jimmy. "We had a big breakfast."

As serious as he could be, Granddaddy said, "What's eating got to do with being hungry, Boy?"

"I could eat," said Wu.

They followed Cap'n Dick into the kitchen. Jimmy couldn't believe that this was his Grandfather watching Shewuma eat a cold chicken leg like nothing else in the world mattered.

"Granddaddy," he said. "Granddaddy!" he said a second time and got his attention. "Let's pull arms."

Cap'n Dick looked surprised, then said, "Hell yeah, Boy. Let's go." Grandaddy sat down at the kitchen table and put his right elbow on the corner, hand open and fingers straight up. Jimmy sat down and matched him. They locked thumbs and then gripped hands. After a ritual of jostling for position, both were ready. "Okay," said Jim. "On three."

"Wait!" said Cap'n Dick. "Let the Kachina count it."

Wu didn't seem surprised that he knew she was a Kachina, but Jimmy was. "How?" he asked.

Granddaddy responded in Creeker fashion, "I don't get much, but I don't miss much either."

"Do you mind, Wu?" Jimmy asked her.

"I would be honored," said Wu. She put both of her hands around the clenched fists and counted down, savoring the sensations of their focus and determination. "Three. Two. One. Go," she said, and released them.

Granddaddy's initial pull got Jimmy's butt off the seat about an inch or so. But the arms were still set and quivering with power. Both men simultaneously adjusted with a Deep Creek trick. A careful turn of the wrist and you were pulling your opponent toward you instead of sideways. Granddaddy made some ground but then Jimmy stopped him cold. They both gritted their teeth, grunted, and began to sweat. After several minutes of no movement, a low growl came from deep in Jimmy's chest and his eyes turned yellow. Cap'n Dick's white knuckles slowly began to lose ground.

"Arrgh!" came from Cap'n Dick as his eyes became lizard-like too. The hollow metal table leg bent and gave way, collapsing the table itself. Both men went to the floor hard. In spite of his girth, Granddaddy was right back on his feet. As Jimmy rose, Granddaddy took Jimmy's head in his hands and said, "I knew it, Jimmy. I knew it. I was never sure about J.R., but you. I'm so proud of you, Boy." Jimmy eyes were tearing up. "Are you crying, Boy?"

"No, sir."

Granddaddy laughed wholeheartedly. "Well, Becky, looks like a tie for now."

"It was epic," said Wu.

"I'll tell ya," said Cap'n Dick. "I was so smitten with you that Jimmy completely got by me. Let's go in the living room and talk."

Wu touched his arm. "Granddaddy, can I have some more chicken?"

"Little girl, you can have anything from me that you want."

"You're a bad man, aren't you?" said Wu as she leaned into the fridge, looking for just the right piece.

They relaxed in the living room as Cap'n Dick told Jimmy the history of Deep Creek, his family, and his clan. When he finished, Jimmy said, "I always knew that you and Papa were special."

"You're special too," he replied. "So, tell me your story."

Jimmy and Wu told Cap'n Dick everything about Enoch, Wu, Bo, the Sanctum, David E., Debbie and Jimmy turning, and the MIB and alien attacks. When they finished, Cap'n Dick said, "Understand something, kids. You're not alone. Ya'll have help if you need it." The men spent the next half hour telling Wu more tales of Deep Creek.

At the front door to leave, Jimmy hugged Granddaddy. "Thanks. I love you."

Granddaddy put a hand on Jimmy's shoulder and touched Wu's cheek. "Are you taking her with you?"

"I have to Granddaddy."

"I understand, Boy. Tell your wife to come see me. It's been too long. I need a Debbie fix."

"Don't we all," said Wu.

Cap'n Dick looked at her and cocked his head with interest. "Something you want to tell me, little girl?"

"No, it just slipped out."

They were silent as they drove home until Wu took Jimmy's hand and asked, "Why did you start crying after you two arm wrestled?"

Looking straight ahead at the highway, he squeezed Wu's hand. "That's the first time he ever called me by my name."

CHAPTER 23

The Show

It was late morning on Halloween day and the air was nippy in the woods out behind the property's privacy fence. Molly, Nicky, and Tippy all seemed particularly unsettled, so Jimmy was very purposely walking an extra wide perimeter. He could hear Debbie and Wu talking on the back deck. "Breathe," Wu was saying. "Slow it down." They were working on Wu's time-sense lessons. Wu had approached Jimmy with it a couple of times, but none of her hocus pocus held any interest for him.

He detected the sound and scent of two critters nearby. Something within fifteen yards—probably in a tree—and something else off to the right. A squirrel and a groundhog were the verdict from his highly cultivated sense of smell. The kids were already reacting. "Leave it," Jim whispered, and they did. It still struck him as odd that from so far away, Debbie and Wu would have heard him speak to the kids, just as he heard their conversation. He stopped and looked down at his hands that were now many times their old strength. He was so different now even though he was still the same inside. Was that how Debbie felt too? He didn't think so. Suddenly Nicky froze, his tail straight up. Molly began growling low and Tippycat was gone. They were onto something that must have gotten by him. From behind, Tippy screeched a sound of alarm, and Jimmy spun around, pulling out his Bowie knife. There, not three feet away, was a creature he'd never seen before. How was it even possible for something to sneak up on them like that? A metallic ticking sound came from within its body. Nicky began to howl. Molly, in attack mode, creeped toward it. Tippycat came out of nowhere and landed on its back. The creature screamed and somehow shook Tippy off, then turned to run. Jimmy threw his knife underhand and it buried in the creature's haunch. Molly and Tippy were back on the attack. By the time Jimmy got close, it was dead. Tippy stood flicking his tail in triumph while Molly straddled the beast, pawing it and looking for signs of life. Debbie and Wu appeared, knives out.

"What happened? asked Deb.

"I don't know what it is," said Jim. "But somehow it crept up on us."

Debbie searched her boundless Cric records. "A Scout," she said.

"Yep, it's a Scout alright," said Wu. "I've never seen one so big."

"Like the thing Tippy killed in Covington?" asked Jim.

"Exactly the same thing," said Wu.

"What? What happened in Covington? You never told me," said Debbie.

Jim said, "There was so much going on that I completely forgot about it until now."

They studied the creature. It was maybe fifty pounds with long legs and matching long arms like a chimpanzee, but the head was more insect-looking with an ant-like face and covered with skin. "The kids killed it before I could get to it," said Jim.

"Good," said Wu. "I'm glad it's dead."

"I'm not sure it's dead," said Debbie.

"How could it have possibly snuck up on us like that?" said Jim.

"That's what they do," said Wu. "They're bred for this. The Greys make them."

"The Greys?" Jim said with concern. Wu just nodded.

Debbie said, "Well, we're definitely still being watched." Debbie told David E. telepathically to meet them in the shop. They took the alien creature with them and placed it on the workbench so they could study it.

David E. got excited when he saw the animal. "A Scout," he said. "I've heard of them, but this is the first one I've actually seen. You mind if I check him out, Debs?" he said.

"Be my guest," said Debbie. "The more you find out, the better."

Jim and Wu looked at each other with the same thought. "Let's go make us some lunch," Jimmy said to Wu.

"I'm in," she replied.

"Can't now," said Deb. "Figure on me not making it till dinner. I want to autopsy this thing."

David E. said, "Yeah, me too."

"Just let us know when you'll be done," said Jimmy, "And I'll make an early supper."

"Okay," said Deb. "We'll see you two later."

Jimmy, Wu, and the kids were on the deck and Wu said, "We're still going to have lunch, right?"

"Of course we are."

"Thank God," said Wu. "You scared me back there."

It was after 4:00 pm when Debbie and David E. came into the house. They were delighted to sit down to a meal of pork chops, brown rice, broccoli, and cornbread. Jimmy passed around a bowl of hot barbecue sauce with honey mixed in, encouraging everyone to put it on everything on the plate. "Did you find out anything about the Scout?" asked Wu.

"Well, we found out that it wasn't quite dead yet. And we know for sure that it was a male."

"You found a winkie?" asked Jimmy, smiling.

"Yes, we did," Debbie answered.

"Was it big and hulking or a tiny little penie?" Jim asked.

"Jim, that's kind of crude for the dinner table, don't you think?" said David E.

In unison, Debbie and Shewuma said, "Not rude, not crude, just nasty." They both laughed. David E. just shook his head and went on eating.

"Anything else of interest?" said Wu.

"Oh, yes. It had no lungs or stomach, like an insect. Also, six legs like an insect. But two of them were up in its body. That was odd. And there was an organ inside its chest that made the occasional clicking sound. I've never seen anything like it. Neither had Enoch."

The way she casually mentioned Enoch struck Jimmy as odd. "Debs, when you brought up Enoch, was that like looking up what Enoch thought in a file? Or remembering like it's your own memory now?" He looked around the table. "Does that make sense?"

"Yes," said David E. "It's a fascinating question. How do Enoch's memories manifest themselves to you?"

Debbie seemed hesitant but said, "I have every memory Enoch ever had since he came to Earth. And if I want to access them, they come to me like I'm actually remembering them myself. That first time in Covington, the flood of his memories almost overwhelmed me. I had to block him out completely for weeks. It's taken a great deal of practice, but I can pull them up now and pretty much keep it straight. But it's complicated and can be painful."

"That explains a lot," said Wu. She sighed heavily and went back to eating.

"So, tell me this, Debbie…"

Debbie stopped David E.'s question. "I would rather not discuss Enoch's memories too much yet, David E. They still confuse me."

"Hmm. I understand…I think. When I was in the remote viewing program at Edgewood Arsenal, we had similar problems with the beginners."

"Wow. That is some wild shit, Debs," said Jimmy. The peculiar expression on her face made him change the subject. "So, what did you do with the Scout?"

"We put it in a trash bag and buried it out behind the shop."

"Jimmy, tell them our idea," said Wu, still seeming a bit down.

Debbie deduced what was causing Wu's despondence. She was wondering if any feelings Debbie ever had for her were real or just reflections of Enoch's emotions. Debbie still wasn't sure herself. But there weren't going to be any discussions of it. She focused on what Jimmy was saying. "So, Wu and I came up with an idea we want to run by you two. We think we should start patrolling the grounds."

"What did you have in mind?" asked David E. "Because I was thinking about that too."

Jimmy laid it out. "There are four of us. A six-hour shift for each person. Each shift would have at least one animal. But David E., you would always have both Tippy and Molly since you don't have the enhanced senses."

"Yeah," said Wu. "Something's coming and we don't want them to take us by surprise again."

"Sounds like a good idea," said Debbie. "We can start tonight at six. Who wants first watch?"

"I'll take it," said David E. "I can go six to twelve. Debbie, you should go overnight. You don't sleep anyway."

Jimmy asked Wu, "What shift do you want?"

"Afternoon. Twelve to six. That okay?"

"Good," said Jim. "I'll take six till noon. I'll make breakfast before and lunch after."

"I have a surprise…martinis," said Wu. The dark mood had vanished. She left and returned with a pitcher of her newly acquired skill from the fridge.

As Wu began filling glasses, David E. waved her off. "Just give me water. My shift starts in less than an hour."

A week of patrolling had gone by with no sightings, flyovers, or incidents of any kind. But they still had to assume they were being watched. It was 6:10 pm when Wu joined the other three at the dinner table. "Oh, man," she said like a child at Christmas, "I could smell this outside. It smells like heaven. Give it to me, Jim." She went straight to work loading her plate.

"For the High Priest. Swiss steak browned and slow cooked in Deep Creek tomato sauce. Au gratin potatoes extra cheesy, of course. And potato bread, a Creeker classic. Taught to me by my grandmother. And a tray of steamed clams for the Dibs."

Knowing he hadn't left the house, she asked, "Where did you get them?"

"Fred across the street. He told me he was going to Newport News today, so I got him to bring me a bushel of clams from Deep Creek. And a peck of oysters. We can have them tomorrow."

With a childlike air, Wu asked if she could have some clams too. "Of course," said Debbie. "What's mine is yours. Except for him." She pointed at Jimmy. The comment prompted laughter around the table.

David E. said, "My compliments to the chef." He gathered his plate and utensils to take to the sink. It was time for his shift.

"Hang on a minute, David E." Debbie had something she felt was important to talk about with them. He sat back down. Since Debbie was in boss mode, everyone just waited. "I think I've had a glimpse of something."

"A vision?" said Wu excitedly. "The sight. You have the sight. I knew it."

Debbie tried to calm her down. "I don't know exactly. But it was so real. Like it was actually happening even though I knew it wasn't, and it doesn't make a lot of sense."

"Maybe you were remote viewing?" suggested David E. "You could have been watching something in real time."

"I don't think so," said Debbie and hesitated.

"So, what was it?" prodded Jim.

They waited. Finally, she came out with it. "It was Secretariat."

"The racehorse?" said Wu.

"You really love horses," said Jimmy.

"Just the horse?" David E. asked.

They suddenly seemed to lose interest. She had to explain it. "No, wait. Secretariat is running for his life through a field of tall grass, and a pack of wolves are chasing him. I know if they catch him," she paused and then said low and quickly, "the world will end."

David E. got up. "I have to start my shift," he said, and left the table.

Debbie looked at Jimmy for some kind of support. "I think it's important," she insisted.

"Well, you really love horses," Jimmy repeated.

She turned to Wu. "Wu, didn't Enoch have, I don't know, visions that were symbolism?"

"No," said Wu flatly. "But maybe you do. Still, it makes no sense to me."

Debbie sighed and turned to Jim. "I'm sure it's important. I just don't know why."

Jim started to speak but Deb cut him off with, "Don't say that I really love horses again." Jimmy stayed silent.

Wu touched Debbie's arm, soaking up her feelings. "I get it, Debs, but it still makes no sense."

"You saw it too?" Jimmy asked her.

"No," said Wu. "But I can tell she saw it. I mean I can feel her commitment to it. Oh, never mind. This is so good." She went back to eating.

Jim started gathering up his and Debbie's dishes. "I'm going to put in Natalie Cole," he said.

They had all but dismissed her vision. "Maybe it was nothing, but it sure seemed important at the time," thought Debbie. She sat doodling a racehorse on her napkin.

At 11:00 pm, Jimmy was in bed, trying to sleep. Debbie lay beside him, obviously bored and humming. He told her something that had been on his mind for a while. "I appreciate that you lay here each night when I go to bed until I fall asleep. But you don't have to."

"I figured it made things seem more normal for you. I just want you to be happy."

He felt Debbie leaving as he drifted off to sleep.

Jimmy sat up in bed alert and wide awake. Why? He looked at the clock. It was 3:00 am. Then he realized that Debbie was mentally calling him to the backyard. He grabbed his .45 Glock and ran outside in his boxer shorts with four startled, barking dogs on his heels. As he came out onto the deck, he saw Debbie in the middle of the yard wearing jeans and a blue blazer. Next to her stood Wu. She was wearing only her moccasins and battle belt. Something was definitely going on. Debbie and Shewuma were looking up at something in the sky. Jimmy took Debbie's hand and he and the dogs looked up as well. After a moment, Jimmy said, "What are we looking at?"

Deb pointed. "There. You see anything?"

Jim took a breath and tried to focus. "Yes," he said hesitantly. "Something. A blur. A shape."

"That's what I see too," said Wu.

The dogs seemed oblivious and went about sniffing the yard. Only Tippy stayed with them, watching the sky. Debbie explained, "It's a big, triangle shaped UFO. Like from the TV shows."

"There are no lights," said Wu. "I can barely make something out."

"I can see it very clearly," said Debbie. They heard David E. coming out of the house.

"If you can see it clearly, why can't we?" asked Wu.

"It's definitely something there, though," said Jimmy.

David E. joined them and saw nothing. He assumed what was going on. "What does it look like?" he asked Debbie.

"It's big, black, and rectangular," said Debbie.

"About a football field long?"

"Yes."

"Can you see it, David E.?" asked Jim.

Daivd E. was amused. "I don't see anything. It's out of my league."

"Wu and I can see something, but it's not clear."

"I'm guessing it's because of Debbie's Cric. She has sonar, radar, and can pick up any wavelength on the UV light spectrum."

"Well, it's been there now for twenty-one minutes," said Debbie. "Wait. It's moving."

Tippy hissed and arched his back. "I think Tippy can see it," said Debbie.

"He senses it," said Wu.

Debbie sighed as it moved out of sight. "Was that random?"

"No way, Debbie" said David E. "They're checking up on us."

"Agreed," said Jim. "That wasn't coincidence."

"We're going to be popular as long as we have the Sanctum," said Wu.

"Is that ship any danger to us?" asked Jim.

David E. shook his head. "I don't know. But I do know it's not alien. It's one of ours."

They stood in silence until it was gone. Then Jimmy said, "Who wants a drink?"

Debbie and Wu were in. David E. laughed and said, "You guys are something. I'm going back to bed."

Debbie said directly to Wu's mind, "You need to go put on some clothes."

Wu had forgotten she was naked. She looked down at herself and laughed. Under the watchful eyes of the others, she ran back to the house.

Sitting in the den drinking PBRs, they listened to David E. snore from down in his bedroom. Shewuma said, "I think we're getting into a rut. All we do is patrol and work out anymore. We should be drinking Golden Monkeys or Miller in the bottle. Who bought the Pabst?"

"You're right," said Debbie. Then she said to Jimmy's mind, "Jimsy, I just had a brilliant idea."

It was 9:30 pm on David E's shift. He was relaxing on the front porch in an Adirondak chair for a moment when he thought he heard something. With the cane in his right hand and the .38 derringer in his left, he slowly worked his way down the steps to the sidewalk. "Molly. Molly girl," he called, knowing the big dog was nearby. His motion turned on the floodlights and there came Molly with something hanging around her neck. David E. slid it up and over her head. It was a card. On the front it read, "To Command Sergeant Major, David E. Major, Retired."

At the same time on Shewuma's side of the house, she was sharpening her Arapaho blade. She paused, feeling, hearing, and smelling an intruder. Then she continued on, realizing it was just Tippy. She greeted him with a Hopi term of endearment. "Hello, Unangwa." She loved her some Tippycat. She noticed he had a card hanging around his neck. On the front it read, "Invitation to Shewuma Hopitu, Kachina." The inside was the same for both David E. and Shewuma:

YOU ARE CORDGIALLY INVITED TO

THE SHOW!

WHEN?

TONIGHT 10:00 pm

WHERE?

BACK YARD LOWER DECK

REFRESHMENTS WILL BE SERVED

FUN FOR ALL, GUARANTEED

BYOW (BRING YOUR OWN WEAPON)

COCKTAIL ATTIRE

As she read it, Wu understood why she'd seen nothing of Jimmy or Debbie all day. At 10:00 pm sharp, Shewuma walked out onto the upper deck, as per the invitation. The backyard was lit up with all the floodlights on the house and shop. On the bottom deck were four lawn chairs in a semicircle, with a plastic end table next to each one. To the left of the deck in the grass was Debbie's fold out table she normally used to trim the dogs. It was covered with a buffet of snacks and alcohol. Jimmy walked toward her from the shop wearing a tuxedo. Instead of a tuxedo shirt, he was wearing a T-shirt under a dinner jacket. Over his shoulder he had strapped his electric/acoustic Epiphone guitar. When he saw Shewuma, he let go with a "Yeow! Wu, you look stellar."

Carrying her bow and quiver, she wore a deep V-neck long white buckskin dress slit up the center past her knee. Around her neck was a silver and turquoise-fringed choker. Her hair was down except for one braid in the front laced with beads and small feathers. Her face was painted blue under the eyes and over the ridge of her nose, with two white hash lines tilting down on each cheek. "I decided to go formal," said Wu, spinning to show off.

"I'm serious. You look sensational." He walked to the deck and held out his hand.

She touched it and said, "Wow! Thanks."

Jimmy was tuning his guitar and Shewuma had just settled into one of the middle lawn chairs when David E. entered through the side gate with Molly. "Welcome, sir. Have a seat," said Jim. "The show is about to start."

David E. sat down next to Wu at the end and said "Wu, you look beautiful. Do you know what's going on?"

"Fun, I think." While Wu and David E. chatted, the dogs found their comfy spots on the deck and Tippy took his usual perch on the upper deck railing. Jimmy was tuning and testing his guitar. "Hey, roadie," Wu addressed him.

"Yes, ma'am."

"I'm assuming that's alcohol over there. Can we have some?"

"Help yourself."

"Do you want something, David E.?'

"Please."

Wu got up and walked over to the table. As she bent over slightly to pour the drinks, Jimmy began zinging some high notes while David E. clapped. "You guys are so juvenile," she said, enjoying the attention. She couldn't help it and wiggled her butt. Once comfortable back in her lawn chair, she asked Jimmy, "So what does your T-shirt say?" He held the guitar up and opened his jacket to show the phrase, "I Heart My Smokin Hot Wife."

"So do I," she said.

Tapping his temple, Jimmy said, "Debbie just told me that she is on her way. And now," Jimmy announced. "The Show!"

He began playing Jimi Hendrix's *Foxy Lady*. Debbie entered the light from the back of the shop walking rhythmically, moving with the music in her stiletto black leather boots. She wore a long white kimono and partially blocked her face with an Asian fan painted with an assortment of spring flowers. When she stepped on the lower deck directly in front of Wu and David E., she closed the fan and tossed it back to Jimmy. She wore bright red lipstick and her eyes stood out with heavy eyeliner, mascara, and sparkling gold eye shadow.

"You look stunning," Wu barely managed to say.

"You ain't seen nothing yet," Debbie said into their minds. Wu slowed her time-sense as Debbie began to move and sway passionately. She swung her head and shoulders, sweeping her long hair back and forth, then pulled off the kimono and threw it aside in one motion. She began to slowly undulate her hips and roll her shoulders. A childhood of tap, jazz, and ballet was about to pay off. Black belts didn't hurt either. Wu and David E. watched her, mesmerized. She wore an American flag themed, tiny one piece. The right side of the front was blue with white stars. The left side was vertical red and white stripes. It was cut perilously high over her lush hips. The sides were cut out. The back stopped dangerously low at the base of her spine, with only two blue spaghetti straps holding everything together. In front, the top was cut low across her generous breasts. Her body so fit and so shapely seemed to pulse with a sensuous muscularity. Her legs were beyond long. They were endless. Her breasts were barely contained and her hips were sumptuously exposed. She looked absolutely ethereal. Debbie's presence was so dazzling it caused Wu to catch her breath. As if far away, Wu heard David E. drop his drink and say, "Holy Mother Mary." Jimmy messed up several chords in a row. Debbie did a back walkover off the deck with one hand and began dancing in the yard. Wu's thoughts came back into focus. She realized Jimmy had moved on to a different song. She touched David E., and it was so intense that she felt a little embarrassed for him.

She wanted to see his reactions but couldn't take her eyes off Debbie. Jimmy played and sang three of his own compositions while Debbie hypnotized them with her movements. The performance was surreally sexy to Wu as she watched in slow motion. Sometimes energetic and athletic. Then sultry and torrid. It dawned on Wu that Debbie was a genuine dancer. Debbie's montage of Brazilian dances. rhumba, samba, and mambo got Wu especially worked up. She even did some disco. And they broke into applause and laughter when she did the robot. The music stopped. Jimmy and Debbie bowed. Shewuma snapped back to her normal reality. "What did you think of that, David E.?" she asked.

He looked at her, speechless.

Debbie opened a case beside the deck and pulled out another guitar. She set it down and reached for her kimono.

"Please don't put the kimono back on," Wu pleaded.

Debbie checked David E. He was nodding his head in agreement but still couldn't talk yet. Jim began chanting, "No kimono. No kimono." Wu and David E. joined in, so Debbie smiled and dropped it. They played the next song together. Debbie played rhythm, while Jimmy sang and played twiddlies and sliding lead. It was called "The Blues in D Minor." He wrote it for Debbie when they were teenagers.

Wu jumped up at the end and said, "Let's do 'Firebird from Hell.'" Debbie put her guitar down and they all sang it while Debbie and Wu danced with each other. Even Petey and Connor joined in, spinning around on their hind legs. After a couple of extra choruses, the music portion of the show was over. Everyone seemed exhausted except Wu, of course.

Jimmy insisted they relax while he made ready for the next part of the show. They were going to watch the Leonid meteor showers. Jimmy made everyone a drink and then headed for the shop. Debbie stood up and put on her kimono.

"No, don't do it," Wu insisted.

"Sorry, Babe." Debbie slipped it on and sat down next to her.

"At least let me take some pictures," Wu said.

"I took some pictures of her earlier," Jim said from the shop.

"He's a good boy," Wu said. She turned to David E. "What did you think of the show?"

To everybody's surprise, he said, "Unfucking believable."

"That's the first time I have ever heard you use the F word," Debbie said.

"Well," said David E., eyeing Wu, "unlike others, I save it for special occasions."

"Why are you looking at me? Do I cuss too much?" Wu asked. That made them laugh.

The lights in the backyard went out. Jimmy returned with his and Debbie's battle belts and a flashlight for David E. After refilling the drinks and giving Wu a bowl full of pretzels, he sat down beside Debbie and sighed with weariness.

"You were great tonight, Jim," David E. said.

"Thanks," said Jim, and set his phone to play *Greatest Hits of Vince Guaraldi.*

Wu jumped up and gave Jim a big kiss on the cheek. "What pictures did you get?" she whispered. "Any dirty ones?"

"You know I can hear you, you nut," Debbie said.

"I'll show them to you tomorrow," said Jim.

"What is this drink?" Wu asked no one in particular.

Deb said, "It's absinthe and white wine. Do you like it?"

"It's potent. Does it have a name?"

"Not that I know of," said Debbie. "It's strong and unpredictable. I say we call it a Shewuma."

The meteors came one at a time and far apart for a while. But by 2:30 am, they were lighting up the sky in bunches. Unfortunately, by then Jim was sound asleep, and David E. was snoring. Debbie looked at both men. "Lightweights," she said to Wu.

"Fuckin A."

Debbie looked at Wu for a moment, then took her dangling hand and sat back. Wu interlaced their fingers. "Anywhere, any time," she said softly, still gazing up at the sky.

Debbie ignored the comment and said absentmindedly, "I think we're going to get David E. to shave his beard."

"Good idea. I'm on it," agreed Wu, and she scooped a handful of pretzels.

CHAPTER 24

THE END AS WE KNOW IT

It was still dark when Debbie and Nicky entered the house and found Shewuma right where she expected—eating. Neither had changed clothes since the show broke up around 3:30 am when they put the men in bed. Debbie had just finished cleaning up from the night's festivities and she had to pee. She passed Wu in the den watching *The Girl With the Dragon Tattoo*. Light was just peeking through the kitchen window. In her stiletto boots and wearing her battle belt over the kimono, Debbie stopped and watched Shewuma eating a bowl of cereal, absorbed with the movie and still in her formal wear. "Jim is right," said Shewuma. "Mixing cereals is much better than eating them by themselves." She wiped some escaping milk from her chin. "Where did he come up with it?"

"You know," said Deb, "most people assume he got it from *Seinfeld*, but he's been doing it since we were kids."

"How long have you two been together anyway?" Wu asked.

"I'm thinking three to five lifetimes so far, plus forty-three years," Debbie said, only partly joking.

Wu indicated the kimono. "You still wearing it?"

"Yes," said Debbie. "I'm going to change now."

"Can I get one more look?" Wu asked, her eyes wide.

363

Debbie sighed—pretending it was inconvenient—and took off the battle belt and kimono and laid them on the chair. None of the glory of the tiny flag outfit had been lost. Playing it up, Debbie put her hand on her jutting out hip.

Wu dropped her spoon into the bowl, causing a splash. She quickly retrieved it and motioned Debbie to turn around. Debbie made a graceful turn, swirling her hair in the process. "You're truly a vision," Wu said, dead serious.

Debbie suddenly felt a little embarrassed. "Enough. Come, Nicky," she said to the beagle, and grabbed her things.

"Wait," said Wu. "Could you take me to Walmart today?"

"I guess so," said Deb. "Why don't you change shifts with Jimmy? We can go this afternoon."

"I already asked him. It's done. I'm going out to patrol as soon as I finish this, and he'll take the afternoon shift."

"Just come and get me when your shift is over." They stood looking at each other a little longer.

Wu stood, took a shot, and asked, "Can we talk about Enoch's memories?"

"No," Debbie said curtly. "Okay, I'm gone." As she left, she called back, "You really do look very pretty, Wu."

"Thanks," replied Wu, watching her walk away. She sat back down and continued eating and watching Daniel Craig at the mercy of the serial killer, while having some very naughty thoughts.

As often happened with their little encounters, Debbie left Wu feeling flustered but aroused. It bothered her that she still couldn't control or suppress those urges. As she entered the bedroom, Jimmy sat up. Connor, Pete, and Molly ran to their mom, while Nicky jumped onto the bed to see his daddy. He was studying her with an odd look on his face. "I thought you would be asleep," she said, feeling for his mood.

"I was waiting up for you. How could I sleep when I know you look like that?"

"You don't sound so happy about it," she said sensing frustration from him.

He jumped out of bed and took her hands, his brow deeply furrowed.

"What's wrong, Babe?" she asked. He wanted to speak, but he seemed stuck. "Tell me," she said softly.

"I don't want to lose you," he said almost sheepishly.

"You're crazy," said Deb, a little stronger than she meant.

Jimmy began to pace slowly, choosing his words. "Look at you. You're turning into a prodigy, an angel, a superhero, or something. It won't take long for you to see that I have nothing to offer you anymore."

She couldn't believe it, but he was serious. "Jim." She grabbed his shoulders, looked in his eyes, and said, "You're my Jimsy. Look at last night. You were a rock star. That was your music."

"That just proves I peaked in my late teens," he said.

"Yeah but look. You have the new DNA," Deb said.

"And still I can't beat either of you," he said, sounding more and more despondent.

"Jims, I love you. What do you see happening?" she asked.

"I kinda see you becoming the owner of this circus and I'm the organ grinder's monkey," was his best analogy.

She pushed him back on the bed. "Wu warned me about this."

He looked puzzled. "About what?"

"She said that as your body adjusts to the Reptilian DNA, you may have problems with adrenaline, testosterone, cortisone, and other bodily hormone imbalances. You're just a little confused and depressed. It's nothing. Just think of it as being on your period." For the first time, he cracked a smile, and the light came back in his eyes. She slowly began sliding the straps over her shoulders and pulling down the flag suit. "We need to give your body chemistry a jolt," she said while pulling off his boxers.

"I'm feeling very patriotic all of sudden," he quipped.

Debbie straddled him. "Yeah, I see you've come to attention," she said dreamily as she began to rock her pelvis against his erection.

"Is this banter?" he asked, consumed by her seduction.

She sat up and pulled her hair to one side. Aggressively wrapping her hand around his hard cock, she said, "I'll show you some banter."

Outside, squatting on the roof over the bedroom, bow in hand, Wu listened to the sounds of their lovemaking. "Oh, you're a lucky man, Jim," she said to herself. "What do you say we go play, little one?" she said to Tippy. He meowed his agreement. Wu ran to the end of the roof and leapt into the trees.

Wu came in from her shift five minutes after noon still wearing her white dress from the night before. Jimmy, Debbie, and David E. were eating biscuits, smoked sausage, and roasted brussel sprouts with white gravy. Jimmy jumped up a little too quickly in Deb's mind and said, "What will you have, High Priest? Biscuits and gravy? How about some eggs? Whatever you want."

"It smells delicious," she said, tempted. "But I have to go change clothes."

"That's a shame," David E. said.

She pointed at him. "We're going to talk later, mountain man."

"What does that mean?' he asked.

"You look so bushy. The beard is out of control," said Wu.

David E. mumbled self-consciously to himself, "I trim it."

Jim made a show of putting his hand on Wu's forehead and pretending to check her temperature. "You okay?" he asked jokingly.

"We're going shopping," Deb said, and Wu nodded.

"I've never seen her turn down food before," said Jim, genuinely surprised. "Well, I've got to go start my shift." He put on his battle belt and a slightly oversized flannel shirt over it. Then he slipped a strapped sword over his shoulder.

"Is that a Samurai sword?" asked David E.

"Yeah," said Jim. "With all these EMPs and LCSs, I thought I should get back in practice."

"It's actually called a Wakizashi," Deb said as she got up from the table. "The middle-sized sword of the Samuri triple threat, you might say." She kissed Jim and said, "Be careful, Babe."

"You guys be careful out there shopping," he countered.

"Oh, we'll be fine. We're just going to Walmart. We'll be back before 5:00 pm."

Jim watched her walk away and said to David E., "Damn."

"I hear you, buddy," said David E.

"Who wants to go with me?" Jim said as he headed outside. Petey and Connor followed him, excitedly jumping up and down. David E. got the dishes and put them in the kitchen sink. When the table was clean, he headed for the computer to check up on China. Whenever things were quiet, check on China. That was his moto.

Standing in the mud room, Debbie called to Shewuma's side of the house, "WuWu, you ready?" Wu stepped out into the hall, and they inspected each other. Wu wore a peach colored mini covered by a very Native American tunic that went just past her hips. It was a V-neck with repeating borders of different colors and alternating rows of beads and embroidered turquoise feathers. In the center was a triangle with a small, animated looking Kachina sewed on. Instead of her usual moccasins, she wore open sandals with straps of twine circling up to the top of her calves. Her hair, which had already grown past her shoulders, hung free. A band of blue color went across her eyes. Setting it off, her eyes were emphasized with generous eyeliner and mascara. Debbie drew in a short breath and remarked, "Wu, you're beautiful." Then she realized she'd been caught. "I mean you're always beautiful, but my goodness." She tried to deflect it a little and asked, "Where did you get the Indian…I'm sorry…Native American tunic?"

"I made it. And listen, that whole Native American/Indian thing is media bullshit. I'm Hopi. Call me whatever you want. Just call me for dinner." She was just happy to be basking in Debbie's praise. "But damn, Deb, look at you." Wu said a sentence in Hopi. Deb searched her Cric for the phrase but couldn't find it. She looked incredibly hot in a white button down blouse open to the third button, causing that button to work awfully hard. It was tucked into a pleated, black and white polka dot skirt that stopped at mid-thigh. No doubt to hide her weapons, she wore a long sleeved, black leather casual coat that stopped just below her knees and zipped up from her belly button to mid breast. All of this on gold, ankle strapped heels.

"I can't find a translation for that," Debbie said.

"It's slang. It means you're a sweet piece of ass," said Wu. "Let's go shopping."

Unfazed, Debbie said, "Alright. We'll take the Muscle," and threw the keys to Wu.

Wu snatched them out of the air and said, "You drive," as she threw them back.

"You don't want to drive?" asked Deb, expecting the opposite, and threw them back again.

Wu said, "No." Seeming annoyed, she threw the keys back kind of hard.

Debbie caught them, looking perplexed. Then it dawned on her. "Don't tell me you can't drive a manual transmission."

Wu held back for a few seconds before admitting, "I've never driven anything."

Having trouble accepting it, Debbie said, "Oh, Sweetie, it's time you learned. You're over eighteen, right?" And threw the keys back again.

"Okay, I'll do it for you. But you back it out. I would die if I hurt Jimmy's baby."

Debbie held out her hand for the keys. "Agreed."

Debbie backed the Muscle out of the garage and pulled it up the driveway about thirty feet. "Okay," she said while getting out, "Let's do this."

Wu sat in the driver's seat at a loss. "Turn it on," Debbie insisted. Wu turned on the ignition and the car lurched forward and stopped. "Oh Jesus," Deb said. "You really have no clue. Let's switch and after we shop, I'll take you to the cemetery to practice. It has miles of empty curving roads. It's kind of a family tradition to learn to drive there." As always at Walmart, Debbie parked the Muscle as far away from the store as possible. The farther out, the less chance of a dent or a scratch. She and Wu took the long walk across the parking lot knowing how good they looked. They entered to the immediate scrutiny of everyone they passed. Women looked at them mostly with suspicion and jealousy, while the men ogled them both furtively and openly. Realizing she had never asked, Deb inquired, "What are we here for, Wu?"

"Cameras," said Wu happily, as if letting out a secret. "I watched *The Girl With the Dragon Tattoo* last night and it occurred to me that we need cameras. David E. looked it up online for me and Walmart has just we need. Six cameras easily installed. They hook to the computer, which, by the way, means they hook up to you. And they're on sale."

"While we're here, I want to get some .30 caliber ammo and some groceries," Deb added.

About an hour later, they were walking toward the front of the store with Wu pushing the cart. "Have you noticed them?" Deb put in her mind. Wu looked at her and nodded affirmatively. As they approached the recently established self-checkout section, Debbie stopped and turned around. Wu followed suit. They stood face to face with a tall, muscular red haired man missing two teeth and a shortish overweight man in a wife-beater T-shirt covered by a stained leather vest with a fixed smile on his face. "Why are you following us?" Deb asked.

The tall man said without missing a beat, "You must work at Subway because when I look at you, I get a footlong." Deb was speechless but Wu burst out laughing.

"You better back away from me, boy," Deb said, her inner volcano building.

"It's okay," he persisted. "I have a friend for your friend." He winked. Wu literally went to her knees with laughter. "I'm Earl," he said, extending his hand. Debbie grabbed it and turned it into a wrist lock, bending Earl over in excruciating pain. His friend began to react when Wu, still on her knees, sent him flat on his back with a heel pick and some pressure on the knee. Debbie released her hold on Earl, and he backed up two steps, cradling his hand. The commotion had not gone unnoticed. A security man showed up and ushered the two assholes away and outside. A manager appeared, apologizing and asking the girls if they were okay.

They insisted they were fine. There was a relatively large group, mostly men, watching the action. They were the focus of whispers and looks through the checkout and out of the building. They left the cart at the first opportunity and headed across the huge lot, both ladened with grocery bags. About three quarters of the way to the car where the lot opened up, they saw five men sitting on the hood of the Trans Am. Next to it sat a running Chevy cargo van at least twenty years old, rusted, and filthy.

They picked up their pace. "That motherfucker," Debbie hissed.

"Debs, look over there," Wu said, pointing many rows over in the very back. Deb saw a man standing by a motorcycle wearing a gray suit with a leather biker jacket over it. He seemed to be watching them.

"What about him?" Deb asked offhandedly, focused on the upcoming bruhaha.

"He has a black aura," Wu said, flabbergasted.

Deb looked at him again. "I got him, Wu, but right now I need to take care of this shit."

A bit shaken by the man she'd just seen, Wu said, "Let's do this, Unangwa." As they approached the car, the girls dropped their bags and stopped as three of the five men faced them while two stood back.

Wu and Debbie pulled their jackets off and tossed them on their bags. "You assholes have no idea what you're in for," Deb said to their minds. They appeared surprised, trying to figure out where the mystery voice came from.

"You bitches are in for a hard night," said the fat man, looking at Wu. Earl pulled his shirttail back, exposing a 9mm stuck down in his belt. Debbie's Beretta was pointing at his face so fast it seemed to appear from thin air. They all froze. "Please take the gun, Wu," Deb said calmly. Wu stepped up to Earl and smelled the pungent exhaust of the idling van. She also smelled their expectations of violence. But when she pulled the gun from his belt, her knuckle touched his stomach. Wu was overwhelmed with his heinous anticipation of cruelty, dominance, rape, and murder. With a complete loss of self-restraint, she tossed the pistol to Debbie and delivered a crushing blow to Earl's solar plexus. Then she spun a kick into the fat one's face. In seconds, she went through the other three. She looked at the bodies that were writhing in pain. Two were on the pavement, Earl was on his knees sobbing for his life, and the last two were limping away. Wu pulled her Arapaho from its sheath, fully intending to finish them.

Debbie filled her head. "Wu, stop! Babe, stop! There are cameras on us." Wu looked at the multiple camera configuration on top of the Walmart building a hundred yards away. She took a deep breath and sheathed her knife, but she wasn't happy about it.

Wu grabbed Earl's hair and pulled his head back so he was looking up at Debbie. Looking into his eyes without speaking out loud, Debbie said, "Tell me, Earl. Tell me everything or you die." The voice in his mind freaked him out but not enough to die for.

"We've been staying at the motel, waiting for any of you to surface. We got a call to come take you at Walmart. We were just going to grab you and get you in the van." Wu tightened the grip on his hair. "No, please. He said we could do whatever we wanted as long as you both disappeared."

"Who?" asked Wu.

"A guy with a scar. I don't know his name. He pays us a lot of money to do stuff." Wu stepped on his right ankle. With a scream, he turned toward the pain, at the same time Wu knocked him out cold.

The sound of a motorcycle starting caught Debbie and Wu's attention. Across the lot, the man in the suit was accelerating out of sight. "Black aura, huh?" Deb asked.

"Black," said Wu. "Let's go before the cops get here." With three out of commission and the other two limping off into the distance, they grabbed their bags and got in the Muscle. As they drove off, Wu said, "So you think he was the guy who sent them?" Debbie blinked her right eye and a holographic projection of the motorcycle man appeared between them. The picture enlarged several times until Wu said, "Earl said a man with a scar. That guy has one hell of a scar."

"A black aura?" Deb asked.

"Yes."

"What does that mean?"

Wu seemed uncertain when she replied. "I was always taught there was no such thing as a completely black aura, but obviously it has to be negative. I need to do some research on this. I'm just not sure."

"Well, let's get home and make sure the boys are safe. Then we'll check it out," Deb said, squealing tires up the ramp to Route 199. On the way home, Deb and Wu passed two county sheriff cars on the way to Walmart, lights and sirens full bore. Debbie looked at Wu and saw that she was smoldering. "What's wrong, Babe?" Deb asked.

Wu said in a caustic tone, "You're not my boss. You don't tell me what to do."

"WuWu," Debbie said, "you would be on camera killing five men. The cops would be at the house within an hour."

"If you knew what they planned to do to us, you would have killed them yourself," said Shewuma, still seething. Debbie touched Wu's arm. Wu felt her sincerity and relaxed a little.

"I believe you," Deb said earnestly. "But I'm not going to lose you either. Besides," Deb said as she held up a brown wallet, "that piece of shit isn't getting away with anything." Wu took it and found his driver's license.

She smiled at Deb. "Excellent," she said, taking hold of Deb's hand. Deb let her do it. This had been an intense afternoon, and she deserved some TLC.

When the girls came in the house they were relieved that all was normal. The guys and the animals, though, sensed something was up. "We had a crazy afternoon," Deb told them. "We've got to do some research. We'll tell you all about it at dinner."

"Dinner will be ready soon," said Jim. "I made it early because you guys didn't eat lunch."

"Thanks, Baby," Deb said. "Just call us. We'll be in the den."

"I'll set the table and break out some scotch," said David E. Jim peeked in the den and saw Debbie and Wu sitting on the couch. They were discussing and manipulating several holographic pictures floating in the air. He went back to cooking, a little concerned.

After a few minutes, Debbie said, "Oh, these shoes are killing my feet."

"Here, put them on my lap," said Wu. Deb laid back and put her feet up. Wu took off the gold strap heels and began deeply massaging Debbie's arches.

Debbie shut her eyes for a minute. Then she opened them and asked in Wu's mind, "Are you looking up my skirt?"

"Yes," Wu answered and kept on rubbing.

It was a dinner of baked bluefish, garlic buttered rice, green bean casserole, and cornbread. When they were done, they all sat back, full and satisfied. The highlight was Jimmy's homemade tartar sauce. Deb even had a little.

"I should get on my shift," said David E. But Deb stopped him, and he asked, "You ready to tell us about it?"

"Yes," said Deb. In great detail, she and Shewuma, alternating the narrative, told the fellows exactly what had happened that afternoon. They sat silent for several minutes, looking back and forth at each other.

Then Jimmy said, "Hey, what if he hired them to see what you guys could do?" They all looked at him questioningly. "To see if you could fight." Jim went on. "Why hire a bunch of assholes just to harass you? He wanted to observe. He just watched and took off, right?"

David E. had a thought. "Deb, can you find his picture in any databases?"

"I don't know," she said. "I'm trying, but I'm just not sure how to access everything out there yet."

"Okay," said Jim. "Let's get back to the black aura. What is it?" He was looking at Wu.

Wu started slowly. "We don't really know. We just know it's not good. I'm assuming it could be something with no soul, like a vampire. Pure evil. Possessed." They were quiet, thinking.

David E. spoke first. "This was obviously planned well ahead of time. They were watching and waiting for any opportunity. And they obviously had no idea what you two were capable of. Seems our options are it was either a planned hit or an attempt to get information."

Jim spoke again. "Why would anyone hire some local dickheads to kidnap, rape, and kill two local girls, then be there as it happens? It makes no sense."

"Whatever it was, they had to react quickly to follow us to Walmart. Which means we're definitely still being watched. All the time."

"I'm telling you, I can feel it," said Wu. "Some shit is going to hit the fan and soon."

David E. filled four Micky Mouse themed shot glasses with Johnny Walker Black. "This is the smoothest scotch you can drink," he said while handing them out. Everyone took a sip except Wu, who just drank hers down. "And now I have a shift," he said as he got up.

"David E.," Debbie said, "you okay out there at night?"

"Are you kidding?" he said. "I have Tippy and Molly and all this firepower." He held up his .38 and his ultimate weapon, the cane. "I'm good."

"One more thing, David E. Those guys from Walmart aren't getting away with that. We're going to pay them a visit tomorrow."

"I take it you want me to stay here," he said.

"Yes, I'd like you to stay here and protect the Sanctum. We'll work out the details later. You remember the code to the safe room, right?"

He laughed. "WuWu is hard to forget." They all laughed, and he went out for his shift.

Debbie asked Wu, "Do you think Earl will be there? You went at them pretty hard."

Wu thought for a second. "One is definitely in the hospital. Three I'm not sure about. But that asshole Earl will be home."

"Do you have a plan?" Jim asked.

"I'm going to look up his address on Google Maps and we'll go from there."

"You feeling better now?" Jim asked Deb. "I saw you flake out on the couch. I haven't seen you tired for a long time."

"I'm okay, Honey. Those shoes made my feet hurt. I think I'm going to go take a shower," said Deb.

"Okay, I'll see you in a little bit," said Jimmy. After Debbie left, Jimmy started collecting the dishes.

"Don't worry, Jim. I'll get the dishes," Wu said. "You go bed your wife. She needs it."

"You're the best, Wu." He jogged down the hall.

At 5:45 am the next morning, Debbie called Wu and a freshly clean shaven David E. to Jimmy's special breakfast. When Wu asked him what the occasion was, he said, "I wanted to wait and have it for Thanksgiving breakfast. But nowadays, you never know." There was a buffet of breakfast tacos set up on the island. There were crunchy taco shells and flour tortillas, scrambled eggs, chorizo chunks, bacon, ham, shredded American cheese, queso fresco, queso cotija, diced onions, green and hot peppers, refried beans, chopped cilantro, and sliced avocados. Sauces included sour cream, Valentina, and guacamole. Three sides were also available: Spanish rice, tater tots, and Elote, tiny corn on the cobs slathered in cream sauce. For Debbie, a tomahawk steak cooked medium rare. As they went through the line loading up, Jimmy warned them how dangerous the jalapenos could be. "Enjoy!" he proclaimed.

The breakfast was a massive hit. Next to Debbie and then secretly Wu, his passion was cooking. And nothing made him feel better than watching a good meal being savored by his family. With breakfast winding down, they discussed the day ahead. Jimmy and Wu started clearing the dishes. "You guys can go," said David E. "I'll do the dishes."

"No," said Debbie abruptly. "I want you to stay in the bedroom near the safe room. You have the TV, the stereo, and some porn tapes hidden in Jimmy's closet. I'll show you where. Okay?"

"Sounds good," he replied. "If I even hear a bark or a meow, I'm in the safe room."

Debbie smiled and kissed his cheek. She knew that from her prompting, Wu had been ragging on him to shave his beard since the show. "I like you clean shaven," she whispered. That made him feel good.

They took Miss Interceptor to Hampton, Virginia. Debbie drove as always. Wu sat in the passenger seat wearing her manta and moccasins. Her hair was in two braids secured by her simple war bonnet. Lightning and her quiver of arrows rested between her legs. Jim took his favorite spot leaning up between the front seats from the back. He wore dark blue khakis and a Captain America T-shirt. Debbie wore a red, skintight, sleeveless cotton jumpsuit. Jimmy said, "You look hot, Spunky."

"Extremely hot," agreed Wu. "Very Mrs. Peel."

"Do you think David E. will be okay?" Debbie put out there.

"Hell yeah," said Wu. "He was kicking ass in Vietnam before you two were born."

"True," said Jimmy. "So, do we have a plan?"

Debbie squinted her left eye and a hologram appeared between the three. "This is a Google Map picture of Earl the asswipe's address. It's a double wide trailer in Hampton near Buckroe Beach."

"Right by the bay," said Wu. "Maybe we could go swimming after."

"Maybe," said Deb. "Let's see how it goes first. I'll drop you two off. Go to the back door. When you hear my signal, go on in."

"When did trailers start having back doors?" Jim asked.

"Doublewides? Since the nineties. He has one. I checked the model," Debbie replied. She held up a flat bar and a key ring in her right hand.

"Trailer keys?" asked Jimmy.

"Yes."

"And I'm guessing that pry bar is a master key," said Wu, remembering the bolt cutters in Covington.

"Thanks," said Jim. "But I have my own master key now." To the girls' amusement, he held his flexed bicep between the seats.

"So, what's the signal?" said Wu.

Debbie answered, "You'll know it."

"We're getting close," said Wu. "I can smell the salt water." Wu took bright red lipstick out of the glove box. On both sides of her face, starting at the hair line, she made red dashes down over her eyes and cheekbones. The marks continued over the curve of her jaw to her neck.

"You're a badass, Shewuma," said Jimmy. Debbie nodded.

Just as Debbie said, there was a back door to the double wide. Jimmy and Shewuma waited patiently on the stoop for Debbie's signal. Jimmy looked Wu up and down and whispered, "Wu, why do you always wear dresses?"

She whispered back. "For comfort and freedom of movement." Then grinning, she bent over and touched her toes. "You don't like it?" She spread her arms, presenting the whole look.

"You know I like it," said Jim, wishing he hadn't brought it up. Then they heard it. Several firecrackers going off out front. Had to be the signal.

Debbie watched three men come out of the trailer, scan the area, and go back in. Jimmy and Wu, unseen from the kitchen, watched the three men reenter the trailer. A tall, muscular, red-haired man with a black eye and a bandage over a swollen, discolored nose sat in a recliner nearest to the front door. It was Earl. A short fat man wearing a "Granddaddy" T-shirt sat across from Earl on a raggedy couch. The whole right side of his face was bruised and swollen. He was joined on the couch by a younger man. Average size with long, stringy blonde hair, he sported an ace bandage around his wrist and was limping heavily.

The front door exploded open and Debbie appeared. The fat guy went for a 9mm on the coffee table. It was his last act, as Wu's arrow went through his ribs and into his heart. The young man darted for a rifle hanging over the fireplace. Long before he could reach it, Jimmy was choking him unconscious with a sleeper hold. "Kill him," came the mental command from Debbie. Jimmy shifted his arm and ruptured the windpipe. Wu disappeared into the back of the trailer for a few seconds and then reappeared. Debbie watched Earl, who was sitting in the recliner and gripping the sides, terrified. A .38 caliber revolver in his belt was untouched. He already knew he had no chance against these people. Wu took his gun and tossed it to Jimmy. "Earl, right?" said Debbie. He nodded. Debbie pointed to his dead friends. "Calm down, Earl. You don't want to be like them. My name is Debbie. I'm going to ask you some questions."

He took a breath and said, "Of course, ma'am. Whatever you need."

"You said you don't know the man with the scar, but he pays you. Explain."

With a trembling hand, he pointed at the dead fat man. Wu was retrieving her arrow as his blood emptied onto the carpet. "Bubba met him only once, three years ago. We do work for him. He emails me when he has a job."

"How are you paid?"

"We have a debit card. After the job, the money is in the account."

"Where is the debit card and where is your computer?"

"Uh. Umm. The card is in the kitchen drawer and the laptop is in the bedroom."

He sounded odd. Debbie thought he might be going into shock. "Okay, Earl. I have one more question. And if you lie to me, it will be very painful. You understand?"

"Yes, ma'am," he answered as he began to tremble.

"What were you going to do to me and Shewuma?"

"We were going to take you to the man with the scar," he said as earnestly as he could. He was watching Debbie for her reaction and didn't see Shewuma moving. She brought her bone knife down through his wrist and into the chair arm. Debbie held a throw pillow over his face until he stopped screaming. She put her finger under his chin and tipped his face up. Tears streamed from his eyes.

"Earl," Debbie said softly. "Earl," she repeated while pushing a nerve in his neck that eased the pain.

He looked at her expectantly while grimacing. "Yes, ma'am," he managed.

"I was told you planned to rape and kill us. Is that true?"

He hung his head and sighed. "I'm sorry," he said as Debbie's Fat Belly Flayer broke through his sternum and penetrated his heart.

She looked at Wu and Jimmy. "All clear?"

"There's a girl asleep in the bedroom. I put her out for a while," said Wu.

"Okay," Debbie said. "Wu, get her and put her outside somewhere. Jim, I'm going to get the debit card and laptop. Burn this sucker."

"You got it, beautiful," he said. They were driving off in Miss Interceptor within minutes. Jimmy had pulled up the stovetop and blown out the gas pilots, then turned on the burners. He found a bottle of rubbing alcohol under the sink. He splashed it on the stove, counter, and microwave. After making sure Deb and Wu were out, he threw a can of roach spray in the microwave and set it for five minutes.

As they pulled out of the trailer park on to Victoria Boulevard, they heard and felt the explosion. "Wow," said Wu, looking back at him.

"I do my homework," he said.

Deb held her right hand out between the seats. "Everybody good?" she asked.

Jimmy and Wu piled their hands on. It felt right. It was another win.

Wu turned and asked Jimmy with some concern, "Did you not know that girl was in the back?"

"Well," Jim began, "I smelled something but not really."

"I need to work with you on your senses. You have so much catching up to do."

"What do you mean?" asked Debbie.

"When the DNA of a Hybrid activates, they need to be taught how to work with it. I was taught for eleven years to learn control of my senses after my DNA was revived. Deb, you have the Cric and the Sanctum and they're guiding you, but Jim is like a babe in the woods. He needs training and direction."

"Start on him tomorrow," Deb told her.

"I will," said Wu, slapping Jimmy on the knee.

Debbie said to Wu, "I have some ideas on how to bring him along quickly."

Wu looked at Jim. "You and me tomorrow, big boy," she said, pointing at him.

"Ten-four," said Jim.

"How about some Ella Fitzgerald on the ride home?" said Wu.

Debbie looked at her and said, "Hit it."

"Where's my children?" yelled Jimmy as they entered the house. They were all over him within seconds. He went to the carpet and was swamped.

"Get your daddy," Wu yelled while randomly grabbing and shaking this one and that one. Tippy came down the hall and jumped into Debbie's arms. She buried her face in his purrs and squirms. David E. walked in, relieved to see them back safely.

"Go get WuWu," Debbie said to Tippy, and he was off. She hugged David E. "I need your help," she said, holding up the debit card and laptop.

"Let's go" David E. answered, and they headed to the office.

Jim and Wu ran to the back door. "Outside," Jim yelled. He and Shewuma played frisbee and tug of war with the kids until Jimmy called her over. "Hey, about tomorrow," he said. "How long do you think we'll be doing this training?"

"Three or four hours," she said.

"Okay, that's good. After that I'm going to teach you how to drive the Muscle."

"Debbie told you, huh?"

"Yes, and it's time you learned."

"Deal. By the way, that was a fine choke you put on that guy today."

"Well let's go practice it some more," said Jim. Wu bolted for the shop with Jimmy close behind.

"Debbie Doodle and David E.! Supper!" Jimmy yelled down the hall from the kitchen. A few minutes later when Debbie and David E. showed up, Jimmy and Wu put the food on the table.

"It smells so good," said David E.

Jimmy laid it out. "Chicken fried steak, french fries, squash casserole, and biscuits." Debbie was wide eyed. Chicken fried steak was a personal favorite of hers. "The breading is from beef flour I found online. So there are no plants in it, Babe." They sat down and dug in.

"Hold it, guys," said Wu with a little hesitation. "Do you mind if I say a prayer?"

"Hell no," said Jim.

"Of course, Sweetie," said Debbie.

"That would be great," said David E.

Wu closed her eyes and made the symbol of her people. She began to speak in her native language.

Directly to their minds, Debbie translated for the others as she spoke:

Make me wise so that I may understand the things that you have taught our people and let me learn the lessons that you have hidden in every leaf and rock. I seek the strength, not to be greater than my brother or sister, but to fight my greatest enemy, myself. Make me always ready to come to you with clean hands and straight eyes so that all we do now must be done in a sacred manner and in celebration. We are the ones we have been waiting for. We are the chosen.

Shewuma opened her eyes and looked up.

"Amen," everyone said together.

"Let's eat," she said, reaching for the chicken. "And you guys should know I can make biscuits by myself now." Debbie and David E clapped while Jimmy gave her a thumbs-up.

Jimmy knew dinner was good because everyone ate silently. When he was done, he asked David E. and Debbie, "So, did you come up with anything on the scar guy with the black aura?"

"Some," said David E., reaching for more meat. "This is the best chicken fried steak I've ever had."

"Thank my mom. She taught me how to make it. What about the guy?" Jim said.

David E. was chewing, so Debbie said, "David E. recognized him from my memory picture."

"You know him?" asked Wu, going for more biscuits and fries.

"Didn't know him per se," said David E., cleaning his plate. "But I used to see him occasionally at meetings at Edgewood Arsenal. Meetings that were only attended by brass with alien clearance."

"Wasn't that in the seventies?" Jim asked.

"Yes," said David E. "And I know what you're thinking. If he was there with me, why does he still look thirty-five years old?"

"A Hybrid?" said Wu.

"Something," said Deb.

"Anything else?" asked Jim while taking his dishes to the sink.

"Yes," said David E. "The money they got for the attack on the girls was paid by the SBA.

"The Small Business Administration?" asked Wu, dismayed.

"Yeah," said Deb. "It's disturbing, isn't it?"

"I'll tell you one other thing about them that's disturbing," said David E. "The Greys are testing a virus and I think it's a bad one."

"Wow. That came out of left field," said Wu.

"I know," said David E. "But they're past due for an outbreak and I've been following the news, the politics, and the money. It seems to be starting in China. They like China. Diseases spread quickly there."

Deb put her finger behind her left jaw and seemed to zone out. Jim said, "Explain, David E. I'm lost."

"Well the Greys are constantly creating and testing new viruses and bacteria. They've been doing it for thousands of years. I've been tracking their work since the seventies when I found out the truth. They've had a good run the last few years. But nothing since 2016."

"What do mean, a good run?" Jim asked.

David E. gave examples. "Swine flu in 2010, MERS in 2012 in the Middle East, bird flu in 2013 in China, Ebola in 2014 in Africa, Zika in 2015 in the Americas, cholera in 2016 in Yemen. It took over a year to get that one under control. And now after three years, here we are in late 2019 and nothing. So, it's coming. It could be big. It could be bad."

"You know about this?" Jim asked Wu.

"Not like David E., but yeah. Human testing, DNA, diseases. That's what the Greys do."

"Come on! Thousands of years?" Jim said skeptically.

"Oh yeah," said David E. "Ever hear of the plagues of Egypt, the Black Death, the pandemic of 1918, mad cow, West Nile, SARS? Come on, Jim."

Deb snapped out of her trance. "It checks out and makes sense," she said to David E. "The Chinese stock market is in a dive."

"There you go," he revealed.

"The Chinese stock market?" said Jim. "What has that got to do with the scar guy and the SBA?"

David E.'s answer was chilling. "I think the same agency probably runs all of it. The Greys, the MIB, the Drach hit squads."

"So, you think this scar guy is part of a government agency?" Jim said.

"He's not just any scar guy," interjected Wu. "Our scar guy is at least seventy-five years old but looks thirty-five, controls government ops money, has a black aura, and has tried to kill us more than once."

"Scary," said Deb.

All the pieces finally came together in Jim's mind. "We're in some deep shit," he said.

"And the Sanctum has to be the focus, the goal," said David E.

Debbie looked around the table. "Can you all ever foresee leaving here? Because I'm like Wu. I see it coming."

Jimmy rubbed his chin and said, "We trust your judgment, Debs. You know that."

David E. asked her, "Is this strategy or precognition?"

Debbie had no answer and shrugged. "I think we should stop the patrolling on shifts," said Deb. "I say we stay in groups of at least two and stay inside as much as possible. We have the kids, the alarms, our senses, the cameras. No one could take us by surprise."

"Okay," said Jim with a clap. "Meals will be easier to plan. I say tonight we drink and shoot pool." The overall feeling was positive, and they headed for the pool table.

Wu went back for bourbon, then quickly caught up.

The next morning, Jimmy made a quick meal for breakfast of Cream of Wheat and a plate of sourdough toast. But he had to have extras. So the kicker was the toppings for the Cream of Wheat. Butter and sugar, of course, but also chocolate chips, dried apricots, cherries, raisins, honey, and maple syrup. There was grape jelly and peach preserves for the toast and a plate of leftover chicken fried steak for Debbie. It was still early and everyone showed up in a robe except Wu. She was wearing a pink bath towel. After breakfast they sat around discussing the day ahead. David E. and Debbie presented their plans to try and better pinpoint the scar man and hack Earl's bank account with his debit card.

Wu told them her plans. "Jimmy and I will be gone for a while today. He's going to get some serious training and I'll be learning to drive the Muscle."

"Wu," said Debbie, "come on back to my walk-in. I need to show you something." They left, and Jimmy and David E. did the dishes without complaint.

Debbie and Shewuma had been gone for a while. "The dishes are done," Jimmy said.

"Are you talking to me?" asked David E.

"No. I was telling the girls."

The super senses. Of course. David E. wasn't sure if he would ever get used to it. One thing for sure. It would always be annoying.

"I'll be in the car, Wu," he added. "I'm ready to go."

David E. didn't hear Wu's reply of, "I'll be right there."

Jimmy went to the garage, backed the Muscle out into the driveway, and waited patiently. Jimmy figured men had two primary crosses to bear in life. One of them was waiting for women.

When Wu finally arrived, Jimmy was both surprised and intrigued by her appearance. She wore a gray, high waisted pencil skirt that hit her right at the knee. Tucked into it was a white, three-quarter sleeve, button down blouse and conservative, round toe black pumps with two-inch heels. She put her battle belt and bow and quiver on the back seat. He meant to just sneak a peek at the dress riding up her legs as she got in. But when she said "What?" he realized he was staring. He cleared his throat and said, "Nothing. You just look so different than I'm used to seeing you."

"Better or worse?"

"Just different. You couldn't look bad anyway. And you're wearing hose and heels and makeup. You look like sexy executive of the year."

"Yeah. Debbie helped me. She said you have a thing for this kind of look and it would help me keep your attention." He put the car in first and took off faster than he intended. Wu touched his arm and smiled. She definitely had his attention.

"Where to, Sensei?" he asked.

"West Point."

Not expecting a forty-five-minute jaunt north, he said, "Really?"

"They have a paper mill. It fills the surrounding countryside with a sort of noxious odor, right?"

"Right."

"Well, this training is all about the sense of smell. So we'll start in an area that will already be distracting to you. Later we'll work on the nuances of scent and scent memory."

"Sounds like a plan. And you really do look lovely." The word lovely slipped out before he could stop it, so he tried to cover. "I like your necklace. Where did you get it?"

She fingered the turquoise teardrop stone with a woven linen necklace. "I made it."

"Of course you did." He smiled. The day was shaping up nicely.

Back at Langley Air Force Base, Mr. Portis stepped off the elevator onto the ninth floor sublevel of the NASA II building. He passed through the outer office and paused in the conference room, where he admired his scar in one of the blank screens hanging on the wall. He enjoyed the fact that it disturbed most people. It was a gift from the Sasquatch leader, Custos, during he and Lucifer's escape from the Erran ship many thousands of years ago. He earnestly awaited the day that he could return the favor. Settling back in one of the luxurious high back chairs, he looked across the table at his two assistants, Will and Grace. Will was a stocky man with angular features and a menacing presence. As Portis watched him, he began to fidget nervously with the lapels on his pinstriped suit. Portis shifted his gaze. "Grace," he said, smiling at her in a navy blue skirt suit and hair in a tight bun as always, "you could be so much more comfortable if you didn't dress so reserved."

"Yes, sir," she answered uneasily. She had fallen for that line from him once before, wearing slacks and a sweater with her hair down. Portis was generally scary and intimidating, but that was the only time he had ever openly threatened her. Only two more years and the contract expired. Her life would be free of this psycho.

Portis continued. "So, we've all been doing our due diligence and I think we're ready to bring this thing home." He nodded to Grace. "Begin."

She began typing on her virtual keyboard over the table. As she spoke, visual aids in the form of 3D holographic pictures would appear. The image of a handsome, white haired Erran came up first. Grace narrated. "Guardian of the Sanctum. Number thirteen and Sovereign of the Skulls. Enoch of Erran. He was tracked for four thousand years and then we lost him. Picked up again in 1902 in Newport News, Virginia, on 22nd Street. The mission target by a team of Drachonians for Operation Long Game. He acquired a Crevetch. A Hopi Kachina named Shewuma. The English translation is White Bird."

Portis interrupted. "You know I prefer Reptilians, Grace."

She was expecting it. No matter how she addressed them, he would insist on the other name. God, she hated him. "Sorry, sir. The plan for the Reptilians to infiltrate and replace the local street gang, kill Enoch, and acquire his Sanctum and Cric went as planned until the random intervention of the property managers. The Erran is dead but the Kachina, the Cric, and the Sanctum are still at large. An apparent clerical error unexpectedly transferred the Kachina from Hampton General to Riverside Hospital." Portis sent Will an accusing glance, causing him to look down in humiliation. "The managers, James and Deborah Archer, liberated the Kachina from Riverside before we could get to her."

"Grace," Portis interrupted, "you're telling me things that I know. Tell me about them. The Archers."

"Yes, sir. I was just being thorough. The Archers recently filed for Chapter 13 bankruptcy on their property management business. He is a local of no consequence. She is local but her background in the sport of competitive martial arts flags her as dangerous."

"Yes, I saw her and the Indian shrew at Walmart. The way they handled those idiots was annoyingly impressive. Go on, Grace."

"We are assuming that they have knowledge of—if not possession of—the Cric and Sanctum. Having gone to ground at the residence of the Archers in rural York County, they were immediately put under surveillance by multiple teams." Grace paused to take a sip of water. She was looking at the holograph showing a picture of the Archers house from above. "A road trip to Covington, Virginia, connected them with Command Sergeant Major, Retired, David E. Major. In the past he was an alien tech and remote viewing instructor for the Army and a Ufologist for a private company. He has been designated a person of interest by NASA II, the USSF, and the Greys for the last sixteen years. The group met in a very isolated area, so the MIB were given a green light to take them out. The MIB failed."

"Why?"

"Inconclusive, sir. The investigation is still open at this juncture. After the assassination of the remaining Reptilians disguised as the KIC gang, a direct MIB approach was aborted by local law enforcement. An assault mounted by Reptilians disguised as local policemen was also unsuccessful."

"Again, Grace. Why?"

"Unclear, sir. Their house is very secure and well-guarded, not only with electronic surveillance, but also well trained guard animals. And there is the Kachina, of course. The subcontractors from the Walmart operation are also dead."

"What!" shouted Portis. "Them *again*?"

Grace winced and went on. "Testimony from a female survivor identified a picture of the Kachina, sir. Three dead and their trailer destroyed. Officially it's being reported as a gas leak."

Portis put his hand up and she paused. "Will, that witness is a liability now. Pick her up. Feed her raisins and dates for the rest of the week. And bring her to me Friday night."

Will's eyes flashed yellow, and he eagerly said, "Yes, Highness."

"I've told you before about the Highness shit in mixed company," Portis snapped.

"Sorry, sir."

Grace was typing. Purposely ignoring them. Portis lowered his hand. "Grace, tell me more about the Indian Hybrid."

"She's from the Hopi tribe."

"Figures. Those fucking Hopi have been a pain in our ass for two thousand years. Go on, Grace."

"She was born in 1862. Turned at the age of five and trained specifically to be Crevetch to Enoch and protect the Sanctum. She is allegedly Combrid of Drachonian and Mantis DNA."

"Mantis," said Portis. "That fills in some gaps."

"Current status. All four still reside at the Archer house in York County under constant surveillance." Grace relaxed a little.

Portis thought for a moment and said, "Okay. This has gone on long enough. We go in hard and heavy."

Speaking for the first time, Will said, "I'll put a team together."

"No Reptilians," said Portis.

"What?" questioned Will.

Portis leaning back in his chair was enough to have Will back peddling. "Sir, I'm sorry. I wasn't questioning you. I don't understand."

Portis stood up. "The Reptilians have failed twice. The MIB will go in with blue lights and plasmas rifles. I want two choppers and twenty MIB on the ground. Also, one Hybrid Black Ops assassin. His only purpose is to find the Sanctum and bring it to me. I want him prepped by the Greys to sense the Sanctum and be able to disarm it. I want them all dead. I want the house and the bodies to disappear."

Will's eyes turned to yellow slits and his cheeks began to harden. Portis looked Will directly in the eyes. Will's face softened and his eyes went back to bluc. "Right away, sir."

"No," countered Portis. "I want it well planned, no mistakes. Wait at least two or three weeks to lower their guard. I want this over. I want it ended." Will and Grace rose to leave. "Wait, Grace." Will walked out, suppressing a smile. Grace didn't know that the game had changed.

"Grace, we know that Will and Grace are code names. But no one else should. I understand you are revealing your actual identity to a *friend*." He made air quotes on the word friend.

Grace thought furiously. She recovered, researched, and proofed every scrap of incoming information to the office from every source they had available. How could he possibly know about Theo? There was no choice but to lie. "No, sir. I would never compromise NASA II."

"Make sure you don't, Grace. You're still mine for two more years."

"Of course, sir," she said stiffly.

Grace went upstairs and straight out of the building. She dialed a number on her cell and ordered a pepperoni and onion pizza to go. Four miles from Langley AFB, Grace turned into a small shopping center and parked in the back behind Anna's Pizzeria. In about ten minutes a tall well-dressed Black man got in the passenger side and handed her a small pizza box. She tossed it on the dash and went in for a kiss.

"So," he said, "this was a surprise. What's the occasion?"

"I just wanted to see you. My boss seems to suspect that I'm having a relationship."

"You know that I don't understand why we have to be secret anyway, Mimi."

"It's my job and clearance. They pretty much own me for two more years. But then I'm free. Can we stay secret for that long?"

"Oh, Mimi. My baby. As much as I enjoy fucking you, you're out of chances," the man said, smiling.

Grace was taken by surprise. "I don't understand."

His face blurred and turned Reptilian for a second, then solidified as the face of Will. She recoiled in horror. A moment of panic found her grasping at the door handle to run. But Will laughed as he pulled her back by her arm. "It was you all along?" Her eyes welled with tears.

"Oh no. Theo has only been dead a couple of weeks. And trust me when I say that he died badly. Very stubborn man. So, I got to nail you twice. I've tried to act shitty so you would dump me…him. Oh well."

"Will, I thought we were friends," she said as she calmed herself in her mind. Remembering her training, she went for his throat without telegraphing, but he was way too fast. He caught her right hand and twisted it, pinning her down against the console. He smiled and his eyes became yellow slits. A claw forced its way through his index finger, and he punctured her skin. "I'll miss you, Grace. The new girl doesn't have your ass."

"You disgust me," she slurred as her veins and arteries began to swell. Her skin turned pale and cracked like mud in the hot sun. With a look of horror on her face, she slowly dissolved into ash.

Will went around to her side of the car, picked up her purse, jewelry, a belt buckle, a hair clip, and what appeared to be a filling. Then he brushed the residue from the bucket seat.

At that same moment, a slightly chubby Korean woman entered Portis' office in NASA II. He looked up from his desk quizzically. "Hello, sir. I am Kameko Yong, reporting for duty."

"Excellent," he said. "I am Mr. Portis. From now on, your name is Grace. I need you to wear your hair up in a bun. And I prefer you dress more professionally." Walking toward the bookcase, he said, "Come downstairs with me. I will explain everything at your orientation."

Jimmy and Shewuma drove around West Point for two hours while she made him identify individual smells of animals, people, and businesses in the context of the paper mill stench. He learned quickly how to pigeonhole and differentiate the smells despite the mask of the plant's strong odor. "Okay," she said. "Stage two. Let's find some roads in the woods, preferably deserted."

"No sweat," said Jimmy. "New Kent is about twenty minutes away. It's perfect." Not surprisingly with Jim driving, they made it in less than fifteen minutes.

Wu picked a spot and told him, "Pull over. Let's go into the woods." He followed. About forty yards in she stopped and looked at him, a question on her face. "I smell something," she said.

"I smell something too," he replied. He clenched his jaw. Then it hit him. "A rabbit?"

"Good," she said. "Feel the smell. Picture a rabbit. You have a sense memory that's like a computer now. Record it. Rabbits have the same scent. Each individual rabbit has a slight variation, but it's still a rabbit. Understand?"

"Yes, I do. He's over there," he said, pointing to the left.

Wu put her finger to her lip. "Shhh." She picked up a small branch that was bent in the middle at about seventy degrees. She began breaking off the ends. Jimmy knew from his survival training that she was making what was called a rabbit stick, an angled boomerang type of object for throwing at small game. She gave him a wink and then slung it sidearm about fifteen yards, hitting the base of a thicket. A large tan rabbit ran for his life. They watched his white tail disappear. Wu nudged Jim's shoulder. He looked at her. She was indicating to him that he breathe in deeply. He inhaled and knew immediately what she meant.

"It got scared," he said.

"You smell the change?" she prompted.

"Yes, I see."

She explained further as they returned to the Trans Am. "Every species has a distinct smell. Every individual has a smell within it, and within every individual there are nuances that can reveal their physical and mental states. Identify each instance and your sense memory will keep it for you to use. Let's go driving. There's much more."

They got back in the Muscle and headed farther into the county wilderness of New Kent. "Can you smell the forest?" Wu asked.

"Yes," he said, after about thirty seconds of testing the air.

"Okay, try this. Smell the left side of the road…You got it?"

"Yes," he replied.

"Now smell the forest on the right side of the road."

He did. "I have it."

"Now slow down a little and close your eyes," she told him. He looked at her like she was crazy. "I'm serious. Smell the left, smell the right, and stay on the road without your eyes."

He slowed to about twenty miles an hour and despite his reluctance, closed his eyes. Within minutes, he was taking curves and driving like his eyes were open. "Wu, this is amazing."

"Okay, keep going. We're going to try something else. Don't open your eyes until I say." Jim nodded. He was into the driving by smell anyway. "Can you smell me?" she asked.

"Of course," he said.

"Can you smell yourself?"

"Yes."

"Okay, keep going, I'll tell you when."

"Okay," he replied.

As quietly as possible, Wu pulled her skirt up around her waist and unbuttoned her blouse completely, exposing her lacy bra. With her right hand, she began to massage her left nipple. With her left hand, she manipulated her genitals through the panties. As Jimmy drove, eyes closed, she asked him, "Do you still smell me?"

"Sure," he said. And then with a furrowed brow, he said, "Wow, it's different."

"Look," she ordered. He looked over. She was wearing stockings and a thong. Her shirt was open, and she was feeling her breast. Her right leg was propped up against the door and she was masturbating. He jagged the wheel and almost ran off the road, then slammed the brakes until they came to a stop. He stared at her, not taking in what she was saying for a second. "Jim?"

"Yeah," he said, coming out of it.

"Do you smell it? Do you smell the difference? It's me, but me excited." A light seemed to go on in his eyes.

"Yeah," he said. "I get it."

"Remember from before. Same scent for each person but with nuances like the rabbit. Happy, sexual, tired, mad."

"I get it," Jim said, understanding but still transfixed by the way she was sitting.

"Jim," Wu said, snapping her fingers to get his attention, "Do you smell yourself? Do you smell it in you?"

"Yes, Wu. I do. You also got me excited. This is pretty amazing," he said, still staring at her.

Wu pulled down her skirt and buttoned her shirt. She was getting too comfortable with the situation. "You've learned years' worth in a day," she told him. "Keep working everything, stay open, and keep your scent awareness sharp. That's our lesson for today."

"You don't think we should keep practicing?" he asked, disappointed.

That evoked a smile from her. "I guess we've learned enough for now."

Jimmy turned off the engine. "Well then, it's time for you to drive, WuWu," he said as he got out. She swapped with him and sat behind the wheel.

"Start it," he said. She turned on the ignition and the car lurched forward, then cut off.

"Okay, we'll start with the basics. First, pull your skirt way up," As she pulled her skirt up, she gave him a haughty look. "No, I'm kidding.

It's a joke," he said, but then happily accepted that she intended to leave herself exposed. "Okay then. With your left foot, push the left pedal. That's the clutch. Now with your right foot, push the middle pedal. That's the brake. That's what stops the car. For the time being, don't stop the car unless you've pushed in both the clutch and the brake. Understand?"

"Yeah, I think so."

"Okay, turn the key." The Muscle roared to life. Wu giggled with excitement. "Alright," said Jimmy, "take your foot off the brake, push the gas pedal slowly and let the clutch out at the same time. You got it?" She did it. There was a little bit of a lurch but she was driving. After seeing her first car over a hundred years ago, she was finally driving.

An hour or so later, Jim had Wu pull into a gas station near I-64. "You're doing great," he said. He went in and returned with two quarts of chocolate milk and an assortment of chips and candy bars. He settled into the passenger seat, looked at Wu, and said, "You should pull your skirt down."

Wu looked at him lovingly. "Now that the novelty has worn off, you think you're somehow cheating on Debbie by watching me, right?"

"I guess so."

"Okay, Unangwa. But just so you know, this was all her idea. She said the clothes and the flashing would keep you focused."

"She was right about that." Wu pulled her skirt down and touched his arm.

As they headed up Route 40 back to the interstate, Jim said, "You have the driving down. Let's get on I-64 and you can open her up. This baby will do a hundred and forty mph."

"Check the glove box," said Wu.

Jim pulled out a CD and read it. "It's a copy of my songs that I sent for a copyright back in 1990."

"Yeah, Debbie made it for me. It's my second favorite CD of all time. Put it in and start it on the giant moose song."

"I wrote that about a place I used to hang out in San Jose, California. They had a giant moose head hanging on the wall over a stone fireplace.

It was the only time I ever spent away from Debbie. I was missing her desperately that night. Sat there and wrote it in less than an hour, swearing the whole time I would never leave her side again."

"Why did you…leave her, I mean?"

"I wanted to try and make it in the music business. Didn't last long."

"That's my favorite song on the CD, right in front of "Firebird from Hell." And you said hole."

As Jimmy searched for the giant moose song, he said, "Second favorite CD, huh?"

"Yeah. My favorite is Carole King's *Tapestry.*" She thought back to her slow dance with Debbie. "It has sentimental value."

"Downshift," Jimmy told Wu. She did and popped a wheel as they accelerated up the entrance ramp to I-64. He began to sing with the song. "The giant moose smiled on his Monday crowd." As the needle on the speedometer passed one hundred, Wu joined in, and they sang their way home.

They turned onto the aggregate driveway toward the house and Jimmy said, "I appreciate what you did today. You've opened up a whole new world for me."

"Hey, I learned how to drive a race car. And you just said hole *again.*" They pulled into the garage and Wu asked politely, "Would you mind opening my door for me?"

"I would be honored," he said, and hurried around to her side. He opened the door and extended his hand. Shewuma then put her leg out very seductively, showing Jimmy everything she could as slowly as she could.

He enjoyed it immensely despite a twinge of guilt. Shewuma took his hand and enjoyed it with him.

Wu went to change clothes and Jimmy went in search of Debbie. About an hour later, Shewuma entered the kitchen in her favorite manta, moccasins, and battle belt. Just for a change, she had braided her hair into a ponytail and swirled it up into a bun on top of her head.

Wearing sweatpants and a Led Zeppelin T-shirt, Debbie was looking in the refrigerator. As always, Jimmy was busy with some type of meal preparation. "Hey, guys," Wu chirped, "I gather from the soapy smell and the abundance of pheromones that you two have had a recent sexual encounter."

Debbie looked up and laughed. "WuWu!" Debbie proclaimed. She rattled off something in Hopi.

"What did she say, Wu?" Jim asked.

"Hello, sweet meat, but dirtier." Jimmy repeated it to himself to try and remember it, then turned back to his preparation of what appeared to be lamb.

"How did the training uniform work on Jimmy?" Debbie asked Wu with a twinkle in her eye.

Wu smelled Debbie's neck. "Like you don't know," she said, slapping Debbie's ass.

Jim put down his knife. "Deb. Wu. Attention please."

"You got it, handsome," said Debbie.

With a speechy air, he said, "Shewuma, I've been planning something for a while and I'm going for it today. It was supposed to be a surprise but I'm gonna need your help." Debbie and Wu were eager, their curiosity peaked. "Our dinner is going to be traditional Hopi cuisine." Shewuma was touched and delighted at the same time. She squealed with glee, hugged his neck, and kissed his cheek. She motioned to Debbie and they both hugged him.

Her eyes welled up and she began to cry. "Oh, Sweetie," Debbie said, taking Wu's face in her hands. Jim put his arm around her shoulders.

Wu sniffled and wiped her eyes. "I'm sorry. My whole life I never felt love like I do in this house. I really cherish you two." She hugged them again and then pulled back suddenly. "Wait," Wu said. "I'll be right back."

Jimmy said, "Wu, I need you to help me plan the menu and go over the recipes."

"I'll be right back!" She said, determined.

"Where are you going?" asked Debbie.

"I'm going to do something for you two. Hang on." She darted off.

A few minutes later, Shewuma strutted back into the kitchen, hopped up on the countertop, crossed her legs, and began to kick her right foot. Jimmy and Deb stared, dumbstruck. She had put the stockings and black pumps back on. For clothes, she wore only the white thong and lacy bra. With a big smile on her face, she slid back to the floor, spread her arms, and spun around. "What?" she said, feigning bafflement.

Debbie looked her up and down admiringly. "How can anyone be so slutty and so innocent at the same time?"

"I'll take that as a compliment," said Wu. "Now let's make a Hopi dinner. What do we have to work with?"

Jim was still watching her, so Debbie elbowed his ribs. "Jimbo, what menu are you planning now?"

Wu said, "Let's get to it."

Debbie told them, "You two get started. I'll be right back," like she had just remembered something and left.

Jimmy looked back at Wu. "You look so hot," he said earnestly.

"Food?" she said and smiled.

"Oh yeah. So I have lamb, squash, pinto beans, green chilis, carrots, onions, and hominy." She nodded at the hominy, impressed. "And corn, of course," he finished.

A glimpse of disappointment crossed Wu's face. "It's a shame we don't have blue corn. That is our mainstay."

"I know," said Jim as he opened the refrigerator. "I have blue corn." He put the corn stalks in the sink. "And blue cornmeal." He handed her a five-pound bag.

"How?" she asked.

"I ordered it online back in August and kept it in the big freezer. It's supposed to last up to eight months if frozen. And don't you start crying again. I also have a recipe for piki bread. It's kind of like making tortillas, except they're blue. So, I was thinking of making hominy and lamb stew. What do you think about blue dumplings?"

"Yeah. We can cook them in the stew," Shewuma said.

"Roast some of the corn on the cob and make some beans with carrots and onions."

"Oh, this is so exciting," she said. "Let's get to work, Jimmy." She turned to the sink and the stalks of corn.

Jim looked at her from the back. "I'll try."

They could hear Debbie coming down the hall. Wu was shucking corn when she heard Jimmy say, "Oh my God." Wu turned, looked at Debbie, and dropped the corn on the floor. Debbie stood there, hand on her hip, in a low cut, skin tight, latex, red mini dress with matching thigh high, three-inch heeled red boots.

"I thought I'd get in the spirit," said Debbie, acting sassy.

Wu spoke a string of Hopi words.

"What did you say to her?" Jim asked.

"I can't tell you. You're her husband," Wu answered.

"So, it was dirty?"

"Oh yeah." Wu walked over and the girls put their arms around each other's waists.

"How do you women expect me to get any work done?" Jim asked while snapping pictures with his cell phone.

"Oh no, boy," Deb held up her clenched fist. "You're not off the hook." She opened her hand, and a blue speedo dangled from her fingers.

Jimmy smiled, shaking his head in disbelief. "You're not serious."

"As a heart attack," she said. "Come on meat," Deb shot back, and tossed him the speedo.

"Does he have a pair of cowboy boots?" said Wu.

"Hell yes! Good idea, Wu."

"So, what happens when I get a boner looking at you two?"

They looked at each other. "We'll just have to live with it," Deb said, and Wu nodded. "Go," said Debbie. "We have a dinner to make." Jimmy headed for the bedroom to change. "You two are so crazy!" he said. "Mostly good crazy. And ya'll should dress like that every day."

Making dinner was a carnival atmosphere. The three—dressed in their revealing outfits—were joking, laughing, and tickling each other while cooking the greatly anticipated Hopi dinner. "Something's missing," said Deb. Mentally, she contacted David E. "Can you come down to the kitchen for a minute?"

He showed up right away and almost dropped his cane. Mouth hanging open, David E. said, "Am I awake?" Working in the kitchen were Debbie looking like a new wave Marilyn Monroe, Shewuma as a porn star he wanted to take home to Mom, and Jimmy just barely covering his junk in a speedo and a pair of cowboy boots.

"How's your research going?" Debbie asked.

"I think I'll get my stuff and work at the table," he said quickly.

"I thought you might," Debbie replied.

"I don't have to change clothes, do I?"

"Not unless you want to, Honey."

David E. detoured on his way back, grabbing a bottle of tequila and putting his new obsession, Eliane Elias, on the stereo. He sat down at the table and filled up four shot glasses with pictures of Marvel superheroes.

"Where's your research stuff?" said Wu.

"This is research, believe me," he said. Like Jim, he began taking pictures. "What's the occasion?" he asked, handing everyone a shot glass. They toasted and drank.

"We're having traditional Hopi food for dinner," Wu told him.

"I love it here," he said in a rare moment of candor. "And I'm not just saying that because of you two unbelievably gorgeous women."

"Here, here," agreed Jim, and they drank again.

"Let's eat," declared Deb.

After dinner, and much to Jimmy and David E.'s dismay, the girls went to put on robes. They met back in the den to finish off the tequila. Wu paused the CD and faced them. "I would just like to officially thank you guys and especially Jim," nodding to him, "for a delicious dinner in spite of a chest hair in my chilis." Everyone laughed. "But I'm serious," she continued. "It was a thoughtful and loving tribute not only to me but also to my people. And as a thank you, I ask you all to indulge me," she said nervously, "as I recite a Hopi prayer." Deb put her two index fingers to her lips and whistled and Jim and David E. clapped. They settled down as Wu cleared her throat. "Debbie, would you translate please?"

"Of course," replied Deb.

Wu began her prayer in her native language using a singsong technique as she read:

> *"Hold onto what is good, even if it is just a handful of Earth. Hold onto what you believe, even if it's a tree that stands by itself. Hold onto what you must do, even if it's a long way from here. Hold onto your life, even if it's easier to let go. Hold onto my hand, even if I've gone away from you. Love and family will always prevail."*

"Oh, Wu, that was beautiful," Deb whispered tenderly. "What do you think, David E.?" They looked at him. He was leaning back in the chair, snoring softly. They roared with laughter.

Jim jumped up. "Hang on, guys," he said as he rushed down the hall. He came back with his and Debbie's guitars. Wu sat down on the coffee table facing them, intrigued. After tuning up, Jim prompted Debbie to strum a C while he told her what he wanted. "Play C for four counts, D for four counts, then keep it going back and forth. I can get some melody lead with some bass notes. Wu, what do you say we turn your prayer into a song?"

"Oh, that would be lovely," said Wu. "I tell you, guys, except for no income and aliens trying to kill us, life couldn't get any better."

Deb started strumming the rhythm. "Let's run it and see where it goes." They spent an hour working on the song. It never sounded very good, but they had a lot of fun anyway.

The next three weeks were relatively uneventful. David E. spent most of his time on the computer, tracking his mysterious virus, while Jimmy, Debbie, and Shewuma spent a lot of time shooting pool, playing cards and games, and just generally having fun. David E. got them engrossed in a new show called *Bosch* about an ex-soldier turned police detective. There were five seasons, and they couldn't get enough of it. Sometimes they would watch three or four episodes a day. They were enjoying life and each other. But there was always an undercurrent of foreboding because they knew something was coming.

They also spent a lot of time prepping for the worst. Every day, Jim, Deb, and Wu trained. They worked out and sparred one on one, two on one, free for alls, on the ground, on the roof, and hand to hand with all manner of weapons. Wu helped Jim and Debbie perfect their knife and axe throwing and created exercises to push Jim's heightened senses to new limits. Deb was mastering her time-sense. But it was their fighting skills that benefited most. The combination of Erran DNA and bodily hormone manipulation through the Cric allowed Debbie to reach the apex of human prowess. Near superhuman strength, foot speed, and reflexes could be summoned by her in an instant and sustained for hours.

Debbie and Wu were astounded by the pace and magnitude of Jimmy's advances. His physiology adapting to the two Drachonian DNAs kept enhancing the density of his bones, muscles, and sinews. They saw dramatic increases in his strength, endurance, and resistance to pain daily.

Jimmy and Debbie's upgrades reaped benefits for Shewuma as well. First teaching and then constant sparing with her two combat prodigies brought her battle skills to a new level she hadn't thought possible.

At meals they would brainstorm on strategy, tactics, and emergency plans. David E. and Wu took turns lecturing on their combined knowledge—which was considerable—of aliens, Black Ops, Men in Black, and government agencies. They discussed weapons, technology, attack patterns, past behaviors, and even how they perceived future trends.

Debbie explained her EMP and LCS options in combat. Men could only achieve these things with nuclear explosions, but her Sanctum could do it at her will by suppressing electron movements with directed celestial energy. It was the same energy that the Errans suppressed to control other alien technology. Only the Crystal Skulls still had access to it. She explained the extent of the EMP. Electricity delivered from out of her range would restart after a time. But batteries and isolated power sources were dead, kaput. The LCS prohibited any and all combustion over a span of at least several minutes and then dissipated gradually.

Jimmy stopped her. "So, Dibs, explain that so a Creeker can understand it."

Debbie obliged. "No guns firing, no cars starting, no electricity, no cellphones, no bombs, no plasma rifles. Hell, you can't even light a cigarette."

Debbie and David E. eventually cracked dead Earl's bank account and acquired $15,411 of probable blood money. David E. split it evenly among the four of them, despite Debbie's insistence that he keep it for himself. They would often stay up late drinking their own alcoholic creations and speculating about alien intentions, government cover-ups, the mysterious Crystal Skulls, and the possible fate of mankind if the Sanctum should be lost. David E. was convinced that China was hiding an already out of control pandemic created by the Greys. The others were skeptical until Debbie accidentally hacked some satellite images of the streets of Beijing filled with angry people wearing medical masks. She was practicing plugging herself into Google Maps with her Cric when the rapid succession of revealing holograms appeared in their den, surprising and startling everyone. Debbie had been trying unsuccessfully to duplicate it ever since. It was just a matter of time, though. Her control of the Cric and her influence over the Sanctum was growing exponentially. Cell phones, radio waves, microwaves, and all manner of electromagnetic radiation were falling to her mercy day by day. They never left the house anymore. Even when Petey got into it with a raccoon and needed a few stitches, Debbie sewed him up herself. Generally, though, the guys and girls were happy, the dogs were happy, and the cat was happy. Debbie enjoyed the fact that everything seemed almost normal. So she was particularly bothered to come in the den and see Wu alone, crossed legged on the couch and moping.

"What's wrong, Wu?"

"I'm pissed. Have I turned ugly or something? Nobody has said anything the least bit nasty to me for days. I feel like I've become Ann Ramsey." Debbie cocked her head. She didn't get it. Wu explained, pouting. "You know. A nonsexual entity."

Debbie could tell this was a real issue, not just a Wuism. She was genuinely upset. Debbie leaned over close to her ear and whispered, "Last night, Jimmy was looking up your dress."

Wu perked up. "Did you catch him?"

"Yes. He got so excited I had to take him in the bathroom and relieve his blue balls."

"How did you do it? Hand? Mouth?" Debbie sighed and stood up. What was she thinking?

"You started it," said Wu.

"My mouth. He was so excited that he shot his load in about ten seconds. Then he bent me over the sink and fucked me silly. Okay?"

Once more happy with her quota of dirty banter, Wu said, "Thanks, Debbie Doodle. You're the best."

Debbie patted her head and walked away. "And you are a nut."

It was early morning on Friday, December 13, 2019, when Shewuma went to the kitchen wearing her new favorite morning attire—a pink bath towel and her turquoise necklace. She was surprised to hear and smell Jimmy, Debbie, and David E. engaged in a rare, heated argument. "I'm going whether you two go or not," Jim said in a loud voice.

"Don't be stupid, Jim," said Debbie.

"Hey, maybe it's stupid but I'm going."

David E. jumped in. "They could be out there right now just waiting for something like this."

"After all this time, you think someone is out there? It's been weeks."

Debbie agreed with David E. "They could just be lying low to get our guard down."

"Yeah," Jimmy said sarcastically. "Or it could be over, and I could go get a job at Walmart. You're supposed to be some kind of psychic, Deb, and you've got nothing." He pointed to David E. "And do you think while they're in the middle of taking out China, they give a shit about us?"

"We have the Sanctum," Debbie stressed.

"I don't care!" Jim shouted. "The Christmas party is tomorrow and I'm going."

Wu finally understood the problem. Jim hadn't seen any of his family for quite a while. In the back of his mind, maybe he was afraid he would never see them again.

They looked at Wu. "What do you think, Wu?" Debbie asked.

"It's tomorrow?" Wu asked.

"Yes."

"It's at your sister's?"

"No," said Jimmy. "It's at Giovanni's Restaurant in Williamsburg."

"That's not very far," she said. "So Deb and David E., you don't want to go?"

"Of course I want to go," Deb said. "It's my family too, but I don't think it's safe."

"David E.?" she said.

"I agree with Debbie. It's not safe. I wouldn't go anyway. I don't know any of these people. I'm really not comfortable being around people anymore."

"Will Granddaddy Dick be there?" Wu asked Jimmy.

"Yes."

"Okay, I'll be honest. I want to go see Granddaddy Dick."

"Cap'n Dick," Debbie and Jim corrected her simultaneously.

"Cap'n Dick," she continued. "But I agree there's a risk."

They looked back and forth at each other. Debbie and Jim's faces were set, David E. was done with it, and Wu was thoughtful as she formed a plan. "How about this? Jim drives Miss Interceptor and Deb and I hide in the back."

"Hide?" said Deb.

"Yeah, fortunately we would have to snuggle up on the floor, maybe under a blanket, and intertwine our legs." Deb and Jim smiled for the first time that morning. "Or maybe we should just get in the trunk of the Trans Am together."

"Okay," Debbie laughed. "I get it. Go on."

"As far as they know, Jim leaves alone. If they're waiting to strike when the house is poorly defended, this isn't the time. Still has David E., Deb, me, and all the animals, as far as they know."

"It's good," said David E. "Even if something happens, I know the plan. I go to the safe room and call you guys. You would be back in fifteen minutes. Of course, they would think Jim is alone. What if they go after him?"

"Not likely in public. But if they did, they'd be in for a big fucking surprise," Wu said, nudging Debbie's shoulder.

Jimmy looked at Debbie beseechingly. "What do you say, Babe? We'll just see everybody, Wu can see Granddaddy, and we leave. We don't even have to eat."

"I do want to see everyone," Deb conceded.

"Wait a minute," Wu interrupted. "Not eat? What do you mean?"

"So, it's a plan. Good. I hate us yelling at each other," David E. confirmed.

"Not until we discuss not eating," said Wu.

The next morning, David E. was sitting on his bed in his tan suit and holding his cane. He stood up and looked in the mirror. "Not bad for an old guy," he said out loud. "David E., breakfast in five," he heard echoing through the house. Perfect timing. He grabbed Debbie's tablet from the office and moseyed down to the kitchen, following the smell of fresh cooked biscuits.

"Good morning," said Jim at the grill.

"Let me see your T-shirt," said David E.

Jimmy turned and stuck out his chest. In black and white letters it read, "I do what I want, when I want, where I want after I ask my wife."

David E. chuckled. "I like it."

Debbie was sitting at the table in black leggings and a T-shirt. No doubt there was something snappy printed on it. "What does your shirt say, Deb?" he asked.

She turned to show it to him. He had to consciously not react to the sight of her large breasts straining against the cotton material. He thought of her as a daughter now, but he still couldn't help enjoying how good looking she was. Her shirt read in black letters, "My husband does what he wants, when he wants and where he wants after he asks me."

David E. laughed out loud. "You match."

"Jim's idea," said Deb.

He sat down and admired her some more before opening the tablet.

Wu entered barefoot in her pink bath towel. "Good morning, big guy," Wu said to David E. as she sat down next to him.

"Good morning, Wu. I always look forward to seeing you at breakfast."

Wu asked, "Is that just a straightforward comment or are you talking about how I look? Or are you being a little dirty?"

"Yes, yes, and yes," he replied, not looking up from his reading.

"Lay it out for me, Jimmy," Wu called out.

While they brought the food to the table, Jimmy said, "For the High Priest, there's cheese and onion omelets, grits, tater tots, fried bologna, and biscuits." He had also made Debbie a couple of thick pork chops.

As he passed Wu going around the table filling milk glasses, she slapped his butt. "All this and he can cook too, Debbie." Debbie winked at her.

"She's right, Jim," said David E. "If Debbie didn't have you and you didn't have a penis, I'd marry you myself."

"Thanks, David E. I don't get compliments like that very often. It's very well thought out."

While they ate, they talked. "So, the big family Christmas party. You guys excited?" David E. inquired.

"I am," said Wu. "I get to see Granddaddy Dick again. He's a Deep Creek Hybrid, you know."

"Cap'n Dick," said Jim.

"Right."

"Any more information on the scar guy?" asked Debbie.

"No, but I read a story that may be connected to aliens." Sounds of interest came from around the table. David E. continued. "At a wedding, about seventy people in Sparta, New Jersey, were found unconscious. The only thing anyone remembered was seeing blue."

"Ahh, the blue light," Wu said with a mouthful of food. "Know it well."

"Me too," said Jim.

"What's the significance?" asked Deb.

"My understanding of blue lights is that they don't use electricity. They use microwaves. So, the blue light doesn't come at you in a linear stream but more like a bubble two or three feet in diameter." He took another biscuit and butter. "But to knock out seventy people at once sounds like a new application or an upgrade."

"Well, if you get blue lighted, you're pretty much screwed anyway," said Jimmy, chewing. David E. shrugged.

"Actually," said Wu, holding up her finger, "there is a technique for dodging blue lights."

"Didn't work too well for you," said Jim.

"No, it didn't," she said. "But I'll show it to you guys next time we spar anyway."

"That sounds good," said Deb. "I'm interested."

"Well, here's some more trivia," Wu said. "When you're facing two MIB, because they always travel in twos, the one on your left is always right-handed and the one on your right is always left-handed."

"No shit?" said Jim.

"And Drachs are left-handed too. Always."

"That's great stuff, Wu. Thanks." Wu offered him a biscuit. "No thanks."

"What time are you guys leaving?" asked David E.

"About 11:00 am," said Debbie. "And I'm not sure when we'll be back, so I'll make you something you can heat it up when you're hungry."

"No, you won't," David E. said. "I can just make a sandwich if I get hungry."

"Too bad. I already did it," said Deb. "There's a plate of leftover meatloaf, mashed potatoes, peas, and carrots in the fridge. Just microwave it. And some of these leftover biscuits from breakfast would be good with it too."

"Thank you, Debbie," he said. "You're a sweetheart."

From the recliner in the den, David E. looked up from the computer tablet and said, "It's eleven o'clock." There was no need to shout since everyone would hear him no matter where they were in the house. He suddenly realized Debbie was standing behind him and closed the tablet quickly.

"Settle down, David E.," said Debbie. "You're a grown man. I don't mind if you look at some porn."

"It wasn't porn," he said.

Then Debbie said, "Oh my gosh, David E. Every day?"

"Look, Debbie," he said, "I love you, but I'll just stop using your tablet if you can't respect my privacy."

"You're right. I'm sorry, David E., I didn't mean to check your history. It was tacky, but online psychics? Is it just research or something? I don't understand."

"My wife was an astrologer," he explained.

"Oh, so you believe in that stuff?" she said.

"When you're around it the way I was, it's not something you believe or not believe. It's just there, like math or gravity."

"Well, it's your business, Sweetie. Forget I said anything."

"Hey, Deb," he said, "do you think you could bone up on astrology and read my chart?"

"I tell you what, Bubba. I'll do some research on it and get back to you. Okay?"

"Okay," he said.

"That helps explain the Chloe thing."

"And look," said David E., "don't tell Jim and Wu. Most people don't understand, or they make fun of it. I would prefer it stayed between us."

"A bit late for that," Wu said as she and Jimmy showed up in the den.

David E. stood up and went command sergeant major on them. "Everybody line up for inspection and concealed weapons check." Jimmy was wearing an oversized brown flannel shirt, hiding his 9mm and an array of sheath knives. "Check," said David E. Debbie was wearing a long-sleeved tunic top with lace around the bottom covering her 40 caliber Beretta, her pair of German throwers, and the Hibben Recon fat belly blade that had become her preference. "Check," he repeated. Wu stood in a denim mini dress laced up the front, wearing her battle belt and moccasins. "You know, your weapons are showing," David E. said. Wu smiled and held up a fringed buckskin coat. "Check," he said.

"Well, I'll go hunker down in the back with the kids. You guys enjoy yourselves. You deserve it." He did his cane fast walk down the hall, waving over his shoulder.

The plan went well. Jimmy made a show of driving away in Miss Interceptor alone, with Debbie and Wu hidden safely in the back under a blanket. It was only a few minutes to the party. He pulled behind a gas station next to the restaurant so Debbie and Wu could slip out and he could go into Giovanni's by himself. When there was no movement in the back, Jimmy jumped out and slid open the side door. The blanket flew off the girls and Debbie climbed out, a bit disoriented. "We're here already?" she said.

"You should fix your hair," Jimmy told her. "It's all mussed." Wu climbed out behind her. Jim looked at her face suspiciously. "You're flushed, Wu."

"It was hot under there," she replied.

"You don't get hot." Then it hit him, and he suppressed a chuckle. "Were ya'll making out?"

"No," said Debbie. Wu was nodding yes and grinning. "We were not," insisted Debbie.

Jimmy started laughing. "Come on, let's go to the party."

Knocking on the back door to the restaurant, Wu asked Debbie, "So I get to meet the Creekers today?"

"No," Debbie explained. "At the summer picnic, the food and booze are free. So, lots of Creekers show up. But at the Christmas dinner, everyone pays their own way. So a lot less Creekers if you catch my drift."

"Cheap, right? I guess this will mostly be people from Jim's mom's side. But I will get to see Granddaddy Dick, right?"

"Oh yeah."

A Giovanni's cook opened the back door, a little shocked to see two beautiful women. He said, "I'm sorry. We don't accept deliveries on weekends after 11:00 am."

Debbie and Wu walked past him, and Debbie said, "I don't blame you. Could you please point me to the banquet room?"

Once inside, they went from person to person, greeting, hugging, chatting, and moving on. They introduced Shewuma as an old friend from school that was visiting them. Mom questioned several times having never met or even heard of her. Many people asked about Bo Dean. They said that he was away on personal business. Willy was especially disappointed that Bo wasn't there. It made them a little sad. But they were determined to enjoy the moment. Who knew when they might see family again? Willy's twin teenage sons, Reid and Fowler, followed Shewuma around like moonstruck puppy dogs. Wu so enjoyed the attention that it didn't take long for the three to become inseparable. Later, when Wu was fending off Uncle Dan's attempts to rub her back, she spotted Jim talking to a well-built, twenty-something brunette. As she hugged his neck, he reached around her waist, picked her up, and spun her. Then they kissed quickly on the lips. Wu pushed Dan out of the way, bumped between the twins, and went straight for her. Debbie had seen Jim and Windy hugging when she spotted Wu, her face set hard, heading for them like a charging bull. Wu was reaching for Windy's hair when Debbie stepped in front of her.

"I'll take care of it, Debs," Wu told her.

In Wu's mind, Debbie said, "It's Jimmy's cousin. It's okay. They're very close. He's kind of a father figure to her."

"That didn't look like any father figure hug and kiss to me."

"It's complicated," said Debbie out loud. "Hey, come on, Wu. Let's go see Granddaddy."

Wu seemed reluctant to drop it at first. But it was Granddaddy. "Okay."

Debbie surveyed the large, packed room and said, "I don't see him."

"He's over in that far corner," Wu said, pointing. "I can smell him. Let's go."

There he was, straddling a backward chair and holding a tea glass full of what Wu could smell was vodka. He saw Debbie coming and his eyes lit up. "Becky," he bellowed.

"Granddaddy!" she returned.

He smiled broadly but never moved while she kissed and hugged him for a long time.

"Where's John Henry?" he asked.

"Oh, he's here. He's coming, Granddaddy."

"He's off dallying with a floosy," Wu remarked, still holding on to the incident.

"He's got a lot of J.R. in him," Granddaddy said, chuckling.

He stood and handed Debbie his drink. "I see you brought my next ex-wife with you."

"Hi, Granddaddy," said Shewuma. She held out her hand. He took it and as they shook, he began to squeeze harder. She squeezed back and he increased his pressure. They kept squeezing more. His strength was incredible.

When Wu grimaced, he let go and nodded his approval. "That's a hell of a grip you got there, girl. Even more than I expected," he said, and then pulled her in for a bearhug. He then did something that Debbie had never seen him do. He turned the chair and sat in it normally. "Now you two girls sit down here on Granddaddy's lap and let's talk."

Wu sat on his left knee and Debbie sat on his right. They put their arms around his massive shoulders, and each put a hand on his large belly. He laughed and joked with them, asking them questions like a Granddaddy would with young children. They rubbed his belly and kissed his cheeks and his neck. Wu fell for him all over again. They were having a ball when Wu looked up and saw a tall old woman not three feet away giving her serious skunk eye.

"Nanny," Debbie said, getting up and giving her a kiss and a hug.

"Hi, Debbie. You look good. And you." Nanny pointed at Shewuma. "Are you a witch?"

"No, ma'am," Wu said, standing up and extending her hand. "I'm a friend of Jimmy and Debbie."

"Don't lie to me," Nanny barked. "I have a Bible in the car if I need it."

"No really, ma'am. I swear I'm not a witch."

"Okay," Nannie relented. "Just take it easy on the old man. I have to go home with him." She turned and walked away.

Debbie turned and hugged Granddaddy again. "I'll see you later, Granddaddy. I have to mingle."

He said, "Okay, Becky." And he pulled Wu back down onto his knee.

Later, Jim found Cap'n Dick and greeted him with a kiss and a big hug. "Why are you sitting this way, Granddaddy?"

"In case she comes back."

"Who?"

"Becky."

"Which Becky?"

"You know. Her." He silently enunciated the word *Kachina*.

"Oh," said Jim. "What do you think of her?"

"I think you two should make babies," he said frankly.

"Granddaddy, I'm with Debbie. You know that."

"Not like that," he explained. "Just babies. You two would make really strong babies. Special babies. She has one hell of a grip…like a gorilla."

"Maybe you two should make babies," Jimmy suggested.

Wu's voice carried from across the room. "You boys know I hear you."

Granddaddy put his finger to his lips. "Shhh! We'll talk about it later."

Wu's voice came once again. "No, we won't."

Granddaddy made a yikes look and Jimmy plopped down on his lap for the first time since he was ten years old.

At Wu's insistence, they stayed and ate dinner. Jimmy ordered a large pepperoni pizza with extra cheese. He gave one slice to Wu and ate the rest. Debbie split a veal parmesan with Wu, who also ordered baked ziti. Then she ate the rest of the manicotti left by Jim's mother. They had a great time and Debbie was glad they'd come.

Back at Miss Interceptor, Debbie opened the side door and reached for the blanket.

"What are you doing?" asked Jimmy.

"We need to hide, right?"

"No, Babe. We're going home now. We can all ride up front instead of you two making out in the back."

"Well, you made out with the slutty cousin," said Wu.

Debbie drove. On the way home, Jimmy leaned up and challenged Wu. "It just hit me. You're jealous of my cousin Windy."

Wu thought and said, "I'm not jealous. I just hate to see a married man make a fool of himself in public."

Debbie and Jimmy agreed. Shewuma was jealous. Wu reclined her seat with a huff and put her foot up on the dashboard.

A little after 5:00 that evening, David E. sat in the den recliner, going through the maze of Amazon programs looking for the show called *Monk*. He was still basking from the chicken salad sandwich on a croissant, dill pickle, and potato salad that Jimmy had made him for dinner when they got home. "Damn," he thought, "that boy could make a bowl of hot water taste like a feast." It made him happy that they had so enjoyed their jaunt to the Christmas party. He went to Season 4, Episode 2 of *Monk*. He was pissed off about Sherona being gone. And the jury was still out on this girl Natalie.

Wearing his battle belt and Samurai sword slung across his back, Jimmy screwed his pool cue together. He turned on the hanging light over the pool table. It was habit since he could see just fine in the dark now. With his new capabilities, pool had become just shy of being dull. So now he would either play the hardest shot on the table or set up trick shots just to keep it interesting. The dogs lay around the pool room, resting and content. Debbie and Wu were sparring in the gym over the shop. They had been at it for almost an hour. Unlike Wu, who never got tired, Debbie was feeling it. Debbie went in for what presented itself as a clean opening. Wu spun out of it and slapped her rubber knife against Debbie's arm.

"Shit," said Deb. "I thought I had you. You're just too tough today."

"Are you kidding?" said Wu, moving her knife and body rhythmically. "If these were real, you would have killed me twice already."

"Trust me," joked Deb. "If it came to that, I would just shoot you. Fuck the knives."

Wu started to laugh and then stopped. "Shhh!" Debbie listened and waited. "Come on," yelled Wu. She grabbed Lightning and her quiver of arrows, and they ran to the backyard, Tippycat on their heels. Shewuma, Debbie, and Tippy scanned the dusky sky. "Do you hear it?" Wu asked her.

"Yes, I hear it. Two choppers."

"From different directions. But I can't see them."

"Oh Jesus," said Deb. "I see them. They're in stealth mode."

Wu looked to her left and her right. "They're coming, Dibs. Twenty-one MIB, I think. From every direction. Tippy, protect Debbie. They may have blue lights and plasma rifles, Dibs. Take out the trash, Babe." And she was off in the direction of the back deck.

In the back of her mind, Debbie wondered why there were twenty-one. MIB always worked in pairs. Telepathically, she sent out the warning signal and then the words, "MIB from every direction."

Wu heard Debbie's voice say "red" and saw the color in her mind as she went from the deck railing to the roof.

Jimmy heard and saw it as well, pulled his samurai sword from the sheath, and went out the front door.

David E. received the alarm just as he heard the front door opening. He grabbed his cane and headed for the safe room as fast as he could. He called the dogs as he went. "Molly, Nicky, Petey, Connor! Come!"

Debbie put her finger behind her ear. She could hear the choppers hovering overhead. She closed her eyes and put everything she had into it. "EMP," she whispered hard. It dazed her for a second. She took off, moving low and ran to the corner where the fence met the shop. She heard the choppers go down, one in front of the house and the other in the trees behind the privacy fence. Two down. Debbie knew that MIB carried standard issue Lugers like the ones used by Nazi officers in World War II. "LCS," she said plainly. They would have machetes as backup, but now it was all hand to hand. Tippy came from around the shop dragging a dead Scout and dropped it at her feet. Then he hissed an alarm. Two Men in Black were coming over the fence. They hadn't even seen her. She pulled her fat belly blade and was surprised at how quickly and cleanly she killed them both. Where was Jimmy? She needed to find him.

In the bedroom, David E. was a few feet from the safe room when the lights went out. *The EMP*, he thought. Contact with the physical hologram made it disappear and the old bowling bag with the Sanctum sat on the floor. Squinting in the darkening room, he punched WuWu into the keypad. It was dead. Something they hadn't accounted for. He would have to wait until the power came back to open the safe room door. The four dogs stood with him. He wondered what was happening outside.

Debbie was making her way to the front yard along the side of the house. Six MIB brandishing machetes rushed her from the woods. She took the two on the left with her throwers, grateful for the months of Wu's persistent practice. She squared off for the other four with her fat belly blade. With her back to the brick wall of the house, they closed in around her. Two went down with arrows through the heart, while Debbie dispatched the other two with relative ease. Wu dropped down beside her on the ground. "You okay, Debbie?"

"I'm good. I'm worried about Jimmy."

"He's doing great," said Wu. "Don't worry about him. I got his back." And then she was gone.

The extra MIB still nagged at Debbie. She sent David E. a thought. "Be careful. There is a single assassin out there. May not be MIB."

David E. heard it And it made no sense until a figure in black crashed through the window, rolled across the floor, and came up toward him. He was wearing a mask that covered everything but his eyes. "Of course," thought David E. "Not an MIB. A Black Ops assassin." David E. knew that the stun gun and the bullet were useless and pulled the sword from his cane. But he was no match for the Hybrid strength and speed of the killer. He was disarmed and in a chokehold almost instantly. He began to pass out. The pressure released and suddenly he was free. In the dim light of the sun setting, he watched the battle playout on the carpet. On the floor, the beagle fought one arm of the killer. The two terriers mangled the other. And Molly was viciously tearing out the throat of David E.'s would-be assassin. The body stopped twitching, but David E. put the sword through his eye just to be sure. He sat on the bed exhausted and the lights came up. The dogs came up to him, excited and wagging their tails. Blood matted into the fur on their muzzles, and he rubbed and hugged them. "Good kids. Good kids," he kept saying, happy to be alive.

Debbie came running through the door. "David E., are you okay?" He just nodded. It hit her like a lightning bolt. "The EMP. You couldn't get in the safe room."

He smiled and said low-key, "Surprise."

Wu came through the broken window with Tippy behind her. She set a bundled blanket on the floor full of Lugers, machetes and two burnt-out plasma rifles she had gathered from the dead. "All good outside."

"They're all dead?" asked Debbie.

"All dead."

"What about Jimmy?"

Jimmy came through the door carrying an MIB under his arm. "I'm here, Babe," he said. He dropped the MIB on the floor like a sack of dirt. The MIB moved and Wu drew her bow. "It's okay," said Jim. "I snapped both of his humorous bones. He's harmless. Kept him alive so we could question him."

Wu rushed over and opened his mouth. She was trying to stuff the hilt of her bone knife in when he opened his eyes and gritted his teeth. They heard a crunch. And he disintegrated within seconds.

"Fuck," said Jim. "He killed himself?"

"He dusted," said Deb. She touched a pinch of the residue to her tongue. "A concentrated form of the Drach poison."

Jimmy looked at David E. "You're not in the safe room."

"I couldn't get in."

"Because of my EMP," said Debbie.

"Oh shit," said Jim. "Never thought of that." Jimmy examined the broken window and the dead assassin's body. "Did you do him?" he said to David E.

"That should have been me," said David E. "Your children saved my life."

Jimmy called them. "Come here, you guys. My badass kids," he said as he rubbed heads."

"Are we sure we got them all?" said Debbie. "I got five."

"I got six," said Jim.

"I got nine," said Wu.

"And this guy that came through the window," said David E. "That makes twenty-one."

"And Tippy got a Scout," said Debbie proudly.

"Good boy," said Wu and scratched his head.

"We have to go," said David E.

"You think they know already?" asked Jim.

"Two choppers down and communications out. Oh, they know. And their backup plan is on the way. Believe it," he said matter-of-factly.

Debbie said, "Jimmy, can we leave?"

"Just say the word Babe."

"David E., can you walk?"

He stood up. "Yeah, I'm good."

She took charge. "Okay. David E., get your bag. Put the dogs in the big van. Then you and Tippy go to the Muscle. Grab a couple of towels to clean off the kids." He limped out heavily on his cane as he called the animals. "Jim, get our bags. Then go retrieve weapons. Arrows and knives. The Lugers should still be loaded. If you see any plasma rifles, they'll be fried. But take them anyway."

Wu pointed to the bundle on the floor. "No need to collect weapons. I already got them."

Debbie smiled. "Of course you did. Okay. Jim, you go in the safe room. Get the Sanctum, the cash, the faraday box, and put them in the van. Wu, put your bags and whatever else you're taking and put it in the van. Then go turn off the water, gas, and set the power like I showed you."

Wu took her hand. "You all right, Unangwa?"

"Yeah. I'm going to cover that broken window, get the laptop, and reboot the security system." Wu looked at her, puzzled. "So we'll have eyes here after we leave."

"Good idea," said Wu and left.

In twelve minutes, Jimmy, David E., and Tippy were in the Muscle and waiting in the driveway. Wu had done her tasks, plus loaded in the van a box full of her homemade arrows, Jimmy's two extra suitcases of knives, and another suitcase of assorted weapons she'd been acquiring from their many altercations. Then she went back in the house and grabbed two bags of chips and a cold six pack of root beer. She put two root beers in the van and then went to the Trans Am. David E. saw her coming in the mirror and opened the door. She put four cold root beers in his lap and held up the chip bags.

"Which one?" she asked.

"Fritos," said Jim.

She gave them to David E. "And the Cheetos for us girls." Tippy stuck his head out from the back seat and she kissed him. "You guys were badass and I love you both."

"Hey, don't get too sappy or I'll have to zap you," said David E.

Then Jimmy chimed in, "If you really loved us, you wouldn't take the Cheetos."

Wu hung her head and laughed. "Creekers. I swear."

She turned to go, and Jimmy stopped her. "Hey, High Priest." She looked back at the car. "We love you too."

She walked away and whispered, "I know."

When Debbie finally showed up in the driver's seat of the extended van, she went over an electronic checklist in her Cric. They hadn't forgotten anything, and she said, "That's it, Wu. You were magnificent today." She sounded tired.

Wu said, "We were already a family. Today, we became a team."

That lightened Debbie's mood a little. Shewuma always knew what to say to make her feel better.

Back in the Muscle, Jimmy picked up a 1970 brick sized walkie-talkie. "Ten-Four, rubber duck. You got your ears on?"

Jimmy's message crackled in Debbie's Cric. "Ten Four, good buddy," she responded directly to his mind.

"Are you talking to Debbie?" David E. asked.

"Yeah."

"Can't the bad guys pick it up?"

"Naw. It's an old walkie-talkie with a half-mile range. Debbie thinks it's safe. Love you," he crackled to her.

"Love you," she sent back. Or had she said it out loud?

"Love you too," responded Wu. So, it was out loud. If she was tired it could still be confusing sometimes.

Jimmy drove away with nervous anticipation, realizing that he may not see his house, his family, or Deep Creek ever again. David E. saw the mangled wreckage of the chopper in the front yard, wishing that they didn't have to leave. After so many years of running and hiding on his own, he had come to love this place and these people.

Connor hopped onto Debbie's lap and settled in. She started the Ford van and followed Jimmy, feeling like she was bound in heavy weights. The past was over, and the future was anybody's guess. Wu touched Debbie's arm, then put her seat back two clicks and put her right foot on the dashboard. Debbie glanced over at her dress riding up and smiled, feeling the weight of the moment evaporate. "Slut," she said into Wu's mind.

Wu took her hand and kissed the back of it. "And don't you forget it," she responded lovingly.

In the beam of headlights, the striking mandarin orange Trans Am tooled down the center lane of I-64. Debbie kept the white extended van close behind. Before they had even reached Richmond, Debbie sent out several texts to close family members. "Heading to Atlantic City for a much needed vacation. Be gone for at least a month. Will be in touch. Love, Debbie and Jimmy." That was not only for the family's sake, but also to throw off the inevitable tracking attempts that were sure to plague them. After passing Richmond a few more minutes later, everyone would expect them to be heading north and up the coast, not west to sanctuary with Corrine and Daniel. Jimmy veered the Muscle onto the first rest stop exit past the Richmond city limits to change the license plates on both vehicles. *Oklahoma, here we come.*

The End (For Now)

Acknowledgments

Mom, thanks for buying me comic books before I could even read. My whole life, you always encouraged me to write. It paid off.

To Debbie, my wife and co-author. I couldn't have done it without you. I love you.

About the Authors

Married co-authors Jimmy and Debbie Parker have been living and working together for thirty-eight years. Between the two, they have been writing poems, stories, and music their whole lives. Only now do we see their first published work. A labor of love for three years, this is just the first of many planned adventures in the world of *Hybrid Lore*. Book Two, *Hybrid Lore: Transformation,* is done. Book Three, *Hybrid Lore: Immortals,* is in the works.